P9-CDE-626

SECRETS IN THE
SHADOWS

BOOK SOLD
NO LONGER R H P L
PROPERTY

SECRETS IN THE
SHADOWS

HEIGE S. BOEHM

RONSDALE PRESS

SECRETS IN THE SHADOWS
Copyright © 2019 Heige S. Boehm

All rights reserved. No part of this publication may be reproduced, stored in a retrieval system, or transmitted, in any form or by any means, without prior written permission of the publisher, or, in Canada, in the case of photocopying or other reprographic copying, a licence from Access Copyright (the Canadian Copyright Licensing Agency).

RONSDALE PRESS
3350 West 21st Avenue, Vancouver, B.C. Canada V6S 1G7
www.ronsdalepress.com

Typesetting: Julie Cochrane, in Minion 12 pt on 16
Cover Design: Nancy de Brouwer, Alofli Graphic Design
Cover Photo: The bombed-out Kaiser-Wilhelm Gedächtniskirche
Paper: Ancient Forest Friendly Enviro 100 edition, 60 lb. Husky (FSC)—
    100% post-consumer waste, totally chlorine-free and acid-free.

Ronsdale Press wishes to thank the following for their support of its publishing program: the Canada Council for the Arts, the Government of Canada, the British Columbia Arts Council, and the Province of British Columbia through the British Columbia Book Publishing Tax Credit program.

Library and Archives Canada Cataloguing in Publication

Title: Secrets in the shadows / Heige S. Boehm.
Names: Boehm, Heige S., 1964– author.
Identifiers: Canadiana (print) 20190072334 | Canadiana (ebook) 20190072350 |
    ISBN 9781553805724 (softcover) | ISBN 9781553805731 (HTML) |
    ISBN 9781553805748 (PDF)
Classification: LCC PS8603.O332 S43 2019 | DDC C813/.6—dc23

At Ronsdale Press we are committed to protecting the environment. To this end we are working with Canopy and printers to phase out our use of paper produced from ancient forests. This book is one step towards that goal.

Printed in Canada by Island Blue Printing, British Columbia

RICHMOND HILL PUBLIC LIBRARY
32972001732637 OR
Secrets in the shadows
Jan.. 10, 2020

for my mother Johanna Boehm
and the memory of my father Rudi Boehm

*"He who fights with monsters should look
to it that he himself does not become a monster."*

—FRIEDRICH NIETZSCHE

SECRETS IN THE
SHADOWS

1

Old Man's Wisdom

— NOVEMBER 1934 —

I GAZED INTO THE BUTCHER'S window, and there sandwiched between a goose and a sheep's head my mirrored image stared back at me.

"I'm perfect," I told my reflection. I thrust my arm forward and clicked my heels. "*Heil Hitler!*"

Frau Silberstein stepped out of the butcher's doorway. "Michael, why are you saluting dead animals? Put your arm down before someone sees you."

Feeling my face turning red, I stared at the cobblestone street, and like a balloon that has lost its air, I let my arm drift to my chest.

"Tell your mama that I will see her tomorrow for coffee," she said as she rode off on her bicycle.

"Michael, Michael!"

I lifted my head, shielding my eyes from the sun, and turned to see who was calling me. From the doorway of the bakery across the street, Frau Bummel was waving to me.

"I have the flour milled for your mama," she called.

As I stepped off the high curb, I stumbled on a loose cobblestone and jetted onto the road just as a hay cart pulled by an ox rumbled past.

"Watch where you're going, little boy!" the driver shouted.

Frau Bummel held the bakery door open, and the tantalizing smell from buttery cakes, sugar-laden pastries and freshly baked bread made me forget about how humiliated I had felt just moments ago.

"*Guten Tag*, Frau Bummel." Her tall slim build cast a looming shadow over me, and as I stared up at her, I marvelled at the neatly braided buns on either side of her head.

"Hello, Michael. How was school today?"

"*Gut, danke.*"

She reached into her display case and handed me a raspberry-filled donut. "Here. Eat, eat! I'll be back in a moment." She stepped behind a curtain into the back room.

I bit into the donut. "We had special doctors come to our school today . . ." Some of the raspberry filling dripped onto my shirt.

"*Ja, ja.*"

I rubbed at the red stain, but I only created a bigger mess. ". . . and the doctor who examined me said, 'you, Michael Boii, are a perfect Aryan!'"

"That's nice." She re-emerged from the back room and plunked a ten-kilogram sack down on the counter. A plume of flour settled over everything. She peered across the display case and her mouth twisted. "Oh, I think you're too small to carry this home."

"I can manage," I said, as I brushed the flour out of my hair. "I'm almost seven and a half!" I reached for the bag and tugged on it, but it wouldn't budge.

"It's much too big for you, Michael. Tell your mama that Herr Bummel will bring it by later today."

I punched the sack. "All right, but one day I'll be strong enough to carry big things."

"You will. Run along now."

"*Aufwiedersehen*, Frau Bummel. *Danke* for the donut." The bell above the door clanged, announcing my departure.

I caught sight of Frau Silberstein outside the florist, two stores up the street from the butcher's shop, placing a bunch of yellow carnations in her bicycle-basket. She got on her bike, wobbling as she manoeuvred her way through a gauntlet of older Hitlerjugend kids who were dressed in their crisp uniforms—brown shirts and black shorts.

"*Jude!*" they yelled after her. "*Jude!*"

For a minute I watched her bumping along the cobblestone street, but she never said a word to those boys as they laughed and joked amongst themselves. My older brothers—the twins, Kurt and Peter, but not Günther—were already in the Hitlerjugend, and my two sisters, Susi and Paula, were in the BDM, the League of German Girls.

As I ran home, taking the shortcut through Herr Zimmermann's farm, I began to imagine how in a few years I too would receive a letter from Adolf Hitler himself, summoning me to join the *Deutsches Jungvolk*. Papa would be proud of me then.

The crisp air filled my nostrils as I ran through the grasses of Herr Zimmermann's sheep pasture. Ahead of me was a wooden fence that separated the sheep from the potato field. I took a deep breath and began sprinting towards it, yelling, "I'm special!" And like a firecracker propelled by gunpowder, I shot into the air and almost—but not quite—sailed over the fence. My trailing leg caught on the top rail, and I found myself dangling from the fence, my head on the ground. I hung upside down like that for a minute or two, and that's when I realized how beautiful Herr Zimmermann's farm was. Then I flipped my legs forward and landed with a thud on my back. I jumped up, pulled my jacket straight and took a deep breath. "Next time!" I told myself as I did a quick surveillance. Good. No one had seen me.

Herr Zimmermann's farm held all my boyhood dreams and secrets. He had forty hectares of rolling land with a brook meandering through the centre of it. He grew thousands of pounds of potatoes, turnips and cabbages on one half of his farm and on the other he pastured a hundred head of sheep, a few cows and pigs, some geese and chickens and two beautiful Clydesdale horses.

In the middle of the farm, a small forest of hazelnut trees stretched out in a grove, and my best friend, Wolfie, and I would make bows and arrows out of the hazelnut branches and use the elastics from the waistbands of our underpants for the strings.

Mama always asked me, "What happened to the elastic . . . ?"

I would only shrug.

She would smile, shake her head and say, "Boys."

But what Wolfie and I loved most on Herr Zimmermann's farm was his magnificent apple orchard. On our way home from school in the fall we would climb the trees and sit in their branches gorging ourselves as we retold one another the adventures of *Max und Moritz* and the Karl May western stories about Winnetou and Old Shatterhand. Inevitably we would end up with stomachaches because we had eaten too many apples—which later resulted in the runs.

Mama would brew up a horrible concoction of herbs—mullein, comfrey and black walnut—and I would hold my nose so I wouldn't smell the odour of the brew, but of course I would gag on it as I swallowed, then gag some more after it was down. But the next day we would be right back up the apple trees.

When we weren't playing the hunter and the hunted or stealing apples, chasing or being chased, Wolfie and I would go fishing or swimming at Trout Lake, a reservoir that bordered Herr Zimmermann's farm just beyond the hazelnut grove. At its deepest, the lake was only ten or twelve metres and it was a mere seven kilometres long, but it was a wonderful playground. On the far side, trees stood right at the lake's edge, and on the north end it was so shallow that bulrushes grew, and that's where we would go hunting for frogs. In the summertime when we went to the lake to swim, we would walk up along old Kliff Strasse, which ran parallel to the Zimmermanns' farm.

"Now, mind," Mama would say, "stay away from the bluffs."

She knew we loved to jump off the six-metre cliffs into the deepest part of the lake, but she preferred us to play where the water lapped gently on the grassy shore.

"Stop cutting through my fields, Michael!" Herr Zimmermann shouted. "You're frightening the sheep. You two boys left the sheep gate open again last night! I spent all morning chasing my animals!"

I shouted back, "Sorry, Herr Zimmermann!" Liebchen, his Deutscher Schäferhund, bounded over to me, knocked me to the ground and licked my face. "Good girl," I said, laughing as I tried to push her way.

Herr Zimmermann helped me up. "Sorry? What am I to do with *sorry*? How about you two close the gates next time! Or better yet—do it again and I won't take you boys fishing or hunting next week." He adjusted the old WWI rifle that he'd slung over his shoulder and reached down to pat his dog. "Maybe I should have Liebchen eat you."

"*Nein*—are you hunting today?"

"Rabbits."

"Any luck?"

"*Nein.*"

"Can I help herd the sheep, Herr?"

"All right."

"Can I hold your shepherd's crook?"

He patted me on the head. "Of course you can." The sun softened Herr Zimmermann's wrinkles.

Liebchen barked and ran after a sheep that had lost its way.

"Does it hurt?" I asked.

"What—my leg?"

"*Ja.*" I stumbled over a small mound of dirt.

"Careful, boy." He reached over to steady me. "When they cut it off with a hacksaw—it hurt like *Scheisse*, and I screamed like a bloody pig."

He had fought in the Great War and lost his leg below the knee, but he sure could manage with that wooden leg.

"You know, it was this place, the animals—and of course, Frau Zimmermann—that pulled me through. There is nothing better than working the land and animal husbandry." He whistled after his dog. "It gives a man purpose and pride, Michael."

"I'm proud, Herr Zimmermann."

"And what makes you proud, boy?"

"Well, there were these doctors that came to our school today, and they told me I'm special because I'm a perfect Aryan."

"Complete and utter nonsense! Special?" He pointed. "You're more like that *Schwarzkopfiges* sheep over there, the one with the black head that Liebchen is chasing. All it's good for is eating."

"But, Herr Zimmermann, they *did*!"

"Whoever they are—they are idiots!" He took my hand. "You might stand out today, Michael, but you're still just one of the flock being herded around. Today you're special, and what about tomorrow? All people and animals are special, Michael. Just treat them with respect and use your God-given brains, boy!"

I pulled my hand out of his.

"You young folk, always doing what you are told to do. Don't ever let anyone take your mind. Foolish lambs."

I handed him back the crook. "But, Herr, they said I was perfect."

"*Ach*, naïve fool you are, Michael. You better run along. I have much work to do." He whistled twice sharply, and Liebchen bolted toward him.

I watched as he limped off with his dog at his side.

I was sure Papa would be proud. He would tell me I was special. And Mama, she too would be proud. I ran over the brick bridge, stopping to stare into the Mulde River to see if I could spot a trout, but all I saw were two white swans before I ran on again.

"Mama, Mama!" I shouted as I flung our front door open. "The special doctors came to our school today, and you know what?"

Mama came out of the kitchen. "Michael, what's all the noise about? And don't slam the—"

The door slammed behind me as I shouted, "They measured our heads and looked at our eyes, and matched our eye colours to a chart. They even took samples of our blood, and samples of our hair and matched them to a hair chart. The doctors wore white coats and the nurse looked us all over." I dropped my coat on the floor. "You know what they said? They said I was a class one. Perfect! They said I was perfect!"

"Wipe your muddy feet! And pick up your coat—we don't live in a barn. And who said what?"

I picked up my coat and hung it on a hook. "The men in white coats—they came to our school!"

"Michael, you're not making any sense. What men? And take off your boots! I don't want mud all over the house! And why is there dirt on your forehead?"

"Real doctors, Mama!"

"Your boots, Michael!" She dabbed her finger to her tongue, and then wiped at the dirt on my forehead. "Where did you get this?"

"I don't know. They just told me I was perfect! And, Mama, the school wants to talk to you about Günther." I pulled my head back.

"When?"

"Tomorrow after school, with the Rektor."

"Herr Kannengiesser, the head schoolmaster?"

"*Ja*, Mama. Papa will be pleased, won't he?"

"*Ja, ja*, but you're going to come with me tomorrow."

"Why? I haven't done anything wrong."

"You haven't, but you're coming with me, and don't argue. After you have washed your face, I want you to go downstairs and bring up some coal."

"Mama . . . Frau Silberstein, the *Jude*, is coming for coffee tomorrow. She asked me to tell you." I trudged toward the stairs.

"Michael! March yourself back here right now." She knelt down and held my hands. "What did you just say?"

"I said Frau Silberstein is coming tomorrow for coffee."

"That's better. I don't ever want to hear you say *Jude* in that way again."

"But, Mama—"

"Don't Mama me. I've brought you up better than that."

"But Herr Hitler—"

"Michael, that's enough out of you." Under her breath she said, "That foolish man will be the death of us all." She sighed as she straightened the single white rose that sat in a small vase on the hall table. "Imagine declaring yourself Führer—Supreme Leader? He's a thug. Nothing more than a foolish postcard painter."

"What, Mama?"

"Nothing, go wash your face, Michael, and change your shirt."

When Papa came home that night, I told him the good news, but all he said was, "That'll serve you well, boy."

The next afternoon I sat in Herr Kannengiesser's office with Mama, tipping my wooden chair back and forth so that the squeaky sound filled the silence of the room. "Mama, how much longer is he going to be?"

She gestured for me to sit still. "Stop that, Michael! He is probably taking care of something important." She adjusted her dress, tugged at her gloves and straightened her hat.

The walls of Herr Kannengiesser's office were painted a cold, putty green. He had a picture of Adolf Hitler on the wall behind his desk. A tall wooden filing cabinet stood in the corner, and the office smelled of floor wax.

I sat fidgeting as the minutes ticked by until the office door opened with a squeak and the Rektor walked in.

"Good afternoon, Frau Boii. Oh, don't get up." He closed the door behind him, its glass pane rattling, then moved directly to sit behind his oversized desk. Herr Kannengiesser was wearing his usual tailor-made grey woollen suit that must have cost a hefty penny. "I hope you're well?" He shuffled some of the papers on his desk.

Mama nodded. "I'm well, thank you."

Herr Kannengiesser kept his head down as he spoke. "I see you brought your son, Michael. Good afternoon, Michael." His ill-fitting glasses were too big for his small round face, and he pushed them back up his beak-like nose.

Mama once more gestured for me to reply. "Good afternoon, Herr Rektor," I said in a flat tone.

"I'm going to get right to it, Frau Boii. The school trustees think it best that you take your son Günther out of school."

Mama took a deep breath and leaned forward. "What . . . what are you saying?"

Herr Beak Face held up his hand, straightened his tie and lightly twirled the National Socialist pin he wore in his lapel. "Let me continue. Since his accident two years ago, we have noticed that your son has been having a hard time keeping up with the new National Socialist curriculum."

"I beg your pardon?"

"The other children are teasing him on a regular basis."

"Günther has never mentioned this to me. He has good friends here in school."

"That may be so, but as I was saying . . ." Herr Beak Face cleared his throat. "As I was saying, the new school board finds Günther . . . not in keeping with the purity of our world to come."

I just sat there like Mama. What did he mean by "purity"? He was talking about my brother. I clenched my fist. I felt hot. "Don't talk bad about my brother, you—"

"Michael!" Mama said.

Herr Beak Face shot me a sharp glance, but I squinted and just ever so slightly lifted my fist. Mama never saw.

Mama leaned forward, tugging at her sleeve cuffs. "I don't think you can do that to Günther. He is only eleven, and surely he needs more schooling than just grade six. I know he stutters, but he is a polite, smart boy."

It did not matter how much she protested, no amount of pleading or arguing was going to make Herr Beak Face budge. She started to fidget with her necklace and her face was becoming red.

He sat smugly behind his orderly desk, and I could see he was taking pleasure in humiliating Mama in telling her to remove her son from his school. Herr Kannengiesser was head of the Teachers National Socialist Education Board of our small town, so he had the authority to determine other people's fate. I knew he had removed Jewish and other children too. He shuffled some papers that lay in a wooden tray on his desk, then picked up his pipe and began filling it with tobacco. "You must understand, Frau Boii, I'm obligated to report any student who doesn't measure up." His steely blue eyes looked as though they were popping out of his head. "I can recommend placing Günther in an institution. You know that is where all the . . . undesirables go, the cripples and the . . . ah, *Untermenschen*, those deemed . . . ah, retarded—"

"My son is not retarded and he is not an *Untermensch!*" she shouted as she clutched her handbag close to her stomach.

I wanted to hit him and tell him that he was dumb and an *Untermensch*, but I knew better.

"Frau Boii, please pull yourself together."

But Mama spoke with determination because she wanted Günther to stay in school. "Herr Kannengiesser," Mama said, puffing herself up much like a hen protecting her chicks, "I apologize for my outburst, but we both know that my son is not—"

Herr Beak Face cut Mama off abruptly. "For several reasons I apologize, Frau Boii." Then with a hint of irritation in his voice, he continued, "But I have responsibilities to the party. I know you do not wish for Günther to go to the insane asylum. However, the state tests are coming up, and that means I will have to report every child's marks. It is only because of who your husband is that I am telling you this, and not putting in for an immediate transfer to have your son committed. Please stop making a scene. Starting to-morrow, keep him at home and indoors as much as you can. I will speak with Frau Zimmermann. She was a teacher here before the National Socialist Party removed her . . ." Then he mumbled, "After she refused to teach the new curriculum." He cleared his throat. "Maybe she will teach him at her home."

Defeated, Mama pulled out a handkerchief from her purse, dabbed her eyes and nodded. "All right."

He leaned forward, his eyes darting back and forth as though he had revealed something he should not have. Then continuing in a softer voice, he said, "It's better this way." He paused. "Truly, my hands are tied."

I sat glaring at Herr Beak Face, but I did nothing to embarrass or bring more shame to my mama. I just sat silently on my stiff wooden chair.

"It is for the greater good," he said.

Mama bit her lip, and then under her breath repeated, "For the greater good."

Herr Beak Face lit his pipe, inhaled, and sucked on it a few times while holding his hand over the pipe bowl. As he exhaled, he said, "Your boy is lucky."

At that moment a sparrow hit the window, and a streak of blood trickled down the glass. Mama and I were startled, but Herr Beak Face continued speaking as though nothing had happened. "Some other children are being sent to work camps, and some lucky ones become street cleaners, and . . . well . . . Let's just say there are others not as fortunate as your son . . ."

He leaned forward, tapped his pipe on the edge of the ashtray, then leaned back in his chair and in a voice that was little more than a whisper added, "Life unworthy of life, Frau Boii . . ."

Mama put her hand up to her mouth and shook her head.

"Please leave quietly and let the matter rest, Frau." A cold placid expression spread across his face. He stood up and directed Mama and me to the door. "*Heil Hitler.*" He saluted and clicked his heels.

In a hushed voice Mama repeated the words, "*Heil Hitler.*"

Once outside the school I took Mama's hand, and we walked in silence for a few minutes. "I'm sorry about Günther, Mama. I know it's all because of what happened in the graveyard!"

She stopped walking, grabbed both my hands, and said, "Michael, sweetie, whatever makes you think that?"

"Because yesterday they said I was perfect . . . I'm blond and Günther's hair is dark . . . so he's not perfect . . . And . . . that day at the cemetery . . ."

"That was two years ago and it was an accident, Michael! And whatever the doctors said yesterday or whatever they believe . . . is ridiculous. All children are perfect."

"*Ja,* but if I hadn't asked Günther to help me climb onto the archangel gravestone, then it wouldn't have fallen on him. His head got crushed because of me. He wouldn't have that metal plate in his head and he wouldn't stutter and his arm would work better . . ." Tears rolled down my face.

Mama wrapped her arms around me. "Michael, you can't think like that. It was an accident."

Between my ragged breaths and tears I sputtered, "He . . . told me . . . Günther told me to get down . . . and I wouldn't." I had wanted to sit between the wings of the archangel—on his shoulders—while Mama was off putting flowers on Opa Odin's grave.

"Michael, it wasn't your fault." Mama held me tighter, kissed me on the forehead and wiped my tears away with her hanky. "Günther will be okay . . . Let's go home and I will make us a nice cup of hot cocoa, and you can have a piece of strudel."

"Okay," I snuffled.

As we walked up our front steps, Mama said, "Michael, everything will be all right." That afternoon she explained the situation as well as she could to Günther. He did not fully understand but seemed to take solace in the promise of being able to spend time with the animals at the Zimmermanns' farm.

After supper Mama sat in the living room with Papa while Günther and I sat on the hallway stairs listening in on their conversation. After Mama told Papa what had happened at the meeting with Herr Beak Face, Papa said, "The Rektor is doing us a favour. By the NSAP standards Günther is retarded and a cripple, and he will never amount to anything. Perhaps being at the farm he can learn something of value."

"Rudi, how can you say that? Günther is your son! You know as well as I do that he's not retarded."

That's when we heard Papa hit Mama. "You know nothing, Frau . . ."

"Rudi, I just—"

"You don't think I care? It can get a lot worse for him."

"But Rudi, I know he—"

I stood up and sneaked into the living room doorway in time to see Papa hit her again.

"You know nothing! Keep your mouth shut . . ."

That's when Papa noticed me, glared my way, and I fled back to the stairs. Günther and I climbed up to the landing, and he put his arm around me as we sat quietly together. We saw Papa emerge from the living room, take his coat from its hook in the hallway and slam the door on his way out.

After a while Mama came out of the living room. "Michael, Günther!" she said as she dabbed at her eyes. "What are you two still doing up?" She climbed the stairs to where we sat. We both stood, and Mama gently placed her hands on our shoulders. "It'll be all right, boys. Up to bed you go."

At two in the morning we awoke to yelling and screaming downstairs. Our sisters, Susi and Paula, tiptoed into our room. Without speaking a word, the twins, Kurt and Peter, lifted the blankets on the big bed they shared, and all five of us huddled together, holding one another till the fighting downstairs stopped.

2

Fritz

❧

"MAMA, WHERE ARE MY SOCKS?" I yelled from the top of the stairs. "I can't find them."

"They're in the wash kettle, Michael. Take a pair out of your father's dresser—but not his good socks. The ones that have been darned will do for you."

"*Danke.*"

"Where are you rushing off to?"

"Mama . . . ! It's my DJV Hitlerjugend meeting."

"*Ach, ja, Deutsches Jungvolk.* It's Sunday already. Don't forget your sister."

"What?"

"Your sister Paula. She'll be waiting for you to walk her home."

"Why can't she walk home by herself?" I mumbled under my breath.

"And don't be late for *Abendessen*. You know how your Papa gets when you are late for supper."

"*Ja, ja.*"

"Michael!"

"Sorry."

"What are you doing up there?"

"I can't find my boots."

"Where did you take them off?"

"I don't remember." I opened the top drawer of Papa's heavy oak dresser. All his socks were neatly folded and lying in perfect rows. "The red and black ones, Mama?"

"*Ja.*"

I picked up a pair of my Papa's darned socks, and there was his World War I Mauser C96 pistol lying under them. Beneath it was a box of bullets. The pistol's handle was made of wood and it had a large red-painted number 9 burnt into the bottom of it. Papa said the number was there to remind the user to load it with 9mm bullets and not the traditional 7.63mm. Careful not to disturb anything, I picked up the gun, opened the box and loaded ten bullets into the chamber. The gun felt cold in my hand as I aimed it into the hallway, away from where the picture of Adolf Hitler was hanging. I smiled, hoping that one day I would make the Führer proud.

"Michael, what's taking you so long?"

"I'm coming . . . !" Minka the cat skittered down the hallway. Quickly I put the pistol back and slammed the drawer shut, and that's when Mama's wedding picture fell over. As I picked it up, I noticed how happy she looked standing beside Papa on her wedding day. I gently placed it back, turned around and sat on Papa's side of their bed to put on his socks. Then I opened his nightstand drawer, picked up a book and read the title out loud: "*Mein Kampf.*" But as I flipped through the pages, a picture fell out: it was of a woman I had never seen before, and she was wearing a bathing suit and sitting on a boulder.

"Michael! Get down here!"

"Coming!" Quickly I put the book back, stuffed the picture into the pocket of my uniform shirt, then stood and tucked my shirt into my black shorts. As I ran down the stairs, I saw Mama standing at the bottom, holding my boots in one hand and my coat in the other.

"Michael, march yourself straight back up those stairs and put on your long pants."

"But they're itchy."

"Do it now before I give you something to really complain about."

As I went back up the stairs, I shouted down, "Why can't the twins or Günther pick Paula up?"

"That's enough out of you. Besides, Susi and your brothers are helping out at the Zimmermanns' farm today."

It only took me a minute to change into my long pants, and I ran back down the stairs.

"It's about time. Here are your boots and coat . . . hurry it up. Wolfie doesn't want to wait all day for you."

Sitting on the stairs, I fumbled as I put on my boots. They had once belonged to Günther and were getting too small for me.

"Let me help you." Mama knelt, placed my foot in her lap and tied my boots. "Stand up, Michael." As she buttoned my grey overcoat, her hands moved over me like a conductor in front of an orchestra.

"*Danke*, Mama."

She sighed. "*Ja, ja* . . . Please don't be late for supper tonight." She stood up and leaned in to brush my hair out of my eyes, then gave me a kiss on the forehead before placing my cap on my head. "You sure are getting big . . . already taller than your older brothers. And you're only twelve. But you take after your Opa Odin."

I felt proud whenever she said that because Opa had fought against the French in 1870, and I wanted to be just like him. "I won't be late . . . I promise, Mama."

"Good, and don't forget your sister. She'll be waiting for you. You know how scared she gets."

"Mama, when are Peter and Kurt going back to their military school?"

"Tomorrow." She stood up, wiped her hands on her apron. "Get going. It's washing day today and I'm up to my elbows in laundry." She picked up her basket and headed down the stairs to the basement to do the washing. But before she reached the bottom of the steps, she turned and shouted up, "Thanks for remembering to stack the firewood for the washing stove."

Mama would pour water into the big copper wash-kettle that sat on the wood-burning stove in the basement. She'd sprinkle Burnus detergent into the water, then fasten a pouch filled with lavender to the side of the kettle. Every now and then, she'd push the laundry down with a big wooden wash spoon when the clothing bubbled. The smell of the soapy lavender brew permeated the house. It was my job to chop wood, shovel the coal into the cellar and keep both the wood piled up and the coal bucket filled by the kitchen stove.

I stood in front of the hall mirror admiring myself before realizing that something was missing. "My armband and neck scarf . . . I forgot to put them on!"

"*Ach*, Michael!" Mama said as she returned from the basement holding a pair of washing tongs.

"Sorry!" I shouted as I flew past her and back up the stairs.

"It's bad enough that Susi isn't here to help with the chores, and with Paula at her BDM meeting . . ."

Mostly the League for Girls just taught the girls housekeeping skills so that they would become good *Hausfraus*, so I shouted, "No one will marry Paula. She's too funny-looking!" Then as I put my Hitlerjugend armband on, I muttered, "What good is it that she's in the BDM anyway? It's not like she'll ever be a soldier. She's too scrawny and—"

"Michael!"

"And she's got fish eyes." I came running down the stairs, still securing my scarf, and tripped on the broken tread. *"Ach, Scheisse."*

"What was that, Michael?" Mama said. "I don't think I raised you to sound like a sailor!"

"Nein, Mama."

As Mama headed for the kitchen, I grabbed up my satchel and stopped in front of the mirror again to check my scarf.

"Paula has very pretty blue eyes," Mama said from the kitchen, "and one day some young man will fall in love with her and she will have a beautiful family of her own."

"Yuck! Why would anyone want kids? Besides, they don't hand out medals for being a *Putzfrau.* Medals are for soldiers." I pulled out my Hitlerjugend knife, ran my fingers over the inscription: Blood and Honour.

"Ja, so they are." Mama came back from the kitchen carrying my two-year-old baby sister, Annalisa, whose birthday was one day before Hitler's. Mama spoke softly, "Medals are given to women, too, for birthing children. The more children the more medals." Papa often scolded Mama that if she had waited one more day to have Annalisa, she would have made Hitler proud.

"Why can't Günther or Susi get Paula?"

"Michael, that's enough out of you. Oh, wait! I forgot your sandwiches." And she returned to the kitchen once more.

Standing in the doorway to our front room, I noticed for the first time how ancient the old family photos that hung on our flocked green-and gold-papered walls looked. "Mama, why do you have a tea towel hanging over Hitler's picture?"

"Oh . . . I don't want it to get dusty."

"That's our Führer, Mama! He wouldn't like that!" I walked over to the picture and pulled the tea towel down, then stood back and saluted Hitler much the same way that Papa always did. I looked around. Our home was small, musty, and more than two hundred years old. The electricity was new, but the toilet was an outhouse that stood in the corner of our garden. Our kitchen had a large metal sink with only cold running water and a long table that we boys would sit at to play cards or Mikado in the evening while the girls helped Mama with the cooking. We had three bedrooms upstairs, one for the girls, one for us boys, and the large room was Mama and Papa's bedroom.

"It's begun snowing again, Michael," Mama called, "so stay bundled up. And your sister—don't forget to pick her up. And for your own good, don't be late for supper!"

"*Ja*, Mama." All of us kids adored our Mama, but none of us dared to cross Papa. I followed him like a shadow—or maybe more like a loyal dog jumping to catch every scrap of approval he threw my way.

Mama came out of the kitchen and tucked two sandwiches wrapped in cloth napkins into my satchel. "I put two liver sausage sandwiches in there—one of them is for Wolfie."

"With mustard?"

"*Ja*. Now get going and don't slam that poor old door on your way out." With Annalisa on her hip, Mama went back down into the basement to tend to the laundry.

I swung my satchel over my shoulder. As well as my sandwiches, it contained some money for the meeting and my official DJV booklet. When we arrived at the clubhouse, our booklets would be stamped, indicating that we had paid our monthly dues. Our books also listed all the tasks that we performed for our community, like collecting scrap paper, metal, old tires and money, as well as how well we did in sports tournaments and fighting and shooting and camping skills.

We were marked on our accomplishments, much like on our school report books, and if we did well, we received badges and medals. I took one last look in the mirror and smiled at myself. The dimple in my chin was just like Opa's and it set me apart from my siblings. It made me look older than my twelve years, and it didn't hurt that I was tall for my age.

"Bye, Mama." As I slammed the door behind me, I whispered, "Watch out, world, here I come!"

It only took me five minutes to arrive at Wolfie's place, which was an apartment in the only social housing building in town, a three-storey U-shaped walk-up with a row of outhouses in the centre of the back courtyard. Only last week Wolfie had a mishap out back, and I had laughed so hard that I pissed my pants. He was doing chin-ups on the bottom rung of a fire escape ladder, but he hadn't realized that the cover on the sewage-holding tank below him wasn't on properly. He pulled himself up, counted fifty, and just as he was professing how strong he was, the rung on the ladder broke. And before I could do anything, he fell right into the sewage-tank. He was standing there up to his hips in excrement, and crying, "Help me out of here! I'm drowning in *Scheisse!*" And I just laughed and laughed.

Now Wolfie was sitting on the front stairs of the apartment building, waiting for me. "What took you so long?" he said.

"Couldn't find my boots."

"Oh." He stood up. "Let's cut through the Zimmermanns."

I put my arm over his shoulder. "Did you pinch some cigarettes from your mutti?"

"Course I did."

"She cut your hair again, didn't she?" I said, tousling his badly shorn hair.

"*Ja* . . . She was drunk again." He pulled two cigarettes from his satchel, lit them, and handed one to me.

"Ah, your hair doesn't look that bad, Wolfie."

"*Ach, danke.*"

I nudged him, "But you still smell like *Scheisse!*" And we laughed.

Wolfgang von Vogel was his full name, but we all called him Wolfie. His birthday was August 5, 1927, just one month after mine, and like me he was tall for his age. He had a mop of curly red hair, his teeth were perfectly straight, and dimples appeared on his cheeks whenever he smiled. We were the best of friends and knew everything about one another. We always had each other's backs.

Herr Zimmermann's fields lay covered in a blanket of snow, and we could see animal tracks before us, heading toward the old brown barn.

Wolfie pointed to where tracks led off to the right. "Looks like a fox killed one of the geese."

"*Ja*. Bet it was Old Red." I led the way to investigate.

When Wolfie bent down to pick up a half-chewed goose wing, some blood dripped onto his shoe. He dropped the wing and winced as he wiped his hand on his shorts. "Let's go."

Though the snow in front of us had been stained with blood, the farm still looked beautiful, cloaked in its stunning coat of pure white.

It took us about twenty-five minutes to arrive at the town square where the regular markets were held, but today and for the rest of the month it was the Christmas market, by far the most beautiful market to attend.

Wolfie reached into his pocket. "Look, I have some money. We can get two pretzels!"

We made our way through the square. Townsfolk were walking about with their Glühwein, some of them munching on roasted candied almonds. The smell of Apfelwein filled the air. A band played Christmas carols, and every vendor tried to entice us to buy their goods—Christmas ornaments, tree decorations, nutcrackers, toys—all made by hand. Children crowded around the booth of one of the toy makers, and Wolfie and I joined them, dazzled by how the man could make his marionettes come alive by just moving a few strings. Finally he wished everyone *Frohe Weihnachten*, and then the marionettes raised their arms in a salute and said, "*Heil Hitler*."

In the centre of the square stood a carousel and a giant Christmas tree that was all lit up.

"Wolfie, want to go for a ride on the carousel?"

"Nah, carousels are for babies, but let's get our pretzels before we go."

"Okay." We walked over to Frau Bummel's stand.

"Hello, Frau Bummel," said Wolfie.

"Hello, boys. Shouldn't you two be at your meeting?"

"We're on our way, Frau Bummel," I said. "We only stopped to get two of your delicious pretzels."

She made the best pretzels from our town of Schadesdorf all the way up to Rochlitz and down to Glauchau and Zwickau. She was known for her delicious baking, and everyone looked forward to one of her pretzels with a tasty grilled sausage, some mustard, and a beer to wash it all down. Of course, I was still too young to have a beer in public, but I would sneak one when Papa had his army friends over for an evening. I liked seeing all the men in their uniforms, but the SS men looked the most regal in their tall black boots and long, beautiful coats adorned with shiny skull buttons. They looked like handsome pirates.

Wolfie nudged me, handed me a pretzel, and we said, "*Danke*, Frau Bummel."

"Now hurry up, boys," she said. "You don't want to be late."

We made our way through the market and down the street. Rushing up the stairs of the town hall, I stuffed the last bit of pretzel into my mouth.

As I pushed open the heavy door, its rusty hinges creaked and squeaked, making me think of the time I watched Herr Zimmermann's two pigs squeal as they were being slaughtered. "The door needs oiling."

Wolfie punched me in the arm. "You sound like your papa."

I punched him back.

The old wood-burning stove in the centre of the room kept the town hall toasty warm, but it left a smoky smell and a heavy blue-grey haze hung in the air. I could see that all our comrades were in attendance, and Jürgen Fassbender was already standing at the podium at the front of the room sorting through his papers. He was getting ready to deliver his final speech to us, and he looked smart in his soldier's uniform. He had just turned eighteen and had been drafted into the Wehrmacht. Next week he was most likely being posted to Poland, and we were all envious!

On September 1, 1939, Deutschland had been forced to invade Poland. Papa said that we had no choice, that after all it was Poland that attacked us first. Papa believed that the war was going to be over quickly, but most of the boys in the DJV hoped he was wrong because we had taken an oath to fight for the Third Reich. Wolfie and I along with the other Deutsches Jungvolk were thrilled to uphold the flag of our fatherland. We loved attending our glorious meetings, going on hikes and camping, but there wasn't anyone in that room who didn't prefer shooting guns and learning combat manoeuvres, because we all wanted to be doing the real thing.

"Michael and Wolfie," Otto shouted, waving his arms at us. "Sit here with Hans and me." He had saved two seats for us beside the stove.

Wolfie pulled me along by my coat sleeve. "Come on, Michael. *Ja, ja,* we're coming, Otto."

I was so busy staring at Jürgen in his new uniform that I stepped on Fritz's feet.

He kicked me. "Watch where you're going, *Dummkopf.*"

I was angry with Fritz for making a scene, and just as I muttered, "*Dummkopf* yourself, Fritzzzzzzzzz!" Jürgen looked up from his papers, his amber eyes glaring at me.

Fritz and Jürgen were best pals, and I was a little jealous of their age and place in life. Jürgen had been our Deutsche Jungvolk leader for two years and Fritz was his helper, though he was almost a year younger. Whenever Jürgen spoke, I became more inspired. I wanted to be like him—a leader, a man's man. We all trusted him, and I hoped that one day I would be brave like him and lead men into extraordinary battles, men who trusted me, men devoted to fighting till the death. After all, I did come from a long line of honourable, dignified commanders like my Opa Odin.

"Sit down, Michael," Otto said. "Jürgen is going to start the meeting."

"*Heil Hitler!*" Jürgen shouted as he raised his arm.

And I wondered if we looked like the marionettes at the market, our strings attached to an invisible puppeteer, as we stood up and thrust our arms forward. "*Heil,*" we shouted.

Jürgen shouted, "*Sieg Heil!*"

And we returned with "*Heil!*"

"Sit! Sit, everyone." He stood in front of our red-and-black swastika banner, his hands dancing in the air as he spoke with authority and pride. We hung onto every word.

"Better to have fought and died in honour than to lose freedom and soul," he said before getting a bit choked up, a tear rolling down his freckled white face. The room fell silent.

Jürgen gripped the sides of the podium. "I will be leaving you shortly, but what I want you all to remember is our oath!"

We stood up and began reciting it. "In the presence of this blood-banner which represents our Führer, I swear to devote all my energies and my strength to the Saviour of our country, Adolf Hitler. I am willing and ready to give up my life for him, so help me God. One People, one Reich, one Führer."

How glorious it felt to say those words, and how happy I felt sitting there with my best friend, Wolfie. And while Jürgen continued speaking, my mind drifted back to April of the previous year when Wolfie had gone with me and my family to Berlin for Hitler's fiftieth birthday celebrations.

During *Abendessen* one night in mid-April, Papa had announced as we were finishing our evening meal, "I have some great news." He could hardly contain himself. "We are all going to Berlin." A smile had crept over his face.

Mama closed her eyes, took a deep breath, and as she opened her eyes, she said, "When, Rudi?"

We were all excited. "Yes, Papa, when?"

"We'll leave here a week from tomorrow. You know it will be Hitler's fiftieth birthday celebration on the 20th?"

"Where will we stay?" Mama said as she set her spoon down.

"With a very respectable family."

"Who, Papa, who?" I demanded as I took another dinner roll.

"The von Frays." Papa looked pleased with himself. "Michael, you have had two buns. Put it back."

Mama glanced my way and gently nodded.

Papa continued, "Herr von Fray is an officer with the SS. I met him at a rally in Berlin."

After we ate, while helping Mama in the kitchen, I pleaded with her, "Mama, can Wolfie please come with us?"

"I don't think so, Michael."

"But the twins won't be going because they're at military school, and if Wolfie's papa were alive . . . Mama, please? This might be the only time we get to see our Führer! Ple-e-ease, Mama . . ."

"I'll talk it over with your Papa."

I hugged her. "*Danke, danke.*"

She handed me a dinner roll with a bit of butter on it. I went to the cupboard to get a plate and sat at the table. Mama sat with me. "A letter from your brothers arrived today," she said as she poured each of us a cup of tea.

"What did they say?"

"Peter is missing home, but he's happy that the school has a lot of track and field games."

"What about Kurt?"

"He's missing his girlfriend, but he's doing well in his studies."

"His girlfriend?"

"Ilsa from next door."

"Yuck!"

Mama was silent for a few minutes and then she said, "You know, Michael, there are a lot of great men in the world to admire."

"Like who?" I asked.

"Well, Charles Lindbergh, for example. He was the first man to fly solo across the Atlantic Ocean . . ." Mama knew how much I wanted to be a Luftwaffe pilot.

"He was? But Adolf Hitler is smarter than anyone, isn't he? That's what Papa says. Don't you think so too, Mama?"

Mama took a sip of tea and stared into her cup. "*Ja*, of course, Michael."

Papa reluctantly agreed to allow Wolfie to come with us to Berlin. The week didn't pass fast enough, but when the day finally came, I woke up early and sat dressed in my DJV uniform on the front step waiting for Wolfie.

After a while, the front door opened. Mama peeked her head out and looked down at me, wrapping her housecoat more tightly around herself. "Michael, what are you doing up so early?"

I turned to look up at her. "I'm waiting for Wolfie."

"Come inside. The cold will be the death of you. Wolfie won't arrive for at least another hour."

"But, Mama—"

"Come inside! You can help me make breakfast."

I stood up and pointed. "There he is!"

"Why is he so early?"

"I told him to come early so he can have breakfast with us."

Mama bent down, brushed the hair off my face and stroked my cheek.

"Hello, Wolfie," I said, grabbing his arm to pull him up the stairs.

But Wolfie stood for a moment smiling up at Mama. "Thank you, Frau Boii, for taking me with you."

"You're welcome, Wolfie. Now you two come inside. Hang your jacket up, Wolfie. You too, Michael."

Wolfie pulled his coat tight around him. "I'd rather keep it on."

"Wolfie, take your jacket off!" Mama insisted. Then she tilted her head. "What are you hiding?"

Wolfie hung his head and mumbled. "I tried to iron my shirt, but ..."

"Take off your jacket, Wolfie, and let me take a look." Mama tried not to smile as she helped him with his jacket. Then she turned towards me. "Michael, take Wolfie up to your room and give him one of your other DJV shirts."

"That's okay, Frau Boii. If I don't take my jacket off, no one will see that I burnt it."

"Nonsense, Wolfie. Go upstairs with Michael."

"*Ja*, Frau Boii."

"And call me Mama!"

After Wolfie changed, we helped Mama in the kitchen. Wolfie handed her some eggs, then leaned in and gave her a gentle kiss on the cheek. "*Danke*, Mama."

She gave his hand a squeeze and smiled. After that day whenever he came over, she taught him little by little how to cook simple foods, iron, polish his shoes, and even sew a button on his shirt.

After breakfast we all put on our boots and grabbed our coats.

"Mama, is Günther coming with us?" I asked as I put on my coat.

"*Nein*. He's staying with the Zimmermanns."

As Wolfie and I stepped off the train in the Lehrter Bahnhof in Berlin, we looked at one another, grinning.

"It's like a palace," I said as I gazed up at the giant arched windows that lined the station and the barrel-vaulted ceiling that seemed to go on forever.

Mama carried Annalisa on one arm, and with her other hand she took hold of my elbow. "Michael, I want you and Wolfie to stay by my side."

"*Ach*, Mama, we're not babies."

Papa slapped me up the side of my head. "Michael!"

Mama pulled me in closer. "I know you're not."

Wolfie grabbed my arm and said, "There's a lot of people here, Michael."

Mama smiled at him. "Paula, take Wolfie's hand and don't let go."

As we stepped out of the station, I saw that Wolfie was right—I had never seen so many people, but for some reason it didn't feel chaotic, just a sea of hats and suits. People everywhere were either saying hello or goodbye, and it seemed everyone had luggage. To our right the Spree River meandered through the city.

Papa lit a cigarette, then tucked Susi's hand into the crook of his arm. "Susi and I will find us a taxi. We'll be back in a few minutes."

Papa and Susi were soon back in a taxi, and as we drove through Berlin, I couldn't believe what I was seeing. Every building had red banners with a black swastika in a white circle, and there were banners hanging from balconies, and so many flowers—mostly red ones—everywhere. I had never seen so many Mercedes and a lot of them were convertibles, too, and there were scores of motorbikes and even people in horse-drawn buggies. There were trams that came in an assortment of colours. I liked the blue ones best, but Wolfie liked the yellow two-tone ones. And Mama pointed to a train that went by and said, "That's the S-Bahn."

At that moment a tram clanked past us, and Annalisa cried out.

"It's okay, Annalisa," said Paula as she bounced the baby on her knee. "Look at all the nicely dressed people."

Just then a bus swerved into our lane, and our taxi driver laid on his horn, raised his fist and yelled, "*Arschloch!*"

Wolfie and I snickered. But as the driver turned onto the street marked Kurfürstendamm, he looked up into his mirror and said to Mama, "Sorry about that."

"That's all right," Mama said.

He pointed out the window. "This street has all the finest stores one could ever want."

Susi, who was sitting up front with Papa, turned and said, "Mama, could we please get new sheet music or some song books while we're here? Maybe they have 'The Flat Foot Floogie?'"

Papa snorted. "No daughter of mine is going to play that black jungle voodoo stuff!"

Mama leaned forward and touched Susi's shoulder. "How about we get some Wagner, darling, or maybe some Hindemith—"

"Hindemith!" Papa roared. "All he makes is noise! Now Wagner— *that* is good music."

Wolfie poked me and pointed. "Do you think we'll get to ride in one of those funny-looking buses?"

Mama smiled. "That's a double-decker, Wolfie."

After fifteen minutes in the taxi we arrived at Herr von Fray's house: Tiergartenstrasse 13A. Annalisa had fallen asleep on Paula's knee, and Mama handed her to me as I stepped out of the taxi. The taxi driver stepped out too, and as he helped Papa with the bags, Mama said, "*Danke.*" Papa paid the taxi driver.

We all stood staring at the beautiful three-storey stone mansion in front of us, and Paula reached for Mama's hand. Not wanting to wake Annalisa, I whispered to Mama, "Is this where we'll be staying?"

Behind a small brick wall was a large flower garden, and the front steps were curved and made out of marble. A carved wooden arch framed the doorway. As Papa marched up to the front door, the rest of us stood at the bottom of the steps. Mama whisked off my cap, then Wolfie's. "I want you two to be on your best behaviour." Then she took out her hanky, spat on it, and wiped a bit of *schmutz* off both our faces. "That's better. Give Annalisa to me, Michael."

The front door opened and there stood the most beautiful woman I had ever seen. She was wearing a Red Cross nurse's uniform. "Good evening, Herr and Frau Boii. Please excuse me. I just arrived home and have not had time to change out of my uniform."

"Quite all right, Fräulein," said Papa as he shook her hand. "That uniform does you justice very nicely."

Blushing, she pulled her nurse's cap off and ushered us into the house. "Come in. I'm Fräulein Margarita, Herr von Fray's daughter. My papa will be home later tonight. He sends his apologies. He had to rush off to attend a meeting."

After the introductions were done, Fräulein Margarita said, "I will get you all settled and then you can wash up. *Abendessen* will be ready for you to eat in about an hour." She took our coats and hung them in a tall wardrobe. "I'm sure you're all tired and would like to rest."

We were standing in the foyer, and beyond it I could see a great big room with a big black piano in it. It looked like a place where people would have ballroom dances.

"*Danke*," Mama replied as she gently removed Annalisa's coat. "I hope we're not putting you out."

Fräulein Margarita shook her head. "Oh, not at all, Frau Boii. It's a welcome change."

"How so?"

"Papa has a lot of his SS men for company, but ever since Mutti . . . Well, it's nice to have some female company." Fräulein Margarita took my hand. "You must be Michael, and you are Wolfgang?"

We nodded, unable to speak or take our eyes off her. She smelled pretty, like summer rain.

She pointed with her free hand at the stairs. "If you two follow the stairs all the way to the top and then open the first door on your left, that will be your room."

We nodded again. Mama smiled and said, "Well . . . get, you two."

As we ran up the stairs, Wolfie stopped and turned. "You can call me Wolfie, Fräulein Margarita!"

She looked up at us and smiled. "Wolfie it is then."

We continued up the stairs and paused at the second floor. "Look, Wolfie." I pointed. "They have a bathroom inside their house!"

"*Ach, ja.*"

We clambered to the top of the stairs and were both startled when a great white poodle puppy with blue ribbons tied in his ears jumped out at us from the room that was to be ours. We knelt on the landing to pet him.

Fräulein Margarita called from the bottom of the stairs, "I see you two have met Bunny."

Wolfie and I laughed as Bunny licked our faces.

That night we all met Herr von Fray, a tall, very bald man with a large scar that began just below his right eye and ran across his cheek and down to the corner of his mouth. When he noticed that Wolfie and I were staring at his face, he took one step closer to us, and when we went to step back, he put his hands on our shoulders. Then he reached up to the top of his scar and with his finger traced it down to the corner of his mouth. "This is a *Schmiss* . . . from a *Mensur* bout."

Wolfie and I just stood not saying a word.

"I was a foolish boy playing tough at fencing during my university years and received this cut." Then he smiled, patted our shoulders and took us to see his fencing swords.

Later that evening Papa and Herr von Fray went to watch the torch-light procession. Papa was delighted because he thought they might possibly catch a glimpse of Hitler who would be on the balcony of the Reich Chancellery. Mama sent us to bed right after dinner so we could be up early to find a good place to watch the parade.

The next morning Papa set off with Herr von Fray while Mama took us with Fräulein Margarita to watch Hitler's birthday celebration from the roadside. The familiar red banners with swastikas were hanging not only from every balcony and every building along the parade route, but they were strung from golden posts as well. Golden eagles were mounted on the highest parts of some buildings, and beneath the eagles hung long red banners also with swastikas on them.

There were other banners with iron crosses—Hitler's glorious symbol. Men in uniform rode horses and beat drums while others were blaring trumpets. Thousands of soldiers marched in formation carrying banners on poles. They were followed by tanks and military vehicles of every kind, and airplanes flew overhead along the parade route.

I could see that Mama was overwhelmed by the thousands of people lining the street and that she was nervous. "I want everyone to hold hands." She shouted to be heard above the music and the deafening cheering.

Wolfie and I looked at one another, and both of us latched onto one of Fräulein Margarita's hands, while with our free hands we waved our own swastika flags.

Suddenly the crowd broke into a thunderous cheer and began chanting, "*Heil Hitler! Heil Hitler!*" Every person saluted as he drove by in his Mercedes convertible, accompanied by his motorcycle brigade.

"*Heil Hitler!*" vibrated through me, sending shock waves through my soul.

"Michael?" Wolfie said into my ear. "Michael?" He kicked the leg of my chair.

I looked at him with a blank stare, and it took me several seconds to realize that I was at our DJV meeting at home and not standing on the street in Berlin several weeks earlier.

He leaned over and whispered, "Look how red Jürgen's face is."

He was right. Jürgen was working himself into a frenzy as he shouted, "We are the future!" Maybe it was just the way the light was coming through the stained glass windows, but his gleaming amber eyes had turned black. I shifted in my chair and lost my balance, bumping my elbow on the red hot stove. "Ow!" I hissed.

"What's the matter?" Wolfie whispered.

"Nothing," I said and focussed on Jürgen, trying not to feel the pain in my arm.

As Jürgen continued his speech, he looked much like Hitler

himself, words and spittle flying from his mouth, and I saw that his hands were grasping the wooden lectern so tightly that they had turned bluish-white.

"Today is the last time I will be speaking to you young men of F66 Hitler Jungvolk division," he shouted. "Tomorrow morning I will be off to protect our great nation! I hope you will also be able to have the honour to fight for the Fatherland!"

Wolfie leaned toward me. "I hope so."

Jürgen glanced at Wolfie but kept on talking. "We are the future! We are the Deutschland of tomorrow! Hitler tried to avoid war, but National Socialism has to be defended. We have to preserve the purity of our people. Our girls too have a duty—theirs is to bear children for Deutschland." Then with great force Jürgen slammed his fist down on the podium. "If you're not with us, then you're against National Socialism."

He lowered his voice dramatically. "Blood will spill." Then he bellowed, "My blood might spill, but I mean *nothing* . . . I count for *nothing* . . . Deutschland is only great if we all fight together. The Fatherland is everything! It is my duty—it is your duty—to defend our flag with our blood. We will inherit and rule the earth for one thousand years!" He ended by thrusting his arm into the air. "Our Führer will lead us to victory! *Sieg* . . ."

And we all shouted, "*Heil!*"

"*Sieg* . . ."

"*Heil!*"

My mind drifted again as I wondered what would happen after that thousand years. Around me the room exploded into the Hitlerjugend banner song, a song sung by boys all over Deutschland as we waited to become men:

> Our banner flutters before us
> Our banner is the new era
> And our banner leads us to eternity
> Yes, the banner means more than death.

It was four o'clock and just about dark by the time we left the meeting, feeling full of purpose, good righteous purpose. Many times after our Hitlerjugend meetings, we boys would roam through the town, shouting Hitler slogans—"We rule the streets, we rule the lands, we children hold the power in our hands!" No one was going to tell us what we could do. No one! But that afternoon when Wolfie and I walked out into the cold air, a wind had kicked up from the north. I felt the chill creeping into my bones, and the burn on my arm stung. I pulled up the collar of my coat and shoved my hands deep into my pockets as we said our good-byes to our comrades. Wolfie and I started for home in silence, but my thoughts where racing.

"Wolfie," I said finally, "light us a cigarette." I smiled, thinking about all the possibilities ahead of us. "You know, we're extremely lucky to be the sons of SS officers. We can do anything."

We paused while he pulled two cigarettes from his brown leather satchel, lit them and handed one to me. "What do you think will happen once we rule the world?" he said.

"Don't know, but we'll be something special."

"I think we'll get to have as many girls as we want."

"You wouldn't know what to do with a girl if she fell on your little Wolfie pecker!"

"Would, too. And it's not that small!"

Just then a snowball hit Wolfie in the face. "What the—"

A snowball hit me too, and we laughed and ran to hide behind a tree. "That's Otto and Hans! Let's get 'em!"

Quickly we made snowballs and fired back at them. After about an hour of playing in the snow, Otto and Hans, wet and defeated, surrendered and went home.

"*Ach, Scheisse!* Wolfie, what time is it?"

"Why?"

"I forgot to pick up Paula from her meeting. *Scheisse!* Come back with me to her BDM meeting hall."

"But, Michael, we're just about home."

"You don't understand, Wolfie! She'll be there waiting for me."

"All right, but you owe me."

I glanced at my watch. "It's already five." Wolfie and I turned around and I began to run as I led us back across Herr Zimmermann's snow-covered fields. I was really feeling bad about forgetting my sister, especially since Mama had told me so many times to pick her up. Dark clouds had rolled in, and the icy wind stabbed at us like a rusty knife. Then, as we ran across the schoolyard, we could hear screaming.

"Help . . . Someone . . . help me!"

"Shut up, you dumb cow, and lie still! Your turn, Fritz!"

Paula was trying to crawl away, and Jürgen Fassbender stood over her pulling up his trousers. When she started to get to her feet, he clenched his fist and struck her in the face. She fell to the ground. "Shut your mouth. Get on top of her, Fritz! Unless you want me to have another turn?"

"*Nein-n-n . . .*!" I shouted as Wolfie and I ran towards them. "*Ach, du lieber Gott!* You filthy rat!" I lunged at Jürgen, catching him off balance. He fell to the ground and I kicked him in the side. "You filthy *Schwein!*" I yelled and kicked him again.

Wolfie jumped at Fritz as Paula crawled to get out of the way.

Jürgen clutched his side as he got to his knees, gasping for air. "Wha—?"

But before he could say anything more, I kicked him in the face. He fell on his back, put his hands up to his mouth, and that's when I straddled him. "You rat!" I shouted as I punched him repeatedly, my knuckles splitting as they connected with his face. I felt no pain, nothing but rage. Blood spurted from his mouth. Just then I heard Paula scream, and I looked to where she huddled under a white oak tree, her face half-covered by her hands. At that moment Jürgen threw me off, stood up, spat out some teeth, then punched me in the head. I was dazed for a moment, but as he ran away, I yelled after him, "I'm going to kill you . . ." and started after him.

But Paula was still screaming my name, "Michael!"

And I turned to see Wolfie lying with his head on the snow-cleared curb with Fritz bent over him, ready to stomp on his face. Struggling to stand upright, I ran towards them and kicked Fritz from behind. He stumbled over Wolfie's body and, as he fell, his head smashed on the curb. He fell across Wolfie, and I grabbed Fritz by the hair and pulled him off. Wolfie scrambled to his feet, and together we repeatedly kicked him. Fritz cried out but he didn't try to defend himself.

I could hear Paula sobbing and begging, "Please stop kicking him, Michael!" She crawled towards us screaming, "You're killing him! Stop!" She pulled at my pant leg. "You're killing him!" She yanked on Fritz's arm, and then at last I realized that Wolfie had stopped kicking him.

In the silence that followed, I heard Paula say, "He's dead, Michael."

The snow was falling gently all around us, but beneath us it had turned an explosive red. Wolfie and I hadn't realized that Fritz wasn't crying out anymore.

3

The Satchel

✍

WE STOOD STARING AT Fritz's lifeless body. My hands trembled. I fell to my knees heaving and retching up everything in my gut.

Wolfie stood at my side and murmured, "He would have killed me, Michael. We had no choice . . ."

Paula was sitting next to Fritz, staring vacantly at the body. Finally, with wobbly legs I stood up and pulled Paula to her feet. Wolfie grabbed Fritz's arm and began dragging his body towards some nearby bushes. I took the other arm. The words *A life unworthy of life* rang in my ears. After we had kicked and piled snow over his body, I bent over and threw up again.

"Michael, we have to go," said Wolfie.

And we all ran . . .

After fifteen minutes of running, I slowed my pace, then stopped. Paula and Wolfie did, too. Out of breath, I sputtered, "My . . . satchel! I've lost . . . my satchel . . ." I bent over and placed my hands on my knees. Still trying to catch my breath, I continued. "It must have . . . been torn off . . . during the fight."

"We can't go back, Michael," Wolfie said. "It's too late. Someone might see us!" He took a deep breath. "My mutti will clobber me. I've already . . . It doesn't matter—I'm not going back there. I have to go home!"

Wolfie was right. Why should he come back with me? I had caused him enough trouble. His mutti drank too much, and if someone connected him with Fritz's murder, she would probably murder him.

"What am I going to do?" I said.

Wolfie pulled out two cigarettes and lit them, and in the flare of the match I saw that his face was a bloody mess. Fritz had punched him so hard that his left eye was swollen shut. He handed me one of the cigarettes and took a deep drag on his own. "I'm not going back with you, Michael! Just tell your Mama that you forgot your satchel at the hall. Besides, it's only a satchel. You can get it tomorrow."

"You don't understand! My name, my picture, address . . . it's all in my Hitlerjugend book." Then for some reason I remembered the liver sausage sandwiches that Mama had made for us and that I had put in my satchel. I took one last drag of my cigarette, threw it into the snow and for a moment watched its orange-red glow extinguish. "Paula, Wolfie will take you home. Don't say a word to Mama or Papa about what happened."

"Michael, maybe we should go to the police," she said softly, her face close to mine, and I could see it was streaked with tears.

"Are you crazy? We'll get hung or shot or—worse—get put into a camp."

Paula looked away. "What am I going to say to Mama?"

"If she asks you about your bruises and your torn dress, tell her that the stairs were slippery at the meeting house. You fell down them . . . and hit your head on the railing. Paula, stop crying. It'll be all right." My stomach was doing flips.

"I don't want to get us into any more trouble than we are already in." Her big blue eyes were pleading with me.

"It'll be all right." Even though she was two years older than me, she had always been more like my little sister . . . and I had failed her.

She held her head down, her eyes full of tears. "It's all my fault."

I put my arm around her and pulled her close. "Paula, it wasn't your fault. It was mine because I was late coming to get you. But it will be all right. You'll see."

A trickle of blood stained her lips. "All right, Michael."

"Wolfie, take her home."

Before she let go of me, Paula whispered, her voice trembling much like her body, "Please be careful, Michael."

She tried to place her scarf around my neck, but I made her take her hands away and pushed her towards Wolfie. "You'll be all right, Paula. Wolfie, take her home quickly."

As she and Wolfie set off for home, her words drifted back to me in the darkness and blowing snow. "Michael, I will tell Mama that you forgot your satchel and that you went looking for it. I'm so sorry . . ."

I didn't look back at them as I ran across the snow-covered fields. Soon my lungs were on fire, but I kept on running, and the faster I ran the angrier I became at Mama and Paula. Why was Paula my responsibility, anyway? "*Scheisse* . . . !" Then over and over I recalled Paula lying helplessly on the path. And I thought about how I had wanted to be like Jürgen. "You filthy pig, Jürgen Fassbender . . . !" I could still feel every blow I had struck, and with each breath my rage grew and grew. Why did he do that to my sister?

By now a northeasterly snowstorm was howling through the town, and I could hardly see where I was going. I pulled my coat more tightly around me as I leaned my body into the barrage. When I came to the path where we had killed Fritz, I stopped in my tracks. Ahead of me I could dimly make out two figures dragging something. Instantly I broke into a cold sweat, and my mind raced.

"Oh, *Scheisse!*" I trembled. I couldn't swallow . . . Who could it be? *Nein! Nein!* I shouted in my head as I crouched behind the old white oak tree, the same tree where Paula had sat earlier and watched helplessly as Wolfie and I killed Fritz. I was sick with fright, wondering who these two people were. What were they dragging?

The outdoor lamp high over the doorway of the BDM meeting-house swung back and forth in the wind, casting a weak light through the darkness and falling snow on what appeared to be an ox-drawn cart. And as I watched the two unknown people, I wanted to scream, I wanted to run . . . I closed my eyes, hoping that this was a dream, but when I opened them, I saw that the two figures were picking up the thing they had been dragging, and with a heavy thud they dumped it into the cart.

"Fritz!" I blurted, then quickly clamped a hand over my mouth.

I saw them climb into the cart and heard one of them say, "It belongs . . ."

The wind whistled, crying with urgency as the two figures vanished into the storm in their ox cart. Still I stayed hidden, my heart beating so loudly that I thought the whole world could hear it. Then I saw something glinting in the snow in front of me. I reached down to pick it up. "Paula's gold cross!" I held it in my hand for a second then quickly put it into my pocket. When I stood up, the shadows on the snow began playing tricks on my mind.

Barely able to see, I crawled on all fours to where we had hidden Fritz's body, desperate to find my satchel. I felt around in the snow for it, terror seeping into me. I didn't want to find his body . . . but would I find it? *Nein!* The two people, those men, they had taken his body! I wanted everything to disappear . . . I bolted, I ran . . .

By the time I arrived home, I couldn't feel my hands or feet, but before I could reach for the door, Mama flung it open. "*Ach, du lieber Gott!* Michael, you're half-frozen!" She pulled me inside and wrapped her arms around me. "All I need is for you to get sick, and look at your coat! It's all torn!"

Her warmth felt different now. What once was comfort no longer felt right. Everything had become different. I pushed her away. "Where is Paula?"

"She's in bed. I want you to get upstairs and into your bed, too. I'll be up with a hot-water bottle for you. And take off your coat so that I can mend it."

I was surprised that Mama was not angry. I said nothing but stripped off my coat and gave it to her.

Susi was standing in front of my bedroom door with her arms crossed. "Michael, what happened? Paula is crying, and she won't tell me anything."

"She's upset that I forgot to pick her up." I pushed past her, opened my door and began taking off my clothes.

She followed me into my room, stood beside my bed and lifted the covers for me. "Get in!"

I jumped into bed. "Do you know if Wolfie made it home okay?"

She picked up my clothes and placed them on the bedside chair. "I think so, but he didn't look so good. Did you guys get into a fight?"

"*Nein.*"

Susi sat on the edge of my bed. "Michael, did you two get into a fight?" she repeated.

"I said *nein!*"

She tried to grab my hand, but I pulled it away from her. "Michael, let me see!"

"*Nein.*"

Once again, she took my hand in hers and looked closely at it with its obvious bruising. "You punched something or someone, didn't you? And how did you get that nasty burn? *Ach,* Michael, it looks painful. Who did you two beat up?"

I pulled my hand away again and turned my back on her. "I said *no one.*"

She placed her hand on my side. "Michael . . ."

"I punched the wall when I saw that Paula was hurt. That's all. Now leave me alone."

"All right, but you're lucky that Papa is working late at Colditz Castle Prison tonight. He would have clobbered you."

"Who clobbered who?" Mama was standing in the doorway holding a hot water bottle.

Susi stood up, and as she walked past Mama, she leaned in and gave her a peck on the cheek. "No one. But Michael has a bad burn on his elbow."

"Susi, will you please see to Annalisa?"

"*Ja*," she said as she left the room.

Mama placed the hot water bottle under my feet, then examined my elbow. "How did you get that burn?"

"I fell against the stove at the meeting hall," I said. "It's nothing. It will be fine." The heat of the water bottle felt good against my frozen feet.

"All right. We'll talk about this in the morning. Susi will bring you a bowl of soup." Mama bent over me and gave me a kiss on the forehead. "The twins are at their friends' house tonight, and Günther is still at the farm. After you've eaten, I want you to go to sleep."

As I was sipping my soup, Paula slipped into the room. The sight of her swollen lips and bruised face took my breath away. "Michael, please don't tell anyone what happened to me. Swear it!"

I put my soup down. "Paula, I swear I won't tell."

She took my hand and held it for a moment. "Does it hurt?"

"*Nein*. And you?"

"A little." She turned to leave, but I grabbed her arm and before I could say anything more she said, "I didn't say anything to Mama."

I reached over to the nightstand and took out her necklace from the small box where I had placed it. "Here, Paula, I found your necklace—the one with the gold cross."

She stared at it for a moment. "You keep it." She pulled her arm away.

"I couldn't find my satchel," I said before she left the room. "Paula, I'm sorry about everything."

As she closed the door, she said softly, "It was my fault, Michael."

The next morning when I went down to the kitchen, Mama had just pulled some hot buns from the oven. "Good morning, Michael."

"Good morning, Mama. Where is everyone?"

She placed a hot bun on a plate and pointed to the table for me to sit. "Susi has left for school already. She has her state exam today."

"Where are Paula and Günther?"

"Eat your breakfast, Michael. Paula is not feeling well. She has a slight fever. Günther is at the Zimmermanns' farm already helping to deliver more sheep to the butcher. And the twins took the early train back to their school."

"Oh."

"Paula told me that you forgot your satchel."

As I cut open the hot bun, a delightful sweet smell rose into the air. I put some butter on the bun and watched it melt. "*Ja.*" But I had no appetite.

"How could you have forgotten your satchel, Michael?" Mama sat across from me. "Did you at least eat the sandwiches that I made for you?"

"I don't remember."

"That's no answer. Where did you leave it? And eat!"

"I don't know." The smell of the bun made me feel sick. I pushed my plate away.

"Did you maybe leave it at the meeting house?" Mama poured me a cup of peppermint tea. "Are you feeling sick, too?"

"*Nein.* I'm just not hungry . . . *Ja*, that's probably where I left it."

Mama reached across the table, placed her hand on my forehead. "You feel okay." She stood and put the kettle back on the stove. "After school I want you to stop in and pick up your satchel. I haven't had time to mend your coat, so you can wear your papa's old coat."

"It'll be too big for me, Mama."

"It will have to do. Now get on your way. Wolfie will be waiting for you."

"Isn't Paula coming?"

"*Nein*. I told you, she has a slight fever."

I stood up and put Papa's coat on. Mama held Annalisa close to her bosom and with her free hand she pulled out a letter from her apron pocket and handed it to me. "Give this note to Herr Kannengiesser. I don't need him to pay us a visit. And please bring home any assignments that Paula might have."

I took the note and stuffed it in my pocket. "I will, Mama." I kissed her and Annalisa goodbye.

I ran down the street to Wolfie's house, my heart racing. I hoped he would tell me that last night was a horrible dream. However, the burn on my arm stung, and my bruised hand felt stiff. How were we going to make this all better, make it go away? Maybe Paula was right, maybe we should go to the police. I spotted Wolfie sitting on his front step smoking. His face looked like a pulverized plum.

He tilted his head back and squinted up at me. "I think Fritz broke my nose last night."

"It looks pretty bad. Does it hurt?"

"*Ja*. Did you find your satchel?"

I sat beside him. "*Nein*. When I got to where we left Fritz . . . there was someone lifting his body into an ox cart."

Wolfie choked. "What? Did you see who it was?"

I didn't answer and Wolfie glanced down at his feet as the fat little postman, Herr Finkel, walked by then came back to take a long look at us. "What happened to your face, Wolfie?" he asked.

"I fell on the ice."

He cocked his head to one side. "Must have been a nasty fall."

"*Ja*." Wolfie kept his head down.

"Shouldn't you boys be off to school?"

"We're on our way, Herr," I said, staring hard at the postman until he finally walked on.

We stood up and I draped my arm over Wolfie's shoulder. Together we walked purposefully in the direction of the school.

"Who was it?" Wolfie asked me again.

"There were two of them but it was dark and snowing too heavily. I couldn't make them out."

"Do you think it was Fritz's papa, Herr Bummel?"

I pulled my papa's black woollen coat tighter around me and stuffed my hands into the pockets. My right hand closed over a piece of paper. At first I thought it was Mama's letter to Herr Kannengiesser, but when I pulled it out, I saw it was a different letter, one that smelled of the sweet orange scent of Kölnisch Wasser no. 4711. Papa had brought some home for Mama, but she only liked wearing White Lily, which she kept on her bedroom dressing table. But the handwriting wasn't Mama's. I knew it was none of my business, but I started to read it. "*Lieber Rudi,*" it read, "*I will shower you with a thousand years of kisses . . .*"

Wolfie studied me. "What's that?"

Quickly I pushed it into my pants pocket. "*Nichts.*"

"Was it Herr Bummel?" Wolfie said again.

"*Nein.* The Bummels don't have an ox cart. Besides, there were two of them, and if they saw us do it, we would have heard by now."

"*Ja,* you're right." Wolfie's face showed a bit of relief. He put his arm around my shoulders, and we walked on not saying a word. When we came to the path where we had ended Fritz's life, there were no marks in the snow.

We both spoke at the same time. "No blood?" Someone had cleaned up the whole mess. Who was it?

We checked the bushes where we had hidden Fritz's body.

"Hey, you two, wait up for me!" shouted Hans.

"*Ach, Scheisse,* Michael," muttered Wolfie as he buttoned up his coat.

We both turned. "Hans."

"What happened to your face, Wolfie?"

"Nothing . . . I fell down some stairs, that's all."

"Oh . . . That was fun yesterday, wasn't it?"

"What was?" I said.

"The snowball fight . . ."

"*Ja,*" we both answered.

"What are you two looking for?"

"*Nichts.*"

"*Nichts?* Then what were you doing in those bushes?" Hans said, smirking.

I couldn't look him in the eye. "We thought we heard a dog yelping."

"Oh. Was there?"

"Was there what?"

Wolfie bent and picked up something that was lying beside Hans's foot.

"A dog."

"*Ach, nein,*" said Wolfie as he put what he had picked up into his pocket.

"Did you guys hear about Fritz?"

We shook our heads. I took a deep breath and said, "*Nein.*"

"He's disappeared. Frau Bummel is worried sick about him, and his papa has been all over town looking for him."

I turned to Wolfie. "We're going to be late for school."

But Hans continued, "I heard the postman talking to my mutti when he delivered our mail this morning, and he said that he saw Jürgen early this morning at the train station wearing his army uniform, so he must have been heading out to join his regiment. But the postman said he was all roughed up. And Mama says that Fritz is a hooligan and probably was picked up by the police and taken to the asylum on account of his stealing from the butcher last week."

I pulled on Wolfie's arm. "We have to go. See you, Hans." And we left him standing on the street looking bewildered.

Once out of earshot Wolfie asked, "Do you think one of the people you saw was your brother?"

"Günther? *Nein* . . . both those guys were a lot bigger." We walked on in silence, then I said, "Wolfie, what did you pick up back there?"

"A couple of teeth."

"They must be Jürgen's! Let me have them."

"Why do you want his teeth? We don't have to worry about him. He's left town."

I stuck out my hand and Wolfie dropped the teeth into my palm.

"What are you going to do with them?"

"One day I'll see that rat again and when I do . . . I'll make him eat them!"

At school everyone asked about Wolfie's face and my hand. I couldn't wait for the day to be over.

Once home, Mama greeted me at the door. "Michael, Herr Bummel came by today, asking if we'd seen his boy. Have you heard anything at school?"

A lump formed in my throat. "Nein, they were talking about it but no one knew anything. I headed toward the stairs. "I have a lot of schoolwork to do."

"Michael, if you hear anything, you'll let me know, won't you?"

No one in our town ever saw Jürgen or Fritz again. At first the townsfolk told all sorts of cock-and-bull stories about Fritz—there were even rumours that gypsies had kidnapped him and used him as a sideshow freak in the circus—but in the end it was decided that he had run off with Jürgen to fight the good war. By then spring was coming and I looked forward to the weather warming up. Soon the apple trees on the Zimmermanns' farm were breaking into bud, the lambs were frolicking in the pastures, and our brave men were marching proudly off to war.

4

Golden Gods

— MARCH 1940 —

❧

I WAS IN THE KITCHEN searching for something to eat when I overheard Mama in the living room talking to Paula. As I buttered a slice of bread, I heard her say, "Paula, this is the third time this week that you have thrown up. What's going on with you?"

With my buttered bread in hand, I went to stand in the kitchen doorway.

Mama was on her hands and knees mopping up vomit, and Paula lay on the sofa. "Do you have a fever?"

"*Nein*, I just don't feel well."

Mama stood up, walked over to her and placed her hand on Paula's forehead. "There is no sickness going around and . . . *Ach*, Paula! *Gott im Himmel!*" Mama struck Paula across the face. "How? When?"

Paula put her hand up to her face to soften the sting. "Mama, what are you talking about?"

"You don't know?" Mama placed her hand on Paula's stomach. "Paula, you're pregnant!"

"*Nein*, I . . . I . . ." Tears began to slide down Paula's cheeks.

"When was the last time you had your *Tage*?"

"My period? I think it was seven or eight weeks, maybe longer. I can't remember. Mama, I—"

"Who was he?"

"Mama, I never—"

"Paula, tell me the truth. I want you to tell me everything from the beginning. Now!"

Paula began sobbing into her hands.

"Stop crying. It won't change anything. We will sort something out, but you need to tell me the truth."

My lungs were clogged with guilt and my mouth went chalk dry. I watched Mama put her arms around Paula and saw Paula slump against her bosom. I slipped back into the kitchen and listened.

"Mama, it was horrible. I was waiting for Michael that night we came home late . . . remember? It was snowing, and Michael forgot to get me."

"But I told him over and over to come for you." Mama's voice rose.

"It happened at the school house, the meeting hall. All the other girls had gone home, and Jürgen Fassbender came with Fritz Bummel, and, well . . . Oh, Mama, it was terrible. Jürgen grabbed me and well, he . . . he . . . Mama, he . . . he . . . Oh, Mama!"

"Did you say anything to make him think you wanted him?"

"Mama, *nein*! I told him to go away. I tried to run, but Fritz held me down!"

"Paula, stop crying."

"Mama, he forced me . . . I can't be pregnant. Mama, what am I going to do? I'm only fourteen!"

"First, I'm going to talk to Jürgen's parents and then to Fritz's."

"*Nein*, Mama, please don't! It'll only make things worse!"

"But we can't hide this."

"Does Papa need to know?"

"He does. Your papa knows Herr Fassbender and . . . Well, he is an SS officer, too."

"Does that matter?"

"*Ja.* I'll figure this out, Paula. Is that why Jürgen and Fritz haven't been seen? Your brother and Wolfie forced them to leave town?"

Paula hesitated. "*Ja.*"

"Well, they did something right . . . Now I think it best you go upstairs before your papa comes home."

I ducked out of the kitchen and ran up the stairs without being seen. Paula's bedroom door was open, and I went in and sat on her bed. I picked up her old hedgehog doll, which was sitting neatly on her pillow.

When she came into her room, she appeared startled to find me there. "Michael . . . were you listening downstairs?"

"*Ja,* I heard everything."

"Mama knows what happened that night . . . But I didn't say anything about Fritz. She thinks you just scared him and Jürgen off." As she spoke, she kept her head down. She couldn't look me in the eye, and I felt her shame.

"Paula, you're going to have a baby?"

"Please don't tell anyone."

"I won't."

"Don't tell Susi . . . No one. Please!"

I stood up and placed her hedgehog doll back on her pillow. "What about Wolfie?"

Paula looked up at me for a second, then burst into tears. I hugged her.

She pulled away, pushed me out of the room and closed her bedroom door.

I stood outside her room and put my hand on her door. "Mama is going to make it all good, you'll see."

That night as I sat in the darkness at the bottom of the stairs with Minka, the cat, in my lap purring, I heard Mama and Papa talking in the living room. I could see Mama walk over to the birch buffet where Papa kept his liquor along with the cigarettes that were in a container with a swastika insignia on the lid. I saw Mama hand Papa a drink and a cigarette as he sat in his overstuffed golden-green chair.

Then Mama told Papa that Paula was going to have an Aryan baby, and that it was Jürgen Fassbender's, but she never told him how Paula became pregnant.

She went on about what should happen. "I think the best place for her is at a *Lebensborn* home, Rudi."

I was surprised that Papa stayed so calm about the whole thing.

"*Ja*, a Spring of Life home is a good place for her," agreed Papa as he stood up to pour himself another drink. He raised his glass of schnapps to the portrait of Hitler above the buffet. "There are a lot of good Deutsche girls there, providing the Reich with the next generation of Golden Gods. Paula is doing something great for the Fatherland." Papa shot back his schnapps.

I couldn't believe that he saw nothing wrong with Paula having a baby as long as it was a strong, wholesome and pure Aryan one. In fact, he seemed happy about it. I saw him light another cigarette and walk to his chair to sit again, but this time he had a stony gaze in his eyes.

"Rudi, it is safe for Paula to go there, is it not?" Mama said.

"*Ach ja*, Frau. I have been many times to a *Lebensborn* home. Pour me another drink . . . Herr Fassbender is a high-ranking officer . . . and his son I believe is a good soldier. Their bloodline goes back to the 1800s."

I jumped up, sending Minka flying, and burst into the living room.

"Jürgen is a coward!" I yelled. Before I knew what I had said, Papa shot up out of the chair, struck me across the face, and glared at me. But I continued, "Jürgen is a rat! And you're sending Paula away?"

"Michael, that's enough out of you," said Mama as she grabbed my arm. "Get up to your room."

For the next week no one in our house spoke much. Paula took all her meals in her room. Papa stopped coming home at night, and when he did, he was drunk. Mama cleaned the house more than ever, and when Papa did come home, I could hear him yelling at her and hitting her.

Three weeks after Paula told Mama what had happened, she left for the *Lebensborn* home. Wolfie and I took her luggage to the taxi cab waiting for her at the curb as Mama stood at the front door holding Annalisa. Paula walked into the hallway, her head down. In one hand she held her hedgehog doll and in the other she carried a small bag.

Mama smiled at Paula. "Do you have everything you need?"

Paula mumbled, "I think so."

Mama teared up. "You'll be home again before you know it."

"Mama," Paula sniffled, "please say goodbye to Susi, Günther and the twins for me."

Wolfie and I stood by the taxi cab, Wolfie holding the door open. As Paula stepped into the taxi, Wolfie leaned toward her and said, "Paula . . ." But she closed the door before he could finish his sentence.

The spring rains had finally ended, and Wolfie and I were on our way to the post office. The path was full of puddles, but the sun was out and it glinted on the grass and the raindrops were dripping from the leaves of the trees.

"Maybe it was your papa," Wolfie said as we walked along. This was at least the thirtieth time we had speculated on who had taken Fritz's body.

"If it was, we'd both be dead by now. Besides, there were two people."

"Maybe it was Günther and your mama?"

"*Nein!* It wasn't Mama!"

We were silent then until we reached the post office. "Have you heard from Paula yet?" he asked as he stomped his feet to get the mud off his shoes.

I stomped my feet too as I opened the door. "*Nein*, that's why we're here. Mama is worried because it's been four weeks and there's been no mail from her."

"How long will she be gone?"

"I don't know, maybe six or seven months?"

"That's a long time."

"*Ja.*"

"You like Paula," I said.

"*Ach, ja!*" Wolfie was blushing. "I kinda like your sister."

"But she's older than you."

"Only by two years."

"That's a lot!"

"Do you think she'll come back with the baby?"

"Can I help you?" shouted Frau Krumpeter, the plump postmistress, who worked behind the mail counter.

"*Ja*," I replied.

She scrunched up her face and rolled her eyes at me as she waved us over. "What can I help you with?"

"Is there a letter for my mama?"

"Let me look."

When the postmistress came back, she handed me two letters—one from Paula and the other an official-looking one.

"Thank you. Oh, and Mama wants to send these letters, but they need stamps." I handed her some money.

"How is your Mama?" the postmistress asked as she reached for the stamps, each with a picture of Hitler on them. She licked the back of each one with her puffy tongue.

"Good, thank you."

She stuck the stamps on the envelopes. "And how is the baby?"

"Oh . . . Paula . . . she hasn't had the baby yet."

Frau Krumpeter's eyes lit up. She leaned forward and fairly shouted at me, "What! Paula is having a baby?"

I just stood there with my mouth agape.

Wolfie pulled on my arm and cleared his throat. "Annalisa is good, thank you." He then grabbed the letters that the postmistress had put on the counter. "And my mutti, she is good too, thank you."

We quickly made our way to the door, but not before everyone in the post office was staring at us and starting to whisper.

Once outside, Wolfie let go of my arm. I closed my eyes and shook my head. "I thought she was talking about Paula."

"Forget about it."

I wanted to go back in and tell them all to stop talking about my sister, but the damage had been done.

Mama was in the garden planting some seeds when I arrived home. "Hello, Michael. Was there a letter?"

"*Ja.*"

"Well, give it here." She wiped her hands on her apron and motioned for me to hand it to her. As she took them, she continued, "What's the matter with you, Michael?"

"I'm sorry, Mama, but I let it slip at the post office that Paula is pregnant." I burst into tears. "Now all of the town will know."

Mama looked at the letters, then at me. "Come over here, Michael." She stood up and wrapped her arms around me. "Let them talk."

I wanted so badly to tell her what had happened that December night, but I couldn't. Wolfie and I worried constantly about being found out. After all, *someone* knew, but who? And why hadn't they told the police? "I promise I won't do anything bad ever again," I blurted out.

She smiled. "Just do your best, Michael. Come, let's go inside and have some chamomile tea."

Mama set the letters on the kitchen table. "Michael, be a darling and open the one from Paula and read it to me while I make the tea."

Liebe Mama und lieber Papa,

I miss you all so much. There are a lot of girls here and they all are lovely and nice. I have a roommate, we are the same age, and her name is Gertrud. She has become a good friend. Us girls talk a lot about keeping our babies or giving them up. Some girls will be leaving their babies to be brought up by the state and a few are giving them to other families to raise. Mama, I want to keep the baby.

They make sure that we do our schooling, and we are being taught how to become good muttis. We go for a lot of walks; they say that fresh air is good for us. I heard that Herr Heinrich Himmler picked all the furniture for the homes. Sometimes SS men, they come to see some of the girls in here. I think they come for a visit and to praise the girls. As Papa said, "We are birthing Golden Gods for Hitler."

I hope my baby will be a girl. Mama, there are girls in here who are excited about having a baby, and they say that if they have a boy, they will name their babies Adolf. I know you said not to be scared, and that everything will be okay, but, Mama, I am scared. How are Michael and Wolfie? Have you begun to plant the garden? I miss your cooking. Even though the food is good in here, it's not as good as yours.

Heil Hitler,
Paula

5

Hear No Evil,
See No Evil, Speak No Evil

— MAY 1940 —

∽

MY FAVOURITE TIME OF year was spring, and it couldn't come fast enough this year. Winter storms and April's long rainy days had only added to my gloomy moods, and so the sunshine of May was a welcome change. I began feeling hopeful again.

Wolfie and I couldn't get enough information about the war. We had heard that the British were calling the war "phony" because not much was happening, but by mid-May 1940, our Deutsche paratroopers had taken the Belgium fortress of Eben Emael along with 20,000 prisoners. The Luftwaffe had sunk the French destroyer *Bison* and the British destroyer *Afridi*—our Luftwaffe dominated the skies—and our troops had entered France. Nothing could stop the Third Reich now. Papa would say to me, "Boy, you're lucky to be alive in such exciting times!"

One day Wolfie and I were walking home from school and decided to stop by the post office to read the list of soldiers who had died or were missing in action.

"Want to go fishing tomorrow?" I asked.

"*Ja,*" Wolfie said. Fumbling around in his satchel, he beamed and said, "Want half of my sandwich?"

I pulled a bar of chocolate from my rucksack. "Want some chocolate?"

We sat on the post office steps, and Wolfie handed me part of his sandwich. "Where did you get chocolate?"

"I pinched it. Papa has a whole box of them. I think it's from the Red Cross care packages given to the prisoners at the Colditz Prison Camp. He must have traded something for it. It's Hershey's!"

Very slowly I unwrapped the chocolate, broke the bar in two and handed half to Wolfie. We took a bite, closed our eyes, and for a moment I just savoured the velvety sweetness in my mouth. I was happy. What more could I want? I had my best friend, food, chocolate, and the afternoon sun melting my troubles away.

"Michael, do you think we'll ever know what happened to Fritz's body?"

I took a breath in, exhaled, and the sun moved behind a cloud. "I try not to think about it."

"*Ja,* but I still do."

"Me too." Every day on my way to school, I walked past Frau Bummel's bakery, and she would always wave at me. Of course I knew she waved to all the school children, but I felt she focussed more on me.

Wolfie took one last bite of his chocolate. "Before I fall asleep is the worst time for me."

I put the rest of my sandwich and chocolate away. "For me it's when the house is quiet." I couldn't stand the silence because it only made me remember what I had done. In my angst I would step out and chop wood, more than we needed. I kept my room tidy, and I became meticulous about my clothing—everything had to be ironed, buttoned up and clean—and even my handwriting changed from almost illegible to crisp and clear. When I bathed, I would almost scrub myself raw.

"How is Günther?"

"I don't see him much."

"How come?"

"He spends his days at the Zimmermanns' farm."

"Who is at the Zimmermanns?" demanded Herr Finkel who had just come out of the post office with his mail bag slung over his shoulder. He looked like a fat dachshund—all belly and stubby legs, and his head melted into his shoulders.

We both turned around. "No one, Herr."

Everyone knew not to say a word to Herr Finkel because he was the town informant. He knew what was going on and knew everything about everyone. It didn't matter who you were, he would turn you over to the Gestapo if he thought it was in his best interests. Most everyone in town stayed away from him.

"Oh," he said as he cleared his throat. "And Paula, how is your sister?"

I stood up and so did Wolfie. "She is good, thank you."

He scratched his armpit and then bored his left finger into his ear. "She is having a baby, *ja*?"

Wolfie stood at my side, not saying a word.

"*Ja*. We have to go, Herr Finkel."

He flicked something off his finger. "Not so fast." He stepped closer and pointed his finger in my face. "Did your mama get the letter from the Department of the Interior Ministry?"

"I don't know. Come, Wolfie. We have to go, Herr Finkel."

We walked around the corner, and there was Günther just about to get into a fist fight with Ulrich Finkel, the postman's son.

"Hey, Günther," shouted Ulrich, "you're going to be taken away soon. That's what my papa said. No one wants a *Dummkopf* around.

And my mutti says you're going to get your balls cut off." Ulrich was always shooting his mouth off.

Günther had a smile on his face as he stuttered out, "Shu . . . shut your . . . your mou . . . mouth, Ul . . . Ul . . . Ulrich!"

My brother had become tall and very muscular, and he always had a tan from working outdoors at the Zimmermanns' farm. His mop of curls was as black as coal and his green eyes were calm, like moss on a rock.

"No, you *Halt die klappe*, Günther! You're nothing but an *Untermensch*!"

"Ulrich, go home!" I shouted as Wolfie and I ran to my brother's side.

"You don't scare me, Michael!" Ulrich shouted.

Wolfie pulled at my sleeve. "Come on, Michael. It's not worth it! Let's go."

I stepped closer to Ulrich. "Go home! We don't want any trouble."

He pushed me and glared at Günther. "Poor *Untermensch* needs his little brother to look out for him."

Günther raised his hand and said, "Go, ge . . . get, Ulrich."

"You're a coward—you're a life unworthy of life!"

There was that phrase again, and that sick feeling came rising up in my throat. My head began to throb and my skin felt prickly.

Wolfie spat on the ground. "There are more of us than you, Ulrich. We don't want to hurt you. Go home!"

Ulrich took a step back. "I'm going to report your brother, Michael, and they'll come and get him—"

I went to lunge at him, but Günther beat me to it and punched Ulrich square in the nose.

Ulrich's head snapped back. He put his hand up to his now bleeding nose and cried, "I'll get you for this!" Then he ran off.

I grinned at Günther. "Guess he won't bug you anymore."

"Guess not." He placed his hand on my shoulder, "You two . . . g . . . go home n . . . now, and stay out of trouble." As he turned to walk away, I saw what he was carrying.

"Günther, that's my satchel!"

Wolfie and my brother both spun around and stared at me.

Günther looked down at the satchel. "Yours?"

My heart raced as I realized what I had just revealed. "Ahh . . . Ah . . ." I couldn't speak.

Wolfie bit at his fingernail, tore it off, spat it on the ground. Then he pulled me by my arm. "Never mind, Günther . . . We have to go."

But Günther reached into the satchel, took out some letters and handed the satchel to me.

I still said nothing.

He turned and walked away.

Wolfie and I scurried off in the opposite direction. In a hushed voice Wolfie said, "Michael, you know what this means, don't you?"

"Günther . . . ?"

We were walking past the butchers' where three sheep heads hung in the window. I felt their eyes watching me.

Wolfie looked at the ground. "But you said there were *two* people that night."

"*Ja.*" We stopped beside the fountain in the town square. "Light us a smoke, will you?" I took the cigarette, and as I sat on the edge of the wall beside the fountain, I said quietly, "Maybe Günther just found it . . ."

Wolfie sat beside me. "But it could have been him that night, couldn't it? But why hasn't he said anything to you, Michael?"

"I don't know. Maybe because it wasn't him?"

"But it could have been him and Herr Zimmermann!" Wolfie flicked his cigarette away.

The warm spring breeze had turned cold. My mind had raced back to the night we killed Fritz. "Well, I can't ask him!" I dropped my cigarette and ground it out under my shoe.

Wolfie stood up. "Of course you can't!"

I felt sick. I wanted to believe that Günther knew nothing because if he did know, surely he would have said something? "Let's go home and forget about it."

Wolfie walked beside me. "I can't forget about it."

Soon we were stumbling through the Zimmermanns' hazelnut grove, where the ground under the trees had been newly tilled.

"Michael, listen."

A roaring began to fill the sky and we both looked up, mesmerized by the approaching planes.

"They're Heinkel-He 111s!" I shouted. I knew all the planes by sight but these were my favourites—twin-engined with a glass cockpit that reminded me of a fishbowl. Now as I staggered with my face turned up to the sky, I was imagining myself piloting one of them . . . And that's when I tripped over a tree root and went sprawling onto my hands and knees.

Wolfie held out his hand, and I started to pull myself up, then stopped. Something shiny had caught my eye. I picked it up and showed it to him. It was a ring.

The bombers were now directly overhead and the noise was deafening, so when Wolfie spoke, I couldn't hear what he was saying. Instead, he pointed to where Old Red, the fox, was running off with something in his mouth. We stepped closer to where the fox had been tugging something from the ground.

Wolfie turned green in the face. "*Ach, du liebe Scheisse!*"

Waves of nausea struck me. We both gaped at the ground, our hands clasped over our mouths.

"It's Fritz," I whispered. The ring I had found was Fritz's.

The grove gradually went silent as the squadron passed, and the only sound was the buzz of the flies swarming around Fritz's partly exposed body.

"Michael, what are we going to do?"

"Cover him."

While we were frantically kicking the dirt over Fritz's body, I spotted a rotten log at the side of the field. "Wolfie, help me," I said. We picked up the log and carried it back to drop it on top of the corpse. It landed with a thud. We wiped our hands on our shorts and for a moment stood in silence staring at the ground. The flies were still buzzing, and the bushes over to our left began rustling.

"Who's there?" Wolfie called out.

A voice replied, "Is that you, Woo . . . Woo . . . Wolfie?"

"*Ja*, Günther. It's me and Michael."

"W . . . wha . . . what are you two do . . . do . . . doing here?"

I realized I was holding Fritz's ring in my hand and quickly thrust it in my pocket. "We're taking the shortcut home, Günther."

Günther shook his finger at us. "You two sh . . . shouldn't be in here. And why are you c . . . cov . . . covered in mud?"

Wiping my hands on my shorts once more, I said, "I fell, that's all."

Günther glanced at the log we had moved. "We better g . . . go. Mama will be wor . . . worried."

The three of us never said a word as we hurried out of the grove, and when we arrived at our house, 27 Schmetterlingstrasse, Günther and I said goodnight to Wolfie.

"I'll see you in the morning, Michael."

Günther and I walked up the back stairs, and Mama opened the kitchen door. "There you are, Günther—and Michael, too? I was worried about you. You said that you would be right back, Günther. What took you so long?"

"So . . . sorry, Mama. I found Michael and Wolfie at the Zi . . . Zimmermanns' in the ha . . . haz . . . haz . . . hazelnut g . . . grove."

"Why are you so muddy, Michael?" Mama asked. "Go and clean up. Your *Abendessen* is almost ready."

I started to walk away to wash for dinner, but Mama grabbed me. Holding my face in her hands, she said, "I don't want you and Wolfie walking in that grove again . . . you hear me?"

I said nothing.

She took Günther by the hand into the kitchen. Did she know? Did everyone know? The smell of food suddenly turned my stomach, and I ran out the back door, heading for the outhouse where I threw up.

After I washed up, I went back into the kitchen. "Where is Günther?"

"He's sorting through some stuff in the cellar," Mama said.

"What for?"

"Never mind, Michael."

The kitchen window was steamed up from the lentil soup simmering on the stove. Mama lifted the lid off the pot. The aroma of the ham bone mixed with onions, potatoes and carrots would normally make my mouth water, but not this time.

Mama dipped a ladle into the soup. "Would you like a taste, Michael? It's your favourite."

I stared into the soup, and saw the ham bone bobbing up and down. "I'm not that hungry, Mama."

"That's not like you. Is everything all right?"

"*Ja*. Just not hungry."

Just then Susi came into the kitchen from the dining room. "Then help me set the table before Papa gets home." She pointed to the white cupboard.

I walked over to it, but just as I began grabbing plates from the top shelf, Susi popped me on the back of the head. "Not the green plates! We're having Herr and Frau Bummel over for dinner. Mama wants us to put out the Meissen dishes!"

With a displeased look directed at Susi, Mama said, "Help your brother. I don't want him to break the dishes. And be nice!" She turned to the stove.

"The Bummels?" I blurted.

The clanking in the kitchen stopped and for a moment all eyes were on me. Even Annalisa who was sitting in her highchair was silent. I couldn't believe what I was hearing. I wanted to run out the door. Fritz's parents were coming for dinner! What was she thinking? Was this an ambush? Did Mama and Papa know? Were they going to make me confess my crime, and if so, would they take into account that I did it to save my sister? Then trying to control my terror, I asked sheepishly, "The white dishes, Susi?"

She gave me a look that said she thought I was completely empty-headed and went back to the dining room.

My hands were trembling. I cleared my throat. "Why are they coming for dinner, Mama?"

"*Ach*, Michael. Your Papa thought it would be nice to have them come for dinner. Stop with the interrogation and finish setting the table."

Mama knew that Fritz had been there the night Jürgen forced himself on Paula because Paula had told her. So why was she all right with the Bummels coming for dinner? Why was she not infuriated? Maybe she was going to put too much salt or pepper in their soup? And Papa had always said that Herr Bummel might be a Communist even if his son had gone off to war. He even said he thought maybe Fritz was working as a spy for the Russians. So why was Mama so calm?

The white tablecloth was laid, the silverware and the fancy glasses were all set. "Can Wolfie come for dinner?" I needed him at my side.

"Not tonight, Michael. Oh, and your Papa wants you to wear your DJV uniform."

I sprinted upstairs. How I wished we had a phone. If we did, then I could call Wolfie and he could—

Peter burst into our bedroom and plunked himself on his and Kurt's bed. "I really hate these dinners." The twins were home for a few days from their school, so the house was once more full of noise. And Mama seemed happier because all her children except Paula were home safe and sound.

Peter picked up a magazine, *Der Adler*, which had all sorts of pictures of airplanes, drawings and stories about the Luftwaffe in it.

I slipped into my DJV shirt and tried to button it up.

"Your hands," Peter pointed. "Why are you so nervous?" he demanded.

Why wouldn't I be nervous? After all, this could be my last meal, and then Papa and the Bummels would escort me to the camp.

"Here, let me help." Peter stepped closer to me, and as he buttoned my shirt, he said, "Michael, what's the matter?"

"Nothing . . . it was just Ulrich today." I couldn't tell him about the Bummels. What would I say? *I killed Fritz and I believe Günther and Mama know?* "Where's Kurt?"

"He's at Ilsa's house for the evening. Don't pay Ulrich any mind. He's a big ox. Besides, I hear that Günther took care of him." Then he flopped back onto his bed and picked up the magazine again.

"Peter, are you scared of dying?" I had no idea why I asked him that.

"I think about it. Why do you ask?"

"The war and all . . ."

"I'm more afraid of killing someone."

I went over to my bed and sat on it to put on my shoes.

Peter squinted and seemed to be scrutinizing what I had on. "Michael, that uniform is too small."

He was right because, as I moved my arms, I felt trapped in it.

"Go show Mama. Maybe you could wear one of Papa's shirts."

"Why not one of yours, Peter?"

"All my shirts are at school."

I went back downstairs and stood beside Mama, who was still at the stove. "Peter thinks this shirt is too small for me, Mama." I put my arms up to emphasize how tall I had grown, but she didn't look at me.

"Michael, don't bother me now. I'm in the middle of making the Späetzle. You look fine. Susi, pass me more flour."

I went back upstairs, but every time I moved, I felt as though my shirt was about to come apart at the seams.

Just before the Bummels arrived, Papa hollered upstairs, "You kids get down here at once."

I took Annalisa out of her crib.

"Michael," she said, and giggled. She had two little red ribbons in her hair.

I held her close to me. "You have to be a very good girl tonight."

"Michael," she said once more and giggled again as she patted my face.

Peter, Günther, Annalisa, Susi and I lined up in the hallway ready to greet the Bummels as soon as the door opened. Papa stood in front of us and looked down at Annalisa. "Now remember to curtsy, Annalisa."

She stared up at me and said, "You ertsy too, Michael?"

"*Nein*, Annalisa." Papa clenched his fist. "Boys bow."

Annalisa took my hand. "*Nein!* I bow, too!"

I wanted to laugh but dared not. I just held her little hand tighter.

Papa turned red in the face. "*Nein!* Annalisa, you curtsy like this." Papa curtsied for her.

Annalisa giggled. "Papa, funny."

Just then Mama came out of the kitchen, wiping her hands on her apron. "Rudi, she is two and a half." Mama picked Annalisa up and gave her a kiss.

Papa gave Mama a stern look. "Open the door, Frau."

My heart raced. What would I say? I couldn't bear to look at Frau Bummel, let alone say hello to her.

Mama's hand shook a little as she opened the door. Then I saw her glance over at Günther and mouth the words, "It'll be all right."

Papa shook Herr Bummel's hand. "*Guten Abend*, Herr Bummel."

"Thank you for the invitation, Herr and Frau Boii."

Mama smiled slightly. "Do come in."

Annalisa began to fuss and Mama put her down. Then Annalisa raised her arms up to me. "Michael, up."

Frau Bummel's chin trembled. She glanced at Mama and handed her a loaf of bread. "Your baby has grown so big, and she is already talking."

I picked up Annalisa and once more held her close to me.

Frau Bummel patted my head. "Hello, Michael. You too have grown. You're almost as big as our boy, Fritz. You remember him?

He was Jürgen's helper in your Hitlerjugend group." She wiped at her eyes.

How could I forget him? I stared at Fritz's mutti and all I could say was, "*Ja.*"

Papa whacked me on the back of my head. "I apologize for my boy, Frau Bummel. Michael seems to have left his manners in a barn. Michael, show the Bummels into the living room and take their coats."

I handed Annalisa to Günther, then went into our living room and invited our company to sit on the sofa.

Papa was in front of me and headed to the buffet to pour some drinks. "Schnapps, Herr Bummel?" Papa asked as he passed the drink to him.

"*Danke*, Herr Boii. It's a lovely spring we're having, isn't it?"

"*Heil Hitler*," Papa said as he stood in front of Hitler's picture and saluted it. "Good weather makes it less treacherous for our soldiers, don't you think?"

Herr Bummel cleared his throat and smiled. "It most certainly does, Herr Boii."

"Let us move to the dinner table," Mama said as she took Frau Bummel by the arm and led her into the dining room.

Once everyone was seated, Mama served the soup. "Frau Bummel, have you had any news from your son?"

I tried not to look at the Bummels, but the more I tried the more I couldn't stop myself from staring at them. And every time I heard Fritz's name, my stomach turned into a knot and my thoughts became paralyzed.

Frau Bummel shook her head while trying to hold back her tears. "*Nein.* He was so eager to leave that he never even said goodbye. We think he went with Jürgen—they were such good friends. We don't want to create trouble for him by requesting information on his whereabouts—he was only seventeen, you know . . ."

Mama filled up Frau Bummel's soup plate. "Perhaps you will get a letter from him soon."

Maybe my secret was safe.

Papa banged his fist on the table. "It's our duty to protect our country. The Jews and the English plutocrats are the downfall of society. Peter and Kurt will put their lives on the line for the Fatherland once they're done with the Napola boarding school." Papa glanced at Peter then gestured to Mama. "Pass the salt, Frau!"

Mama's and Peter's faces drained of colour. Clearly rattled, Mama's hands shook as she passed the salt.

Kurt and Peter had been studying for the last four years at a national political academy where they were taught how to become SS soldiers and Deutschland's future leaders. But they had their hearts set on going on to a medical university. They really wanted to be doctors, and hoped that the war would end soon. Neither of them wanted to serve in the army.

Herr Bummel sat straighter in his chair. Looking at Mama, he said, "This is tasty soup, Frau Boii."

Faintly under her breath Mama said, "*Danke*, Herr Bummel."

Everyone nodded and said, "*Ja*, it is a good soup."

Mama cut up the bread that Frau Bummel had brought. "Bread, anyone?"

Everyone kept their heads down staring into their soup, and every clank of a spoon and slurping of soup felt like someone was scratching the skin off my body right to my bones.

All through dinner, Papa kept extolling Hitler's virtues and how there was nothing more important than being devoted to the Third Reich. Herr Bummel listened politely, agreeing to whatever Papa said.

After supper, Susi played the upright piano, and Papa sang with Peter and Günther. Even though Günther stuttered when he spoke, he sang flawlessly, his voice deep and velvety smooth. Often when Papa was not home, Günther would sing while Susi accompanied him on the piano. Then Annalisa and I would dance to the latest tunes, and sometimes Mama would join in.

The last song of the evening was the Horst Wessel song, and Papa demanded that we all sing it:

The banner high! The ranks are tightly closed!
The SA march with a calm assured step.
Comrades shot by the Reds and reactionaries
March in spirit within our ranks . . .

After Fritz's parents went home, Peter went to sit with Papa in the living room to listen to the news on the black Volksempfänger radio. Papa was proud of it because it cost him only thirty-five Reichsmarks. He thought that the eagle in the centre and the two swastikas on the dialing knobs made the radio look classy. Mama called it Goebbels' Beak, but Papa didn't like us calling it that.

I was just about to join them to listen to the radio when Peter came rushing out of the living room, knocking me into the side of the doorframe.

I watched him run up the stairs, and I thought I heard him crying. I went into the living room. "Papa, why is Peter so upset?"

"Be quiet, Michael. The Wehrmacht news is about to start. Turn the radio up."

As I turned the volume louder, the radio hissed and crackled. I sat on the sofa, and Papa sat in his chair, a glass of schnapps in his hand. The tall reading lamp behind him made his black hair shimmer blue. I knew he used pig fat to slick his hair back, and the light illuminated the graying hair on his temples.

The announcer's voice, full of excitement, blared from the Goebbels' Beak. "People of Deutschland, as I speak, the Luftwaffe is raining down bombs on the city of Rotterdam, and for two days our paratroopers have been steadily advancing on the ground . . ." He went on to describe all the troop manoeuvres in meticulous detail, and Papa listened intently, not even raising his glass of schnapps to his mouth.

The announcer ended with "People of Deutschland, we are winning this war! The Kriegsmarine, the Luftwaffe and our soldiers along with our Panzer corps are the best in the world and most certainly will keep us from harm's way. Sleep well tonight, knowing that this war will end soon. Good night and God speed to our soldiers. *Heil Hitler.*"

After the news ended, I sat quietly for a moment. "Papa, why doesn't England join Deutschland in this war?"

Papa shrugged, lit a cigarette and sucked on it mercilessly before exhaling. "I suppose they don't know any better. But they are the enemy of every country in Europe. They believe they are the Herrenvolk. But I tell you, boy, they are not the people chosen to rule! They are ruled by *Juden*, and that's why this war is a good thing."

"So it would be better for England if they fought with us?"

"It would, but look around you! Everywhere men are working, roads are being built, and everyone is employed. And we are ridding our country—and who knows . . ." he paused to take another drag on his cigarette ". . . maybe the world—of these filthy, good-for-nothing *Juden. Untermenschen!*"

There was that word again, and a bitter taste rose in my mouth.

Papa poured himself another drink. "It's the fault of the *Juden* that we are in this war!" He shot the drink back and poured himself yet another. "They were the reason we lost the Great War. They pretend to be our friends, just like Herr Silberstein, and before you know it, they have your job and everything else they can get their dirty hands on. The *Juden* have infested everything and are everywhere. Animals! They will never stop! You give them a bit, and before you know it they have taken over whole cities. *Juden* only think about their own kind. Vermin! But, no more! No more! . . . You will see. Life unworthy of life!" Papa sat in his chair staring ahead and smoking his cigarette furiously.

I turned my head and saw Günther standing in the doorway. He met my gaze, then lowered his head and ran up the stairs. The bitter taste rose in my mouth again.

The radio began playing *"Heil Hitler Dir!"* and under his breath Papa sang along: *"Deutschland erwache aus deinem bösen Traum . . ."*

Then he stood up, walked over to the front window and kept repeating, "*erwache aus deinem bösen Traum . . .*" At last he turned to
me, looking as if he were himself waking out of the song's evil
dream and whispered, "Up to bed with you . . . Leave me in peace."

"Papa—"

"Boy, I have much work to do . . . Get."

I didn't understand why Papa was sad or maybe he was angry, but
I breathed a little easier knowing that I wasn't going to be sent to a
work camp for ending Fritz's life. For now my secret was safe . . . and
so was I.

I stood in the hallway. "*Gute Nacht*, Papa."

But he didn't say a word back to me. The music ended and he
shouted for Mama as he sat back in his chair.

I started up the stairs with the words of the song still ringing in
my head. "Deutschland: wake up from your evil dream . . ."

"Gretchen, come in here!" Papa called. "I want to talk to you."

"Rudi, what is it?" she shouted back from the kitchen. "I'm doing
the dishes."

"Frau, don't make me call you again. Get in here!"

I ran up the stairs so Mama wouldn't see me, but once she stepped
into the living room, I crept down again and sat at the bottom of
the stairs to listen in on their conversation. As usual, Minka soon
found me and curled up on my lap.

"What is it, Rudi?"

"I received word today about a job for Susi."

"Where?"

"I put in a request to have her taken on at Ravensbrück."

"What sort of work is it, Rudi?"

"It's a camp for women: Communists, Gypsies, Poles, Jews . . .
And there's some children there, too."

"Children?"

"Does it matter, Frau? It's a good camp. Susi will work there as a
guard."

"A guard? Not our Susi!"

"Why not Susi? She is too much like her Papa so making babies may not be her calling for now."

"But what about her music, Rudi?"

"Music? Music isn't going to do anything for her!"

"Rudi, please."

"Frau Helga is the head warden at Ravensbrück."

"Helga Hegal? The Frau that attended the party at the von Frays' house when we were in Berlin, the one that smelled of oranges?"

I remembered the picture of the woman sitting on a rock in her bathing suit, and the letter I found in Papa's coat pocket. I felt sick.

"*Ja.* She will make sure that Susi moves up in the ranks. It will be good if she sets her sights on becoming one of the SS *Totenkopf.* Her training will be three months, and she—"

"Rudi, I don't know about this . . ."

"What do you mean you don't know about this?"

"It's just that she's never been away from home and—"

"Nonsense! Ravensbrück is a lovely town. It has lakes, forests . . . Besides, it's done. She's going."

How could Papa do this to Susi? He knew she wanted to go to music school.

"Have you told her, Rudi?"

I stood and crept closer to the doorway of the living room and saw Mama holding Papa's drinking glass.

"Please let me tell her, Rudi."

"*Nein,* I will tell her tomorrow myself. And Peter and Kurt are signing up for military service." They are eighteen now. I have told them already that they will be assigned to barracks next month."

The glass that Mama held slowly slipped out of her hands, landing on the floor and shattering into a hundred small pieces. "Next month . . . What about university . . . ?"

Mama's hands were trembling as she knelt to pick up the shards of glass.

Papa frowned at her. "It is their duty to serve the Führer." He put on his reading glasses, crossed his legs, and then, with a snap, opened the newspaper.

As Mama stood up, she saw that I had heard and seen what had happened. She motioned for me to go upstairs, but I didn't. Instead I walked into the kitchen and waited for her.

Once in the kitchen she sat at the table still holding the bits of broken glass in the palm of her hand. "All my children are leaving." She gazed up at me, searching my face as though she were seeing me for the first time. "You will leave, too. But promise me, Michael, promise that no matter where you go, you'll always come home."

"I promise, Mama."

The morning didn't come fast enough. I tossed and turned all night because I couldn't calm my thoughts. My brothers, Susi, and images of Fritz's corpse haunted my dreams. When I came downstairs, Mama was in the kitchen making breakfast. Susi, Peter, and Günther sat quietly at the table with Annalisa in her high chair. I could tell by Susi's red eyes that Papa had told her where she was going. He had already left the house before I had awakened, and Kurt was, as always, at his girlfriend's house.

Mama said, "Good morning, Michael. Did you sleep well?" She placed a hot bun on my plate along with a soft-boiled egg and kissed me on the top of the head. "I'm taking you to the shoe shop today."

"*Ach*, Mama. I want to go and see Wolfie."

"He's coming, too, Michael. Susi, when you're done, I want you to get Annalisa ready to go with me."

"*Ja*, Mama."

"Günther and Peter, are you going over to the Zimmermanns' today?"

"*Ja*, Mama," they both replied at once.

"Michael, when you're done, please get ready to go. There is a lot I have to do today."

"*Ja*, Mama, but after we buy the boots, can I go over to Wolfie's?"

"You can, but I want you two to go to the barber's and get your hair cut, and I want you home before *Abendessen*. I am making the supper now. Hurry it up."

As I pulled on my boots, I realized why I was getting new ones. My hand-me-downs were all worn out and too tight. Funny that I had barely noticed how uncomfortable they had become.

When we arrived at Wolfie's apartment building, I lifted Annalisa out of her carriage and carried her up the three flights of stairs. In every corridor toys and baby carriages were neatly parked outside people's doorways along with their shoes.

"Apartment number 363. Here we are, Annalisa." I had to knock several times before Wolfie's mutti opened the door, and we were greeted with a waft of cigarette smoke and the smell of stale booze.

"*Guten Tag*, Frau von Vogel," Mama said. "I am taking my son to get some new boots this morning. I noticed that your boy was in need of a new pair as well. I thought . . ."

Wolfie's mutti was already half-drunk, and before Mama could finish, she pulled some money from her apron pocket and pushed it into Mama's hand. Her speech was slurred as she said, "*Ja, ja, danke*. I would take him myself but I have much work to do today. Wolfie, get your coat." She smacked him up the side of the head as he passed her. "And mind your manners with Frau Boii. I don't want her to think that you are badly brought up."

Mama took Wolfie's arm and smiled at him, then we said our goodbyes and marched down the stairs. Wolfie pushed Annalisa's buggy all the way to the shops. She was a happy baby in that stroller. She clutched Paula's old doll and she had Wolfie as her chauffeur.

A small bell rang as we opened the door of the shoe store, and Annalisa pointed and said, "Bell." The store smelled of new leather and shoe polish. The walls were lined with handcrafted oak cases displaying boots and shoes for men, women and children. Most of the men's and boys' boots were in sensible browns and blacks, but the section for women's shoes was full of every colour, shape and style.

While Mama was explaining to Herr Schumacher that she wanted good ankle boots for us boys, we sat on the bench with my sister on my lap. She kept reaching up to pull on Wolfie's curly red hair while he made faces at her, and she responded with little girl giggles. I bounced her up and down and said to Wolfie, "She likes you."

"Of course she likes me. I'm handsome."

Annalisa pulled on Wolfie's arm so that she could climb onto his lap. "Wolfie pretty," she said and chortled.

"Thank you, Annalisa," Wolfie replied as he gave her a little kiss.

She blew a kiss and said, "Wolfie kisses."

We all laughed. Mama glanced over at us, grinned, and continued studying the ladies' shoes.

Herr Schumacher measured our feet. "You kids have big feet. I will see what I have."

He went to the back of his store, and while he was there searching for boots to fit us, I whispered to Wolfie, "We have to do something."

"Do what?"

"Do something about Fritz."

Annalisa looked up at Wolfie and said, "Fritzzz, Fritzzz."

"Shh," he said as he put his hand over her little mouth.

I handed Annalisa her doll. "Here, play with your dolly."

But she pushed it back to me. "*Nein!* Fritzzzz."

This time I put my hand over her mouth. "Shh."

Wolfie began to bounce Annalisa on his knee and sang a song about a rider on his horse. "*Hoppe, hoppe, Reiter,* if he falls, he'll cry out ..."

After he finished the game with her, all she said was, "Again!"

Just then Herr Schumacher came out of the back room holding up two pair of boots. "They are one size too big, but they will last you boys for some time."

We put on our new boots, Mama paid Herr Schumacher, and then we all said our thanks and off we went.

"*Danke* for taking me, Frau Boii," Wolfie said as we stepped outside.

"You are welcome, but you must call me Mama, Wolfie." She gave him a small kiss on the cheek. "Michael, here is 80 pfennig." She tousled my hair. "I want the two of you to go to the barber and get haircuts. Now be good and have fun. And don't lose that money!"

"*Danke*, Mama."

"And don't be late for supper!"

When we were safely around the corner, I said, "You'll never guess who came for dinner? The Bummels!"

Wolfie looked as though he were going to choke. "*Ach*, did they say anything?"

"*Nein*. All they said was that they hadn't heard a word from Fritz, and that they believed he had taken off with Jürgen."

"Why did they come to dinner?"

"Papa invited them. Herr Bummel didn't talk about the war. Later, Papa said he thought they were *Kommunisten*."

"Why would he think they were *Kommunisten*?"

"Don't know, but Papa said he will find out if they are, and he will have them sent to a camp."

"*Ach was, Scheisse*, Michael. We have bigger things to worry about than the Bummels."

"*Ja*." We walked in silence for a few minutes. "Do you think it was Herr Zimmermann and Günther that put Fritz's body in the grove? If they did, why hasn't Herr Zimmermann said anything to the Gestapo?"

"I don't know. You think they want to blackmail us?"

"My brother? I don't think so!"

We were confused. We walked to the post office and loitered there, reading the posters and hoping to hear some local gossip, but we heard nothing.

"Look, Michael!"

"At what?"

Wolfie pointed to a poster, "At this!"

I had never noticed the poster before. It had been up there for some time because the edges were curled, and it was torn. It showed a cigarette shaped like an alligator with a man in its mouth. Under the image it said, "He does not devour it, it devours you."

Wolfie laughed. "That's pretty funny, don't you think, Michael?"

"*Nein.* Cigarettes can't eat you." I think it's dumb.

Wolfie nudged me in the ribs. "Michael, don't let anyone hear you say that," he whispered, checking to see if someone had been listening to us.

"Why?"

"You know why."

"*Ja.* Mama says talking gets people killed. Come on, let's go. We have to get our hair cut."

"I'm going to get mine cut like Heini Völker in the movie *Our Flags Lead Us Forward.*

"Me too."

Once inside Leopold's barbershop, Wolfie and I took off our jackets, hung them up and sat on the high-backed wooden bench to wait. I stared up at the ceiling where six lights hung down on long cords while Wolfie stared at the black-and-white floor tiles. Then we silently admired the three barber chairs upholstered with red leather, the counters made out of white marble with black porcelain sinks, and the large mirror with its carved wooden frame that ran the length of the room.

Pointing at us, Leopold the barber said, "Okay, who's next?" He had a long mustache that curled up on the ends, and he wore a short white smock with a metal comb poking out of the pocket. He had all sorts of potions, sprays, pomades and lotions on his counter.

I settled into the barber chair. "Can I have my haircut like Heini Völker in the movie, *Our Flags Lead Us Forward?*"

"You mean Jürgen Ohlsen? Sure thing, boy. A Nazi cut it is! Did you want a shave with that?"

I glanced over at Wolfie and he grinned. I said, "Sure!" Then I turned in the chair to look up at Leopold. "Wait! How much will it be? My Mama only gave me 80 *pfennigs* for the two of us."

"That'll do it, boy."

"Okay then! Nazi it is." My first shave! I knew there was nothing there to shave but I was hopeful. With a snap, Leopold shook out the cape and fastened it over me, reclined the chair, and placed a warm towel over my face for a few minutes. When he took it off, he put some oil on my skin before he lathered up a shaving brush and applied a lot of shaving foam to my face. It smelled sort of like lemon mixed with pine. Out came the razor, he sharpened it on his leather strop—*swish, swish, swish*—then I held my breath as the blade slid like butter over my face.

A half-hour later Leopold had magically transformed Wolfie and me. As we left the barbershop, we walked taller and prouder.

Wolfie touched my face. "Smooth . . . Really smooth," he said.

Our hair was cropped short on the sides, parted on the right and it was left long on top. I grinned and ran my hands through his hair. "Very classy Nazi."

"*Guten Tag*, Michael and Wolfie."

We turned to see who was talking to us, and my eyes grew large. "Hello, Herr Zimmermann," I stammered. I couldn't say anything more because my mouth suddenly felt as dry as though I had been sucking on an old sock.

He placed his hand on my shoulder and pulled me in closer. "Let us take a walk." When we were about a block from the barbershop, he began. "Did you know, Michael, that your Papa and I . . . we fought in the Great War together—the war to end all wars? We were in the same division . . ."

Wolfie and I glanced at one another. Why was he telling us this?

"We fought in the trenches of Flanders, the battle of mud. We were young men then, not much older than you are now. It was nothing but a slaughter. But your papa saved my life. I was badly wounded, and I would have died because half my leg was blown off. I went into shock. He cinched his belt around my leg, and he dragged me back into the trenches. He could have left me there for the rats. But he managed to pull me . . . half-carried my wretched self to the field hospital.

Two other young men and I—your papa's old friend Herr Silberstein and I don't remember the other one's name—we all were hit that day, one in the groin and Herr Silberstein almost lost his arm. I don't know if the other man made it, but it was your papa who saved all of us that day. Who knows what would have happened had it not been for his bravery? So you see, I owe him . . ."

Wolfie and I stood in silence. Papa had never talked about the Great War, and he had certainly never said anything about saving lives.

I just shook my head. I felt as if I had been punched in the gut. As I looked past Herr Zimmermann, I caught a glimpse of Herr Finkel, the postman, staring at us from a distance.

"You know what I am getting at, Michael, don't you?" Herr Zimmermann said. "Günther and I saw what happened that snowy day . . ."

6

Lullaby

— MAY 1940 —

⁓

"MICHAEL, HURRY UP," Mama called from the bottom of the stairs. "Wolfie is waiting for you!"

I came running down the stairs. "Where is he, Mama?"

"In the kitchen having breakfast."

"Hello, Wolfie," I said as I sat next to him.

Mama hung my knapsack over the back of my chair. "I want both of you boys to behave while you're in Berlin."

Wolfie stuffed a hard-boiled egg into his mouth and mumbled, "We will, Frau Boii."

"Don't talk with your mouth full, Wolfie, and don't forget to call me Mama."

Wolfie took a sip of coffee. "Sorry, Mama."

"Michael, you won't see your papa for some time, so after you have eaten breakfast, I want you to say goodbye to him."

"Where's he going?"

"Poland." Mama placed a roll on my plate.

Wolfie reached over, grabbed it and put some jam on it. "He's overseeing the expansion of a camp."

"How do you know that?"

Mama placed another roll on my plate. "Early this morning your papa was in the kitchen having some coffee, and Wolfie had already let himself in."

"And Papa told *you*?" I said, staring at Wolfie.

He wiped his mouth with the back of his hand. "*Ja.* Your papa said it's a big job and he'll get a big promotion." He stood up, placed his dish in the sink and gave Mama a kiss. "Hurry it up, Michael. We'll be late meeting our class at the train station."

"Not so fast, you two. Michael, go into the living room and say goodbye to your papa. He's waiting for you. And, Wolfie, do you have a change of clothes with you?"

"*Nein.*"

I pushed my plate away, stood up and walked over to the living room doorway. "Good morning, Papa."

Papa nodded then motioned for me to step closer to his chair. "Michael, you're going to be the man of the house while I'm gone."

"What about Peter and Kurt?"

"Most likely they will be sent to France next week."

"*Ja*, but they'll be home again soon . . ."

"I don't know that."

"But Susi, she'll be back, and what about Günther?"

"The people from the institution are coming to take Günther for an examination."

"Mama never said anything about—"

"That's enough, Michael. You're not a little boy anymore. You're what—thirteen? Anyway, you're the only one left on the home front. Do you understand what I'm saying?"

"I'm almost fourteen. Papa, how long will you be gone?"

"However long it takes to expand the camp. The *Juden* can't all be sent to Madagascar."

"What camp? Will the Silbersteins move to Madagascar?"

"*Schluss*—never mind."

Just then Wolfie stepped into the living room doorway and mouthed the words, "Let's go."

I wasn't quite sure what I would have to do as the man of the house, but I would ask Mama later. I felt sick. Why did Papa not care about his friend? After all, Herr Silberstein gave him a job at the bank after the Great War when no one else would . . . Of course, Papa had saved his life so he had owed him, but . . .

Wolfie pointed to his watch and once again mouthed, "Let's go!"

Papa stood up. "All right, Michael. Remember what I have taught you. *Heil Hitler.*"

I raised my arm. "*Heil Hitler.*" We shook hands and I said goodbye. I went into the kitchen, gave Mama a kiss and assured her that Wolfie and I would be on our best behaviour.

Wolfie gave Mama a hug and a kiss goodbye, too.

We closed the door behind us, and as we hurried along the street to meet our classmates at the train station, Wolfie said, "What did your papa say?"

"Peter and Kurt are going to be gone for a long time."

"Wonder if we'll ever get to go."

"Probably not."

"Why would you say that?"

"Yesterday the announcer on the radio said that the war would be over soon. And Mama . . . well, I think she needs me to look after things while Papa's gone."

"Michael, it doesn't work that way. If the time comes, no mutti can keep her boy home. We'll all have to go."

"*Ja*, I know. But what about Mama?"

"I don't know."

As we came around the corner, I pointed. "*Scheisse!* Herr Kannengiesser is waving at us."

"Hurry up, boys! Wolfgang, I take it that your mutti knows you are going on this trip?"

Wolfie hung his head and mumbled, "*Ja*, she does."

Truth was, she didn't know because for the last three days he'd been coming over to my house for every meal, and when he did that, it always meant that she'd gone off on a binge and would be gone for at least a few weeks.

"Good. Get into line with the rest of the boys."

The station conductor shouted at us. His front teeth had a big gap between them, so that his spit went flying as he shouted. "*Achtung!* Boys, please, stand in an orderly manner. That means no pushing. The train will pull into the station in two minutes. You'll be travelling for about three hours with Wehrmacht soldiers from a Panzer unit. Stay in your seats at all times. We don't need to lose anyone!"

Herr Kannengiesser stood beside the conductor, clapping his hands to get us to line up on platform F7. He peered over his glasses and bellowed, "Come along now. Hurry it up!"

Wolfie buttoned up his jacket as the incoming train rumbled into the station, bringing a gust of cold air with it. He said, "*Ach*, Michael, that's a marvellous train! Did you see the big swastika on the front of it?"

We walked beside the train, excited at the sight of it.

"*Ja*, I like the yellow stripe on it." I pointed to the back of the train." Look at the tanks on the flatcars at the end!"

"Wow!" Wolfie shouted as the train screeched to a halt. "It's just like Hitler's train, the *Führersonderzug*. Wow!"

"Everyone line up in twos!" shouted our teacher. "No pushing! Michael and Wolfgang, get in line and stop talking."

As we joined the rest of the group, Herr Kannengiesser peered over his glasses at us, shook his head, and lightly smacked us on the backs of our heads. Then as he pushed us into line, he said, "I sincerely hope you two will not give me any trouble. Now get!"

We didn't dare glance at each other as we would have burst out laughing for sure. But Wolfie pulled a funny face mocking Herr

Kannengiesser. I snickered and Herr Kannengiesser caught me.

"Boy, one more stunt from you and this trip will end so fast . . ." Shaking his finger in my face, he added, "Not one more sound out of you two. Am I making myself clear?"

"*Ja*," I said. "I'm sorry, Herr Rektor."

Wolfie and I were the last to climb aboard, and we took the seats by the door that led to the next passenger carriage. Wolfie pointed at the soldiers, "Bet they're a replacement unit."

I nodded.

The conductor checked his pocket watch, blew his whistle as he must have done a thousand times before and shouted for everyone to get in: "*Alle Einsteigen!*"

Once everyone had boarded, the train whistle sounded, black smoke billowed forth, metal rasped on metal, churning, grinding, and we were on our way.

The countryside began rolling by, undulating hills of green, sheep dotting the land, Hitlerjugend workers out sowing fields to serve the Third Reich. By the time we pulled in to the next train station, we were all sitting quietly. And then I saw her. She was holding her mother's hand as they stood close together beneath the great flowing swastika banners that hung from the station. There was something so different about her. Her hair was a beautiful shade of chestnut brown, and her features were perfect. My face felt hot. I became short of breath, and my hands felt clammy, no matter how much I wiped them on my shorts.

She boarded the train, coming towards me, floating as if she were walking on air. Closer and closer. I couldn't take my eyes off her . . . and now I could see that her eyes were hazel-coloured. She noticed me staring at her and softly bit her lip. As the train started up again, she bumped into the seat in front of her, and in so doing dropped her handkerchief. Then she floated past me as though she were in another world altogether. I leaned over to pick up her hanky. What was her name? I had to talk to her . . . I just had to.

The train rolled on, metal on metal, through rolling hills that led to quaint little villages. I lifted her hanky to my nose. The aroma of white lilies.

"What have you got, Michael?" Wolfie demanded.

"Nothing . . . nothing." I stood up. "I'll be back in a few minutes."

"We're supposed to stay in our seats. You'll get us in trouble."

"I'll be back in a few minutes. If Herr Beak Face asks, tell him I went to the toilets." I turned and followed the pretty girl and her mutti into the next carriage, but most of the seats there were filled with soldiers.

A Sturmbannführer glanced up at me as I passed. "Are you lost, boy?"

"*Nein*, I'm looking for someone," I said as I caught a glimpse of them ahead.

"Oh, there they are!" I waved at them, but they didn't see me. However, I was determined to speak to the beautiful girl.

The Sturmbannführer turned, looked at them, then back at me. "Friends of yours, boy?"

"*Nein*, Herr."

"Then what business do you have with them?"

I was both annoyed and made nervous by his questions. My face grew hot. Perhaps I had no business speaking to her? I glanced at them, took a deep breath. "I don't. The girl dropped her hanky, and I want to return it to her."

The Sturmbannführer held out his hand, motioning for me to hand it over.

I reached into my pocket, pulled out the white hanky and handed it to him. He looked at it carefully, stood up and handed it back to me. Then he clicked his heels. "*Heil Hitler!*"

I saluted. "*Heil Hitler.*" But before I finished speaking, he was already headed toward the next carriage of the train. I approached the mutti and her daughter with my heart pounding. Smiling, I held out my hand to the mutti: "*Guten Tag.*"

Startled, the mutti cleared her throat, looked over her shoulder, then back at me. She held out her hand. "*Guten Tag.*"

"My name is Michael Boii." I shook her hand, which was cold and delicate, almost skeletal.

Her daughter kept her head down at first and then shyly looked up. "May I sit with you?"

The mutti nodded and gestured for me to sit on the bench across from them.

"I'm Helena Engel, and this is my daughter, Erika." Frau Engel then took her daughter's hand and held it to her breast.

I nodded. "I am pleased to meet you, Frau Engel and Fräulein Erika." After we introduced ourselves, I leaned down to pull up my socks. Frau Engel nervously shuffled her feet to the side, trying to conceal her well-worn shoes, which were covered in mud. I sat up and gave her a smile. "It is a very nice day," I said.

Frau Engel straightened her linen coat and proceeded to comment on the weather, but I kept staring into Erika's hazel-brown eyes. Fortunately the rhythmic clatter of the train was like a sweet-sounding lullaby that soon put Frau Engel to sleep, and Erika and I were free to talk. I told her that I was with my school and we were taking a tour of Berlin, and we talked about our friends, our favourite movies, where we loved to go swimming and the sort of music we liked. We laughed at one another's stories. I fell in love in that short hour. "Erika, where are you and your mutti going?"

"We are going to stay with my Onkel Franz and Tante Clara. They live in Berlin. My Tante is not well. I love Onkel, but he is old and has trouble looking after Tante Clara. He has a long gray beard, and he walks with a cane. Mutti and I will help look after Tante Clara."

"Oh. That's good of you. Have you been to Berlin before?"

"*Nein.* It's my first time. Have you?"

"*Ja,* for the Führer's fiftieth birthday celebration. It was quite the spectacle! Where do your relatives live?"

"Kurfürstendamm. Above the big shoe store." She then glanced at the floor and in a hushed breath said, "I don't like Herr Hitler."

It was such a strange thing to say because everyone loved our Führer, but when she said nothing more, I asked, "Are you hungry?"

She nodded. "A little."

I reached into my satchel and pulled out the sandwich that Mama had made for me. I gently unwrapped the clean crisp napkin and handed her half. She took it eagerly as if she had not eaten in days.

She seemed on the verge of tears as she said, "*Danke.*"

"You're welcome." I dropped my satchel and leaned over to pick it up, and that's when I saw Erika put part of the sandwich into her pocket.

Just then an SS officer approached with the Sturmbannführer I had spoken to earlier.

"Fräulein, may I see your travel papers?" he asked with what I thought was a smirk.

With trembling hands Erika handed her papers to him.

He flipped through them, then stopped and said her name out loud. "Erika Engel?" He said it as if posing a question, then looked her over from head to toe. "What a nice name. Good, all is in order." He handed the papers back to her, and leaned into her, smiled, and in a whisper said, "*Jude.*"

Erika's eyes opened wide, and she clasped her hand over her mouth. At that instant Frau Engel awoke, terror spreading across her face. The Sturmbannführer reached out and pulled Erika roughly to her feet, shouting, "Get up, you filthy *Jude!*"

I pulled on his arm. "Take your hands off her!"

He hit me across the face, knocking me to the floor. Then as he pushed Erika and her mutti along the aisle toward the next carriage, he shouted back at me, "Are you one of these rat Jews, too, boy? You better shut your mouth!"

Some of the people in the carriage had become alarmed, and they stood up to see what was happening. But several of the soldiers in the car rose to their feet and pulled out their pistols, waving them about at the passengers. "Sit down!" they shouted.

The Sturmbannführer looked down at me. "Get back to your seat, boy! Now!"

Erika turned back to look at me. Her eyes were full of fear and her voice trembled. "My name is Rebekah Schapiro . . ."

I scrambled to my feet, wiping blood from my lips. Some of the passengers shook their heads at me and some pushed at me or called out, "Shame!" Others looked down as I walked past them. When I returned to my seat, I couldn't speak.

Wolfie asked, "What was all the commotion about back there?"

I only shrugged.

At the next small village the train stopped, and I stared out the window in horror as Rebekah and Frau Schapiro were dragged and kicked onto the train platform. The Sturmbannführer had Rebekah by the scruff of the neck now, and two soldiers held onto her mutti. Wolfie and my other classmates pressed their faces to the windows to watch, and I rose to my feet, mouth open in silent protest.

Then I saw Rebekah struggle free and start running away, but the Sturmbannführer pulled out his Luger and shot her. She stumbled and fell and tried to get up. He shot her again. After that she didn't move. All this time Rebekah's mutti was screaming and struggling to get free to run to her daughter. The Sturmbannführer nodded to the soldiers to let her go, then he shot her dead, too.

"Okay, that's enough!" shouted Herr Kannengiesser. "There is nothing more to see! Sit down, everyone!"

I sat down, not saying a word, just staring at nothing.

"*Ach*, Michael, why did they shoot them?" Wolfie asked.

I shook my head. It was my fault . . . I pulled out the hanky that Rebekah had dropped. In the corner of it, embroidered in pink thread, were the initials R.S. It was my fault . . . my fault. I plunged my hand and the hanky back into my pocket. The train started up again, and the grinding and turning of the wheels, metal on metal, lulled me into the world of untold truths.

My fault, my fault, my fault . . .

7

Berlin and the Angel

— MAY 1940 —

⁓

"MICHAEL, WAKE UP! We're here."

I awoke, my hand in my pocket still clenching Rebekah's hanky.

As we stepped off the train, I looked up and saw a giant clock. It was one o'clock in the afternoon. Hundreds of people were coming and going, some stopping in front of the train schedules, others joining the orderly lines on the platforms. And I was unable to move. I had grown leaden feet.

Wolfie pulled at me. "Keep up, Michael! You're going to get us sent home or worse . . . What's wrong with you?"

"Her name was Rebekah."

Wolfie stared at me.

Under my breath I said it again. "Her name was Rebekah . . ."

"Who?"

"No one, Wolfie. No one . . . now." As we stepped out of the station, it began to rain, and the world fell silent. All I heard were the hollow drops of water exploding on the pavement. And suddenly I was standing there saluting and shouting, "*Heil Hitler. Heil Hitler . . .*" But while one hand was raised, the other was deep in my pocket. Tears rolled down my face.

"*Heil Hitler.*" An officer from the Wehrmacht Panzer unit saluted back. The soldiers marching behind him out of the station were wearing black jackboots and grey overcoats, the same grey that was on display in the heavens above us, and as they marched by, they sang the song, "Erika."

"*Heil Hitler,*" I continued shouting hardly knowing why.

"Come on, Michael," Wolfie urged, pulling me along by the arm. "And keep your enthusiasm for Hitler under control."

Herr Kannengiesser called a halt and shoved Otto to get him back into line. "All right, boys," he shrieked at us, "you will be split into three groups." While giving us orders in his ear-piercing squawk, he rose onto his toes and then rocked onto his heels, trying to appear taller. "All of you with red name tags go and stand with Herr Braun. Those of you with the green name tags go to Herr Schmitt. The rest of you are with me."

The ten of us with black name tags groaned at the realization that we were going with Herr Kannengiesser.

"*Ach, Scheisse!*" Wolfie muttered. "It's raining and we're stuck with Herr Beak Face."

"*Ja,*" said Otto. "Guess he wants to keep an eye on you two."

Wolfie scratched his head and said under his breath, "We're not going to have any fun with that fat-headed imbecile."

Herr Kannengiesser marched over to us. "Would you like to share your comment with everyone, Wolfgang?"

Wolfie pulled his head back to avoid the teacher's flying spittle. "Sorry, Herr Rektor. I just said that we should—"

"Shut your mouth, boy, before I shut it for you." Herr Kannengiesser's face was all sweaty, and his glasses as usual had slid to the bottom of his beaky nose. "I better not hear another peep out of you. And that goes for you too, Michael! Now get in line!"

I wanted to scream and tell Beak Face to shut up. Instead, I threw up onto his shiny black shoes. He lurched back and in doing so tripped and fell into the path of a well-dressed Fräulein who was wearing a veiled hat and shielding herself from the rain with a large black umbrella. Before he could scramble to his feet, the Fräulein accidentally stepped on Herr Kannengiesser's hand.

"Ow! You stupid cow!" he yelled.

We all burst out laughing, but Otto ran over to help Beak Face up.

The Fräulein, whose back was turned to us, stopped in front of Herr Kannengiesser and slapped him across the face. "Maybe you should learn some manners." And she walked on.

Wolfie poked me in the ribs. "That was Margarita!" he said. We both turned to stare after her.

"Are you sure?"

The other boys were still laughing at Herr Kannengiesser, who stood red-faced and humiliated. He shouted, "That's quite enough from all of you!" Shaking the vomit off his shoe, he walked over, smacked me in the face and whispered, "One more stunt like that and I will see to it that you are sent home. Do I make myself clear?"

I clutched Rebekah's hanky and wiped my mouth with the back of my hand.

Wolfie put his arm over my shoulder and whispered, "Your aim was pretty damned good."

Herr Kannengiesser lined us up again and proceeded to outline the route we would be taking to our billet and what we should watch for along the way. The only thing that stuck in my mind from all that he said was Kurfürstendamm. We would be going down the street where Rebekah's uncle had his shoe store.

"All right, boys, follow me." Herr Beak Face began marching us towards our accommodations. He was wearing his small National Socialist pin on his lapel, and he marched ahead of us like he was some high-ranking officer.

Wolfie whispered in my ear. "Look at him showing off."

But my mind was on how Papa had said that all Jews were rats. I'd heard him say that so often, but Herr Silberstein was a Jew and he had given Papa a job ... "Wolfie," I said, "keep your eyes open for a big shoe store once we get to Kurfürstendamm."

"What?"

"A shoe store on Kurfürstendamm."

"I heard you, but why?"

"Just keep your eyes open."

As we marched over a bridge, the rain stopped briefly, and Herr Kannengiesser told us to halt. "Listen up, boys!" he said. "Take a look to your right." Obediently we all turned our heads. "That is the Reichstag. Kaiser Wilhelm II inaugurated it in 1890, and in 1933 Marinus van der Lubbe, a Dutch communist ..."

Wolfie and I leaned against the bridge railing. "Do you need laces for your boots?" Wolfie asked.

I shook my head. "*Nein* ... It's just that her uncle ..."

As an ambulance raced shrieking toward us, Herr Kannengiesser began speaking louder. "This communist set fire to the Reichstag and tried to burn it to the ground! He was put to death by means of a guillotine."

Wolfie leaned into me. "Whose uncle?"

The ambulance's siren was so loud that I screamed her name at the top of my lungs. "Rebekah's!" And just as I shouted, the siren went silent, and everyone in my group turned to stare at me. Herr Kannengiesser began rocking on his heels, but he continued his lecture. "And over here is the beautiful Brandenburg Gate. Notice the Goddess of Victory on top of the structure, on a chariot driven by four horses. It is called the Quadriga." He took out his handkerchief and wiped his forehead. "In 1806 Napoleon took this statue to the Louvre—that's in Paris, boys—but the glorious Prussian army defeated Napoleon and brought her back home to Berlin in 1813."

Wolfie whispered, "Michael, what's the matter with you?"

"Nothing," I said and felt for her hanky again. Did no one in our group care about what they had witnessed from the train? Or were they just scared to think about it?

As we walked through the gates, we stared up at the white pillars with their golden eagles and the swastikas mounted on top. There were throngs of people everywhere as we made our way to Wilhelmstrasse where Hitler's flags lined the street. Parked in front of the NSDAP headquarters were a lot of BMW cars and Citroens. Berlin was so alive. But I felt numb.

"Boys, this is where our great Führer, Adolf Hitler . . ." As Herr Kannengiesser pointed at a balcony of the NSDAP headquarters, his eyes welled up. "It is from this balcony that our Führer addresses thousands of people. Remember this address—Voßstrasse 4."

"*Ach*, did you see that?" Wolfie pulled a sad face, mocking Herr Kannengiesser. "I think he has lost his head."

When we turned into the Kurfürstendamm, Wolfie stopped in his tracks. "*Ach*, Michael, I don't remember all these stores from the last time we were here, do you?" He and the rest of our classmates just stared, their eyes wide with wonder, but I was only looking for the shoe store.

"Come now, boys!" shouted Beak Face. "No time to stare. We are only a few more minutes' walk to the grand house of Officer von Fray. I want all of you to be on your best behaviour. It is a privilege that he is taking us in for our time in Berlin. Michael's papa, Herr Boii, arranged this for us, and I want everyone on their best behaviour. Do I make myself clear?"

Wolfie nudged me. "Did you hear that, Michael? We're staying at Margarita's house! Did you know we would be staying there?"

"*Nein.*" But at that moment I spotted the big shoe store just up ahead, and as we got closer, I saw that there was an old man, with a long grey beard standing with a cane in front of his store, and he seemed to be searching the crowd for a familiar face. Rebekah had described him so well to me. "It's the uncle," I said under my breath.

"What?" Wolfie asked. "Michael, where are you going?"

But I ignored him and ran ahead to where the old man waited. I pressed Rebekah's hanky into his hand as I softly said, "Rebekah and her mutti are not coming. They were . . ." I did not need to say any more.

He looked off into the distance, turned, and began walking toward the door.

Then Herr Beak Face was standing beside me and demanding, "What do you think you are doing, boy?" And he clipped me across the back of the head again. "Get back in line!"

As I fell into step beside Wolfie, he demanded, "What was that about, Michael?"

"*Nichts.*"

"Can you believe it?" He punched my arm. "We get to stay with Fräulein Margarita!"

"What?" I was watching Rebekah's uncle as he vanished into his store.

Fräulein Margarita's grand white brick house with its small flower garden out front and its pink roses felt familiar and safe, and we followed Herr Kannengiesser up the marble staircase that led to the glass door.

"Wow!" Otto shouted. "Bet it's all fancy inside."

"*Ja!* Officer von Fray must have a lot of money," said Fred.

I adjusted my pack and took off my cap, and then, just as Mama had done, I pulled Wolfie's cap off, too. He bent down to pull up his socks, and then straightened his coat.

"Do you think she'll remember us?" he asked.

"Sure," I said, but I was thinking of Rebekah. Would anyone remember her?

Herr Kannengiesser rang the doorbell, and Fräulein Margarita opened the door.

She was just as beautiful as I had remembered her. She glanced at us boys, then glared directly at Herr Kannengiesser. "Have we met before?"

"*Ach, du Scheisse,*" Wolfie whispered. "Michael, it *was* Margarita at the station!"

Herr Kannengiesser stumbled over his words, then stuck out his hand. "Hello, Fräul . . . ?

"I'm Herr von Fray's daughter, Fräulein Margarita."

She shook his hand, smiled politely, and stood to the side of the staircase. "Oh my, you boys look as though you had a good walk. You must all be hungry. Do come in." As our troop filed past, she suddenly smiled and reached out to stroke first Wolfie's face and then mine. "And how wonderful to see you two boys again!"

I blushed and Wolfie nudged me. I said, "It's nice to see you, too."

"Michael, how is your mama?"

"She is fine, *danke.*"

Herr Kannengiesser cleared his throat. "I think these boys would like to have a rest, Fräulein Margarita."

"I'm sure they do. Come in, boys." She led all of us into the foyer where her papa greeted us. We all saluted him, but it was obvious that Herr von Fray frightened some of my classmates, most likely because of his large scar.

He saluted us back. "It's my pleasure, boys. I hope you will make yourselves at home." Then he smiled broadly at Wolfie and me and put a hand on each of our heads. "Well, hello, you two. You have grown since the last time I saw you!"

"*Ja,*" I said.

"You will say hello to your mama for me, Michael."

"I will, Herr von Fray."

Herr Kannengiesser once again cleared his throat, but this time he smiled at me. "These two are my best students," he said.

Herr von Fray winked at Wolfie and me. "Herr Kannengiesser, why don't you join me and my guests in the next room, the Herrenzimmer. They are mainly army officers, but Herr Professor Albrecht Haushofer from the University of Berlin is also here. I'm sure you'll enjoy talking to him."

Our teacher followed Fräulein Margarita's father into the smoke-filled gentlemen's room, but I saw that the SS officers in the room looked much like the men who shot Rebekah, and I felt queasy. Just before he closed the door, I heard Herr von Fray say, "Would you like a drink, Herr Kannengiesser?"

As soon as the door closed, Fräulein Margarita turned her attention back to us. "All right, boys. Follow me."

As Wolfie pushed me to move along, he whispered, "Did you see how guilty old Beak Face looked when he was offered a drink?"

Fräulein Margarita led the way up the stairs to the second floor and opened the door to a room with two double beds. In an adjacent room with a connecting door were two more double beds. "All of you but Wolfie and Michael will sleep here." Then she pointed up the stairs that led to the attic room that Wolfie and I had stayed in the last time we visited. "You two will be staying in your old room," she told us. "I trust you will be comfortable there?"

We nodded and thanked her. "*Ja, danke*, Fräulein Margarita."

She winked at us and smiled. "Now all of you get washed up, and I will come for you when *Abendessen* is being served." We watched her as she seemed to glide down the stairs before we climbed the last flight to our room.

"Are we ever lucky to get our old room," Wolfie said. "Fräulein Margarita must like us." He went to look out the little window. "Just look at us! We're hot-blooded Deutsche, and all the women want us!"

I swung my pack at him. "Let's have a smoke."

"Not yet. I bet Herr Beak Face is going to come up here to inspect our Shangri-la." Wolfie fell back on the bed, put his hands under his head, closed his eyes and exhaled the words, "Ahh . . . Fräulein Margarita."

"I get the left side," I said, flopping onto the bed beside him. "And you better not fart tonight."

We laughed and both of us passed wind just as Herr Kannengiesser walked in. He was hit by an unpleasant waft.

He screwed up his face. "*Ach*, you two are disgusting."

Just then Fräulein Margarita arrived and said softly as she slipped past him into our room, "Herr . . . at it again, are we?"

He stepped out of the room past her, with an angry glance directed at us.

She smiled at us. "You two darlings, wash up. The other boys are on their way downstairs. Supper will be served in ten minutes. You do remember that the washroom is on the second floor?" She closed our door.

"I'm going to put on a clean shirt. You should, too, Wolfie."

"She called us *darlings!*" he said, then added, "I didn't bring another one."

"That's all right." I reached into my pack. "Mama put two shirts in here." I threw the extra shirt at Wolfie and carefully laid my own on the bed and ran my hands over it to smooth out the wrinkles.

"*Danke.*"

"Can you light us a cigarette now?"

"*Ja,* but let's put on our clean shirts first."

"Nah, they'll smell like smoke."

"*Ja,* you're right."

As I leaned on the windowsill smoking and gazing out over Berlin, I wondered if anyone would bury Rebekah's body. Or would it just be left to rot? I flicked my cigarette butt out the window.

Wolfie ran his hand through his hair. "Let's sneak out tonight."

"What? You know how much trouble we can get into?"

He shrugged, took one more drag from his cigarette and blew a smoke ring as he looked out over the city. "Who knows when we'll get to come back here again, so we better make the most of it." He slapped me on the back. "Let's go and wash up."

We were the last to arrive in the dining room with its big mahogany table dominating the room and the large crystal chandelier hanging above it. At one end of the room a set of glass doors led onto a terrace that overlooked the back garden, and at the other end another set of glass doors separated the dining room from the living room where the piano still stood. In front of them lay Bunny, Fräulein Margarita's big white poodle, still wearing those baby-blue ribbons tied to his ears.

As soon as we entered the room, Bunny jumped up on Wolfie and me to lick our faces. "Hello, boy!" Wolfie said. "You remember us, don't you?"

Fräulein Margarita came over and pulled Bunny away from us. "Bunny, get down."

We took our seats, and Bunny slipped under the table to lie at our feet. Soup was served in rose-patterned china bowls, and we ate with silverware.

My classmates sat at the table staring around the room, hesitant to pick up their spoons.

Fräulein Margarita said, "Come, boys, it's only cabbage soup and bread. Dig in." She walked behind my chair. "Is everything all right, Michael? You look a little pale."

"*Ja.* May I be excused for a moment?"

"*Ja, ja.* You remember there's a bathroom at the end of the hall?"

I nodded. As soon as I reached the bathroom, I threw up. Afterwards I went to the sink, splashed cold water on my face and stared at myself in the mirror. *Is the world mad or is it full of madmen?* I asked myself. *Why did she have to be a Jew? How could I have not known? She was so beautiful . . .* I sat down on the toilet seat and stared at my feet. It was my fault. *Why had I insisted on talking to her?* Just then someone tried the bathroom door handle. I opened the door, and there stood Herr Beak Face swaying and reeking of some sort of schnapps. "Get out of my way, boy."

He stumbled forward and I stepped out of his way.

When I returned to the dining room, Fräulein Margarita said, "Are you feeling better, Michael?"

"*Ja, danke.*"

After supper we were told we could play cards, *mikado* or board games until ten o'clock and then we had to go to bed as we had a big day ahead of us. Fräulein Margarita came up the stairs and asked us if we had everything we needed. She reminded us not to forget to brush our teeth.

We nodded. "*Ja*, Fräulein Margarita."

"Where is Herr Kannengiesser?" Wolfie asked.

"Oh, he's not feeling well. And I don't think he'll come up to see you boys any time soon."

Otto stood up. "Is he sleeping?"

"*Ja*. I'd like it if all you boys put on your nightshirts and jump into bed. I will come by later to say goodnight."

We said goodnight to our classmates and went to our room. When we got there, Wolfie produced a flat silver pocket flask out of his knapsack. "Look what I got!"

"Where did you get that?"

"It was my papa's." He unscrewed the cap, took a swig, scrunched his face up and shuddered before handing the flask to me. "I filled it with my mutti's vodka."

As I drank from the flask, Wolfie, still talking, pulled on his night-shirt over his clothes so Fräulein Margarita wouldn't be suspicious when she checks on us.

"I think we can sneak out the bathroom window, Michael. I stuck my head out, and there's a trellis that we can use to climb down."

Our eyes locked for a split second as we caught the sound of someone coming up the stairs. I quickly pulled on my nightshirt too, then we both dove into bed moments before there was a knock on our door.

"Come in!" I called, and Fräulein Margarita poked her head into our room.

"I thought you might like a bed-time snack," she said.

"*Danke!*" Wolfie and I chorused.

She placed a tray of cookies and cups of chamomile tea on our nightstand, then took a book off the tray and handed it to me. "And I thought you might like to read about the adventures of Old

Shatterhand by Karl May—unless you think you're too old for this sort of stuff . . ."

"*Ach, nein!* We're not too old for Old Shatterhand," Wolfie said.

"It's from my papa's library so take good care of it."

"We will, Fräulein Margarita."

"Well, don't stay up too late because remember that Herr Kannengiesser has planned a full day for you tomorrow. *Gute Nacht.*"

"*Gute Nacht*, Fräulein Margarita."

She closed the door as she left our room, and we heard her going back down the stairs.

Wolfie took the book from me. "Look, Michael! It's *Der schwarze Mustang*, one of my Karl May favourites!" He reached for one of the cookies on the tray and began leafing through the book. "Oh, remember this part, Michael? It's where—"

"Wolfie, where's the vodka?"

"Oh, *ja.*" He brought it out from under the blanket and handed it to me.

I had just started to take a swig when he said, "Did you hear that?"

"What?"

"Listen."

We both jumped out of bed and stood by the open window. There were two men smoking on the back patio directly below us.

"It's Herr von Fray," I whispered, "and one of the SS officers." In the cool evening air their words rose up to us quite distinctly.

"Herr Schellenberg, do you mean this . . . this brothel is just around the corner *from my own home?*" Herr von Fray said, sounding shocked.

"*Ja.* They have moved into the Pension Schmidt at 11 Giesebrechtstrasse. You just tell them 'I come from Rothenburg,' and that gets you in and you take your pick . . . Any one of twenty delightful, clean girls. Two, if you'd like."

"And they've moved into this neighbourhood?"

"Well, it's a classy salon. Count Ciano from Italy visits whenever he is in Berlin. He told me he likes Kitty—she's the owner."

Wolfie turned to me and whispered, "That's what we'll do, Michael!" He put the flask on the night table, reached under his nightshirt and into his pocket and pulled out a wad of money. "Look!"

"Where'd you get that?"

"I took it from my mutti."

I took a gulp from the flask.

"Hey, leave some for me!"

Wolfie grabbed the flask and took a big gulp. "We need girls!" he said. "What's the password?"

"Rothenburg."

"I think we should wear our sunglasses." He dug into his knapsack and put his sunglasses on.

"Why?"

"They will make us look older!"

We drank some more before pulling off our nightshirts and combing our hair. Wolfie dug my sunglasses out of my knapsack and stuck them on my face. I started to put on my boots when he said, "*Nein!* They'll make too much noise. Tie them together and wear them around your neck." And he laughed. "We'll be like Old Shatterhand and Winnetou—we'll leave no tracks and make no noise."

Wolfie crept to the door, slowly opened it and stood listening for any sound. Then he signalled me to follow him. "All clear."

He went first, tiptoeing down the stairs and clinging to the bannister. I was tight up against his back, but it was hard to see with my sunglasses on. "*Ach, Scheisse!*"

"Sshh."

"Sorry, can't see . . ."

"*Ja!* Careful, Old Wobble-Legs, don't knock us down."

Herr Kannengiesser's room was directly across from the bathroom, but all was quiet there. Neither of us breathed as I pushed the bathroom door open, pulled Wolfie inside and whispered, "All good, no one's in here."

"Did you bring the booze?"

"*Ja*, it's in my pocket. Want some?" I pulled the flask out and handed it to him.

Wolfie took a swig and wiped his mouth with the back of his hand. "*Ach*, that's good stuff. Think we can make it down the trellis?"

I peered out the window and assessed the situation. There was only a scraggly bit of vine growing up it as far as the first floor. "*Ja*, it's not that far. I'll go first, then you throw me the flask."

"Wait . . . I have to piss."

"Not now. Can't it wait?"

"*Nein . . . Ach, du Scheisse*, someone's coming!"

Before I knew what had happened, Wolfie and I had climbed out the window and were hanging from the rose trellis, and Herr Kannengiesser was at the bathroom window above us, calling out, "Who's there?"

We clung to the trellis, not moving. When everything remained quiet, he closed the window and turned off the bathroom light. Slowly, feeling our way, we started down the trellis, but when my feet were still about three metres from the ground, the trellis pulled away from the wall, and with a thump we fell the rest of the way. Winded, we lay there for a moment on our backs, not sure what to do. Just then the lights at the back of the house went on and Fräulein Margarita stepped out onto the back porch. In the light from the kitchen and the one above the door we could see that she was wearing some kind of filmy négligée, and the slight breeze moved it, revealing her silhouette. We held our breath. She was so beautiful.

"Michael, I really have to piss—now," Wolfie whispered close to my ear.

I put my hand over his mouth.

"Hello . . . Hello . . ." Fräulein Margarita was about to step off the porch into the garden when a cat streaked across the lawn and disappeared into the shrubbery. "Oh, cats!" she said. She went back inside and switched off all the lights, except for the one over the back door.

Wolfie stood up and watered the grass. "Ahh! That feels better."

I brushed myself off, put on my boots and pushed my hair out of my face. "Come on!" We needed to be on our way before someone else came out.

I waited while Wolfie pulled on his boots and then took out a couple of smokes and lit them. While handing me one, he whispered, "How about we have a drink?" Then he pulled me close and said, "The flask . . . do you have it? Please say *ja*."

"The flask, ahh . . ." I scanned the grass and there it was, lying under the trellis. I pointed to it.

Wolfie picked it up, wiped off the dirt, took a swig, and handed it to me. This time the liquor running down my throat made me feel warm inside.

"Now we're all good to go and get us some girls!" With a swagger to his step, Wolfie began marching around the corner of the house and heading for the front gate.

I trailed along behind, but as he reached for the gate, I stopped him from opening it. "It squeals," I reminded him and started climbing over the four-foot stone wall instead.

Wolfie followed me, and we toppled over the wall to land on the cobblestone sidewalk, with me lying on top of him. Laughing, he pushed me off then helped me up, and we began marching along Kurfürstendamm staying close to the buildings and ducking out of sight when anyone came along.

He stopped and tipped the flask up to his mouth. "*Ach*, Michael, that's the last of the vodka, and if I do say so myself, I think we're skunk as drunks."

"*Nein-n-n*," I said. "We're drunken skunkens . . ."

He put his arm around my shoulder and broke into a silly song about a hat with three corners:

Mein Hut, der hat drei Ecken,
Drei Ecken hat mein Hut.
Und hätt' er nicht drei Ecken,
So wär's auch nicht mein Hut.

I grabbed his arm and pointed at the street sign. Giesebrecht-strasse. "We need number eleven," I said. And there it was, three houses up and across the street from us—number eleven, a big white four-storey building with a woman standing in the doorway.

"*Ach*, it's the Pension Schmidt. How do I look, Michael?"

"You look drunk. How do I look?"

"Drunk."

"What were we supposed to say, Wolfie?"

"Ah . . . I come from Frauingburg?"

"Frauingburg?" I laughed so hard I fell down. Wolfie extended his hand to help me up, but instead I pulled him to the ground. "More like Badrunkenburg. Do you think she can see us, Wolfie?"

"*Nein.*" He managed to stand then pulled me up.

"It's Rothenburg—that's what we're supposed to say."

"*Ja*, that's it." He started forward but I stopped him.

"Light us a cigarette," I said. "That way we'll look smarter, sophisticated."

With our cigarettes dangling from our mouths and our sunglasses straightened, we marched up to the madam, who was having a cigarette of her own. In his deepest voice, Wolfie said, "We come from—" And just as he was saying the secret word, his voice jumped up several octaves.

I nudged him and, blowing out cigarette smoke, said, "Rothenburg."

The madam looked us over and lifted up her dress to reveal a pair of lovely long legs. "My, my, you men look so handsome." She reached between her legs and caressed her hand provocatively. "And I guess you want some of this, do you?"

Our mouths dropped open. Finally we breathed in unison, "*Ja.*"

She came closer, reached over to run her hand through my hair while blowing smoke into my face. "I tell you what, boys . . ." her voice was slow and sultry, and we were both aroused. "I'll take you both on and do whatever you want . . ." We stood transfixed. Then she lifted my sunglasses and looked me in the eye ". . . when you come back in five years. This is not the place for you. I don't know how you found us, but go home. You are lucky there are no officers around." She patted Wolfie on the cheek, stepped back into the building and closed the door.

"Wha . . . ? What happened?"

"Don't know. Could be that your voice sounds like a monkey, Wolfie, or maybe your breath smells."

He punched me in the arm. "*Ach,* she was too funny-looking anyways. Let's get us some good-looking Fräuleins." He laughed and began singing, "*My hat has three corners . . .*"

An hour or so later we found ourselves in the seedy part of Berlin where everyone slid silently through the darkness or scurried like cockroaches through the pools of street light. But we heard music coming from a basement window and we peered in. The place was full of smoke and people were drinking and dancing.

"*Ach, du lieber Gott.* Look . . ."

"Let me see. Oh—"

Just then a voice behind us said, "Hello, boys. Looking for some fun?"

Wolfie stood up, swaying from side to side. "*Ja.* What did you have in mind?"

"Depends how much money you have . . ." She was older than the woman on Giesebrechtstrasse and she was heavy, but her face was pleasant and she had a big smile.

Wolfie pulled out some bills and showed them to her.

"That'll get you some fun," she said, taking the money and grabbing Wolfie's hand. She pulled him behind her up the nearby stairs to a down-at-heel apartment, and I followed, scared to let Wolfie out of my sight. Inside, a bunch of scantily dressed women lounged about, some of them on an old blue sofa. The heavy odour of alcohol, cigarettes and stale perfume was almost suffocating.

A tall, older, skinny woman grabbed me. "Want a drink, fella?" she said.

Before I could answer her, I saw Wolfie grab a bottle of rum and disappear behind a floral curtain with a full-figured woman.

As my tall lady of the night pushed a drink into my hand, I noticed she had a bruise beside her right eye, yet she had a soft look about her. Pulling me behind a green curtain, she pushed herself up against me. "They call me Ivy. What's your name, darling?"

I was too scared to talk. I saw a narrow bed, a nightstand with a flickering candle, and at the foot of the bed a table with a washbowl. She gave me a little push and I found myself sitting on the edge of the bed.

Ivy knelt in front of me and ran her hand up my leg. I jumped, spilling some of my drink. My heart was racing, and sweat had started to bead up on my forehead.

She caressed my face. "Surely you have a name, darling."

"Ah . . . Michael?"

"Michael! That is a lovely name."

She pulled off my boots, pushed me onto the bed, then slipped off her négligée to reveal a bony, bruised body. I placed my hand gently onto her thin droopy breast. As I closed my eyes, I heard Wolfie laughing just a few feet away from me. The chubby woman that he was with said, "My name is Gretel. So are you ready for some fun, boy?"

"*Aber klar doch!*" Wolfie said, still laughing.

When we stepped out from behind the curtains, the ladies of the bordello all clapped. Smiling, one of them said, "Now you are men."

We both blushed. Ivy leaned over and gave me a kiss on the cheek and said to the ladies, "This boy is a respectable gentleman."

Wolfie put his arm over my shoulder and we bowed. When we stumbled out onto the street, I held Wolfie's bottle of rum while he lit cigarettes for us. As he handed the cigarette to me he said, "I couldn't do it."

"But I heard you laugh."

"*Ja.*" He shook his head and took a long drag of his cigarette. Off in the distance we heard the sounds of circus music. "Hear that, Michael?"

"*Ja.*"

We walked for a few minutes, and then as we turned the corner, there in glorious splendour stood a yellow-and orange-striped circus tent. The entrance was like the façade of an East Indian temple, with towers on either side, and in the centre hung a sign that read: SARRASANI—TATTOOS.

Wolfie slung his arm over my shoulder. "This'll be fun . . ."

Somehow in spite of our drunken stupor we found our way back to Herr von Fray's house before daylight, but after we climbed over the wall, I grabbed Wolfie's arm. "How are we going to get back inside? That trellis is *kaput.*"

"Maybe the back door is open." I led the way around to the back of the house where the light still shone above the kitchen door. "*Ach,* what if the dog is there?"

"Bunny . . ." I went over to the trellis, pulled off one of the broken slats and gave it to Wolfie.

"What's this for?" Wolfie whispered.

"You can throw it for him and . . . and distract him."

Wolfie held the stick, I held onto him, and slowly we crept up the back stairs to the porch. We took off our boots, opened the kitchen door and there was Bunny, guarding the house, wagging the stump of his tail. Wolfie and I ran as fast as we could into the hall and up the stairs with the dog in hot pursuit. Quickly I pushed Wolfie into the room and Bunny pushed me in. I grabbed the door just before it slammed shut and closed it carefully. When I turned around,

Bunny and Wolfie were already in bed. I climbed into my bed after them.

Wolfie fell asleep almost instantly, but I lay there wide awake, my mind going backwards through the day's events—the circus, Ivy, the high-class brothel on Giesebrechtstrasse. Climbing down the trellis. Dinner with Fräulein Margarita. The train ride to the city. Rebekah's slumped-over body. I felt the tears well up in my eyes.

Bunny awakened me, licking my face. Moments later Herr Beak Face burst into our room yelling, "What's the meaning of this? All the other boys are at the breakfast table!"

Bunny jumped off the bed, growling and holding our teacher at bay. Wolfie and I grabbed the feather duvet and pulled it up to our chins.

"Herr Kannengiesser, we don't feel well. It must have been something we ate last night."

"Get up this minute!" Beak Face turned red as he shouted, "*Schnell!* And what is this filthy mutt doing in your room?" But as he reached for the dog's collar, Bunny growled and bit Beak Face in the ankle, then pulled off his shoe and tore down the stairs with it. Beak Face hobbled after him, shouting, "Get back here, you bad dog!" Then we heard him shout back up the stairs, "You two get down to breakfast immediately!"

Holding his head, Wolfie said, "*Gott im Himmel*—my head hurts, and so does my chest."

I rolled out of bed and managed to stand. "*Ja*, so does mine. I need a cup of coffee."

As I peeled off my shirt, Wolfie said, "*Ach, du Scheisse!*" He was pointing at my chest.

"What?" I turned to look in the mirror over the wash basin.

Wolfie took his shirt off too. "Oh, *du grosse Scheisse!*" He put his hand over the black swastika that was tattooed on his left pectoral. "Do you remember how—?"

"The circus . . . Some guy named Bobo with tattoos all over . . ."

Wolfie laughed nervously as he placed his hand over his tattoo. "At least it looks good."

"*Ja*. I think my papa will like it . . . but Mama . . ."

We splashed water on our faces, changed our clothes and hurried down to the dining room. Herr Kannengiesser and all the other boys were already there eating breakfast. The sideboard had a spread of buns, boiled eggs, cuts of delicatessen meats, and a pot of coffee. Hoping that coffee would clear my head, I reached for the pot, but Fräulein Margarita's reach was faster than mine.

She poured me a cup. "*Schönen Guten Morgen*, Michael and Wolfie. You both look a little under the weather. Is everything all right?"

I smiled up at our angel. "*Guten Morgen*, Fräulein Margarita. Wolfie and I feel a little unwell . . ."

Herr Kannengiesser cleared his throat, and wagging his finger in our direction, said, "Those two are fine. Hurry it up, boys. We have a long day today. And tuck in your shirts!"

His voice rang in my ears making my head throb, but as I began cutting open the warm breakfast roll, and smelled the freshly baked bread, I took pleasure in smothering it with butter and jam. As we were hurrying to stuff our faces, Wolfie asked, "Herr Kannengiesser, where are we going this morning?"

But it was Otto who answered. "We're going to the Kroll Opera House and then to the Island of Museums and to the circus tonight. Tomorrow we will go to the soccer game at the Olympic stadium."

"Very good, Otto." Herr Beak Face stood up and rocked on the balls of his feet. "Now hurry up. The bus won't wait for us all day." He clapped his hands, and we jumped to attention and quickly put on our coats. But as we walked out the door, Wolfie and I stopped to thank Fräulein Margarita, and she gave us both a hug.

We walked until we came to Friedrichstrasse, and as we came around the corner we saw a big movie house. Wolfie read the sign out loud: "The *WINTERGARTEN!*" None of us had seen a movie house that big before.

"Here comes our bus, boys. Make a straight line!" Herr Beak Face puffed out his chest to show off his NSDAP pin.

Otto stood beside our teacher and counted us to make sure that we were all present, and as we walked past him, Wolfie and I made faces at him. Once we were all seated on the bus, Otto, who was sitting in front of us, turned. "So, Michael and Wolfie, I went up to your room last night, but you weren't there."

"*Ja, und?*" Wolfie smiled.

"That's probably when we were in the bathroom. Wolfie was sick."

"Oh," he said and turned around to look out the window.

We arrived at the Reichstag, and once again Herr Kannengiesser began lecturing us. "The Reichstag was burned, remember I told you about that fire earlier? Because of the fire, the Kroll Opera House, directly across from here, is being used as the parliament building. And, because of the fire, our glorious Führer has enacted a decree that prohibits unauthorized assembly, the publication of irresponsible . . . in other words, for those of you who are *stumm im Kopf* . . . it means no public gatherings, unless you have been approved. Does every dumb head understand?" Herr Kannen-giesser went on and on, not just insulting us, but lecturing about the great merits of Hitler and his party. He was particularly grateful for the Jewish decrees. "It's good that we have laws against Jews . . ." he said, because they could weaken our proud Aryan lifeline.

I found myself remembering Papa saying that the Führer's new laws were a good thing because they would destroy all lying cor-rupt men. And then I remembered the picture of the woman in Papa's copy of *Mein Kampf* and the love letter in his coat pocket . . . All pumped up, Herr Kannengiesser pointed to the front entrance. "You boys are very lucky to see the new seat of the Reichstag parlia-ment. When we go in, I want all of you to stay together. And not one word out of anyone! Do I make myself clear?" He glared directly at me and Wolfie.

I turned to Wolfie, bent down and pulled up my socks. "Once inside, let's sneak away. I need a smoke."

"Sounds good."

We were greeted inside the building by a petite brunette woman holding a clipboard in one hand and a fountain pen in the other. "*Guten Morgen*, boys," she said in a cheery voice. "My name is Frau Alderman. I'll be leading your tour of the Kroll Opera House today."

As soon as she began leading our troop down the first hallway, Wolfie gently nudged me, pointed to the washroom, and pulled me towards it. He pushed open the door and we slipped inside.

"Wow, look at this place," he said as he checked the stalls.

"Yeah, it's really fancy." I looked at my reflection in the long mirror over the wash basins, and all I saw staring back at me was someone I didn't like. A coward. "Come on," I said, pushing open the window over the urinals, "hurry up with the cigarettes."

"Lock the door," he said. He handed me a lit cigarette, and we stood by the window sucking back the smoke.

Wolfie smiled at me. "I like Margarita."

I was thinking about Rebekah.

But then there was a loud banging on the door. "Michael, Wolfie! Are you two in there? Why is this door locked?" Herr Kannengiesser yelled.

"*Scheisse!*" We threw our cigarettes out the window. "Quick!" I said. "Stand at the urinal and piss!"

"I can't piss on demand."

"Just do it!"

"Open the window wider, Michael."

Herr Beak Face banged on the door again and shouted, "Open this door at once! You boys are in a lot of trouble!"

I ran to open the window wider, then headed for the door to unlock it just as Wolfie turned from the urinal and pissed on the floor.

Before I knew what was happening, my feet had slipped out from under me and I hit the floor with a dull thump, smacking my head on the cold, wet tiles.

Wolfie laughed. "Are you all right?"

I began to laugh too, but my laughter turned to crying. "*Nein!*"

He ran to unlock the door and our teacher pushed into the room. I sat up in Wolfie's puddle of piss and stared at Herr Beak Face.

"What is the meaning of this?" he exploded.

"We . . ." I tried to reply.

But he just kept on yelling. "Get up off the floor, Michael! Wolfgang! Button up your trousers!"

"It was an accident, Herr Rektor," Wolfie shouted. He handed me his hanky, but as he tried to help me up, he slipped too, though he managed not to fall. "It was an accident!"

"Is that so! And what about the smoke in here?"

"Smoke?" Wolfie answered.

He tried to help me up again, but I pushed his hand away and managed to stand up myself. "Oh, *ja*," I said. "There was a man in here sporting a mustache and wearing a brown uniform. He said he didn't like the no-smoking law."

Wolfie snickered.

"Do you take me for a fool? Do you think I have *Tomaten auf den Augen*? I am certainly not sporting tomatoes on my eyes! I'm not blind! It was you two smoking in here!" Herr Kannengiesser waved his hands furiously at us. "I will call the authorities! The two of you are good-for-nothings!" Then he scowled directly at me. "Just like your dumb, dumb brother, Günther! And you are dumb like your *schlampige* . . . your floozie sister Paula . . . A real *Dummkopf* you are! I am going to call the authorities and they can deal with the two of you!" He turned to leave.

Wolfie linked arms with me. I took a deep breath and shouted. "You think you're a big important man! Well, you're not! You hide behind your stupid NSDAP pin! My brothers are fighting for this country and so is my papa! Even my sister Susi is doing more than you are! All you do is bark orders and hit us! You are a coward, Herr Kannengiesser!"

He squinted and his face turned purple, but Wolfie grabbed his arm before he could strike me. "I would think twice about hitting him, Herr Kannengiesser! You wouldn't want us to go to the authorities and let it slip that you have spoken ill of the Führer, now would you?" Wolfie pushed his face close to our teacher's face. "And Paula is ten times the man you are!"

His mouth dropped open and he pulled his hand out of Wolfie's grasp. When he found his voice again, he snarled, "Don't think you'll be coming with us to the circus tonight!" He turned toward the door, straightening his jacket and tugging at his lapel.

Wolfie reached out to open the bathroom door for him. "We prefer to keep Fräulein Margarita company anyway, Herr Kannengiesser." For the rest of the day, Herr Kannengiesser did not look at or speak to Wolfie and me. When we all returned to the house for supper, Fräulein Margarita greeted us and inquired about our day, but it was Otto who blurted out the day's events and told her how Wolfie and I were not well, because of which we would have to miss the circus that night.

8

Max and Moritz

— MAY 1940 —

༄

AFTER OUR COMRADES LEFT for the circus, Wolfie and I sat eating poppy-seed cake at the kitchen table with Fräulein Margarita while Bunny slept at her feet. Eventually we told her how Herr Kannengiesser had threatened us in the Kroll Opera bathroom, but we didn't tell her that we had been smoking or that we had threatened him.

"Would you like me to talk to him?" she asked.

It felt wonderful that our angel wanted to protect us, but I said, "*Nein*, it would only make matters worse for us."

Wolfie pointed to the last piece of cake, and with Fräulein Margarita's approval he took it. "*Ja*. Besides, Fräulein Margarita, things aren't that bad."

"If you say so. But if there is ever anything I can do for the two of you, you just have to ask."

Wolfie and I smiled. "We will."

The kitchen radio was on, and the evening news was about to start. As usual it began with the war news, the announcer assuring listeners that we were winning the war and it would be over soon. Then he said, "Today the news has come that our Secret Police, the Geheime Polizei, has apprehended a large number of Jews who were running a money-counterfeiting ring. It is expected that there will be more arrests."

Fräulein Margarita reached over and quickly turned off the radio.

"Why did you turn it off?" I asked her.

Wolfie, who was still stuffing his face, looked up. "Maybe she doesn't want to hear anything more about the Jews. There was a Jew mutti and her daughter on the train, and the SS shot them." He took another bite of poppy seed cake. "The Führer says—"

I felt like throwing up. "Shut your mouth, Wolfie. You know nothing about them."

Margarita sat in the chair beside me. "Why the tears, Michael?"

Wolfie leaned in on the other side. "Michael, they were Jews, and the Führer says—"

"Wolfie, I said shut your mouth! You know nothing."

"Michael, what is it?" She used her hanky to wipe at my tears. "You can tell me . . ."

I took a deep breath. "Her name was Rebekah . . . and she was beautiful . . ."

Wolfie looked confused. "Rebekah? Who are you talking about?"

"The Jews! Her name was Rebekah. And her mutti's name was Helena. They were the ones who were shot by the SS men."

Wolfie said, "But Michael, how do you know who they were?"

Then I told them everything that had happened on the train, about the hanky, about how it was my fault they were found out.

Wolfie leaned in closer. "Why didn't you tell me?"

"I don't know . . . Because it was my fault . . . Because they were Jews? Why would a man as smart as Hitler be okay with killing girls and their muttis?"

Margarita reached across the table to put her hand on my arm. "I don't know the answer to that question, but I do know that you had no way of knowing what would happen. It wasn't your fault."

"It was." I tried to hold back my tears.

Margarita squeezed my arm. "You really liked a girl. There is no fault in that."

I sat up straight, wiped my nose on my sleeve and my eyes with the back of my hand. It felt good to finally tell others about what happened.

Margarita said, "My mutti died when the Luftwaffe bombed Poland. I thought it was my fault, too."

"Why?" Wolfie asked.

"My oma lived there and she was not well, so Mama had gone to visit her. She also was not well and wanted me to come with her, but I was sweet on a boy, so I begged not to go. She was at the market buying food when the planes dropped their bombs."

Wolfie looked stricken. "We're so sorry, Fräulein Margarita . . ."

She stood up, wiped her hands on her dress and patted Wolfie on the shoulder. "Oh, look at the time. Boys, will you be all right for a few hours without me?"

Wolfie blushed. "*Ja*, Fräulein."

"Well then, I'll be back by eight." She went to the hall wardrobe to get her coat.

I followed and helped her on with it. Bunny stayed close to her side, clearly planning to go with her, but as she moved towards the front door, she said, "Please hold onto Bunny, Michael. I don't want him to follow me."

I crouched down to hang onto the dog. When she opened the front door, I could see out through the front gate that a black Mercedes was waiting at the curb, and a tall, dark-haired man stepped out of the car and came around to open the door for her.

"Margarita, thank you for . . ."

She leaned down and gave me a kiss on the cheek. I said nothing but blushed just as Wolfie had. I stood at the door for a moment, watching her step into the car.

I turned to face Wolfie. "She kissed me!"

"Guess you won't ever wash your ugly face again?"

I punched him in the arm. "You're just jealous."

"*Ach, nein.* She just feels sorry for you."

We didn't say much as we washed our dishes, but as we started to put them away, we noticed that Bunny was scratching at the door that probably led to the cellar.

"What's the matter, boy? What's down there?" As soon as I opened the door, Bunny flew down the stairs.

Wolfie and I followed. We discovered the dog sniffing at the corner of a cupboard that was pushed up against the far wall. "What's up, boy?" I said. "Hey, Wolfie, I think Bunny's cornered a rat behind this cupboard."

Wolfie moved his hands along the side of the case. "*Ja,* look here. There is a space here that I can get my fingers in. Help me, Michael."

Together we pulled, prepared to stand aside when the rat came running out, but to our surprise, when the cupboard moved, a piece of the wall came with it, and Bunny ran past down a long hallway. We saw that he was wagging his stumpy tail and scratching at a door at the far end. We hesitated for a moment. "Maybe we better go back," Wolfie said.

"*Nein.*" We followed Bunny to a door at the far end. To my surprise it opened when I pushed on it. And as we stepped into the small room, a faint smell of perfume struck me. Wolfie along with Bunny stood still as we all heard a door lock to the right of us.

"Did you hear that?" Wolfie said.

"*Ja,* that door must lead outside." There was a table in front of us, with two typewriters on it, and what looked to be a small machine of some sort in the corner.

Wolfie walked over to it. "It's a printing press."

I pointed to the door. "Someone just left. We should get out of here."

"What do you mean?"

"Whoever that was might come back."

Wolfie shrugged, and reached into the wastepaper basket, and pulled out a scrunched-up ball of paper. He unfolded it, and uncreased the leaflet. "Hitler and the National Socialist party are dividing our country. They are poisoning . . ."

"Wolfie, stop reading that. Someone might hear you."

"You know what this is, don't you?" Wolfie held the paper up waving it in the air.

"Doesn't matter. Let's get out of here."

The door handle rattled. Wolfie scrunched the leaflet up and threw it at me. I stuffed it into my pocket, and together we bolted out of the room.

An hour later, Fräulein Margarita arrived home. We never asked about the secret room or what we had discovered. We didn't want to get into any more trouble, and we certainly didn't want to see our angel be dragged off to a prisoners work camp.

"Boys, did you have a nice evening?"

We nodded.

"Well, run upstairs and jump into the bathtub. Your teacher will be back within the hour."

In the tub I splashed Wolfie and we laughed. "Do you think Margarita's papa knows?"

Wolfie soaped up his hair. "Maybe it's her papa, and Fräulein Margarita doesn't know?"

"*Ja*. But the room . . . you smelled it, didn't you? It was her perfume, I'd know it anywhere."

Wolfie splashed water at me. "*Ach*."

Once out of the tub, we wrapped ourselves in towels and carried our clothes to the bedroom. We were just getting into our nightshirts when we heard our schoolmates coming up the stairs chattering about the circus. I opened the door a crack and stood listening as Herr Beak Face spoke with Fräulein Margarita in the foyer below.

"Are those two boys in bed? Did they behave themselves?"

"*Ja*, Herr Kannengiesser. They were delightful. We played cards until it was time for them to go to bed."

"Would you see that the rest of the boys go to bed, too? I have arranged to take a stroll with my schoolmasters, Herr Braun and Herr Schmidt."

"Certainly, Herr Kannengiesser."

When the house was quiet at last, Fräulein Margarita knocked on our door, opened it a crack and whispered, "Are you asleep?" She came into our room, "I'm sorry, my darlings, for leaving you alone in the house." She walked over to my pants that I had left on the floor.

"It's okay, Fräulein Margarita, I'll pick them up." But before I could jump out of bed, the crumpled leaflet fell to the floor.

She bent down to pick it up. "What's this?"

"It's nothing, just garbage," I blurted out.

She glanced at us then down at the crumpled paper as she closed her hand over it. "Well, boys, you had a busy day, best go to sleep now."

The next morning Fräulein Margarita gave us each a copy of *Max und Moritz*. She had inscribed mine with "Lieber Michael, you will forever be my trusted Max. I will always be yours forever—Fräulein Margarita." She wrote the same inscription for Wolfie, only it said, "You will be forever my trusted Moritz . . ."

"Max and Moritz!" we said, smiling at each other.

Wolfie and I walked home together from the train station, but after he left me at his house, I ran the rest of the way, excited to tell Mama everything we had seen—of course not about Rebekah or the brothel or . . . But when I threw open the front door, I could hear crying coming from the kitchen.

"Mama," I called, but it was Annalisa who came running into the hallway and sprang into my arms. "Michael, you home!" She buried her head into my chest, sobbing uncontrollably.

I carried her into the kitchen, hugging her tight. "It's okay, Annalisa." I sat at the table and looked up at Mama. "What's happened?"

She was near tears, too. "Günther is gone, Michael." She pulled out her hanky and dabbed her eyes.

"I don't understand . . ."

"Last week . . . when you brought the letter home from the post office . . . it wasn't good news." She nodded toward the letter lying on the table. Annalisa was gradually sobbing less and less and falling asleep on my lap, and Mama spoke softly. "It says that the authorities want to take Günther to Sonnenstein."

"Why? I don't understand. What is this Sonnenstein?"

"It's the psychiatric hospital in Prina."

"Why do they want to take him there? Günther's not crazy."

"They say he will receive treatment for his stuttering and his hand."

"What's wrong with him getting help?"

"People who go there never come out, Michael."

"Have you spoken to Papa?"

"*Ja*, but by the time I heard from him, Günther had run away. Herr Zimmermann and I have searched for him everywhere, but no one has seen him. He left his St. Francis medal in an envelope with your name on it. He wanted you to have it."

I looked at the pendant lying on the table. "He always wears it."

"It means a lot to him. That's why he wanted you to have it."

"How do you know he wanted me to have it?" I picked up the pendant and let it fall into my hand.

"Michael, he put your name on the envelope."

"What will happen if the authorities find him?"

"Let's hope they don't."

That night I sat quietly in Papa's green chair to listen to the news. The announcer greeted all dutiful Deutsche with joy in his voice.

"Our Führer Hitler is making Deutschland great again! This war is good for our glorious country. The Wehrmacht armies invaded

Denmark and Norway! The government in Copenhagen has surrendered. Their military was no match for our might. At Narvik in Norway, German destroyers have sunk two Norwegian coastal cruisers, the city of Trondheim has been captured. The Swedish ore is safeguarded, and we will destroy Britain's naval blockades of Deutschland.

"It will not be long now before we have conquered and secured the Atlantic waters. Meanwhile, the Kriegsmarine are doing an outstanding job sinking the merchant supply ships coming from Canada. We will starve the British people, they will run out of fuel, and no Canadian soldier will set foot on British soil. We have trapped the British army at the town of Dunkirk in France, and our Führer has ordered a halt to the advance. The British will surrender to the glorious armies of the Third Reich. The German armies dominate the ground and the Luftwaffe dominates the skies . . ."

I wondered why Hitler had given orders not to continue the attack at Dunkirk? Maybe he knew that the English would accept Deutschland's offer of an alliance? As the nightly news continued, my thoughts drifted to Fräulein Margarita, and the fact that she must be helping the Jews. I knew, too, that Rebekah's young life had ended far too soon. And I could see that women like Ivy had to endure men's violence to make a living. And my brother Günther had run away. Where had he gone? Had he found safety?

9

More

— AUGUST 1941 —

⁓

A YEAR HAD PASSED. The Wehrmacht had swept across Europe, Operation Barbarossa—the invasion of Russia—had begun on June 22, and Peter and Kurt along with another four million soldiers had been sent to the Eastern Front. There was still no word from Günther, but Paula had come home with her baby, Waldemar. Mama, when not helping out at the Zimmermanns' farm, spent her days glued to the radio. But summer was at its peak, and all I wanted was to be outdoors with Wolfie. When I came bouncing down the stairs with my bathing towel in hand, I peeked into the living room. Mama was sitting on the worn green sofa, listening to the Wehrmacht news on the Goebbels' Beak. She motioned for me to sit beside her.

The radio broadcaster sounded sullen. "Last night Berlin, our capital, was bombed by the Russians . . ."

"Fräulein Margarita!" I turned to Mama. "Do you think she's all right?"

"I hope so. I will try to call her later today from the neighbours." She stood up to turn the radio off, and as she walked toward the kitchen, she said, "Michael, everything will be fine. Don't worry."

"But, what about—"

"Aren't you meeting Wolfie to go swimming?"

"*Ja*, but—"

"Michael, go. There is nothing we can do."

I hugged her and felt for the first time how thin she had become. "I'll be back by two o'clock and do the garden then, Mama."

She placed her hands on either side of my face. "Michael, please don't go jumping off the cliffs. It's really not safe. You know how deep the water is." Her eyes were red and tired. Some nights I could hear her crying.

"I won't, Mama."

She smiled. "Now, go and have fun."

As Wolfie and I lay on our towels by the lakeshore, watching the dragonflies darting over the lake's clear surface, the sun glinting purple and blue off their wings, it was almost possible to forget for a while that Deutschland was at war. The sweet scent of wild roses and the soft laughter of the girls lying on their towels nearby had me spinning with desire. They would stare at Wolfie and me and ask if our tattoos hurt, but most of them said they thought having a tattoo made us look all grown up. One of the girls was Otto's sister, Sophie, and Wolfie whispered that he wanted to be with her . . . or at least steal a kiss from her. "Hear that, Michael?" Wolfie sat up and raised a hand to shield his eyes from the sun. "That's a Russian plane."

We jumped to our feet as it came into view over the far end of the lake. It was flying very low.

"It's a TB-7. A heavy bomber!"

Wolfie had become quite good at identifying planes, and together we would read *Die Wehrmacht* magazine. It only cost 25 Reichspfennig and it told us everything we wanted to know about planes and guns. It had great war stories in it too.

"On the radio this morning they said Russian planes had again bombed Berlin in the night," I told him.

"I bet this dummy is lost from that bombing run," Wolfie said scornfully. "Look!" He was pointing to another plane higher up. "That a Messerschmitt and it's chasing that piece of Commie junk."

The pilot of the TB-7 must have seen the Messerschmitt, too, as he started unloading his bombs over the lake, and as a succession of explosions shook the ground, the girls screamed and jumped up, gathering their blankets and towels.

"Our guy's shooting at the Commie!" I yelled as Wolfie and I struggled into our clothes.

"Run to the bomb shelter!" Wolfie shouted at the girls.

But Wolfie and I had to see what was going on. We grabbed our boots, and with our hearts in our throats, we started to run towards the blast area. We stopped in our tracks as we heard the whistling sound of another bomb and threw ourselves down just as the ground ahead of us convulsed.

As we scrambled to our feet, I yelled back at the girls who were still milling about, uncertain which way to run, "Go to the town bomb shelter. Run!"

We started running toward the blast as fast as our bare feet could take us, but soon Wolfie had to stop to put on his boots. "Wait, Michael!" he yelled and I stopped too and put on mine. Then together we ran on again through the Zimmermanns' hazelnut grove and down the gentle slope that overlooked their orchard.

We stopped when we heard gunfire overhead, and Wolfie grabbed my arm as he yelled and pointed. "They got him! Wow!"

The Russian plane was in a nose-dive now, black smoke trailing behind it.

Wolfie kept hitting my arm. "We got him! We got him!"

"He's heading for Otto's farm!"

Otto's family lived a kilometre beyond Herr Zimmermann's farm, their land separated by a strip of forest.

"It's the Russian!" shouted Wolfie, jumping up and down. He pointed and I could see that a Russian had parachuted out of the plane. "Michael!" Wolfie lunged at me.

We hit the ground together as the plane whizzed over our heads, and the earth heaved as it crashed behind the small forest that divided the two farms. A ball of flames sprang up and a plume of endless black smoke followed it into the sky. We jumped up, hollering, "Whoo-hoo!"

"Hurry, Wolfie, before someone else gets to that Commie!"

As we ran, the town's air raid siren began roaring with a deep growl that rose into a high-pitched prolonged cry. We knew the Russian pilot must have landed in the sheep pasture near the Zimmermanns' apple orchard because the sheep were running frantically in all directions.

"Hurry!"

"Michael, that was—"

"Otto's farm. I know." We stopped running. The air smelled like roasted apples because the plane had scorched the tops of the apple trees. The crackling sound of the fire and the distant siren filled my ears and, for a moment, the smoke blinded me.

"Where did he go?" I said, but as the smoke parted, we could see the Russian sitting in the centre of a grassy patch, his parachute spread out beyond him.

"Wolfie, it's the Commie!"

"What are we going to say to him? We should go to Otto's . . ."

"We will, but let's capture that Commie first."

"What are we going to say to him?"

"How about—you're under arrest, Bolshevik!"

"Why's he just sitting there like that?"

As we approached him, I realized his head was hanging at an odd angle. "You!" I shouted. "You, Herr Russian—"

Wolfie shoved me. "Herr Russian?"

As we made our way closer, I yelled at the Russian again. He didn't move or even turn to look at us. When we got up close, I kicked his leg. "You! Get up!"

When he still didn't move, I knelt down beside him and put my hand on his shoulder. "Do you speak Deutsch?" But as I shook him, his head wobbled forward, and we saw that his body was scrunched up like an accordion and his spine jutted out just below his skull.

"*Ach, du lieber Gott!*" I turned away and retched.

"Michael—"

"His spine . . . his spine went straight through," I said, wiping my mouth. "His parachute must have deployed too late."

"Guess we can't take him as our prisoner now."

I gazed at the crumpled body. He wasn't much older than Wolfie and me. "What are you doing?" I asked Wolfie who had crouched down beside the Russian.

"Searching his pockets—and taking his pistol. Look, it's a Tokarev." Wolfie held the weapon up. The sun glinted off it.

"Don't wave that thing at me! Give it here before you kill us both." I tucked the pistol into the back of my shorts and pulled my shirt down over it.

"What should we do with him?"

"Nothing." I knelt and reached into the Russian's jacket and pulled out a small red book.

"What's that?"

"What's it look like? It's a book."

"What's it say?"

"I don't read Russian, Wolfie."

"Open it."

I flipped through the pages and a photo fell out. "Must be his mutti," I said, handing the book and picture to Wolfie. I gathered the dead Russian in my arms and carefully laid him out on the ground and closed his eyes. As I cradled his head in my hands, blood spilled from his wounds, drenching my hands and the green grass below him. I stared at the blood on my hands, the same way I had stared at Fritz's blood.

Wolfie nudged me. "Let's get going before Herr Zimmermann or someone else comes." He handed me the Russian's belongings.

I wiped my hand on the grass.

"Michael, we should go over to Otto's."

"Don't think I can stomach much more."

"*Ach*, Michael. Pull yourself together. He was a Commie."

"*Ja*, a Bolshevik." I tucked the little red book and the picture into my pocket.

As we approached Otto's farm, we could see an old woman standing near a hole in the ground. "*Mein Got im Himmel . . .*" she screamed. "*Mein Gott—mein Gott.* My cow, my cow!"

I looked away, pointing in the other direction. "It's Otto."

"*Ach, du Scheisse!*"

Otto was standing with his sister Kattie in his arms. His little brother and Sophie stood by his side crying. They were staring at the burning pile that had been their house. The Russian plane had crashed into it, and all we could see was the tail with its red star sticking out of the centre of the burning house. The heat was sweltering.

We ran towards him.

"Otto—Otto! Where's the rest of your family?" I took his sister from him and laid her down. Her smouldering body was barely recognizable. I heaved at the stench of burnt flesh.

"Are you all right, Otto?" Wolfie asked. "Otto—?"

He just stood there, his mouth wide open. His eyes were almost swollen shut, his skin was hanging like sheets from his body. Most of his hair was burned off.

Finally he said, "Kattie ran into the house just before . . . Mutti was in the house. I tried to help . . ."

"Otto, sit down. You're hurt." I didn't want to touch him because I was afraid of hurting him more. "Wolfie, get some water from the brook."

As Wolfie ran for the water, an ambulance swung into the farmyard. Wolfie stopped and guided them back to Otto and his sisters. The ambulance attendant leapt out and began unloading a stretcher, although it was plain that there was little he could do to help Otto.

I put my arm around his little brother. "It'll be all right."

Wolfie grabbed me by the shoulder. "Michael . . ."

"What?"

"It's a bomb!"

"What is she doing!"

We watched in horror as the old lady, clearly in shock, began pushing at an unexploded bomb, trying to free her entangled cow.

Wolfie yelled, "Stop! Don't do that!"

The ambulance attendant, seeing what was about to happen, yelled, "Take cover!" And threw his body over Otto. I gathered up Otto's little brother in my arms as Wolfie dove at Sophie. A thunderous explosion roared over us. The ground shook, and the smell of cordite filled the air once more. A moment later we were all covered with debris, mud and guts. We lay there, not sure if we were alive.

When I finally looked up, I could see that Wolfie was shouting at me, but I could barely hear him. The smoke was thick as mud, and as I tried to stand, I felt myself swaying from side to side. Everything around me moved in slow motion.

"Michael . . ."

"What?"

Out of nowhere a BMW came barreling towards us, then abruptly stopped. Two Gestapo men stepped out of the car and ran toward us. Wolfie stood up, and the cow's tail slid down his face. He screamed.

I clambered to my feet, still carrying Otto's little brother, but when I put him down, he just wrapped his arms around his knees and began rocking back and forth. He didn't make a sound.

Sophie was kneeling and holding her arm. "My hand! My hand!" she screamed over and over.

The ambulance attendant had a large piece of metal sticking out of his back. I went to help him but he was dead.

Wolfie stood staring at Sophie's arm. Her warm blood gushed out like a spewing water pipe. Then her eyes rolled to the back of her head, and she slumped over. Why hadn't she gone to the bomb shelter?

One of the Gestapo men motioned for us to help. "You, what's your name?" He was pointing at Wolfie, but Wolfie only stood staring stupidly at Sophie.

The Gestapo man yelled again. "Hey! Snap out of it! Give me your belt."

"What?"

"This little girl's bleeding won't stop on its own. Just do what I say."

Wolfie pulled the belt from his brown shorts and handed it to him, and he put it around Sophie's arm.

After that, one of the Gestapo men drove the ambulance with Sophie and Otto and Otto's little brother to the hospital.

Over the next few days, things settled down. Gradually our hearing returned. We learned that Wolfie's belt had helped save Sophie's life. But it turned out, as expected, that Otto's burns were too severe; he died from complications in the hospital the next day. Everyone in town attended the funeral for Otto, his mutti and oma, as well as his sister, Kattie and his little brother.

"Michael, come down here, please," Mama called from the bottom of the stairs.

I was busy admiring the Russian pistol. "What!"

My bedroom door swung open and there stood Mama. "I have

been calling you . . . What on earth do you have in your hands, Michael?"

I tried to hide it, but it was too late. "Ah . . . nothing."

"That's a pistol! Where did you get that thing?" Mama grabbed the weapon out of my hands.

"I found it."

"You found it?"

"Ah . . . When we were at Otto's. It was on the grass. It belonged to the Russian."

"Michael, you know the law. Why didn't you give it to the Gestapo?"

"I didn't think of it, and when I did, it was too late. I thought I would get into trouble."

"You have a point. We won't speak of this, but only because your papa doesn't need to know."

"What are you going to do with it, Mama?"

"Don't you worry about it. Besides—with Paula and her baby home, I don't want this dirty thing around. Now, go wash up, dinner is ready."

I was surprised how calm Mama was about the pistol. I thought for sure she would be furious with me.

As she turned to leave my room, she asked me, "What sort of bullets does this thing use?"

"I think it can take Deutsche bullets . . . But it's already loaded."

Mama put the pistol in her apron pocket. "Go wash up."

Our lives became more and more regimented, each day filled with collecting scrap metal or money for the war effort. In mid-August we all had to help bring in the harvest from the surrounding farm fields. Only the women, old men, girls and the young boys were keeping our town alive now. And when we boys weren't working, we had to attend our HJ meetings. I longed for the old days when I didn't have to be the man of the house.

Every day Mama would ask the postman if there were any letters, but it was always the same. "Not today, perhaps tomorrow."

At 3:00 on Sunday afternoons I would sit with Mama and drink coffee as we listened to the *Haus des Rundfunks* broadcast of the *Wunschkonzert*. Our soldiers could call in to request a song and dedicate it to their loved ones at home, and people at home could do the same for them. Mama hoped that perhaps she would hear a song that Kurt or Peter had dedicated to her, letting her know that they were alive. But weeks of hoping and listening to the radio only left her more and more saddened.

Then one Sunday afternoon, I sat in Papa's chair and waited for her, but instead she began climbing the stairs. "Mama, don't you want to listen to Goebbels' Beak?" I asked.

"*Nein.* I'm going to lie down."

"Are you all right, Mama?"

"Just feeling a bit weary."

10

Schnapps

— DECEMBER 1941 —

‹⁓›

SUMMER SLOWLY TURNED to fall, and winter followed on its heels, bringing with it a bitter cold. Paula no longer looked tired and she had grown to be rather pretty. We never received news from the twins and we tried not to assume the worst, but the radio said that our soldiers were having a hard time with the Russian winter. Rationing had become much stricter, and we depended increasingly on our rabbits and chickens, though Mama's garden provided us with summer-canned goods. Christmas was coming in a few weeks, and she still clung to the hope that her children would come home in time for the holidays.

One day as I came in from chopping wood, stomping my feet to shake the snow off my boots, I heard Paula talking to Mama in the kitchen.

"I'm really thinking of moving to the wild East like Gertrud, Mama."

I poked my head into the kitchen. "The wild East?" I hung my coat on the hallway hook.

"Michael, have you chopped all the wood?" Mama asked as she removed the towels that covered the rising bread.

"*Ja*, it's all chopped," I said. "What do you mean the wild East, Paula? Will you take Waldemar?" I sat at the table and watched as Mama began putting the loaves of bread into the oven.

Paula pulled a small poster from her pocket and unfolded it. It read: *You can achieve great things. Come to the wild new East.*

Mama took the poster from Paula's hand. "You want to go to the Ukraine?"

I took the poster from Mama. "The wild East?"

Paula tucked her hair behind her ear and leaned in. "*Ja.* Remember my friend Gertrud? The Deutschen Red Cross is training her to be a nurse, and she's going. She says it's a great opportunity."

"Opportunity for what?"

Mama put her hand on mine. "Hush, Michael. Why would you want to move there, Paula?"

Annalisa, now almost four, climbed onto my lap. She put her hands on my face. "Michael, you going to get us a Christmas tree?"

"Soon."

Paula pulled the poster from my hand. "Because . . . Mama, there is nothing here for me. What am I to do? Work on the farms or in the weapons factories or have more babies! I can become someone out there."

"But why go to the Ukraine?" Mama put the last of the bread into the oven. "You can be a nurse here."

Paula poured herself a cup of coffee. "Well, a lot of girls are going and . . . the government is creating a living space for Deutsche settlers." She placed her cup onto her saucer very carefully. "Mama, I want to become a nurse . . . You see, Waldemar is just shy of a year and a half, and . . . I thought perhaps you could look after him while I get settled, and then I would send for him."

Annalisa interrupted with, "The Christmas Angel is coming soon, isn't she, Michael?"

"She is."

She slid off my lap and with her hedgehog doll in hand went to her bedroom singing,

> *O Tannenbaum, O Tannenbaum,*
> *wie treu sind deine Blätter!*
> *Du grünst nicht nur*
> *zur Sommerzeit,*
> *Nein, auch im Winter, wenn es schneit.*
> *O Tannenbaum, O Tannenbaum,*
> *wie treu sind deine Blätter . . . !*

Her sweet voice filled my heart as she trotted off to her room. I got up to pour myself some coffee. "Where did all the people that lived there go?"

She shot me a dirty look. "I don't know. Mama, please say you'll think about it."

There was a knock at the front door and I went to answer it. "Hello, Wolfie."

"Hello, Michael. Is it okay if I stay for a few days?"

I opened the door wider to let him in. Wolfie spent most of his time at our house now as his mutti had stopped coming home. We never really knew where she went, but we thought maybe to Dresden to take a cleaning job.

Before we went up to my room, Wolfie stuck his head into the kitchen. "Hello, Mama, Paula."

"Hello, Wolfie," they replied.

Once in my room Wolfie flung his rucksack onto the twins' bed.

"Paula wants to move to the Ukraine," I told him.

"And do what?"

"Be a nurse or something." I sat on my bed and pulled an old book from my nightstand drawer, Karl May's *Winnetou*. I flipped through the pages, then tossed the book onto my bed. "When did your mutti leave?"

"Two days ago . . ."

"Did she say when she'll come back?"

"*Nein.*"

Minka rubbed herself against Wolfie's leg, but when Annalisa burst into the room, screeching, "Wolfie," the cat scuttled under the bed.

Annalisa sprang into Wolfie's arms and kissed him on his cheek. "Wolfie, I missed you so much . . ." She hugged him tight.

He laughed and tickled her. "I missed you too, little frog."

"The Christmas Angel is coming soon, and you know what?"

"What?"

"We will have candles on our tree!"

"You will?"

"*Ja.* And you know what?" She began to bounce on the bed while Wolfie held her hands.

"What, Annalisa?"

"Mama told me maybe Günther will come home for Christmas!"

"That would be nice, Annalisa."

She bounced off the bed and began singing *O Tannenbaum* once more as she hauled Minka out from under the bed, tucked the long-suffering animal under her arm and went back to her room.

"Want to go downstairs and listen to the radio, Wolfie?"

"Sure."

In the living room I sat in Papa's old green chair, and Wolfie sat on the floor holding Waldemar. Paula sat close to Wolfie. They were both playing with the baby when the announcer broke into the program to say there would be a special news bulletin. I shouted, "Mama! Mama! Come quickly." I startled the baby, and he began to cry.

Wolfie handed him back to Paula.

"Mama, come!"

"What is it?"

I motioned for her to sit down. "Come listen."

The radio broadcaster sounded surprised. "Yesterday, December 7, at precisely 7:55 a.m. Hawaii time, the Empire of Japan attacked the American island of Oahu. Over 350 Japanese warplanes flew over Pearl Harbor and launched a powerful and fierce strike on the American naval base there."

Mama's hands flew to her face, and she shook her head. "*Ach, du lieber Gott.*"

The voice on the radio continued. "The attack has killed over 2,000 men, and about nine destroyed battleships now lie at the bottom of the ocean . . ."

Mama had clasped her hands over her mouth. Tears ran down her cheeks and spilled over her fingers.

"Mama, why are you crying? The Japanese are on our side, aren't they?"

She whispered, "All those young men . . ." She took a deep breath then pulled her hanky from her apron pocket and wiped at her tears. "This attack will draw the Americans into the war." She stood up and began to shout, "War is not how we should solve our problems!"

I stared at her. "The Amis—the Americans are not going to come over here, are they?"

"They did in the last war." She disappeared into the kitchen.

Mama was right. America declared war on Japan the next day, and on December 11, Deutschland declared war on the United States of America, and after a few hours the United States declared war on Deutschland.

Christmas came and although there was little in the shops, somehow Mama was able to give each of us an orange and a pair of knitted socks. But we still had no word from the twins, and there was no news about Günther either. At night whenever I heard a noise outside, I hoped it was him coming home. Susi wrote often, begging Mama to help her to come home. But Mama dared not disobey Papa, and even if she had, the Wehrmacht did not make allowances. Mama would write back and tell her that maybe she would fall in love with a nice boy there and get married and perhaps start a family. Paula started her training with the Red Cross, and now she talked about nothing but moving to the wild East.

January held nothing but misery for our soldiers and for us at home. Wolfie's mutti had still not returned and a rumour began—spread by Herr Finkel, the postman—that the Gestapo had picked her up for being drunk and disorderly and that she was in a concentration camp, assigned to hard labour.

One Sunday afternoon Wolfie and I sat in his cold apartment listening to the *Wunschkonzert* on the small radio that sat on his kitchen counter.

He handed me a cigarette. "Turn the radio up."

I tipped my chair back, reached behind me and turned the music louder. *Helenenmarsch* blared forth, the glockenspiel ringing out over the flutes, the snare and the bass drum keeping a strong rhythmic pulse. We banged our hands on the table, keeping to the beat, and I imagined our soldiers marching on toward Moscow.

Wolfie was always amazed at my music knowledge. He would say, "How do you know all that music stuff?"

And I would reply, "Susi taught me." And then I would think about Susi in far-away Ravensbrück . . .

A bottle of Jägermeister or Göring-Schnapps—so-called because Göring was the Reichsjägermeister—stood in the middle of the table between us, and we took turns drinking hits of it. Then as we slammed our empty shot glasses down, we would shout, "Again!" and take turns refilling each other's glasses. Cigarette smoke engulfed the room as one marching song after the other continued uninterrupted. Finally, just as we drained the last of the Göring-

Schnapps, the music ended and the radio announcer spoke. "To warm their hearts, this next tune is for our soldiers on the Russian Front. This is to let them know we are with them as they prepare to push forward."

"*Scheisse* to those Commie pigs!" Wolfie pushed his chair back, stood up and swaggered over to the pantry cupboard. He pulled out a half-full bottle of vodka and plunked it down on the table between us. "We better have another drink."

I nearly tipped backward. "*Wo in Gottes Namen* did you get that?"

"Mutti left it behind."

The music began once more with the song "Lili Marleen."

> Underneath the lamp post by the barrack's gate.
> Standing all alone every night you see her wait.
> She waits for the boy who marched away . . .

Wolfie filled our glasses, "To Kurt, Peter and Günther!"

I raised my glass. "To my brothers!"

"Again!" Wolfie shouted. "To Margarita!"

"Margarita—and Ivy! To your mutti, to all muttis . . ." I shot the vodka back.

Wolfie lifted his glass. "To all muttis."

By now the radio was playing Beethoven's "Agnus Dei." My head started spinning. Wolfie poured me another and did himself the favour, too.

"To Hiedler!" Wolfie slurred and fell off his chair.

"*Ach, Scheisse* on Hiedler . . ." I leaned over to help him up and instead passed out on the floor beside him.

11

Good Night, Mama

— SPRING 1942 —

☙

BY MAY OUR TROOPS WERE engaged in a counteroffensive to retake Kharkov, Rangoon had fallen to the Japanese and they were marching north in Burma, and for the last three months the Americans had been landing troops in Britain. Then Paula got her wish and was ordered to the Ukraine with the Red Cross, leaving Waldemar with Mama. We all went to the train station to say goodbye.

Mama hugged Paula. "I want you to write often, and don't worry about the baby. I'll take good care of him." Mama wrapped a blue shawl around Paula and kissed her on the forehead.

"I know you will . . ." Paula knelt down and hugged Waldemar, who was now a toddler, kissed him goodbye and told him to be good. She hugged Annalisa and told her she would have to be Mama's helper around the house.

Annalisa nodded solemnly.

Wolfie stood at Paula's side, holding her suitcase. He hugged her to him and whispered something in her ear. She blushed.

Mama dabbed at her eyes.

Annalisa took Waldemar's hand in hers.

I stepped close to Paula and said, "Give me a hug, you pretty goat." We embraced. "Don't fall in love and get married out there," I said into her ear, "because Wolfie will be waiting for you here." I slipped her necklace with a gold cross into her pocket.

She pushed me away. "Don't grow up too fast, Michael, and watch over Mama."

She boarded the train, and we all waved her off.

Soon after Paula's departure, as Wolfie and I were walking home from Herr Zimmermann's farm where we had helped with seeding the fields, he said, "Did you hear about Mexico, Michael?"

"*Nein.* What?"

"Mexico has declared war on us."

"They have an army?"

"They must."

We had brought our fishing rods so we could go fishing before heading home. We hadn't ventured to the lake since the awful day when the Russian plane had crashed, but now it felt good to be there again. The croaking of the frogs, the warmth of the last bit of the day's sun, and a soft wind that carried the sweet scent of the summer to come felt heavenly.

After a time and we had caught a few fish, Wolfie reeled in his line and while I packed up the fish we had caught, he started walking toward the shallow end of the lake. "Want to catch some frogs?" he said.

"Sure. We have enough fish."

At the shallow end, he slipped off his boots and stepped carefully into the water between some bulrushes. I was taking off my boots to follow him when I heard a big splash. He had slipped on the muddy bottom and fallen in. I started to laugh.

But Wolfie screamed, "Aghh! Get me out of this *Scheissdreck* piss-water!"

I laughed so hard that I too slipped on the muddy bank and nearly fell into the water. "Relax, Wolfie! It's only water."

But he just kept yelling, "Get me out! Get me out!"

"Stop screaming!" I continued to laugh as I pulled him out and we sat together on the shore.

"I could have died!"

"Don't think so." But I knew why he was so scared. There was a story that a boy had fallen into this muddy end of the lake long ago. The more he struggled the deeper and deeper into the mud he had sunk till he eventually drowned.

I put my boots on and picked up our fish. "You look like a drowned rat," I told him.

"*Ja, ja.* Let's just get home. I'm cold!"

Mama was in the kitchen reading a letter. "Michael, come sit here beside me . . . You, too, Wolfie—oh, you're soaking wet!" She stood up, leaving the letter on the table. "What happened? Never mind, get upstairs and take those clothes off. The last thing I need is for you to get sick!"

Wolfie did as he was told, while I dumped the fish into the sink. "He fell into the lake, Mama, the murky part where the bulrushes grow."

The letter was from Papa, and I sat at the table to read it while Mama turned the fish we had caught into fish soup. Papa talked mostly about the weather. He never asked how we were, but he said that he thought it was time for me to go to military school so that I could get proper training and become a worthy soldier.

Later Mama took a bowl of soup up to Wolfie, but when she came downstairs, she put the kettle on the stove and said, "I'm worried about that boy."

"Why?"

"He won't stop shivering," she said.

She sat Annalisa and Waldemar into their high chairs, and I tried to feed them the fish soup, but they wouldn't eat it. No one liked fish soup. Meanwhile, Mama poured hot water into the hot water bottle and went back upstairs. I put the children to bed, but Annalisa begged me to read them the adventures of *Max und Moritz*.

Afterwards, I must have dozed off in Papa's old green chair because I woke to hear Mama in the kitchen. "Mama, what are you doing?"

"Wolfie is running a fever."

"But he only got wet."

"Can you pull the tub down from the kitchen rafters and bring up a bucket of coal? And when you're done with that, I'll need you to help me bring him downstairs."

"You're going to give him a bath? Is he that sick?"

"Please, just do as I ask."

Once the tub was full of warm water, she poured in half a cup of cider vinegar. We brought Wolfie down, I helped him undress and he sat in the tub. Mama knelt at the side of the tub and put a cold cloth on his forehead.

"Wolfie!" she screeched suddenly. "What have you done?" Mama looked up at me. "Did you know about this?" She bolted up and crossed the room to where I stood and tried to tear my shirt open.

I held it closed, but she knew what I was hiding.

"Michael! How could you?" She slapped me across the face. "A swastika! Of all things!" She stared at me for a moment, her eyes filling with tears.

I couldn't tell her how or where we had done it. I just said, "I'm sorry, Mama."

Wolfie apologized too.

The next morning the doctor came to the house. He too saw the swastika when he unbuttoned Wolfie's nightshirt. He glanced at

Mama with a raised eyebrow and shook his head. "Stupid boys."

I held Waldemar in my arms, and Annalisa stood close to my side. She pointed and said, "Wolfie has a black sun on his heart. Michael, do all big boys have black suns?"

I took her hand. "Not all boys."

The doctor told Mama to keep an eye on Wolfie's fever and call him if his condition worsened.

But no matter how many mustard poultices Mama applied to his chest and back, Wolfie just kept getting sicker. The doctor came back to the house but stayed only long enough to say that Wolfie had pneumonia and must go to the hospital immediately.

"Michael, I want you to try to find Wolfie's mutti," Mama said.

I made inquiries all over town, but I couldn't locate her anywhere.

Mama said, "Perhaps Herr Finkel was right."

We called a taxi to take all of us to the hospital, and as we carried Wolfie to the car, Annalisa said, "Is Wolfie going to die?"

"Don't say such things, Annalisa," Mama said as she tucked Wolfie into the car.

I climbed into the front of the taxi and sat Annalisa on my lap. "Wolfie's going to be as good as new in a few weeks, you'll see." Waldemar, who sat on Mama's lap in the back of the taxi beside Wolfie, cried for his mutti all the way to the hospital.

After that Mama or I went every day by bus to visit Wolfie, and after a long three weeks he finally came home. About that time we learned the authorities really had sent his mutti to a work camp for being drunk and disorderly in public. And in late summer she finally came home.

By mid-fall there was talk that sixteen-year-olds could volunteer to enlist in the SS, but Mama didn't think that I should. Papa, however, wrote another letter home telling her that I had to enlist as soon as I turned sixteen. He had not, he wrote, raised me to be a coward. While Wolfie and I had been working to bring in the harvest from the fields, we had talked about enlisting in the Luftwaffe and becoming fighter pilots, but now it seemed that we were both going to be in the Waffen-SS. The war hadn't missed us after all.

That Sunday I sat with Mama to listen to the afternoon radio show *Wunschkonzert*. The announcer spoke softly: "The next song is for all you *Mütter* who have lost your sons while they were fighting to defend our fatherland. This song is for you—'*Gute Nacht, Mutter.*'"

12

Goodbye

— AUGUST 1943 —

⁓

IT WAS LATE AUGUST, and I couldn't tell if I was nervous or excited about getting out of our town. Of course, I hated to leave Mama and Annalisa. But now that I was sixteen, Papa had ordered me to volunteer with the Waffen-SS for combat training, and when I told Wolfie, he responded by slapping me on the back. "Looks like we get to fight after all." Wolfie had volunteered along with me, and he was as excited as I was.

A few days later, Wolfie and I were taking the first train of the day, heading for Beverloo in Belgium, the camp set up to train Hitlerjugend boys to become SS soldiers. The sun had not yet warmed the morning air when Mama and I arrived at the station to find Wolfie already there, his rucksack slung over his shoulder as he leaned against the red brick wall of the train station, smoking a cigarette. He nodded and flashed a smile at me, revealing the dimples that always drew the girls to him.

"*Schönen Guten Morgen*, Frau Boii—Mama." He butted out his cigarette. "I didn't know you were coming to see us off."

"*Guten Morgen*, Wolfie. Did you sleep at all?" Mama asked.

"*Nein*. I was afraid I'd miss the train."

"*Ja*, me too," I chimed in.

Mama kissed Wolfie on the cheek. "Where is your mutti?" She looked around, expecting to see her.

"*Ach*, she doesn't like goodbyes."

Mama fussed with his shirt. "Well, never mind."

Gently he took her hand. He knew she was worried about us. "Frau Boii—Mama, we'll be back before you know it."

She turned to me, grabbing my hand. "Michael, it's just . . ." She tried hard to smile, but the pain of possibly never seeing us again was too much for her. "You boys, please keep safe and always look out for one another, you hear me?" She squeezed my hand, then let it drop to pull out her handkerchief.

Just then a black Mercedes, the kind known as the *Totenwagen* or death-mobile, drove up with two Gestapo officials inside. The one behind the wheel stepped out of the car and pulled a booklet from his pocket. "Excuse us, Frau, we are looking for the Zimmermanns' farm. Do you know where it is?"

"*Ja* . . . why?"

"We are not permitted to discuss the matter. Do you know how to get there?"

Mama began giving directions, but she didn't make any sense. Wolfie looked from Mama to the Gestapo men, then lit two cigarettes and handed one to me.

Now the second Gestapo man, who had pockmarks all over his face, stepped out of the car. He looked annoyed and pointed his finger at us. "You two look familiar. Have we met before?"

We had, but I wasn't going to admit it. "Don't think so."

"I remember. You're the kids who were there when the Russian plane crashed out at that farm . . . that boy Otto. The Keller place."

Wolfie put out his cigarette. "*Ach, ja*."

"Then you boys know where the Zimmermanns' farm is."

I glanced at my mama. The sadness on her face had changed to fear.

Wolfie put his hands in his pockets. "*Ja*, we know where it is."

Pockmark opened the rear car door. "You two, get in."

Mama stood rubbing her hands together. "I'm sorry, officer, but these two are on their way to the Beverloo training camp. It's almost six, and their train will be here any minute."

"Stand back, Frau! You are interfering with official business. They can get the next train out."

Mama took my hand and mouthed the word, "Günther."

"Frau! I have told you once." Pockmark pushed her to the side. "Stand back."

I wanted to hit him for pushing my mama, but, Wolfie glanced over at me and shook his head. I bit my lip and resisted the urge to sock the man.

He shoved his pitted face into mine. His breath was foul, like salami and stale booze. He grabbed my arm pushing me towards the car and telling me to hurry. "*Schnell, schnell!*" he shouted. "Get in!"

What was so pressing and why was the Zimmermanns' farm of such importance? And why did Mama call me Günther? My head was spinning and I felt ill.

From within the car I saw Mama turn and run in the direction of home.

The car sped off, leaving a cloud of dust behind. As we drove, the tall yellow grasses on the side of the road swayed in the gusts of wind that came from the passage of the *Totenwagen*.

We passed the post office, and up ahead I could see Herr Finkel, the nosy postman, walking towards us with his head down. As we came abreast of him, he glanced up, then turned and walked off in the other direction.

An unsettled feeling crept over me. Something told me to stall, and I began directing them the long way to the Zimmermanns' farm. Now, though I had not thought about Fritz Bummel for some time, the memory of finding him buried in the grove came flooding back.

"Why the farm?" Wolfie asked the Gestapo officials.

Gestapo Man turned his head and said, "We have been informed that—"

Just then the car swerved to the right, then to the left, and with a loud thump we came to a jolting stop. "*Ach, du Scheisse!* What was that?" Gestapo Man stepped out of the car. We waited for a moment, then followed.

A burst of bitter bile rose to my throat. They were dragging a flailing sheep by its head to the side of the road.

The sheep's eyes were wild with fear, blood trickled out of its nose, and a rhythmic moan was spilling from its bleeding mouth. All the while, its front legs were frantically thrashing the air.

"One of you boys want to put this mutton out of its misery?" Pockmark said.

Wolfie took a step back. "*Ach, nein!*"

Laughing, Pockmark pointed his pistol at me. "What about you, boy?"

The sour bitter taste in my throat surged into my mouth. I swallowed the bile, and nodded my head and reached out my hand. "*Ja,* I'll do it."

Pockmark handed his Luger to me. "Take a deep breath in, exhale half, aim at the target and slowly pull the trigger. That's how you execute something—or someone. It's all the same."

With a calm hand I took his gun, took a breath in, and watched for a moment of calmness in the animal's eyes. Once the creature showed that the storm within him was no more, I gently pulled the trigger and shot him between the eyes. The stony grey roadside, where now the sheep lay dead, was slowly transforming to a red slough.

I handed the Luger back to Pockmark. "Here is your pistol."

Wolfie slapped me on the back as we stepped back into the car. He nodded toward Pockmark and whispered, "*Schwein.*"

I directed the driver along the old Kliff Strasse, the winding back road that led to the Zimmermanns' house. The hazelnut grove was to our right, and to our left stood the remnants of the apple orchard that once had branches bursting with blossoms, but now was a field of burned and broken trunks.

Frau Zimmermann, who was carrying a pail of milk, saw the car approaching and walked quickly toward the house, calling for her husband. Just as Herr Zimmermann opened the door, we stepped out of the *Totenwagen.*

Liebchen, their Alsation, stood between Herr and Frau Zimmermann. Its ears were back and its teeth bared.

Herr Zimmermann studied the two officials standing beside us, while his wife stood holding her pail of fresh milk. As she wiped her free hand on her mustard-coloured apron, she said calmly, "Hello, Michael and Wolfie."

Herr Zimmermann reached down to hold Liebchen by her collar, as by now the dog was growling. "Can I help you?"

"You are Herr Isaac Zimmermann?"

"*Ja.* Is everything all right?"

"We have orders to bring you to the Reich security office," said Pockmark.

"May I ask regarding what?"

Gestapo Man reached for Herr Zimmermann's arm, but Liebchen went to lunge at the Gestapo Man, and Herr Zimmermann pulled back on her collar.

"We have our orders," said Pockmark. "If you don't want to be arrested, I suggest you come with us at once."

Frau Zimmermann turned to her husband. "Best you do as you're told."

Herr Zimmermann nodded, and she bent to take Liebchen's collar from him, but at that moment Liebchen broke free and began running across the grass. Gestapo Man turned and we all spotted a small, dark-haired child running into the barn.

"Who was that?" Pockmark asked.

Before any of us could say or do anything, he pulled out his whistle and began blowing it as he ran after the child. The other Gestapo man stopped briefly at the *Totenwagen* to grab a pair of semi-automatic machine guns from the trunk, slung them over his shoulder and then followed him, yelling, "*Halt! . . . Halt!*"

I turned to Frau Zimmermann, but before I could ask her anything, she dropped the pail of milk, spilling it over the doorstep, and ran after the two men.

Herr Zimmermann said, "The children, your brother . . ."

Wolfie and I ran toward the barn, not knowing what would happen. When we bolted into the barn, we saw at the far end Liebchen barking wildly, and she had placed herself between the child and Pockmark. He pulled out his pistol, shot Liebchen, then grabbed the child by the hair and dangled her in the air. As the girl screamed, she clasped her hands around her head, trying to release herself from his grasp, her dark brown eyes frantically searching the room for help.

"Well, well . . . What do we have here?"

Wolfie and I stopped dead in our tracks. Liebchen lay on the barn floor dead. Wolfie whispered. "That's Sarah!"

He was right. It was little Sarah, the Silbersteins' youngest daughter. She was only about five. We had all assumed that the family had moved to Madagascar.

Frau Zimmermann, an arms-reach from us, stood helplessly beside Gestapo Man, who held tight to her arm. "So you're hiding *ein Judenkind*?" he said. With his free hand, he backhanded her across the face, then knocked her to the floor.

I tried to help her up, but Gestapo Man pushed me out of the way and then kicked her in the ribs.

Pockmark pulled out his pistol, then he released his grip on Sarah's hair so that she fell to the floor on her knees. Before she could scramble to her feet, he aimed his pistol at the back of her head and shot her without so much as a moment of hesitation. She fell partly on top of Liebchen. Disgusted, he punted her legs out of his way. He pointed his pistol at Frau Zimmermann, "Are there any more, Frau?"

I went to lunge at him, but Wolfie stopped me. "He'll only shoot you."

Gestapo Man pulled Frau Zimmermann up by her hair and slammed her repeatedly into the wall.

Herr Zimmermann came running into the barn wielding a shovel and cracked Gestapo Man over the head with it. The man's knees buckled, and he dropped his Luger, but he quickly retrieved it.

Frau Zimmermann tried to struggle free as she screamed, "*Nein!*"

Pockmark shot from across the barn, and Herr Zimmermann's wooden-leg splintered into a hundred pieces. He dropped to the floor, his head hitting the plough blade, a pool of blood spreading out from under his head, but we could see he was still alive.

Pockmark stepped over the lifeless bodies of Sarah and Liebchen as Wolfie and I stood looking helplessly on. "You two, look for the *dreckigen Juden*," he snapped at us as he helped his partner to his feet.

That's when it hit me—Günther! He was hiding somewhere in this barn. Not only had Günther been helping the Zimmermanns, this is where he had gone into hiding. And Mama knew. That's why she came out here so often.

A shaft of morning sun streamed into the barn, illuminating the trap door to the root cellar below the barn floor. Pockmark jumped up and down on it, and it reverberated with a hollow thumping pulse. He knelt down then and pointed at Wolfie and me. "You two, get over here! Open this door."

My hands were trembling. "It's only the door to their root cellar . . ." My voice quavered.

Pockmark pushed me out of the way and whistled a slow strange tune as he pulled up on the door. There looking up at us were Herr and Frau Silberstein and Günther with his arms around Esther Silberstein.

"Please don't shoot," begged Herr Silberstein.

"Please, please," Frau Zimmermann pleaded desperately with Gestapo Man. "Please let them go!"

He turned, pressed his Luger to her forehead, and with not so much as a word or a blink of an eye, he took a loud breath, exhaled, and pulled the trigger. Her body slid down the wooden wall as if someone had stolen her bones, leaving a trail of bloody skull fragments and hair on the wall.

As Pockmark pulled Günther and then Esther's family from their hiding place, Gestapo Man shouted at them to get out, "*Raus! Schnell! Schnell!*"

Günther looked straight into my eyes, shaking his head and motioning me not to say anything. I clasped my hand over my mouth. The stench of the horse manure, urine, hay, cordite, and the iron smell of blood became overbearing. The room spun, my heart raced frantically, but my mind stood still.

And then we were all walking toward the hazelnut grove, and the sparrows were chirping in the tree branches overhead. The morning sun flooded the grove and glimmered on the dew-covered grass. Some of the leaves had turned colour and were gently falling on us. A song filled the air. It was my brother, and he was singing in a soft, deep, voice.

Why should I feel discouraged, why should
                    the shadows come
Why should my heart be lonely, and long for
                    heaven and home
When Jesus is my portion? My constant friend is He,
His eye is on the sparrow, and I know He watches me . . .

Gestapo Man shoved Günther, who was in the front of the line, and shouted at him to shut up. "*Halt die Fresse!*"

But Günther just kept on singing.

"I said shut your mouth!" Gestapo Man knocked Esther to the ground, and Günther rushed to help her up. She was crying now, her hand on her stomach, and Günther held her close to his side and began singing once more.

Let not your heart be troubled, His tender word I hear
And resting on His goodness, I lose my doubt and fear . . .

And then there we were standing right beside the log that Wolfie and I had dragged over to cover Fritz's body. "Down on your knees," Pockmark ordered my brother and the Silbersteins. "And you two, get over here!" He waved his pistol at Wolfie and me. "You're going to shoot these muttons."

I glanced at Wolfie. He was as white as the milk that had spilled on the Zimmermanns' doorstep. Günther turned, gazed at me with a smile, his green eyes soft. I clutched at his St. Francis medallion that I wore around my neck. Frau Silberstein had an empty look about her. I remembered her buying yellow carnations, and how the Hitlerjugend boys had shouted after her, "*Jude!—Jude!*"

I reached for Wolfie's arm and through clenched teeth I whispered, "We have to do something." I didn't realize that tears were streaming down my face.

"They'll kill us," he whispered back.

"We can't do this," I whimpered.

He glanced my way, and I knew by his look that he too could not shoot Günther or the Silbersteins—even to save our own lives.

"Hurry up, you two." The Gestapo officials were laughing now just as they had when they goaded me into shooting the sheep. They handed us their Lugers, shoved us forward, and said, "Now, boys, let's see what kind of men you are. Stand here behind them and aim at their heads. Just like you killed the mutton." Then together they shouted, "*Erschiesst sie . . .* Shoot now!"

Günther, Esther, and her parents knelt before us quietly, awaiting their fate. Behind us, the Gestapo men readied their semi-automatic machine guns to shoot. Pockmark stood behind me. I could feel his breath on my neck and the barrel of his gun in the small of my back. "*Schiessen* or be shot!" he said in my ear and then yelled, "I said *schiessen!*"

My hand was trembling, and I heard Pockmark inhale. Then out of the corner of my eye I saw someone to my left and heard Herr Zimmermann shouting, "*Nein . . .*"

I turned, and at that moment Wolfie knocked me to the ground. The grove was filled with gunfire and Pockmark landed on the ground beside us. Gestapo Man had fired his weapon, but he too had dropped to the ground.

The sparrows in the trees had stopped their song, and the hazelnut grove had fallen silent. As we stood up, from behind us a scream shattered the stillness.

"Günther . . . !" It was Mama running towards my brother who was slumped forward with his face in the dirt. Herr Zimmermann was behind her. He had a cloth wrapped around his head, and he was leaning on a crutch under one arm, while clutching his old WWI rifle with his free hand.

Wolfie and I were stunned. I felt a movement at my feet. The two Gestapo officials were still alive and flailing in the dirt just as the sheep had. Wolfie shouted as he kicked Gestapo Man. "*Schwein—Schwein!* This is for Frau Zimmermann, the Silbersteins and Günther. You *Drecksack!*" He pointed the gun at the top of Gestapo Man's head, took a breath and pulled the trigger.

Pockmark grasped my ankle, his eyes full of fear. My hand had stopped trembling, and my tears had dried. I pointed the Luger between his eyes, not waiting for Pockmark's storm to subside and, just as he had taught me, I took a breath in and shot him dead.

We turned to Mama, who now sat on the ground with Günther's head in her lap, rocking him back and forth. He had taken a bullet to his chest. The Russian pilot's gun lay in the dirt beside her. Herr Silberstein stayed kneeling, staring vacantly. His wife and daughter lay dead beside him. The leaves of the hazelnut trees fell softly on them.

"Fahrkarte, bitte." I felt a nudge at my side from the train conductor. "You two, train tickets, please!" In a haze I handed him our travel cards, then stood up and placed our luggage on the overhead racks.

"Travelling to Unna, Westphalia?" he asked.

Wolfie vacantly stared at the conductor and nodded.

We sat for hours after that, Wolfie and I, not saying a word. I thought about the two Gestapo men and wondered if Hitler would have pinned medals on those two killers. At Unna we stepped off the train and waited at the bleak station until our connecting train arrived just after midnight.

At every stop the train picked up more boys, all of them around our age. The jubilation on their faces and their excited chatter about going off to war made me want to scream at them, "Go home to your muttis!" After a while I calmed myself and looked out the window. There were thousands of stars in the sky, and as I stared up at them, I realized that I had never truly understood who my mama was. I took Günther's watch from my pocket. It had his initials beautifully engraved on the back, G.C.B. Mama had given it to him for his nineteenth birthday and for completing his education with Frau Zimmermann. I opened the case—on the inside it read: *You are more than you will ever know.*

Mama had pressed the watch into my hand before we buried Günther and the others in the grove. He had thrown his body in front of Esther, but the bullet that killed him had also gone through her chest. Mama told me that he and Esther had fallen in love while he was in hiding, that they had married in secret last May, and that Günther had wanted to become a teacher.

Wolfie pulled the Luger that had belonged to Gestapo Man out of his knapsack and placed it on the seat between us. Ever so gently he would put his hand on it from time to time and stroke it. Mama said it was okay for him to keep it. She wanted nothing more to do with guns. It was enough that she had shot one of the Gestapo men with the Russian's gun.

Although Herr Zimmermann had been limping badly even with the help of his crutch, he and Herr Silberstein had worked hard to help us bury all the bodies and push the *Totenwagen* off the cliff and sink it into the deep end of the lake. After we had finished, Mama had insisted that we catch the last train of the day so that we would not be reported absent from training camp.

"Everything will be all right," she had kept saying to me when we had got to the station and picked up our rucksacks. "No one will ever find out what happened at the farm."

Herr Finkel was the only one who knew that we had gone to the farm with the Gestapo, but Herr Zimmermann said that he would take care of the nosy postman. And we were not to worry about the Gestapo, he said, because there weren't that many of them, and it was not common for them to visit small towns. It was only people ratting on one another to the Gestapo that brought them around.

The last words Mama had spoken to me before we had left on the train were "Esther was expecting a baby."

13

Training

— AUGUST 1943 —

∽

IT WAS MORNING WHEN we arrived at our next stop where we were organized into groups, and a day and a half later we set out again by train for the Deutsche–Belgian border. This time when we piled off the train, we were lined up in orderly formations with hundreds of Hitlerjugend, who all seemed to be in high spirits. Then we began marching to the quarters of the Aufklärungsab-teilung, our reconnaissance unit.

Wolfie and I had eaten very little for the past few days so my gut was empty, and the light stung my eyes. My Hitlerjugend uniform smelled like sour milk. And while the warmth of the morning air brushed ever so gently against me, it left me feeling cold. I could hardly breathe.

Wolfie marched beside me. "Basic training won't be so bad," he said. He held his head high and joined in singing the Horst Wessel song with everybody else.

I clenched my jaw and thought about Günther.

"Just sing, Michael, sing!"

But I hung my head as I marched with the rest of the boys. It was as though I had stepped into quicksand. How would I ever get home again?

After six weeks of basic training just outside of Turnhout, we were shipped to the troop grounds at Beverloo, 72 kilometres southeast of Antwerp in the Dutch-speaking part of Belgium. As Wolfie and I jumped off the transport truck, an officer shouted, "Listen up! You are now part of the Hitlerjugend 12th SS Panzer Division. Over twenty thousand boys have volunteered for active duty. You will all train here. Life will be hard, and being hungry and tired will become the norm. Food, after all, is difficult to come by for everyone. Sturmbannführer Hubert Meyer, our first general staff officer, is trying to have our rations increased."

But more food never came. We were, however, given candy in our rations instead of the cigarettes that the older soldiers received, and the younger boys loved that. I suppose it gave them some comfort. Wolfie, on the other hand, always managed to find a way to get cigarettes.

Wolfie and I were assigned to the reconnaissance unit in the 25th Panzer Grenadier Regiment where we would be responsible for scouting enemy positions and terrain, and then reporting back to our commanding officers. We threw ourselves into the daily training exercises, trying to forget what had occurred at the Zimmermanns' farm.

One day Lars Wildmann, who had lied about his age in order to volunteer, ran into the mess hall shouting, "The mail has arrived!" He held a stack of letters in his hand and waved them above his head. At fourteen, he was the smallest and youngest boy at the training school. "Michael, you got a letter, and you too, Sugar Boy."

Wolfie reached up and grabbed for the letters from Wildmann. "*Mensch*, give it here then!" He handed me my letter. "What does Mama say, Michael?"

"Wait till I open it . . ."
Wolfie read over my shoulder.

> *Dearest Michael and Wolfie,*
>
> *I hope you boys are keeping well.*
>
> *I tell you my news with the saddest of hearts. There is no easy way to say this. Your sister Susi has succumbed to typhus. She contracted the disease from some of the prisoners at Ravensbrück. Your Papa said she got too close to the women there, but he says she did our Führer proud. I miss her dearly. I seek solace in knowing she is playing all her favourite music now. I sit sometimes at the piano to feel close to her.*
>
> *Wolfie, your mutti is doing well and sends her love. I still have no news about the twins, but I hold out hope for them. Paula might be coming home early next year as she has put in for a position with Margarita. Waldemar is growing fast and is well. Annalisa talks about you two boys non-stop. The other day she sat on the stairs petting the cat and said, "I remember when Michael and Wolfie got new boots. I'm going to marry Wolfie when I grow up." I guess, Wolfie, you have someone waiting for you when you come home. Please watch out for one another and come home safely.*
>
> *We have a new postman. Please write home soon.*
>
> > *Heil Hitler,*
> > *Your liebende Mama*

Wolfie put his arm across my shoulder. "*Ach*, Michael, I'm so sorry about Susi."

I looked around the cafeteria and saw that other boys had received bad news as well. I stuffed the letter into my pocket. "*Ja* . . . Wolfie, I need some air." We stood up, and so did two of the other boys, Sugar Boy and Wildmann.

Once we were all outside, I took a deep breath, but the air still felt suffocating. "Wolfie, light me a cigarette, will you?"

None of us had much to say. Off in the distance to my right, I could hear the birds singing in the forest. The leaves were now falling from the trees. I wanted to shout, but who would I shout at? Maybe Hitler himself? I took a drag from my cigarette and remembered how much Susi had loved playing the piano.

"Sugar Boy, what was your news?" Wolfie asked.

He plunged a hand into his pocket, lowered his head, and as he rubbed his eyes, he mumbled, "My mutti . . . She died in a night bombing. I hate those *beschissenen* Tommies and the *Dummköpfe* Amis."

Wildmann put his arm around him. "*Ach, du lieber Gott.*"

Sugar Boy shrugged Wildmann's arm off his shoulder. "I'll kill them all!" he whimpered. "Hitler would want that! He'd give me a medal for that."

I lifted my head and studied Sugar Boy. He had tears rolling down his face. He was a skinny boy with sunken cheekbones, but we called him Sugar Boy because he would devour anything with sugar in it.

Wildmann shrugged. "My family all died in the bombing."

Wolfie asked, "Where?"

Wildmann stared off into the distance. "Cologne."

"Last year?" Wolfie asked.

Wildmann nodded.

"Amazing you lived through that," Wolfie said.

"My papa lowered me into the sewer hole in the street in front of our house."

"What happened to your family?" Sugar Boy asked as he wiped his face with his hands.

Wildmann was silent for a while, watching Sugar Boy kicking at the cobblestones where a buttercup grew between the cracks. Then he explained, "There was no time for anyone else to follow. It felt like days before I crawled out of that filthy hole. What I remember most was the animals walking around, starving to death. Dogs roamed in packs . . . I still think about the animals."

Wolfie stepped a bit closer to Wildmann and pointed at his head. "Is that how you got that scar?"

"*Nein*. I got this when my mutti asked me to bring in the wash. I tripped and hit my head on the back stairs."

The boys all laughed. I wiped at my eyes. "Sugar Boy, we're your family now." I handed him a cigarette.

Sugar Boy shook his head. "Do you have any candy?"

I reached into my coat pocket and handed him my last chocolate. "We can all count on one another and our rifles to get us through this. And if that fails, we can at least die knowing that we've done our families proud." I believed Susi had.

"There you guys are," said Joop. He had just come from the barracks.

I flicked my cigarette to the ground. "Hello."

We couldn't tell Joop and his twin brother apart, so we called them both Joop. They were tall, lanky boys, and they were much like my two brothers, always finishing one another's sentences. Their papa was Danish and he had joined Denmark's National Socialist Workers Party in 1930.

"Panzermeyer wants us all ready in five minutes," he said.

"What for?"

"We're going to start firearms training."

I pulled my jacket around me and stuffed my brother's watch deep into my pocket. "What did you say we're doing today?"

"I just said it—shooting rifles! Strauss is ready, and he's waiting with my brother. So, if you *Fräuleins* are done here . . ." He flashed us a smile and turned, and we all followed him to our barracks room.

Jochen von Strauss was sitting on his bed, putting on his boots. "Hello guys, thought you would be late."

Strauss was twice the size of any one of us and must have weighed at least ninety kilograms. Wolfie called him Tiger Tank.

I sat on the chair in the corner of the room and pulled out Günther's pocket watch again.

Wolfie flung himself onto his bed and put his arms behind his head. "Not us, Tiger Tank."

In my mind I could hear Susi playing the slow march from Paul Hindemith's Piano Sonata No. 1. Papa said that Hindemith was not worth listening to or playing, but Susi would play his music and other forbidden tunes when he was not around. And Günther would sit in Papa's chair, his eyes closed, his head swaying to the music that filled our home. Sometimes he would sing to the melodies. I always wondered what he thought about in those moments of peace while Susi played.

"Where are Rudolf and Heinz?" Wolfie blurted.

Just then a scuffle erupted outside the room, and we all jumped up and headed for the door. But Strauss beat us there and stood in front of us, his arms outstretched to either side of the doorframe.

Wolfie tried to push him out of the way. "Mo-o-ove—you big—fat—Tiger Tank!"

Strauss was not exerting any effort, and he just stood there laughing. "Oh, sorry, madam."

Wolfie pushed Strauss once more, and this time I pushed up against Wolfie, the twins pushed up against me, and Sugar Boy and Wildmann pushed up against the twins. "Push . . . guys," Wolfie yelled, "and we can move this tank."

Just then, Strauss moved abruptly to the right, and we all fell to the floor in a heap, laughing like crazy. Heinz, whose nose had been bloodied by Rudolf, stuck his head in the door. "*Ach,*" he said, "what a fine bunch of Fräuleins you are." Rudolf and Heinz, whose full name was Heinrich Richter, were best friends, but they always fought with one another.

"What's going on here?" shouted Obersturmführer Ritzert.

"We're all waiting for you boys. Perhaps you think this war is going to be all fun and games?"

Wolfie reached for my arm so that I could pull him up. "*Nein,*" I said as I helped my friend to his feet.

The Obersturmführer smiled at us. "Hurry it up and get yourselves to the shooting range. Richter, wash your face."

Sugar Boy took a four-day leave so that he could be with his aunt and bury his mother.

Our combat training at Beverloo continued, and now more than ever we felt that we had to give our best. The squadrons of enemy bombers flew overhead just about every day and every night en route to Deutschland, and we felt incredibly helpless because we knew that they were dropping their bombs on our families.

Then, after endless weeks of combat training, we were finally scheduled for a free day. I was sitting on one of our Italian Guzzi motorcycles smoking and thinking about what I wanted to do on our free day when Wolfie walked towards me. "*Ach, Mensch,* are you dreaming of pretty girls?"

"*Nein.* I was just thinking maybe . . . we could take one of these motorcycles into town tomorrow night."

"And?"

"We can have us some fun."

"What if we get caught?"

"We won't. Besides, Joop is on guard duty, and he knows what to do." I threw my cigarette butt down on the much-worn grass path. "Don't you want to see Lorelei and her sister?"

We had met the sisters when we'd been taken into the town of Balda to meet up with our comrades of the 26th regiment who were housed in the local high school. We were allowed to get together with some of the local girls in the town's coffee shops, and that's where we met Lorelei and her sister.

"Felicia? Sure . . ."

I stood up and patted him on the back. "Good, we'll go after supper tomorrow."

He pulled his coat tightly around him. "Looks like it might rain for tonight's combat training."

"Wolfie, don't you like Felicia?"

"*Ja*. What about you and Lorelei?"

"I kissed her."

"When?" he said in disbelief.

"The day we all went to her father's bakery."

"And you said you were going to the bookstore?"

"*Ja*."

He pulled out two cigarettes, lit them, and handed one to me, giving me the look that told me to get on with my story.

"Well, she works at the bookstore, and she said she needed to pick something up there. So I went with her."

Wolfie scrunched up his face. "*Und?*"

"I was looking at some books when I accidentally knocked one of them off the shelf. She picked it up and placed it back in its spot . . . And that's when I stole a kiss."

"A stolen kiss. Lucky," Wolfie said.

That night at training the rain came down like miniature bombs exploding on our helmets. As we were crawling through the mud, Wolfie was in front of me, and Manfred Müller—Fred—one of the other boys in our battalion, was beside me. Poor old Fred's glasses were so covered in mud that he couldn't see in front of him, and when he stood up to get a better look, he accidentally fired his gun and shot Wolfie. Wolfie rolled in the mud with his hands up to his face, yelling, "I've been shot! Who shot me?"

I threw my gun down, got up, and ran over to him. "*Ach, du Scheisse!* Are you okay?"

Fred went running in the other direction.

I pulled Wolfie's hands away from his face. "Let me see, Wolfie."

"I'm bleeding!"

The Obersturmführer came running over. "What happened here?"

"Fred shot Wolfie," I said. "It was an accident."

The Obersturmführer knelt down. "Are you all right, boy?"

"I think so."

He helped me lift Wolfie from the mud. "Where's Fred?"

I pointed to my right. "He ran that way."

"Take Wolfie to the first aid station."

"It's all right," Wolfie said. "I think the bullet just grazed me. I'll be fine."

"I'll keep an eye on him," I told the Obersturmführer.

"You two are good soldiers, but you do need to go to the infirmary."

Wolfie needed a few stitches. Back in our room and once our comrades had returned from training, we stood around admiring Wolfie's newly acquired wound. I grabbed his chin and turned his face so I could look at the stitches. "With that on your face, you're going to look like Fräulein Margarita's papa."

"You think, Michael?"

"Sort of. But yours is smaller."

Wolfie checked himself out in the mirror, turning his head back and forth. "Has anyone found Fred?"

Joop, who was lying on his bed flipping the pages of his pay book, looked up. "*Ja*, the commander found him hiding in the woods. Poor kid."

"Poor kid? You must be kidding . . . he could have killed me!"

Joop threw his book at Wolfie. "Ah, he made you better looking."

14

Lorelei

— SEPTEMBER 1943 —

∽

IT RAINED ALL THE NEXT DAY, but after inspections we played Foosball and watched a boxing tournament. When *Abendessen* was over and we had eaten our full, Wolfie and I walked casually out back to the motorcycle garage. I grasped the cold metal handle and slid the door open. The sky was still mainly overcast, but the wind had come up and a shaft of moonlight shone into the building that housed about ten motorbikes and a dozen bicycles. A few of the motorbikes were in pieces, and we could make out countless nuts, bolts, wrenches, a pair of wire cutters and rags lying on the workbench, but I spotted a Guzzi that was all in one piece.

"That's the one, Wolfie. I'll drive and you get on the back."

"All right, but I'll drive on the way back."

"We'll push it to the start of the trail so no one will hear us."

"The girls will be thrilled when we drive up on a motorbike. You're sure that Joop is on guard duty?"

"*Ja.* Help me push this thing."

"Does it have gas?"

"I think so . . ."

Wolfie twisted the gas cap off and peered into the tank. "*Scheisse!* It's empty."

"Empty!" I looked around the room.

"Maybe this is not a good idea, Michael. You know how tight we are for fuel . . . Every drop has to be accounted for."

"No one will know." I pointed to a green metal gas can. "What's that?"

Wolfie picked it up and shook it. "There's not much, but it'll get us there."

"Good then. Fill her up." I slipped the wire-cutters I had seen on the workbench into my pocket.

Wolfie noticed what I had done. "You should put them back."

"They might come in handy."

He shrugged. "Do you even know how to drive one of these bikes?"

"Never have, but how hard can it be? You?"

"*Nein.*"

"Let's push this beast to the trail then."

Once we were on the narrow trail through the pine forest and far enough away from camp so no one could hear, I kick-started the motor. As we drove off into the night, the moon would make an appearance for a moment or two in the west and then hide behind the fast-moving clouds.

Behind me Wolfie was laughing, and I figured he probably had his eyes closed as we bounced over the trail. "Good driving, Michael," he said in my ear.

After a few kilometres the trail broke out of the pine forest and began skirting the edge of the trees while to our left lay farm fields. In the west the clouds parted briefly, revealing stars hanging in the sky by the thousands. For a moment I felt free and as if I could do anything. "Think I can jump that log in front of us?"

"Don't even think about it! I'll go flying," Wolfie said, laughing. "Okay! Do it, Michael!"

"Hang on tight . . ."

But instead of flying high up over the log, I put on the brakes. Wolfie lurched forward, almost falling off the bike.

Beneath us the bike spun sideways and then came to a full stop. I cut the engine. "Wolfie, look! There in the sky!"

"What is it?"

"Not sure . . ." Crates were parachuting silently from above and landing in the nearby field.

"It's a drop! It must be for the Belgian Resistance."

"We've got to get it, Wolfie."

"What if the Resistance catch us?"

"Let's just pick up a box of whatever, and get the hell out of here! We'll drive back to camp with it and say we found it in the woods."

"Michael, they'll ask us why we were in the woods."

"Shh! Listen!"

Wolfie's eyes grew large.

"Quick, help me push the bike behind those rocks." I pointed to some huge boulders on the edge of the pine forest.

"*Nein!* Let's get out of here."

"Too late. We've got to hide."

"*Scheissdreck.* They're coming."

"Come on . . . Help me hide the bike behind those rocks!" But Wolfie was pointing back toward the camp, shaking his head.

"Wolfie-e-e!" I growled. "Push . . ." He snapped out of it and together we pushed the motorcycle through a large mud puddle and into a gully behind the largest boulder, and there we stayed hidden.

The moon was now high in the sky casting a cold, bluish light over the forest floor. The dirt smelled of mushrooms, and the dampness of the soil slowly seeped through my clothing, keeping me uncomfortably alert.

Wolfie wriggled a few inches forward. He glanced back at me and signalled with three fingers up, opening and closing his hand twice.

I mouthed the word, "Six?"

He nodded.

"Belgians," I mouthed.

Wolfie nodded again.

I too crawled forward until I could make out the silhouettes of their caps. I turned to Wolfie and mouthed again, "Belgians." They had come running out of the forest to collect the crates that had been dropped from the plane. When sudden gunfire erupted around us, we pressed our bodies into the ground, almost not breathing.

"*Scheisse*," Wolfie mouthed.

I grimaced and motioned for him to get back. "The Resistance," I said under my breath.

We slithered farther behind the boulder, leaned our backs up against it and tried to stay calm.

Wolfie pulled out his Luger.

"Halt!" We heard a Deutsche shout, and a shot rang out over our heads. One of our patrols must have seen the drop too.

Just then someone else ducked into our hiding place and tripped over us, and Wolfie and I threw our bodies on him pressing him into the earth so that he couldn't move. I grabbed his pistol and tucked it into the back of my pants.

Wolfie put his hand over the person's mouth. "We won't hurt you."

After two minutes of gunfire, our boys all veered off to the right and ran deeper into the woods. The person beneath us stopped struggling, and so we eased our hold on him. However, as I lifted my hand from the back of his neck, I knocked off his cap. The moon once more showed its face casting a light onto the golden hair of our captive as it fell around his shoulders. He struggled to grab for his cap, but not before I saw—her face.

"Lorelei?"

"Michael?"

"*Ach . . . Du?*" Wolfie said under his breath.

We lay barely breathing in the gully, hoping no one would discover us, both of us holding Lorelei down. But the tighter I held her the more she struggled to get free. "Be still," I whispered.

"And be a coward like you?"

"*Halte die Schnauze,*" Wolfie hissed at her.

"My *vader* and my *broer* are out there!" she said softly.

"Your papa would want you to live."

"You know nothing about my vader."

"What would you have us do?"

"Kill Hitler!"

Wolfie and I just stared at her.

The moon peeked out from behind a dark cloud, and Wolfie pointed out into the open field. Ten metres from us, all tangled up in a white parachute, lay one of the crates that had been dropped from the plane.

At that moment we heard noises off to our left. Wolfie peeked from behind the boulder and his head snapped back. He held up two fingers, then one finger, and mouthed the words: "Two of them and one of ours."

I took a stealthy look and there were indeed three people running through the trees toward us. I pulled out Lorelei's pistol. "Wolfie, cover me." I lay on the ground and slithered out from behind the rock to take cover behind a nearby tree. I motioned for Wolfie to hang onto Lorelei. Now we all had a good view of the three people running towards us. One of them, a tall skinny man, was returning fire with our guy, who looked more like a child than a soldier. Meanwhile, our guy was gaining on the smaller Belgian, so I rolled onto my side and fired two shots over their heads. Startled, our guy lost his footing and slid to the ground, giving the smaller man a greater distance between them. The tall man paused for a moment, uncertain where the shots had come from, then turned and ran the other way, deep into the woods.

The small Belgian kept coming in our direction, and as he ran past us, Lorelei called out "Jasper!"

He turned just as Wolfie let her go, and she ran toward him. Then seeing us, he raised his pistol.

"*Non!*" she shouted. As he hesitated, she grabbed his hand, and together they ran off into the woods.

Our guy scrambled up and fired after them but missed.

Wolfie crawled up beside me. "That's Fred!" he whispered.

"*Ja*, the boy that nearly blew your head off!" We grinned as we watched Fred getting to his feet and begin running back the way he had come.

"What do we do now, Michael?"

"We become heroes."

"And how do we do that?"

"We grab that crate of guns and bring them to the Zugführer—then I guess he'll let the Kommandeurs know about our heroic effort. Then they'll tell Standartenführer Kurt Meyer."

"That's not going to work ... Why are you looking at me like that?"

But I was looking past Wolfie where I could see another Belgian running towards Fred. We saw Fred turn, slip on the wet ground and fall backwards. Wolfie and I took aim, but we were too late. The Belgian shot Fred in the chest and then escaped. We sprang up and ran to help Fred. But the Belgian's bullet had torn Fred's chest open, and blood was spewing from the wound.

"Did I shoot him?" Fred asked, his voice very faint.

"*Ja*. You shot at him." I pulled off my jacket and tried to stop Fred's bleeding by pressing it against his wound.

"Am I going to die?" Fred's breath came in gasps. He began to spit up blood.

"*Nein*. Everything will be all right," I said.

"I'm sor ..." Fred's head fell to the side.

"Michael— he's dead. We have to get out of here."

"We can't just leave him." I removed Fred's glasses and tucked them into my pocket. I took the Belgian's bicycle pump pistol. I hadn't seen one before, had only heard that these pistols were silent when fired. Then just as I bent down to take Fred into my arms, a bullet whizzed past us. We dropped to the ground and quickly crawled behind a tree. I peered out from behind the trunk and held up three fingers.

Wolfie nodded and we both rolled onto our bellies. I checked the chamber of Lorelei's pistol—four bullets left. The three men retreated, and as Wolfie and I sprang to our feet and pursued them, the rain began again. Through the trees we ran, taking cover whenever a bullet came our way. At last they disappeared in the direction of the town, and we too turned and made our way back to where Fred lay, the rain falling on his upturned face. I picked him up. He felt so small in my arms.

"Michael," Wolfie said. "I know there's guns in that crate and I'm going to get them."

"Wait!" But he had already run off.

When he came back ten minutes later, Wolfie handed me three Sten guns. I slipped their straps over my shoulder while he dumped some boxes of bullets and a radio into the bike's saddlebags. Then we laid Fred over the bike seat and pushed the motorbike back to camp in the pouring rain.

Two days after we reported to the Kompanieführers, we were escorted to see our commander, Standartenführer Meyer. We stood at attention as he sat at his desk with his hands clasped behind his head. He was not pleased with us for stealing the bike but chose to overlook our "borrowing" it.

"So," he said, "you boys mean to tell me that Fred Müller alerted you two to the airplane drop, he shot one of the Belgian Resistance and sacrificed his life to save you two? Is that what you are telling me, Wolfgang von Vogel and Michael Boii—that he sacrificed himself—and because of him, you two were able to prevent the Resistance from collecting the guns?"

I kept a stony stare on Meyer. "*Ja.*"

"And you think he should get a medal for his bravery?"

Wolfie stepped forward. "*Jawohl*, Standartenführer. We think he should. His mutti would be proud of him."

The next week we had a small ceremony where Fred was awarded a posthumous Iron Cross 2nd-class medal for outstanding bravery in combat.

After the ceremony, the weeks passed more slowly, and Wolfie and I stayed on our best behaviour. News finally arrived that we would be leaving this place. Beverloo had become home to us during our nine months of training, but we were itching to get out of training school.

I took one last look around our room, knowing I would never see the place again. We had grown from boys into soldiers and had formed strong bonds with our comrades. I had even stopped thinking so much about home, Mama and my dead siblings.

Now we were all excited about being redeployed near the city of Caen. "Wolfie, do you have everything?"

"*Ja.* Did you bring your bicycle pump pistol?"

I went back into the room and reached to the back of the top shelf in my locker. "Do you think Lorelei was captured?" I asked him.

"Her? *Ach nein!*"

We lined up behind the Opel Blitz truck, and Strauss reached down for Wolfie's arm to pull him up. "Here, let me help you, Fräulein."

"Very funny."

Once on the truck Wolfie reached for my arm, and both he and Strauss hoisted me aboard so fast that I went sailing through the air. "Thanks a lot," I said after I smacked against the wooden slats of the truck.

As the truck rumbled along the streets, the gearbox making a grinding sound whenever the driver changed gears, we all lurched back and forth. I peered out at the passing scenery. The trees in the forest where Fred had died were bursting their buds and unravelling their soft green April leaves. Soon we were driving through Balda, the town where Wolfie and I had met Lorelei and her sister.

Wolfie cinched his belt. "*Ach*, they don't feed us enough." Then he looked up and pointed to a group of Belgians who were standing by the small bookstore. "Michael, look."

"It's Lorelei!" I said, half under my breath.

Wolfie elbowed me in the side.

For a brief moment her eyes met mine. I raised my hand to wave at her but quickly stopped the gesture. That was the last time I saw her. But her words still rang in my ears. "*Kill Hitler.*"

15

Battle

— JUNE 1944 —

℗

BY THE BEGINNING OF JUNE we had been in France for almost two months, where we had trained a great deal in the area of Bernay-Orbec-Vimoutiers about 50 to 70 kilometres southeast of Caen. We knew the area like our own town. Every hiding place and every shooting vantage point we had sought out. Our comrades were excited, wanting to get into the battle, and that excitement rubbed off on Wolfie and me. But in the early hours of Tuesday, June 6, a lot of confusion was spreading through our camp, and the commanders seemed on edge.

"Wolfie, you awake?" I whispered.

"*Ja.*" He said.

"What's going on out there?" I lifted my covers and sat on the edge of my bed.

Wolfie jumped off his bunk. "I'm not sure, maybe RAF paratroopers have landed?"

Some of the other boys who were now stirring, said, "*Ja*, that's probably it."

Joop said, "Those Tommies will feel like real dummies once we get to them."

As I climbed out of bed, Unterscharführer Eric Koch came running into the bunkhouse and shouted, "It's official—the enemy has landed."

We all stopped what we were doing. Wolfie slapped me on the back. "This is it."

I turned to him. "*Ja*."

Like the trained soldiers we had become, we swarmed to collect our gear, the same way ants would retrieve their eggs when the nest has been disturbed. I strapped on my supply belt, secured my ammunition pouch and took a quick look in my field pouch, rearranging my wire cutters that I had taken from the garage, pointing them down. I adjusted my gas mask and blanket, along with the rest of my gear.

Once we received our orders to deploy to the assembly area in Bernay-Lisieux-Vimoutiers, our excitement was hard to contain. But as we marched along the road southwest of Caen, Wolfie and I didn't exchange a single word. It was windy. The rain came and went, and our heavy gear slowed our pace.

"Cover!" yelled our Unterscharführer Koch, and we all plunged into the bushes as the Mosquito fighter-bombers dove towards us.

But they weren't trying to get us. I raised my head and pointed. "Look, it's that bridge ..."

"Michael, keep your head down!" Wolfie screamed.

An explosion shook the ground, dirt spewed up, some falling on our helmets with sharp pinging noises. At the head of our column Standartenführer Panzermeyer, as we had now nicknamed him, leapt out of his VW jeep moments before a bomb demolished it.

Wolfie scrambled up and so did the rest of the boys. "*Ach,* look at Meyer's jeep!"

But a grain of dirt had worked its way into my eye, and I stayed sitting on the ground, sucking my finger clean and poking at my eye, trying to dislodge the dirt. No matter what I did, I could not get it out.

"Good thing they missed the bridge," Wolfie said. "What's the matter with your eye?"

"On your feet!" Koch yelled.

We marched on, but we were increasingly slowed down by the attacks of the fighter-bombers and had to dive into the ditches and bushes each time they appeared overhead. Around noon the rain let up. The clouds were moving as if they were in a hurry, hiding the sun and only allowing it out briefly to warm us. The farms we passed reminded me of home, despite the fact that the fields were cratered, the barns and houses blown apart.

All the small towns we passed through were on fire, and the roads in and out of them were clogged with fleeing civilians along with burned buses, trucks and tanks, all in bizarre twisted shapes. The smoke irritated my eye even more. Along the roadside, dead soldiers lay with their eyes and mouths gaping, their bodies torn open and their guns still at their sides. We began picking up the dead and draping their bodies over the jeeps. The wounded cried out for help, and we tended to them the best we could, although the only thing we could do for now was put them on the tanks to take them with us.

For the rest of the march, the grain of dirt continued to scratch and embed itself deeper and deeper into my eye. With every step we took, and every small town we passed, the not knowing of what lay ahead made me hyper-aware and frightened. I tried to swallow my nervousness.

We had stopped in a small town to rest when we heard another squadron of fighter-bombers overhead. I grabbed Wolfie and together we ran for cover. "Stay alert!" I yelled at him over the sound of the strafing. We pressed up against the wall of a small house. Around us we could see our soldiers running, trying to take cover. I saw bullets hit Sugar Boy, saw his back arch, his arms rise, and disbelief fraught with anguish flood over his face. He fell to his knees and hit the ground as more bullets riddled his body. We also dropped to the ground and aimed our light automatic rifles at the planes, but the sun blinded me, and my eye wept from the grain of sand in it.

Wolfie shouted. "Stay down, Wildmann!"

I looked in the direction that Wolfie was waving his rifle, and without thinking I ran in a crouched position, with my rifle pointing halfway to the sky. A fast-approaching plane released bullets that struck the ground beside me. I yelled at Wildmann, who stood shooting at the plane. "Get down!" I ran at him with everything I had and tackled him. We both fell to the ground and just in time rolled into the bushes. "You could have died, Wildmann."

He sobbed, "Sugar Boy . . ."

My eye wept.

It was our baptism by fire and it was nothing short of a blood bath. We were all in disbelief. No one said a word. Three of our boys were dead and twelve wounded, and we couldn't find two of our comrades.

Once we had regrouped, we saw that Wildmann was marching in front of us with his head down. After a long while he wiped his nose with the back of his hand and turned to look back at me. His face was covered in dirt, and two tear streaks ran down his cheeks like lines drawn in sand. "Do you know where we're going, Michael?"

"*Ja*. It's a small village called Missy." I handed him a piece of chocolate. "Here. Eat this. It'll make you feel better."

"*Nein, danke*," he said. "He died for our Führer," he mumbled then lowered his head again and marched on.

Wolfie marched beside me, his rifle slung over his shoulder. He lit two cigarettes and handed one to me. He took a long drag on his own, then exhaled. "That was brave of you to save Wildmann like that. You could have been killed."

"Didn't think about it." I punched Wolfie in the arm. "I would do the same for you."

"*Ja.*"

By nightfall when we set up camp in the woods southeast of Missy, the grain of dirt had finally worked its way out of my weeping eye.

"Listen up, men." Unterscharführer Koch pulled out a map.

The Joop brothers stood beside Strauss, Koch and Hans. Wolfie and Wildmann were sitting with their backs against a tree, trying to sleep. I bent down and grabbed Wolfie's shoulder. "Wake up."

"Everyone gather round." Unterscharführer Koch shone his flashlight on the map, and we listened intently to what he had to say. "We'll be marching to the railroad line at Noyers. That's right here," he said, tapping the map. "That's where we'll take up our positions. From there we will await further orders."

At 2300 hours we finally arrived in Noyers. The night air was cold. There was radio silence so no one was sure what was to come because Panzermeyer wasn't with us, having driven to Caen. We rested as best we could, but at 0300 hours on June 7, Unterscharführer Koch received our new orders. We all gathered round, and once more he pulled out his map. "Our orders are to defend the railway line between Bayeux and Caen. There are a number of small villages all around this airfield." He called them out: "Bretteville, Rots, Authie, Buron, Cambers and Cussy. Along with the rest of the divisions we will set up a defence perimeter." He started to fold his map, then added, "It is our job now to push the fish back into the sea."

We all looked at one another. Why hadn't we been sent into action sooner? I wondered.

"The enemy is advancing and is fighting to get inland. Our goal is to stop them at Buron. It's only a kilometre-and-a-half north-west from here." He reopened his map and pointed. "Here!" And with that, he rolled it up and put it into his coat pocket. "Collect your gear. We leave in five minutes."

Wolfie turned to me. "Tommies, I bet."

Koch, overhearing him, corrected him. "Canadians."

When we arrived at Buron at first light, we were ordered to dig in just outside the village, but Panzermeyer had sent orders that we were to hold our fire. After an hour or so we could see the Canadians and their Sherman tanks advancing in the distance, rumbling across the fields toward us like a herd of metal dinosaurs.

They'll be easy pickings, I thought, and we waited like wolves for our prey. Once they crossed the road between Bayeux and Caen, we would pounce.

Wolfie lay beside me in the tall grass. We had stuck branches and weeds on our helmets for camouflage. Our tanks and 88mm guns were hidden in the hedgerows, and they too were adorned with branches and weeds. Wolfie pointed at the Canadians. "The poor bastards."

I nodded. They had no idea that we were waiting for them. My heart raced. I looked up. The sky was clear now, and in my head I repeated the words, "Wait, wait . . ."

Unterscharführer Koch who lay beside the Joop twins shouted, "Ready!" and then signalled . . .

Our camouflaged Panzer IVs began moving forward, looking like rolling bushes. I was glad not to be inside one of them. I preferred to walk beside or behind them. Earlier that morning in the fields, I had watched as a Sherman tank was struck by the 75mm gun that was mounted on one of our Panther Panzers. The tank crew had emerged out of the turret, screaming. One by one they came out, half of them on fire and the others mowed down by our gunfire. The Shermans were no match for our Panther Panzers.

They were called "Ronsons" because they went on fire so easily.

As the battle continued, there was no rest for us. Every bone in my body felt like lead. I was beyond exhausted, the constant air strikes being relentless. The fighting never let up throughout the day and continued into the night. The Canadians were far more ruthless and fierce than we had expected. During the night, and once we were inside the village of Buron approximately four kilometres north of the airfield, we quickly realized that the Canadians and now the British had made it through our defences, and almost every village in the area, including Buron, was under attack.

Wolfie, Strauss, Wildmann and I crouched in the corner of the stone wall that surrounded the back garden of an old grey house, while Unterscharführer Koch, Hans and the Joop brothers holed up in a house just around the corner. I put my hand up to my mouth, signalling the boys to stay quiet. As I peered over the wall, a black cat jumped up from the other side. Startled, I fell back, and the cat meowed. Wildmann had to put both hands over his mouth so that he wouldn't laugh out loud. We tried shooing the cat away, but instead of being scared of us, it sat on the wall and continued meowing.

Wolfie crouched tight up beside me, and I whispered to him, "There's no one in the garden next to us. We have to jump over the wall." I motioned for the other boys to follow me. I jumped safely over to the other side, but as the boys followed, a shot rang out, and a bullet whizzed past my head. The cat scurried off.

Wolfie pointed to a large tree beside a gate at the other side of the garden. He leaned over to whisper, "If one of us climbs that tree, maybe we can see where they are."

I crouched low, ran to the tree and managed to climb it without being spotted.

Signalling again for the others to come over, I jumped down. "Okay, there's two of them across the street behind a garden shed. They can't see us from back there, so we can take them."

Strauss, leading with his rifle, said, "I'll go first."

"Wolfie, you go second," I said. "Then you, Wildmann, and I'll be behind you."

Gunfire erupted as soon as Strauss kicked the gate open. He hit the ground and rolled over behind some bushes in front of the stone wall, but he was now on the same side as the Canadians. One after the other, we slipped out of the gate and ran for the bushes, taking cover between the shrubs and the wall.

I motioned for Wolfie and Strauss to go left. "Stay tight to the wall." I put my mouth close to Wildmann's ear. "We'll go to the right," I whispered. "When I give the signal, shoot."

More gunfire was exchanged, but the Canadians soon knew we had them surrounded, and so they came out from behind the garden shed with their hands up.

"*Schweinehunde!*" Wildmann yelled and raised his rifle to shoot them.

"*Nein!*" I shouted as I pushed his gun down. "*Nein!* They are not to be shot. We'll take them to headquarters at the Abbaye d'Ardenne. That's where Sturmbannführer Waldmüller and Panzermeyer told us to take them."

"But they killed Sugar Boy!"

"Those guys in the plane killed him, not these guys."

Along with some other guys from our regiment who also had prisoners, we made our way back to the Abbaye with our Canadians. We were just outside of Authie and still a couple of kilometres from the Abbaye when one of the Canadians said to me in broken Deutsch, "You're all just kids!"

"You speak Deutsch?" I said.

"My mother came from Dresden. She went to Nova Scotia with her parents in 1915."

Wolfie pulled out a cigarette, lit it, and handed it to him.

He took it and pointed to his coat pocket. "May I?"

I nodded.

He pulled out a packet of cigarettes and handed them to Wolfie.

The other prisoner snarled, "Fucking pussy Nazi kraut." All I understood was "Nazi kraut," and thinking that perhaps he wanted some food, I shook my head. "*Kein Kraut.*"

Wolfie took two cigarettes from the Canadian's packet and lit them, handing one to me.

"*Danke,*" I said to the Canadian.

Wolfie handed him his smokes back.

We arrived from Authie at the Abbaye in mid-evening and handed our prisoners over to the Feldgendarmerie, where they joined over 130 other Canadian prisoners who stood in the courtyard. Wolfie said goodbye to the Canadians, and I shook the Deutsch-Canadian's hand, but the other man turned his back on me.

"Michael, what do you think the military police will do to them?"

"Send them to a POW camp."

We made our way through the orchard where our wounded and the enemy soldiers lay side by side, being attended to by our medics. The groans and cries of the wounded faded the further we walked away. We crossed the street to join the rest of the boys who had gathered around a fire where a couple of guys were cooking soup. I sat beside a young soldier I hadn't seen before. "What's your name?" I asked.

"Jan Jesionek," he said as he continued slurping his soup.

Wolfie gave him a light punch in the arm. "Jesionek? *Ach*, Polish SS?"

"*Ja.*" Jesionek finished his soup and started back towards the Abbaye.

I grabbed my gear. "It's getting late, guys. We better get back to our battalion and report to Sturmbannführer Waldmüller."

Wildmann reached into his pocket, pulled out some chocolate and took a bite. With a mouth full of chocolate, he turned and said, "Guess the fish didn't get pushed back into the sea today."

As we walked down the street, I turned to look back at the Abbaye.

It had two high towers, a great vantage point for Meyer to observe the battles as they unfolded. Suddenly we heard a series of shots. Wolfie grabbed my arm. Wildmann stopped in his tracks and turned to face us.

I looked back at the Abbaye. *Gunshots!* But before I could say anything we heard six more shots being fired. They all came from the Abbaye. "*Ach, Gott . . .*"

Wildmann looked from Wolfie to me. "What? What is it?"

"They shot our prisoners," I said.

"*Nein!*" cried Wildmann.

"We have to go back," I said.

"To the Abbaye?" said Wolfie.

"*Ja!*" I began to turn around.

Wolfie tightened his grip on my arm. "There is nothing we can do."

A shiver ran through my body and I felt ill. Off in the distance across the fields I could see the Sherman tanks still burning. Tracer bullets streaked the evening sky with their green and blue light, and to the west we could hear artillery shells exploding, and yet the sounds of war were muffled by my thoughts of home. I took a deep breath and closed my eyes.

16

Wolfie

— JUNE 1944 —

∽

WOLFIE SAT BESIDE ME ON the back of one of the Panther Panzers as it headed west in the growing darkness along the old N-Thirteen Road. Our section had been ordered to accompany the Panzers and recapture the village of Bretteville. The rest of our division had moved on to Cussy.

"Did you hear that Panzermeyer is up ahead, Michael?" Wolfie said. "He's riding in a motorcycle sidecar driven by Sturmmann Schmidt."

I took a drag of my cigarette, wondering if Panzermeyer had ordered the shooting of the prisoners at the Abbaye d'Ardenne.

Wolfie's hand trembled as he drew on his cigarette. "Hope the next battle is as quick as Rots was."

"*Ja*. We blitzed through that one all right." I straightened my helmet.

"Hope it's as easy when we get to Bretteville," he said. He was silent for a minute or two before adding, "Wonder how much longer till we get there?"

Trees lined either side of the road. Beyond the trees I could see untended fields, and I wondered where all the farmers had gone. I leaned out and craned my neck to see around the turret of the Panther.

"Wolfie." I pointed at the silhouette of the church spire straight ahead. "That's Bretteville." I took another long drag of my cigarette, exhaled, and let my thoughts stray back to Herr Zimmermann's farm and our running through the fields playing the hunter and the hunted. I could hear his voice now. "Nothing good will come from this war, boy."

Wolfie slapped my leg. "Come on, Michael. Time to jump off."

Again we regrouped, and after Panzermeyer had given us his orders, we split into our sections ready to retake Bretteville. I grabbed my Panzerfaust and secured my fire belt by tucking the last seven inches of it into the belt of my jacket so it would not fall off when I had to run. My section assembled on La Reu Street, taking cover against a high brick wall that encircled a grand old house. I took a gulp of water from my canteen, hoping to settle my stomach. The sky was beginning to cloud over from the north, but the moon was still sailing high in the sky, and its light fell onto a vine with sweet-smelling flowers climbing over the wall. I put my hand out to touch it.

Wolfie grabbed my shoulder, almost knocking me to the ground. "Michael, what are you doing? Come on!"

Before I could get my bearings, I was running down a side street with my section and Unterscharführer Koch was leading the way. Around us, all the buildings were burning, and the smoke bit at my sore eye and made it difficult to see and breathe. But we ran on, taking cover only when a shell exploded near us. Up ahead, enemy planes were constantly dropping bombs, and every so often

Unterscharführer Koch would shout, "Take cover!" and we would all dive into doorways or behind garden walls. After a while I stopped reacting to the explosions, but the Joop twins were jumpy whenever the ground around us shuddered from a violent blast. I stepped between them, trying to ease their fear. "It'll be over soon." But the truth was, whenever the ground shook, I too tensed up and felt scared.

Staying close to house walls and leading with our rifles, we came at last to the main road just as one of our Panther tanks came around the corner up ahead. Wolfie grabbed my arm and pointed. A Sherman tank had entered the street from the other direction, heading straight for our tank, and we saw its gun swivel around to point directly at our Panther.

"Why isn't it firing?" I said under my breath.

We took cover in the nearest house where Wolfie and I crouched by a window, riveted by what was unfolding. I reached for my Panzerfaust and placed the end of it in the crook of my arm. Wolfie pulled out a hand grenade, ready for the barrage of gunfire that would surely ensue from the infantry who were following the Sherman. I made sure no one was standing behind me. I had a perfect shot, and when I pulled the pin, the sight guide popped up, releasing the lever at the same time. The tank was still about thirty metres in the distance, and I took careful aim, waiting until I was sure it was within range. The other boys had their rifles ready. I pressed the lever.

The blast tore through the Sherman like a warm knife through butter, and the men running behind the tank scattered, looking for cover. The Sherman's turret popped open, one crewman spilled out, another followed, his clothes on fire and his right leg smoldering where it had been blown off just above the knee.

I looked away and vomited.

When I looked again, I saw the Panther had turned to its right just as another Sherman came around the corner from the left, but now the Panther was stuck because the street was too narrow for it to turn around. We could see it was trying to swing its gun around, but there was not enough room, and when it fired, it only blasted a house to smithereens. That's when the Sherman fired on the Panther. It heaved into the air with the blast, fire spewing from the turret, and a second later it exploded. And there it sat amongst rubble, blocking the street, all of its crew dead inside.

We withdrew from the house and gave chase down a narrow street, only to see two Sherman tanks chasing another Panther. We ran over to the next street, ducking bullets and mortar fire. There we saw one of the Sherman tanks blasting one round after the other at the Panther. Strauss had a perfect shot. He aimed his Panzerfaust and fired at the Sherman. It burst into flames.

By now the town was ablaze, casting flickering light on the houses. We continued to fight our way through the streets, but finally we were coming under constant rifle fire, and we couldn't tell where it was coming from. Unterscharführer Koch put his hand up, signalling for us not to move. He pointed to a very large, white, three-storey villa with six small dormers projecting from its black slate roof. "There," he mouthed, pointing to one of the dormers.

I pulled my helmet strap tighter.

He pointed at Wildmann, one of the Joop twins and me. Then he signalled that we should go around the left flank of the house. Then he pointed at Heinz and Wolfie and mouthed, "Go right."

Koch put his hand on the other Joop twin's shoulder. "You and Strauss, you're with me." He pointed at our necks, indicating that all of us were to hand our fire belts for the machine gun to Strauss, who would provide cover for the five of us.

Before Koch began setting up the MG42, the beast, as we had named it, he whispered, "When I see that you're all in the clear, we'll make our way to the front of the house."

Wildmann took off his helmet to scratch his head.

I reached for his helmet and plunked it back on his head. "Keep your helmet on your ugly *Schädel*," I whispered.

The Joop twins embraced.

Strauss got into position, lying beside Koch, ready to feed the beast. I took a deep breath, bent down and smeared some mud on my face. Then I studied the house and its gardens. The path winding between the chestnut trees would provide the best cover from anyone in the upper floors of the house, I thought. We waited. There was no movement in the house or its grounds.

Wolfie stood close to me and leaned in. "Our Panthers could blast that house to smithereens."

I tensed up and clenched my teeth. By now we both knew the streets were too narrow for the Panthers to manoeuvre.

He patted me on the back. "See you in the house, Michael."

I took a deep breath, "You bet," then turned to Joop. "Ready?"

"*Ja.*"

"You, Wildmann?"

"Ready!"

Unterscharführer Koch gave the awaited signal, and we all ran, zigzagging between the rows of chestnut trees. No one shot at us.

Wildmann yelled, "This is easier than I thought."

I turned to look at him just as gunfire erupted all around us. Dirt and debris flew as the bullets struck the ground.

"Hit the—" I hollered, but before I finished, Joop, Wildmann, and I had already hit the ground and rolled under the cover of a laurel hedge. Grenades exploded to our left and right, followed by more gunfire.

Wildmann managed to get himself up and squat behind one of the trees. He shouted, "Michael, can you see where that gunfire is coming from?"

"*Nein!*" It was definitely coming from the house, but I couldn't see which window it was coming from. I caught a glimpse of Wolfie as he disappeared around the other side of the house.

Wildmann shouted, "Joop!"

"Follow me!" I shouted. I fired a few rounds at one of the top windows of the house, then ran as fast as I could towards a woodpile neatly stacked close to the house. Several bullets just missed me. I slid behind the pile with Wildmann sliding in right behind me. We were scrambling to sit up when, with a big thump, a dead Canadian soldier landed across our legs, obviously having fallen from the window above us. As we pushed him off us, blood trickled from his mouth. Koch and the boys had done their work well with the covering fire.

"*Verdamnit.* That was close." Wildmann crouched against the woodpile, trying to disappear into it.

"Where's Joop?"

Wildmann pointed.

Joop lay in a fetal position under the chestnut trees, twenty metres from us.

"Joop, get up! Run!" Wildmann and I shouted.

Bullets ripped into the ground around him, but he wouldn't move.

Wildmann grabbed my arm. "*Scheisse!* Michael, we can't leave him there!"

For a split second the world slowed down. I noticed a little red tricycle lying on its side on the garden path, all twisted up from bullets hitting it. All I heard was the squeaking of its rear wheel as it spun gently in the wind.

Wildmann elbowed me in the ribs. "We have to do something."

"I know, I know." I shouted, "Get up, Joop!" Then I shot to my feet and ran to him as bullets whizzed over me. I grabbed him by the scruff of his neck and began dragging him back to the wood-pile. I wanted to slug him. "What's wrong with you? You almost got us all killed! Pull it together!"

He looked up at me, unable to say a word.

"Wildmann, we have to get into the house." I pointed to the side of the house. "There's the cellar door . . . see it?"

Thin clouds had drifted across the moon, but there was still enough light to see the few steps leading down to a wooden door.

"*Ja*," he said. He leaned down, shook Joop and shouted into his face. "Are you with us . . . ? Michael, what are we going to do with him?"

I tried again to get through to him. "Joop, either snap out of it or stay here! Do you understand?" He just stared vacantly into the distance.

"We don't have a choice," I told Wildmann as I bundled two grenades together. "The others are counting on us. We have to leave him." I looked down at Joop and straightened his helmet. "Okay, Wildmann, on three we'll run, kick the cellar door in, throw the grenades, and once they explode, we'll go into the house. Ready?"

Wildmann nodded.

"Remember—wait for the explosions."

I took a deep breath and together we counted. "One, two, three!"

We ran as fast as we could towards the door.

I kicked the door in.

We both stood tight to the house on either side of the door.

I unscrewed the bottom sticks, pulled the cords and threw the grenades.

The next thing we heard was a bloodcurdling scream as Joop ran straight past us through the door opening and right into the explosion. He was thrown backwards from the blast, landing not two feet from us. He bounced to his feet with a smile on his face, not realizing that his arm had been blown off, and shrapnel had torn into his chest. He teetered there for a few seconds and then fell to the ground, convulsing just as Frau Zimmermann had on that barn floor.

"*Scheisse!*"

The air was still and that sour taste that lingered in the back of my throat lurched forward. I gulped to force the vile contents of my stomach back down.

"He's still alive," Wildmann said, his voice filled with horror.

"I know . . . We have to go in!" I stared at Joop. In the distance the

squealing of the tricycle wheel screamed in my ears. "No time."
And I thought, *once this house is secured, we'll come back and help
him.*

"*Nein!* We have to help him!"

"There's no time, Wildmann!"

My ears were ringing.

At that moment I heard what I thought was Unterscharführer
Koch and Strauss kicking in the front door, and I hoped that Wolfie
and Heinz had made it to the back of the house. I pushed Wildmann into the room that lay in ruins, and through a hole blown
through the ceiling I could see some of our guys were already on
the first floor.

I pointed. "We have to get up those stairs . . . what's left of them."

As we were about to clamber up what remained of the staircase,
a soldier appeared at the top of them and turned his gun toward
Wildmann. But Wildmann just stood frozen, staring up the barrel
of the gun. I pointed my rifle, clenched my teeth, and shot the soldier dead. His body tumbled down the stairs, landing at our feet.

"Don't just stand there, Wildmann!" I yelled. "Move it!" I stepped
over the dead body, held onto the tattered banister, scrambled up
the stairs, and reached my hand down to pull Wildmann up beside
me. We rushed up the stairs.

At the top Koch pushed past us. "We have to get to the top floor.
Where's . . . ?"

More gunfire erupted around us, drowning out his question. The
firing was coming from two doorways. Strauss sprayed the first
with bullets while Wildmann and Joop's twin fired into the other. I
spotted a Canadian coming down a staircase that led to the upper
floors, and I split from the group to chase him to the end of the
long hallway. When he disappeared around a corner, I followed
close behind, trying to get a shot at him.

"Eat this, you fucking Nazi!" he yelled, firing at me before he
ducked into a doorway. I followed him, still shooting, and managed

to slide behind a huge old oak desk. That's when I realized we were in the library of this villa, and as the Canadian fired at me and I at him, our bullets were tearing up the books that had been placed so neatly on the shelves. The firing stopped for a moment, and hoping that he was reloading his gun, I sprang to my feet and shot him. He fell to the floor, landing on top of a pile of old books. The room was silent. And so was the house.

"Everyone out!" Koch poked his head into the library, gesturing with his rifle. He glanced at the dead soldier. "Let's go!"

"Did we take the house?"

"Let's go!"

As the other guys ran past the doorway, I asked, "Where are Wolfie and Heinz?"

"We're it."

"What do you mean, *we're it*?"

"They didn't make it." Koch pushed me forward. "Move!"

"What happened?"

"Canadians are coming!"

I went to turn back. "*Nein!* I have to get Wolfie!"

Koch pushed me harder. "Move it! Now!"

"*Nein!*" I turned to Wildmann. "Where's Wolfie?"

Koch grabbed Wildmann by the scruff off the neck and pushed him. "Move it!" Then he thrust his rifle into my back. "Move it, Boii!"

I spun around and punched him in the face. He fell to the ground. "I'm not leaving without Wolfie! Understand?"

Rubbing his jaw, Koch shot to his feet, gave me a stern look, and realizing it was useless, continued down the stairs.

Strauss grabbed my arm. "We'll come back for him."

"Let me go!" My heart was racing. Why was Koch not telling me what had happened to Wolfie? Strauss pushed me along the hall, down the stairs and out of the house. Gunfire erupted around us again.

"Take cover!" Koch shouted.

As soon as Strauss let go of me, I ran back into the house and scrambled up the stairs. As I came around the corner by the library, I stopped dead in my tracks. Wolfie and Heinz had their hands on their heads and behind them were three Canadians with their guns trained on them.

Wolfie shouted, "Michael!"

I heard the shot and fell to the ground, my rifle landing beside me. I reached out toward it . . .

"Boii! Boii! . . . Michael!"

Someone was calling my name and I felt a smack across my face. "Boii . . . I thought you were a goner."

A large blurry figure stood over me. "Strauss . . .? What happened?" I was sitting propped up against a tree. My head throbbed.

"A bullet went straight through your helmet. Lucky for you it just grazed your thick *Schädel*."

"Where is everyone?" I tried to stand, only to wobble back down. "Where's Wolfie? And Heinz? What happened?"

"We had to pull back."

"What . . ."

"We don't have much time. Are you okay to walk?"

"I think so."

Strauss hoisted me up and handed me my pistol and some bullets. "They took Wolfgang and Heinz with them."

"The Canadians took them? Where are we?"

Strauss handed me more bullets and some grenades. "Not far from our command post. I ran in after the Canadians left the house and carried you here."

I put the bullets in my pocket. "But we had the house—" As I looked around, I could see that Strauss had found good cover for us in a hedgerow.

Strauss shook his head. "We didn't have the house. Koch had us retreat."

"But we have orders . . ."

"We did, but the enemy overran the house and more were coming. Wolfgang and Heinz got up to the third floor, and they were the ones that yelled for us to get out. Guess they could see more soldiers were coming to storm the house, but they couldn't make it out themselves."

I removed my helmet and reached my hand up to the side of my head. I felt caked blood. "But we had orders . . . Why didn't we keep fighting? Is he alive?"

"Koch got scared," said Strauss grinning. "As I said, the Canadians took Wolfgang and Heinz as prisoners. I followed them partway."

"How?"

"Well, after everyone ran outside and you ran back into the house, all hell broke loose. I ran after you. I saw you get shot and I hid, then after they left with Wolfgang and Heinz, I hauled your ass out. We almost didn't make it. They had us surrounded. Koch and the others retreated."

"Joop?"

"We stumbled over him when we ran out . . ."

"Was he still alive? Did you get help for him?"

"Koch ordered Wildmann and the other Joop to take him with us."

"And Koch?"

"One of the Canadians got him."

I stumbled over something and Strauss caught me. "Easy, boy."

I pushed him away. "I'm fine. We have to find them quickly— Wolfie and Heinz!"

"We will."

We headed away from the town by working our way along the hedgerows. Once we came out into the open, I turned back and saw the church in the centre of town being devoured by dancing red flames that seemed to have come straight up from hell.

"The Canadians have managed to hold onto Bretteville." Strauss had pulled out two cigarettes, lit one and went to hand it to me.

I shook my head. "*Nein.*" I still didn't feel well enough to handle a cigarette.

He nodded, put it into his mouth and put the unlit cigarette back into the pack. He gave me a slight smile.

"So where did they take Wolfie and Heinz?"

"They were going in the direction of Putot-en-Bessin. It's only about twenty-five minutes from here."

"Do you have a map?"

"It's straight ahead. We have to hurry." He set off across the grain field beside us. The grain was tall enough that it gave us cover, and we were helped further by the darkness of the night. We stopped at a small creek, and Strauss whispered in my ear. "This is as far as I got. We're in enemy territory now."

As we began scouting the area, there was a break in the clouds, and for a few minutes the moon provided some light.

"What makes you think that they're on their way to Putot, anyway?"

"I heard one of the Canadians say, 'Putot-en-Bessin.'"

"They can't be that far ahead of us, can they?"

"*Nein.*" Strauss pointed at an old farmhouse. "We'll cut across the field and go through that farmyard. We'll probably catch up to them."

"Better if we skirt around the house."

"Why?"

"Some of the Canadians could be holed up in there, and if we have to shoot, we'll draw the attention of the rest of them."

Strauss nodded.

"We should be able to see the main road from that shed—see, by the wall." The house and farmyard were surrounded by a stone wall, and an old garden shed stood up against the wall on the far side. We ran across a narrow field, and I jumped over the wall. As

Strauss went to jump over it, a phosphorescent flare lit up the sky.

"Get down!"

Strauss stayed perched on the wall like some enormous ostrich on a wire. The moon disappeared, and the flare burned out, leaving the dark to engulf us.

"Strauss!" I reached up and pulled him off the wall. He landed with a thunk on his side, and as he hit the ground, his rifle accidentally fired.

"*Ach, Scheisse.*"

Strauss pulled his rifle close to his body.

"You okay?"

"*Ja-ja.*" He groaned.

"Stay down." We lay there for perhaps thirty seconds, hoping that the darkness would conceal us.

"Strauss, we have to get to that shed."

"You go first, Michael. I'll cover you."

"*Nein.* We'll go together. Stay on your belly."

We began to slither across the garden, but when we reached halfway across, I bumped up against something. I stopped.

"What is it?" Strauss whispered.

I reached my hand out to feel the object. It was wet and cold. I quickly pulled my hand back. My gut turned over.

"Michael, what is it?"

The air had taken on a foul smell. I tried going to the left, and again I bumped into something. I reached out, and as I touched it again, I was sure what it was. I pulled my hand back.

"Strauss!" I turned to him just as the night sky lit up with another flare, casting a blue haze over the garden and revealing an earlier slaughter. Corpses and body parts were strewn everywhere. I took a deep breath. We continued crawling. Shots rang out in the distance, then closer to us I heard voices.

"Stay down!"

But Strauss shot to his feet, clutching his side as he laboured to run toward the shed. Footsteps approached closer. I pressed my body into the blood-soaked ground and lay still like the dead around me. I hoped that Strauss would stay still too. Another flare lit the sky, and the Canadians caught a glimpse of him. They fired several shots at him and he responded. I reached for my rifle, but the strap was tangled in the arm of the corpse beside me. Just as the flare burned out, I saw that Strauss was still clutching his side as he crumpled to the ground.

"You cocksucker Nazi piece of shit! Drop your weapon! Come out with your hands up!"

Strauss yelled, "Yes! Yes! No shoot!"

At that moment the moon broke through the clouds again. The scene was not much different from when we had caught the two Canadians in the small town outside Authie. This made me nervous because I knew what had happened to them at the Abbaye d'Ardenne, and I was certain that Wolfie, Heinz, and now Strauss would meet the same fate.

"These milk-baby fucking Nazis are everywhere," one of the soldiers said, and when Strauss stood before him, towering over the Canadians, the Canadian drew his arm back and punched Strauss in the face as hard as he could. Strauss, not even flinching, smiled.

The other soldier reached out a hand. "That's not necessary, Jim."

"Fucking tough guy, eh?" Jim punched Strauss again.

"Jim, that's enough."

Strauss again only smiled and wiped his sleeve across his nose.

Jim spat on the ground and yelled, "Keep your fucking hands in the air! You piece of shit! I'll blow your ugly pussy Nazi head off!"

"Jim!"

"I didn't sign up to save Nazis! This fucking Nazi killed our guys."

The other soldier motioned for Strauss to begin walking, which he did, along the gravelly road that headed in the direction of Putot.

As soon as they left, I carefully untangled my rifle strap from the corpse's arm, then took out the bicycle pump pistol that I had grabbed from the Belgian resistance fighter. I got slowly to my feet and began following the Canadians, hoping they would take Strauss to where Wolfie and Heinz were being held. I knew I had to stay as far back as I could without losing sight of them. As I passed the barn, a cat scurried across my path, then stopped and snarled at me, and I stumbled and fell against the wall. Quickly I slipped into the barn's open doorway. The Canadians stopped, looked behind them, and fired a round of bullets in my direction.

Damned cat, I thought. There was silence for a long time. I stayed in the doorway until I heard their footsteps on the road again. Quietly I set off after them and soon discovered that there was a deep, grass-covered trench running parallel with the road. This was perfect for me because I could walk in the trench without making any noise. We walked for a full twenty minutes, and though I strained to hear, I'm sure not a word passed between Strauss and the Canadians until the nicer Canadian said, "There they are—there by those bushes. You'll soon be rid of your friend."

"Fuck you, Marshall." Jim shoved Strauss. "This piece off shit is no friend of mine."

Marshall laughed. "Hey, if times were different, maybe you two would be playing on the same hockey team!"

"This pussy crap probably doesn't know what hockey is." I could hear Jim slap Strauss across the back of the head. "Eh, asshole?"

Marshall took off his helmet and called out, "Hey, Eddy. Where's Dave and Fish?"

"They went on to Putot," a voice called back. "Looks like you found yourself another Kraut."

I crawled closer but stayed behind some bushes growing in the trench. That's when I saw Wolfie and Heinz sitting on the ground with three or four other soldiers. They were guarded by a single soldier with a rifle. Jim shoved Strauss toward them, and he stumbled and fell to the ground. "A big fuck of a Kraut." Jim kicked Strauss in the ribs. "Get up, you piece of shit."

"Jim!" Marshall helped Strauss up. "This guy's bleeding."

Strauss turned his head in my direction and smiled. I think he knew I had followed them.

"Good!" Jim said. "And what the fuck are you smiling at, eh?"

"That's enough outta you, Jim!" Marshall opened Strauss's jacket. He turned to the other Canadian. "Shit! Eddy, do you have a first aid kit?" Marshall pointed to the ground and helped Strauss to sit down. "What's your name?"

Strauss looked confused, but after a few gestures from Marshall, he understood and said, "Jochen."

Marshall smiled. "I'm Marshall."

Jim aimed his gun at Strauss's head. "What—now you're going to help that fuck stay alive?"

Marshall rose to his feet. "Jim, put your gun away!" A shot rang out and Strauss fell back, still smiling.

Marshall pushed Jim so hard that he fell to the ground too. "You didn't need to do that!"

Some of the prisoners got up, scrambling to help Strauss, but they could see he was dead. Eddy, looking nervous, quickly pointed his rifle at them. "Sit down—now!"

Jim scrambled to his feet and pushed past Marshall. "It ain't like we haven't shot our prisoners before! Just fucking shoot them!"

Marshall went to stop him. "No, Jim—! No ..."

Two shots rang out. Two more Deutsch soldiers fell dead. I couldn't stay hidden any longer. I leapt up, aimed my bicycle pump pistol at the back of Jim's head and fired. The shot made no noise, and all Eddy and Marshall saw was Jim dropping dead at their feet. They both spun around, but I had slipped back into the trench. They shot in my direction, but at that moment the remaining prisoners lunged at them, knocking them to the ground. They stripped Marshall and Eddy of their guns. I scrambled up out of the trench. "Tie them up," I said, "and let's get the hell outta here!" I bent down and took Strauss's tags from around his neck.

17

Revenge

— DECEMBER 1944 —

❦

SIX MONTHS AFTER THE enemy landed in Normandy, our Hitler-jugend SS unit had lost more than half of its boys. Some had good sense and just ran away but most, sadly, were shot, the lucky were wounded, and the unfortunate were killed. There were no more than 10,000 of us left. Our commanders told us that we had fought courageously in Normandy, that we men should feel proud because we are fighting for the Fatherland, but I just thought about all our boys who lay dead. I took no solace in the commanders' praise.

Since the end of the summer we had been officially "strategically retreating," but I felt more as if we were running from the enemy. I didn't care that we were retreating. I just wanted to go home. Death was all around me and there was no escaping it. I wasn't fighting for Deutschland and most certainly not for Adolf Hitler. I was fighting to keep my promise to Mama that Wolfie and I would come back home to her.

In the fall we had been moved back to Deutschland for a few weeks. And I had been more than ready for rest and relaxation, but now it was early in December, and we were back in the line just east of the French-Deutsche border. All around us we could see a skim of ice-coated puddles, and the ground was a mess of frozen mud. The early morning air pricked my face as Wolfie and I walked from the small field kitchen back to our group. We were taking a break from the march to our assembly area near Hollerath. I leaned against a Panzerjäger. It felt icy cold on my back.

Wolfie took a gulp of his coffee, then lit two cigarettes. As he handed one to me, he smiled and said, "Here, Unterscharführer Boii," teasing me about my recent promotion to section leader.

I shrugged. "I can't believe it's December already." I wrapped my scarf round my neck and flipped my coat collar up.

Wolfie tightened his hands around his coffee cup. "And now we're here."

"Where exactly are we?" asked Veit.

Veit, along with Oskar and Bernd, none of them more than fourteen years old, had joined our battalion back in Cologne when thousands of inexperienced recruits—just young kids really—had joined our division, along with a bunch of old men.

Heinz reached for Wolfie's cigarette, took a drag from it, exhaled, and leaned into Veit. "We're in hell," he said, "guarding its gates to keep them open." He handed the cigarette back to Wolfie.

"We're in the Eifel, Veit," I said and stomped my frozen feet on the muddy ground. My boots were covered with brown sludge, and I tried to knock it off by scraping one boot against the other. It didn't work. "We can feel proud about guarding the gates of hell when we held the Falaise gap open," I said.

Wolfie nodded. "I still have some fragments of shrapnel in my back."

At Falaise we had fought with a vengeance, and for our comrades who had died, but by August 16, the 12th SS had been but a skeleton of its former strength—fewer than 400 infantrymen, eleven Panzers and just over a half dozen 88mm anti-tank guns. We had struggled and prevailed in the sweltering heat and the putrid stench of the dead. Thirst, dust, and hunger: nothing had stopped us. We had helped over twenty thousand soldiers of the 7th Army to escape death and worse: the clutches of the enemy.

Wildmann reached for Heinz's coffee. "That airfield in Carpiquet—that's where the fires of hell burned. Remember how the boys screamed . . ." He looked at the ground and shook his head. He handed the coffee back. "Hope to never see one of those hellish flame-thrower tanks again."

We all nodded. Veit crouched to loosen his bootlaces. "My feet are killing me."

Oskar, who looked exhausted, said, "Mine too. When we were in Euskirchen, that's where my feet got blistered. I don't think I can keep my boots on anymore—they're too small."

"You better toughen up," Wolfie told him. "If you think two days of marching is tough, then you might as well call it quits now. Not only are we marching on, but you'll be in your first battle soon enough."

Wildmann took a drag from Heinz's cigarette. "Didn't think we'd still be at war by now."

Wolfie laughed. "Didn't think the four of us—Michael, Heinz, you and me—would still be alive, especially with what happened at Caen."

I put my arm over his shoulder. "Ja." We had lost our hold on Caen, and almost half of our boys were killed there, and some ran home to their muttis. We had fought to keep the Carpiquet airfield, a crucial strategic position in the defence of the city, out of the enemy's hands, and we had held the British and Canadians at bay for almost a month. But after a heavy Allied bombing of the city, we were ordered to retreat southwards. That had led us into the Falaise Pocket, and that was pretty much the beginning of the end of our hold on Normandy.

Wildmann stomped his feet, took out his last piece of chocolate, and handed it around. "*Ja*, but a lotta good all our fighting at Caen did us. We lost that one, remember?"

We all laughed, though I'm sure none of us found anything amusing about any of this. Seeing comrades and foe lying dead side-by-side, bodies ripped apart, horrified me. And I thought about Strauss and how he had come back for me in Bretteville. He had been one of the good guys, and I wanted to say, "Remember how he always had a warm smile for everyone?" But I dared not.

"Hello, guys," chirped Joop. "What's up?" A fresh uniform hung on his skinny body.

"How do you like the new assault rifle?" Wildmann asked him.

Joop smiled. "This Sturmgewehr 44?" His eyes were sunk deep into their sockets. "Wish I'd had this beauty back in Bretteville." He stroked his rifle and pointed it in my direction. "But it would have been great back in Plomion too."

The rest of us exchanged glances because, when we were in Plomion on the last day of August, the Hitlerjugend had been ordered to eliminate fourteen civilians, and Joop had volunteered to be one of the shooters. The men and young boys were beaten and then taken to a meadow and shot. Wolfie, Heinz and I had been ordered to scout the edge of the village that day and only heard about what had happened later from Wildmann. It reminded me of the shooting at the Zimmermanns' farm.

Now I threw my cigarette butt on the ground and gave Joop a shove. "Shut your mouth, Joop! It's nothing to brag about."

But he only stood taller. "What, you're going to cry about it, like you did in Ascq?" He stepped closer. "Like a little baby . . ."

"Shut your *Schnauze*." But Joop was right, I did cry that day. I thought back to April 1, 1944. In the town of Ascq, France, our train en route to Normandy had been derailed. Two compartments were blown up. Obersturmführer Walter Hauck had ordered us to eliminate eighty-six men from that town. He had held them responsible for the sabotage.

Joop shoved me a tad. "What's wrong with you? I'm proud to have protected my Fatherland! And my name is Klaus. Joop is my brother's name! You remember my brother?"

He had changed after seeing his twin mutilated, and he hated us because he felt we had not protected him and had just left him to die. I raised my hand. "If you don't shut your *Klappe* . . . I'll do it for you."

Klaus spat on the ground. "*Du bist eine Sau*, Boii! You are a disgrace to that uniform you're wearing!"

Heinz and Wolfie went to jump him.

"*Nein!*" I said. "If he is so proud to have taken part in the killing of innocent civilians, then let the devil keep him."

Klaus slung his assault rifle over his shoulder. "Maybe I should report you?"

The four of us turned our backs as he walked off, and Wolfie patted me on the back. "What an *Arschloch*."

Wildmann threw a stone after Klaus and called out, "*Verpiss dich!*"

I pulled my camouflage jacket on over my grey coat. "Everyone get ready. We're on the move again."

We marched through the night with the II/25th battalion and made it to our assembly point at Hollerath early the next day. Obersturmbannführer Richard Schulze stood in front of our ragged and worn battalion—a mix of old veterans, raw recruits and children—and shouted, "Soldiers, listen up. I have a letter from the Deutsche Army Command in the West."

"Generalfeldmarschall von Rundstedt writes to us: 'Soldiers of the western front! Your decisive hour has arrived . . . it is now or never . . . to perform superhuman feats for our Fatherland and our Führer.'"

"*Ach, du lieber Gott!*" Wolfie shouted. "This is it!"

It was Saturday, December 16, and before dawn the entire sky over the Ardennes was lit up. Our artillery streaked across the sky while our floodlights illuminated the low clouds, blinding the enemy, we hoped. The combined weight of three armies—all of Army Group Centre—began moving forward in those early morning hours. In our area, the preliminary artillery attack lasted for half an hour while I and other section leaders received our orders for the assault.

"Guys," I said as I returned out of breath, "we're to take the twin towns of Rocherath and Krinkelt, then go on to Elsenborn and Antwerp—all within four days. We have to move fast."

I really hoped we could take these villages, but we were already exhausted, and now I had to look out for my four new boys. They had no experience; they barely knew how to hold a rifle. I understood we were in a war, but this seemed crazy to me. Why was Hitler okay with this, and was he going to have girls fight too?

Our march started off slowly because of the heavy fog and deep mud. We had to constantly stop and pull artillery and vehicles out of the muck as they blocked the narrow roads moving west, but by mid-afternoon we had assembled in the area west of Hollerath. All too soon we found ourselves under harassing fire and we lost a few good boys. But we had no time to mourn, and we hurried on till we stood at the edge of the Dreiherrenwald—the forest—where we had been told that the Americans had positioned themselves throughout the trees, hoping to hold us back.

Obersturmführer Zeiner, the officer I reported to, appeared beside me in the fog and explained that we were under orders to break through the enemy defences in front of us and move on to Rocherath. I glanced down our line of soldiers and what was left of our tanks. They seemed ready to enter the dense forest ahead of us, but I saw that all the younger boys were being sent into the woods first, and not the older, more seasoned troops. Soon I heard screams along with rifle fire and grenades going off, and it became clear that the first ones going into the forest were being mowed down. Zeiner, however, reassured me that this was the battle that would turn the war back in our favour, and that we should all remain strong.

I waited along with my boys behind the line for my final orders. And then they came from Obersturmbannführer Schulze. I was to scout the area to our right, going roughly a kilometre into the forest, and report back by radio.

"Stay spread out but don't lose sight of one another when we go in," I said. "The fog is thick, and we have to move fast." A chill was creeping into my bones even though the sun was out, and a small tickle in the back of my throat began to bother me. My head was pounding. Only the fact that I was responsible for seven boys gave me courage. "Guys!" I pulled out my map, and they huddled around it. I pointed to where we were going. "Is everyone clear on what we're doing?"

They nodded.

"Get your weapons ready. Wolfie and I will go in first. I want Heinz, Helmut and Veit to stay a good distance behind us. Wildmann, Oskar and Bernd, I want you three to go in on that small path to our right. Don't shoot unless I give the signal. I need all of you to stay very, very quiet and alert." I took a deep breath.

As we advanced toward the woods, the deafening hush alerted my senses.

"This is not good," whispered Wolfie.

The terrain was rugged, and ahead of us we could see the fog winding its way among the firs and spruce trees. We were on a small muddy path, shaking with fear and cold, stopping whenever we heard the slightest sound. As soon as we entered the forest, a shot rang out, and we aimed our guns at an enemy that we had not yet spotted. The cracking of twigs on my left caused me to turn my head, and I caught a glimpse of a soldier. The next bullet went straight through the head of Helmut who had been on my right. He dropped to the ground dead.

"Get down!"

Behind me another shot rang out. Wildmann had taken out the

sniper who shot Helmut. Just then the sun broke through the heavy fog, and I could look up into the trees. I tapped Wolfie on the back and pointed to a huge fir tree fifty metres straight ahead. "Sniper!" I mouthed. I aimed my gun and so did Wolfie. I fired but missed him.

Wolfie fired and shot him out of the tree. "You okay?" he whispered.

"*Ja*, just a bit of a cold. Let's keep moving." But I was feeling weak and had trouble seeing straight. I glanced back and saw that the others were bunched together. Veit and Bernd had stopped and were just standing there staring at Helmut. I reached for Wolfie and whispered, "We need to spread out."

I signalled for the guys to spread out, and Wildmann and Heinz began pushing the others to get back into formation. In the confusion, Oskar had wandered far to the right near a small path that ran parallel to a creek. I beckoned for him to come towards us. We waited for him in silence, and then without warning an explosion sent us diving to the forest floor.

"*Ach du Scheisse!*" screamed Veit.

The fog took on a red hue. Body parts, guts and blood rained down on us. Oskar had stepped on a land mine.

"I want to go home!" cried Veit. "I want my mutti!"

I reached for his shoulder and pulled him close to me. "Shut your mouth," I whispered, "and stop crying. Your mutti can't help you now." He had pissed his pants.

Veit got down on all fours and threw up, tears streaming down his blood-covered face. He kept muttering, "I'm scared, I'm scared . . ."

"We all are." I stood up, pulled him to his feet and pushed him in front of me. "Now keep moving."

I felt a poke in my ribs. Heinz had come up quietly beside me. "There, by that ridge," he whispered and pointed over to his left. "Can you see them?" He took a look at Veit. "You'll be okay," he said, patting him on the shoulder.

I tried to see, but I was sweating and everything was spinning around me. I had to shake my head to see where Heinz was pointing. Dead ahead were a couple of Americans dug into a foxhole, and just as I saw them, their mortar fire began raining down on us. Once more we dove to the forest floor.

Wolfie crawled up beside me and pointed. "See that guy there to the left?"

"*Nein.*"

"There . . . by that little hill just off to the left. And there's another one."

I rubbed my eyes. "*Ja*—I see him now." I turned my head to Heinz. "Can you get him?"

"*Ja*," Heinz said calmly. He took careful aim and fired. We heard a scream.

I shouted, "You three!" I pointed to Heinz, Bernd and Wildmann. "Cover Vogel, Veit and me." I lowered my voice to a whisper. "Wolfie, when I say go, head for that partly blown-up log, and stay down." I glanced to my right and then back to my left. "Veit, stay with me. You'll be all right."

He nodded.

"Go!" Hunks of dirt and mud spewed up from the ground as Wolfie ran. I came right behind him, exchanging fire with the Americans while pushing Veit to run faster. Once I had made it to the log, I motioned for the others to follow. When we were all hunkered down behind it, we opened fire again at the two guys in the foxhole.

"Michael, throw the grenade!" Wolfie shouted.

I bundled three grenades together. "Give yourselves up," I called out to the Americans, but they only fired back.

My head throbbed, and the fog claimed most of my vision.

Wolfie nudged me. "Michael, throw it!"

And so I did. The two Americans were blown from their foxhole. There was silence.

Wildmann reloaded his rifle. "That was close."

Heinz put his hands up to his mouth, blew on them for warmth, and as he rubbed them together, he said, "Now what?"

I shivered again as the wet fog soaked into my already frozen body. Every time I swallowed, it felt as though I had a toothpick piercing the side of my throat. Sitting there on the wet, muddy forest floor with my head pounding, I just wanted to curl up and sleep.

Wolfie peeked over the log. "Michael, we can't just sit here."

"There." I pointed. "There's no gunfire coming from that direction. Let's follow that path. The fog will hide us. And from there we'll radio our position."

I could hear gunfire to our right, and some of the other guys in our battalion were calling out, but we couldn't see anything through the dense trees and the thick fog. Bernd walked beside me. "Shouldn't we help them?" he asked.

"Keep your voice down," I whispered. "We can't. They're as good as dead. Besides, our orders are to get to Rocherath and report back." The trees got taller and thicker as we trudged deeper into the forest. We walked in silence, although every now and then we would hear gunfire echoing in the distance. As we weren't sure of the direction, we couldn't tell whether it was their gunfire or ours, but after a while I began to feel as if we were being followed. I signalled for everyone to stop. Looking around I realized that one of my boys had gone missing. "Where's Bernd?"

"He was right behind me," Heinz said, looking puzzled. "He must have wandered off into the fog."

"*Ach, nein.*" Straining to see in front of me, I caught a glimpse of something moving in the woods. "Wildmann, you're with me. I want the rest of you to stay put." I pulled Wolfie close and said into his ear, "If we don't come back in half an hour, I want you to keep moving west."

"Where are you going?" he whispered back. "Shouldn't we stay together?"

"*Nein.* Wildmann and I will look for Bernd."

"*Ach*, I don't like this, Michael. At least let me go with you."

"I need you to take charge in case I don't make it back. And Wolfie . . . be careful. I think someone is following us."

"Since when?"

"A while."

"Why didn't you say anything?"

"It's one of our guys."

"Who?"

I shrugged.

"Bernd?"

I shook my head.

"Who?"

"It doesn't matter. We have to go." I coughed and wiped my nose on my sleeve. "Just be careful."

Wildmann and I set off. The underbrush was thicker here, and I kept an eye on the branches to see if they had been broken. I looked down as we came to a muddy creek bank. "Wildmann, look . . . footprints."

"Bernd's?"

"Don't think so. He was wearing the new boots."

"Americans?"

"*Nein*. The prints are like ours."

Wildmann looked surprised. "You think it's . . . ?"

Before he finished, I replied, "*Ja.*"

"That's why you chose me, not Vogel?"

"It's for us to settle."

"*Ach, du Scheisse,*" he said.

The footprints veered off to the right. "He's around here someplace."

Just then Wildmann was struck in the head from behind with the butt of a rifle. He fell against me, knocking me to the ground.

"Joop?" I scrambled to get up but he had already straddled me, pinning my arms under his knees.

"*Nein, Arschloch!* I'm Klaus—you killed my brother Joop!"

"Get off me, *Blödmann!*" I struggled to get up but he was holding a knife to my throat.

"How does it feel to be helpless?"

"It wasn't our fault, Klaus. Your brother ran into the explosion."

"You shoulda stopped him." Klaus pushed the tip of his knife into the side of my neck.

"Klaus, stop . . . there was nothing we could have done."

"You didn't need to leave him there!"

"Killing me isn't going to bring your brother back!" I had wiggled my right arm free from under his knee and now I slid my Hitler-jugend knife carefully out of its sheath.

"*Nein*, it won't, but . . ." He pushed harder on his knife blade.

I forced my knife into his gut piercing his abdomen, and with one push I thrust it deep into him. He let out a deep moan, and at that moment I saw that Wildmann was standing over us holding a small boulder. Without saying a word, he smashed it into Klaus's head. Klaus fell on top of me, and I pushed him off.

Wildmann stared down at Klaus and then at me. "You okay?" He reached up to touch the gash on his head.

"*Ja*. I think so." I could feel something trickling down my neck.

"You're bleeding." He helped me to my feet.

"I didn't think he would do it. He was one of us."

"What should we do with him?"

"Take his identification tags and rifle."

"What will we say to the others?"

"The truth . . . *ach, nein*! Here, give me his rifle." I released Klaus's magazine clip and took the bullets. "Just leave him."

"We can't do that . . ."

"We don't have a choice . . . unless you want to be court-martialled."

We didn't say another word about Klaus to one another. By now I felt terribly ill, and I wasn't sure whether it was because we had killed Klaus. "We better find our way back to our guys."

Wildmann nodded. "We'll look for Bernd when we get back?"

"Okay."

The fog had begun to lift, and the early evening light that streamed through the trees gave the forest a sombre glow. I had no idea where we were as the fog had not only hidden us from the enemy but allowed us to get completely lost. The only good thing about it was that, wherever we were, it was relatively quiet. But just as I thought this, we heard a rustling in the bushes to our right.

Wildmann jumped back. "*Scheisse*. What is it?"

I aimed my rifle as the bush shook more violently, but I began coughing and just at that moment a boar came charging at us. I aimed but before I could pull the trigger, the animal hit me in the shins, knocking me to the side. Wildmann ran as fast as he could. I shouted after him, "Run! Run!" I rolled onto my belly and aimed my gun at the boar just as Wildmann tripped. I took a breath in, and as I exhaled I squeezed the trigger, shooting the animal dead.

I shouted as I ran towards Wildmann. "He just about had you, Wildmann! Wildmann?" My heart pounded. "Wildmann . . . this isn't funny." I stepped closer and stood over him, but he just lay there. I knelt beside him and wiped my nose on my sleeve again. I put out a hand to touch his head. "Wildmann?"

At that exact moment he sat up and started to laugh.

"*Dummkopf*. I thought you were dead." I punched him in the arm. A shot rang out. Wildmann's head jerked back, and he fell into my arms. I turned and there, covered in blood and holding one hand on his stomach, stood Klaus, whom we had left for dead. He was pointing a Luger at me. "Klaus," I said.

"*Schweinehund*, Boii!"

He raised the Luger just as another shot rang out. Klaus fell to the ground.

"Michael, are you okay?" shouted Wolfie.

I looked up at my friend and back down at Wildmann and Klaus. Fragments of Klaus were clinging to my face. "*Ja*."

After we dug the shallow graves, we stood staring at the two mounds of dirt that concealed the latest savagery of war.

Heinz nudged me. "You should say something, Michael."

"I suppose." What was there to say? Words weren't filling my head. My mind was flooded with images of Herr Zimmermann's hazelnut grove. "Rest in peace, boys ... It's getting dark. Let's hunker down for the night. Wolfie and Heinz, why don't you two gut that pig so we can have warm food tonight? Veit, let's collect some firewood."

Veit didn't let me out of his sight as we collected wood. "Will we ever get home, Unterscharführer?"

"Don't know. Some of our commanders have said we should think of ourselves as already dead."

"Why would I do that?"

"Guess so you don't dream about the future."

Veit look at me vacantly. "I think we have enough wood. Should we head back now, Unterscharführer?"

Poor Veit wasn't made for war. "Where are you from?" I asked.

"Schlesien. It's a beautiful place. It has mountains and rivers and many churches. I want to be a priest when I grow up."

My thoughts turned to home and Mama.

"I have a small sister—her name is Johanna—and a baby brother—his name is Peter. They're both very young. My other two brothers and my papa were conscripted into the Volkssturm in November, and I have three step-sisters ... but I don't know them very well ..."

I nodded. I didn't want to talk, but Veit didn't seem to need me to say anything.

"My mutti died seven years ago, and my sister was only nine months old when my two brothers and I were put into an orphanage ..."

I leaned over a small log and threw up, then wiped my mouth with the back of my hand.

"Papa remarried, but I'm not sure where everyone is."

"Why is that?"

"Last I heard, they were on the move."

"Oh."

We had arrived back to our makeshift camp, and the skinned pig hung from its back legs, with its guts lying in a heap. I placed the wood on the ground.

Wolfie handed me a cigarette. "Wonder if we can get that wood to burn?"

"We won't make a big fire. You having trouble getting the pig's head off?"

"*Ja.* My knife's not big enough."

"*Ach*, Wolfie, just twist the head around till it snaps. The same goes for the feet."

He smiled. "Guess helping Herr Zimmermann on the farm all those years has paid off."

"Guess so."

He leaned in close. "Michael, I think we should keep moving."

"I know. I've tried to establish radio contact but I can't get a signal in here. I'm exhausted. I know that's no excuse, but you know as well as I do we are as good as dead. We'll be lucky to make it through the night. At least let's give the kid one last meal and some sleep." The sky had grown very dark, and I sensed a snowstorm coming.

Wolfie nodded. "You know, I haven't seen this much meat . . . since that last Christmas at your mama's house. Remember?"

"We chopped all that firewood so Mama could cook that big goose." I took a drag from my cigarette. "That was the night you kissed Paula in the living room."

As Wolfie twisted the head off the pig, he smiled. "*Ach . . . ja.*"

Veit started the fire while Heinz began cutting up the pig. "If you two ladies are done chatting," Heinz said, "we can start cooking."

I turned to Veit. "Come and help me make a shelter . . . a lean-to."

"I know how to do that," Veit said. "We learned how when I was in the Hitlerjugend." He took out his Hitlerjugend knife and read the inscription on it aloud: "Blood and Honour." He reached up to a branch over our heads. "Should I cut some pine branches down?"

"*Ja.*" We strung a long branch between two trees and then placed branches vertically against it. Finally we dug a small pit under the shelter then lined the pit with the remaining branches.

Veit looked pleased with himself. "That looks good, doesn't it, Unterscharführer?"

Once the shelter was up, we sat around the small fire with our blankets wrapped tight around ourselves, as we inhaled every morsel of food. No one spoke about Wildmann, Klaus or our three other comrades.

Veit smiled, his face covered in dirt, as he gnawed at a rib from the pig. "This is like camping," he said.

I pulled my scarf tight around me. "*Ja*, minus the war." The night became bitterly cold and, as I expected, it wasn't long before the snowstorm began. "We better keep each other warm, guys. I'll keep first watch, then you, Wolfie, and then Heinz."

"What about me?" asked Veit.

"Not tonight. I need you to be alert for tomorrow."

The boys huddled together. I sat as close as I could to them, and although I knew the cold still ripped through their hardened young hearts, sleep captured them. A small glow from the fire danced over my comrades' faces as they slept. My head still throbbed and my throat burned. Distant shooting and bombing rang out through the night, but somehow the artillery fire felt soothing. And why not? I had grown so accustomed to it that I was just numb. After a while our small fire burned out, but the thunderous cracking of the war god's whip continued to rip across the sky, lighting it up in explosions of blues, orange, and yellows. The earth trembled beneath me.

18

Sorrow

— DECEMBER 1944 —

❧

HEINZ SHOOK ME AWAKE. "Michael!"

"What?"

"Tanks."

Quickly I shook the other two awake. "Wolfie, Veit! Wake up."

Veit rubbed his eyes. "What time is it?"

"Around 0200," I said.

Wolfie sprang to his feet, then hopped from one foot to another trying to shake the cold off. "Tanks! *Scheisse*, it's cold."

"Grab your stuff, guys." I was shaking, not from fear but from being sick.

Wolfie stood beside me. "What are we going to do?"

"We have to take a look. Maybe they're our guys."

Veit moved to my right. "And if not?"

"If not . . . then we'll have to take them out."

Wolfie checked his rifle, took a deep breath in, and exhaled. "Let's try the radio again?"

"It won't work. I tried it in the night. We don't have a choice. Besides, we have grenades." I hoped that the morning would not fully break. I tried to take one last look around, but when I stood at the edge of the creek, all I saw among the trees were the ghostly silhouettes of the boys we had lost.

Wolfie appeared beside me and handed me a cigarette. "Michael, what are you looking at? We have to go."

Slowly I turned to face him. "They're down there."

The four of us set off, following the creek and the sound of the grinding-squealing of the tanks' treads. The trees thinned, and we saw a narrow road ahead.

"Stay put, guys. When I signal, come slowly."

I crept to the edge of the woods, hoping that it would be our guys, and as I lay on my belly, I spotted the tanks. Raising myself slightly, I motioned for my boys to come forward slowly.

Together we waited for them to come closer. "Michael, listen . . . that's our guys," Wolfie said.

I felt relieved. "Yeah. Let's go and greet them."

A tall guy who was walking beside a Tiger tank stopped when he saw us. "*Ach* . . . you boys look like *Scheisse*. Who's in command?"

I stepped forward. "I'm Unterscharführer Michael Boii. We're with the 25th SS Panzergrenadier Regiment. And you?"

"They call me Muskel." He smiled. "This is Kampfgruppe Peiper. You guys are way off track."

I was not sure why he was called Muskel as he was a short, skinny guy. There wasn't a bit of muscle on him. "*Ja*, we were on patrol and got lost."

"Well, stay with us."

"Where to?"

"Honsfeld, then on to Meuse."

Veit's eyes sparkled. "We get to fight with Peiper!"

"I don't think you'll see him."

"Why not?"

Muskel lit a smoke. "Boy, just keep your eye on that gun of yours."

Veit pointed to the tank in front of us, and still with that sparkle in his eye, he asked, "Michael, can I hitch a ride on that Tiger tank?"

I smiled, slapped him on the back. "Go. Heinz, you go with him."

As Wolfie and I walked with the Kampfgruppe, he nudged me. "You feeling better now, Michael?"

"*Nein.* And I don't have a good feeling about where we're headed."

"Don't worry. Just look at how many tanks we've got, half-tracks and soldiers. Besides, we're with Peiper and he's a legend! The youngest and greatest tank commander in the whole army!"

"Yeah, but I'd feel better if we were with our own regiment."

"But, Michael, think about it. Any battle we get into will be over in no time. Peiper always wins!"

He was right. When we entered Honsfeld around 0400, we marched alongside Peiper's paratroopers. We soon discovered, however, that the town was full of Amis. As we moved forward, Wolfie, Heinz and I took up a position pressed against the wall of a small house. Wolfie said, "The Amis are taken completely off guard." And he was right again. As we stealthily moved from house to house, we were able to take many prisoners and march them out into the street where we destroyed their weapons.

Heinz pointed his rifle at one of the prisoners. "*Hände hoch!* He shouted as he ordered the men to begin marching.

But before we knew what had happened tracer bullets rapidly flew back and forth along with cannon fire. We took cover in the ditches, I pointed my rifle, and began shooting, but all hell had broken loose. I hoped Veit was okay.

As I went to reload my rifle I heard an explosion. I looked down the street and saw one of our tanks go up in flames. But the Amis were not able to stop the might of Peiper's column, and as his tanks kept rolling in and firing into the houses, some of the 1st SS division, seeing their comrades dead or wounded, opened fire and began shooting the captured American soldiers.

Once the shooting stopped we were ordered to round up the remaining American soldiers and have them in formation.

"Michael!" Shouted Veit as he stood beside me.

"Where were you," I said.

He pointed at a Panzer, "I was with—oh no—they're running over dead men."

Then orders came down the line that we were to make a little detour to Büllingen to take a small gasoline depot.

This time the four of us were marching at the back of the *Kampfgrüppe*, tasked with watching over some Americans who had been taken prisoner at Honsfeld. When Heinz came up beside me, puffing away on a cigarette, he pointed at a tall black soldier.

"Michael, look how black that man is."

"What, never seen a *schwarzer Mann* before?"

"Not like this guy."

"I bet he's never seen a face as ugly as yours either."

Wolfie slapped Heinz on the back. "Go and see if he wants one of your smokes."

Heinz looked intimidated, and I was sure the black soldier knew it. But finally, puffing away on his cigarette, Heinz walked up to him. The soldier glanced at him and lurched toward him. Heinz jumped back. We all laughed, but the black soldier did not.

"Cigarette?" Heinz extended his packet.

The black man took it but began muttering something to the American soldier walking beside him. It clearly wasn't complimentary about Heinz.

We didn't understand what he was saying, but for the rest of the trek Heinz believed he had found himself a friend.

After we took the depot, and the prisoners had helped refuel our tanks, we moved on.

"Wolfie, you got any of that pig left?"

"*Ja.*" He reached into his pack and pulled out some meat—it was frozen solid. "Here, and give some to the others." Heinz shared his with Tucker, his new friend.

It was close to noon when we heard the tanks shelling something at a crossroad up ahead. "What's that all about?" I asked Muskel.

"Probably an American convoy. Boii, you and Vogel run up ahead and see what we're supposed to do."

Once we made it to the front, Wolfie pointed at a troop of about a hundred American soldiers. "Look! More prisoners."

I started to feel sick again, the way I always felt when something bad was going to happen.

"Michael, you all right?"

"I don't like this."

As we were walking, an officer stopped us. "You have some prisoners at the back, do you not?"

Wolfie nudged me "Michael, look. That's Peiper up ahead."

"Boy, I asked you a question."

I caught a glimpse of Peiper, and just as he drove off in his tank, he turned and shouted, "It's a long way to Tipperary!"

"Boy!" the Sturmbannführer said again.

"We have about twenty prisoners, Sturmbannführer."

"Bring them up front, and make it quick!"

We hurried back and gave the orders to Muskel. "The Sturmbannführer wants all the prisoners brought to the front of the column."

"You four boys can do it."

I felt Veit pressing into me, and I had to nudge him to give me some space, but as soon as I did that he would cling tight to me.

Heinz walked beside Tucker. "Don't worry," he told the black American. "Nothing will happen to you."

Wolfie gave me a cigarette. "Michael, do you think . . . ?"

"Just like before."

Heinz looked at Wolfie and me, and then at Tucker—understanding all too well the implication. As their eyes met, Heinz quickly glanced down at the frozen mud beneath his feet.

We marched our prisoners up to the front of the column that had now stopped at the crossroads to Baunez. There was a café on the side of the road, which three SS soldiers were setting on fire, and I saw that the other prisoners were now standing in the field beside the burning café. The officer that I had spoken to ordered our prisoners to join them.

Heinz looked scared. "What are they going to do, Michael?"

We were standing at the side of the road among a bunch of SS soldiers, and I saw that some of the prisoners were being searched. Just as I was about to say, "Don't know," a scuffle broke out on the field, a shot rang out, and I heard the commander order, "*Erschiesst sie alle! Erschiesst alle!*"

The SS men opened fire with their machine guns on the prisoners. Veit stood frozen, and Heinz turned to walk away. The Sturmbannführer in charge grabbed him by his jacket collar and spun him around. "Where do you think you're going?"

Heinz looked at the man, threw his rifle down, and said, "I don't want any part of this madness."

Some of the prisoners who had not been gunned down ran into the woods. Shots were fired after them. I ran to Heinz's side, my heart racing. I shouted, "Pick up your rifle, Heinz!"

The officer pushed Heinz. "Boy, do as you're told!"

A tear ran down Heinz's face. He spoke softly. "You can take your *Scheisse* war and shove it up your dirty ass, Sturmbannführer!"

The Sturmbannführer pulled out his Luger and held it to Heinz's temple. Heinz looked at me and said, "I'm sorry, Michael."

The Luger barked once and Heinz dropped to the ground dead.

"*Nein!*" I shouted, and fell to my knees beside him.

Wiping some of Heinz's blood off his face, the Sturmbannführer motioned with his Luger. "Get this piece of *Scheisse* out of my sight." He turned and walked away.

Wolfie went to rush him, but I stood up and put my hands on his chest. His heart beat wildly beneath his uniform. "*Nein!*"

19

Grace

— DECEMBER 1944 —

⁓

AFTER TWO DAYS OF FIGHTING with Peiper's Kampfgrüppe, we finally rejoined our unit. As we marched exhausted, wet and cold through the snow to our next battle, I thought about home and summer days.

Wolfie leaned in to me and whispered, "We need to do something about Veit."

"I know. He won't survive another battle."

"Michael, I have to stop for a minute." He sat at the edge of a ditch, took off his left boot and peeled off his sock.

"Wolfie, your toes are purple! You should have gone to the first-aid station two days ago."

"I know but it was always so crowded."

I helped Wolfie up. "And how's your arm?"

"*Ach*, it hurts like stink. I think some of the metal is still in it.

"We'll have to get it looked at soon."

I looked around and seeing that Veit seemed stunned, I pulled him out of the marching line. "Stay beside me."

Veit had taken the coat from one of our dead comrades—it was warmer but it hung on his small frame like a potato sack. Now he stood watching the last of our troops march by while Wolfie pulled his holey socks back on and forced his swollen foot into the boot that he too had taken from a dead soldier.

"*Ach*, poor Veit," Wolfie said. "Michael, what are we going to do with him? Just look at him. He's completely out of it."

"Come on," I urged Wolfie and Veit. "We'd better hurry. We're getting too far behind."

The snow was coming down heavily now, nearly blinding us. When we reached the top of the next rise, I realized we had lost our unit—or they had left us behind.

"Wolfie, they're gone!"

"What do you mean gone?" He turned and took a few steps forward, but as he put weight on his left leg, he winced. "*Ach, Scheisse.*"

"Are you okay?"

"*Ja.* Let's keep going. I'm sure they're just up ahead."

"I can't see or hear them." I nudged Veit. "Can you hear them?"

He just stood looking at nothing and not saying a word.

"Veit!"

"Michael, it's no use," Wolfie said.

"Guess we're on our own."

We three walked on for another hour before Wolfie said, "I have to stop."

I helped him to sit down beside the road. "Is it your foot?"

"*Ja*, but I'll be okay."

"Take your boot off."

"There's nothing you can do, Michael."

"Just take your boot off and let me see." While Wolfie did what I asked, I tore a piece of the lining from the inside of my coat. "Here, give me your foot. What a mess." I gently wrapped the cloth around his foot, and he pulled his sock over it.

"Thanks, Michael."

Just as we were about to start walking again, we heard the sound of tanks. "Those are Ami tanks up ahead, I think." I pointed to a small rise not far on our right.

"Can you make it to that hill, Wolfie?"

"I think it's Kampfgrüppe Peiper," Wolfie said and stumbled.

Veit turned to look at me, his little face pinched and white as the snow around us.

"*Nein*, they're American. Listen to the engines. Wolfie, let me help you." I placed my arm under his and half-dragged him through the snow-laden trees and up to the top of the hill. Veit trailed behind us. Once we reached the top, he plunked himself down in the snow.

We peered down through the trees. "See," I said. "It's the Americans."

All around us the snow had settled heavily on the branches of the trees, and a hush crept through the forest.

"Should we do something?" Wolfie mumbled.

"There's nothing we can do."

"But we have to do something, Michael . . ."

"You can't walk, and I don't think you can shoot with that arm. And Veit is no help."

"We better alert the guys?"

"We don't know where they are! Let's just stay here till I figure something out. In the meantime, let's stay quiet."

We lay on the hill for a good hour, and the snow took pity on us, covering our frozen bodies with a protective white blanket. Below us, the American tanks had come to a halt.

I looked over at Wolfie. "The Americans aren't moving, so we'll have to stay in the forest and try to find our unit in the morning . . . Wolfie!" When he didn't answer, I shook him. "Wolfie!" I touched his face. "*Ach*, you're burning up."

"*Nei-n-n*, I'm okay."

"Veit, get over here. We have to find help."

"Michael," Wolfie murmured, "what are we going to do about Fritz?"

"Wolfie, you're delirious. Take his arm, Veit."

"I didn't know we were killing him," Wolfie muttered.

"Enough, Wolfie."

But he wouldn't shut up. "Where's Paula? . . . beautiful Paula . . ."

I had no idea where we were going to find help, but together Veit and I half-carried Wolfie through the woods. The snow quickly covered our tracks.

"Are we going home, Michael?" asked Veit.

"*Ja.*" I couldn't believe it. Veit hadn't said a word for the last two days.

"It's this way," he said, pointing to the right. He seemed happy, oblivious to the snow that clung to the bottom of his coat giving him the appearance of Father Christmas.

"Okay, you lead the way."

Wolfie faded in and out of consciousness, and I told him, "Just stay with us. We'll find help soon."

Veit didn't seem bothered by the cold or that we were again lost. "We'll be home soon, Michael," he said.

"*Ja*, we will." I wanted to believe him. "But we have to stop and make a shelter, Veit. It's going to be dark in another hour."

Veit pointed straight ahead. "But we're home, Michael. See!" He was pointing through the trees to an old hunting lodge.

"Did you know this place was here?"

Veit just smiled.

The roof was partly caved in so there was no reason for anyone to be living in it, but I could see a thin line of smoke coming from the chimney.

"Veit, stay with Wolfie."

I had my rifle ready as I climbed to the porch and gently pushed the front door open with my foot. I stepped into a large foyer. A chandelier made out of antlers hung above me, and to my right was a reception desk with a tattered guest book on it. I expected someone to appear any minute and say, "May I help you?"

The dining room had tables and chairs all neatly set up. To the left was a sitting room with a large fireplace in which a small fire burned. Overstuffed chairs had been placed on either side of it, and one of them had a blue knitted afghan across it.

I crept up the damaged stairs and checked the upper rooms, but no one seemed to be home. Whoever was living here had left in a hurry. I went back outside and brought Wolfie and Veit into the lodge.

"No one's here." I sat Wolfie in the chair by the fire, took off his boots, and covered him with the blanket. "Veit, look for food in the kitchen cupboards. I'm going to check around outside."

Maybe there are some Americans here, I thought. *Nein.* I would have seen their footprints as we approached the lodge. Then I looked down and saw them—fresh footprints in the snow. "*Scheisse.*" I breathed slowly, trying to calm my nerves. I had my rifle ready. Then I felt the barrel of a gun in my back.

"Don't move or I'll shoot!" It was a woman's voice, and she spoke in French-accented Deutsch.

I put my arms in the air, still holding my rifle. "I won't hurt you. We need help."

"Are there more of you? How many?"

I started to put my arms down. "You're French?"

"Keep *ze* hands up. How many?"

"Mademoiselle, my friend is sick. Please help us."

"Why should I help you?"

She moved so I could see her. A small, half-starved woman stood before me, her trembling hands holding a shotgun, her cheeks rosy from the cold. "Keep *ze* hands where I can see them."

"My name is Michael, and my two friends are Wolfie and Veit. They're in your house. Please . . . We need help."

"Have you hurt my maman?"

"Your maman?" How could I have missed her? The kitchen! I never looked in the kitchen. "*Non*, mademoiselle. I did not see your maman."

"Get moving."

"You don't have to point the gun at me. I won't hurt you."

"*Bougez!*"

She kept the shotgun pointed at my back, prodding me to move along. Then without warning she stumbled, thrusting the gun deeper into my back. I turned around just as she fell into the snow.

"Are you okay?" I asked, helping her up.

"*Oui*," she said.

I held onto her arm as we climbed the snow-covered stairs. When I pushed the front door open, there standing in the foyer, embracing and lavishing kisses on Veit, was an old woman.

"Maman, get away from that boy!" The small woman beside me half-raised her gun to point it at Veit. "*C'est un Boche, Maman*, a Hun!"

"It's Gustav, Catherine! He's come home for Christmas! *C'est un miracle!*"

"*Maman, il est un soldat allemand!* Get away from him."

Catherine attempted to push me out of the way, but I grabbed her shotgun. Clumsily she tried to pull her maman away from Veit, but she had no strength.

Veit just stood there as the old woman held his face and continued to kiss his cheeks, saying, "I knew you would come home, Gustav."

With tears in her eyes, Catherine turned to me. "Please don't shoot us."

"We won't hurt you or your maman." I saw that she had the same softness and beauty as Margarita.

"Maman is old and confused."

"It's okay. My friend is confused, too. Besides, they both look happy."

Catherine took a deep breath and dried her eyes on her sleeve. "Where's your other friend?"

I leaned my rifle against the wall and placed her shotgun on a table by the front door. "He's sitting by the fire in the living room."

Before Catherine left the foyer, a small smile crept across her tired face. "Maman, leave the poor boy alone. Go make some tea."

"There's no more wood," the old lady said as she took Veit by the hand and led him into the kitchen, chattering like a happy bird.

The smile that had made Catherine's face look softer quickly vanished, and worry took its place.

"I'll go and chop some wood," I said. I grabbed the shotgun from the front hall and added, "Who knows? Maybe I can shoot us something to eat."

As I stepped out into the snow, I took a deep breath in, looked up at the falling snow, and felt tears begin to roll down my cheeks. I thought of Mama, how whenever I felt bad, she had made me chamomile tea. Then together we would sit at the kitchen table where she would say, "Don't worry. Things will get better." And I always believed her.

But this war wasn't going to get better. I knew that. I wiped the tears from my face and set off for the woodshed. As I picked up the axe and began chopping, I could see my mama wagging her finger at me. "Michael," she would say, "I'm not going to ask you again! Get outside and chop that wood or else!"

"Michael, I . . ."

"*Scheisse*, Veit! Don't sneak around like that! I just about clobbered you."

"Sorry. Let me help you with the wood."

"Are you feeling better, Veit?"

"We're home."

I piled wood onto his outstretched arms. "Take it back to the house. I'm going to see if I can find some food for us."

"Okay, Michael."

I realized that Veit was reminding me of Paula. She too was small and helpless and had the same anxious look in her eyes. But his blue eyes, which had not so long ago sparkled at the thought of going into battle with his hero Peiper, had dulled to a stormy grey, just as my sister's had after that awful night. Their thoughts were battered, I was sure of that.

What was left of the daylight gave me some comfort. I made my way through the woods until I found some animal tracks that looked to be deer, maybe three of them. I followed the prints to a small rock outcropping, and over to the right I could see two small, almost black roe deer standing with their ears twitching. They looked up at me with their sad brown eyes, snow clinging to their noses.

The forest was calm, though I could hear the faint echo of ruthless, explosive firepower in the far distance. I squinted along the barrel of the gun. I had a perfect shot, but I couldn't bring myself to shoot them. Not yet anyway. Just as I put the gun down, a couple of rabbits bounced gaily out of the bushes, startling the deer, and lightning fast, they dashed away.

And just as fast as the deer fled, so I followed after the rabbits for about twenty minutes down a steep narrow trail.

About half an hour later, I walked into the living room holding two dead rabbits in my hand. Catherine was sitting on a small ottoman with a bowl full of steaming water beside her. The smell of chamomile and clove scented the air.

She looked up. "You're all just boys, aren't you?" She shook her head and continued washing Wolfie's foot. "Take your boots and that coat off. You're covered in snow."

"How is he?" I asked.

"He is asleep so I am not sure. I removed some shrapnel and put a clean bandage on his arm, but it's badly infected, and he has a fever."

"What about his toes?"

As she bandaged his foot, she said, "We can just pray."

"He'll get better." I didn't dare think anything else.

Catherine wiped her hands on her apron as she rose, holding the bowl of dirty water out to me. "Take your stuff off in the foyer." I took the bowl and she reached for the rabbits. "I'll make a stew." As she walked away, she said, "Supper will be ready in a little while."

I threw the water out the front door. As I came back inside and closed the door, a voice behind me said, "Will you be staying long, monsieur?"

I turned. Catherine's *maman* was now standing behind the front desk. She had brushed her gray hair back from her face and fastened it into a bun high on her head. When I didn't answer, she stepped out from behind the desk, walked towards me, stopped and looked at me for a long moment before saying, "Let me help you with that, monsieur." As she reached for my coat, she added, "You may call me Grand-mère." She hung my coat on a hook by the front door, then turned and said again, "Will you be staying long?"

"*Non-n.* Just a few days."

"Have you met my grandson, Gustav?"

"*Oui*, Grand-mère . . . he's a fine boy."

"Would you and your friend like a cup of tea?"

"*Oui*," I said and followed her into the kitchen.

She walked over to a wooden shelf mounted on the wall above the sink. She stared at the jars on it the same way she had stared at me moments earlier in the foyer, swaying back and forth as though some beautiful melody was dancing in her head.

I too stared at the jars, wondering which one contained the tea.

"It's the third one from your left, Michael," said Catherine, who was standing at the table peeling wild onions. I reached for the container and handed it to Grand-mère. "This is the one you want."

"*Oui*," she said. She put the jar on the table and began ladling tea leaves into a porcelain teapot. "Such a good boy," she said, smiling at Veit, who was helping Catherine by preparing the rabbits.

Veit said not a word.

I picked up the kettle of hot water from the stove and poured some into the teapot. Grand-mère placed teacups on a wooden tray, and I placed the teapot in the centre. She handed me the tray. "Now, go and sit with your friend."

Catherine looked up and smiled.

I put the tray down on the ottoman and lightly shook Wolfie. "Are you awake?"

"*Ja.*" He didn't move but he opened his eyes.

"How do you feel?"

"Where are we?"

"In a hunting lodge deep in the woods. We'll be safe here till you get better." I wasn't entirely sure this was true, but I handed Wolfie some hot tea. "Here. Drink this."

"Where's Veit?"

"In the kitchen. There are two women living here, but don't panic—they're nice."

Wolfie took a sip of tea, coughed, and handed the cup back to me. "Good then." And he fell asleep again.

For a while I sat watching the blue blanket rise and fall with each breath he took, then got up to place another log on the fire. The flames danced like tiny fairies as they effortlessly ascended the chimney. The shadows lapped across Wolfie's weary face, and I saw that stubble had sprouted on his cheeks, making him look years older. We had grown into men on the battlefield and hadn't even noticed that we were no longer boys. I turned to stare into the flames, reviewing the last year and wondering about my two brothers in Russia. Were they dead or in a POW camp?

Wolfie flinched and moaned as he turned in the chair, then lunged forward, screaming.

I reached out to him. "It's all right."

Catherine stood in the doorway. I hadn't noticed her dark brown hair before—I guess she had been wearing a scarf over it—but now her hair fell around her shoulders and framed her soft face. "Michael, I think it best if we take Wolfie up to one of the bedrooms. He'll be able to rest more comfortably."

"*Oui*."

She placed an arm under Wolfie's arm and I did the same. As she leaned forward to pull him to his feet, I could see the top of her lacy champagne-coloured camisole. She caught me sneaking a glance. I could feel my cheeks turning red. I looked quickly at the ground.

"On three we'll pull him up." She started counting. "*Un, deux, trois*."

Wolfie moaned and opened his eyes but did not say a word. His head fell forward. We started to climb the broken stairs, and I could see that Catherine was struggling.

"It's the door on the left," she said.

I turned my back to the door and pushed it open, then we dragged Wolfie to the bed.

"Oh, *excusez-moi*, we are tangled," she said as we laid him on the bed.

I reached over and gently untangled the lace on her sleeve that had caught on my sleeve button. As she pulled her hand out from under mine, I could feel the softness of her skin against my rough hand. Again our eyes met, but this time it was Catherine who looked down with flushed cheeks. She pointed to a tall black dresser. "There are nightshirts in there."

I cleared my throat. "*Oui, mademoiselle*."

Before she closed the door, she turned to me. "Michael, you boys are safe here."

"Thank you."

I peeled Wolfie's uniform off and saw all the scars that were etched into his body. I could read them like the story of our lives together.

After dinner Grand-mère went to bed and so did Veit. But I stayed to help Catherine with the dishes. "What happened to your son . . . to Gustav?"

She sank into one of the kitchen chairs. "It was only two years ago . . . He was not much older than Veit. We were living in Paris at the time. Maman and my sister Colette had come up to our lodge here because they thought it would be safer. My husband, Jean, had been taken away by the Gestapo—" She stopped, looked at me for a long moment before continuing. "He was part of La Résistance française. Colette thought it best that Gustav and I come here, too, but the night we were to leave, Gustav received word where his papa was being held. So he and my brother went to get him out. But everything went terribly wrong. They were caught, and they— along with my husband and five others—were executed." She wiped her hands on her apron, stood up, and began pulling a large galvanized tub from under the table, then walked over to the hot water boiler on the stove.

I was holding a plate in my hands, but now I put it down and went to help her lift the boiler from the stove. "I'm sorry."

As we poured the hot water into the tub, she said, "It was not you. This war is the doing of old men and their love of fighting."

"And Colette? Where is Colette?"

"Colette . . ." Catherine tested the water. "It is good. You can undress and get in the tub."

The steam from the water hid my shame. "Undress?"

"*Oui.* I will not look. Hurry before the water gets cold. I will bathe after you." She hauled the boiler out the kitchen door, and through the window I could see she was scooping up snow to refill it. Quickly I took my clothes off and slipped into the tub moments before she returned with the boiler and put it on the stove. Then she came toward me holding a bar of soap and a scrub brush and knelt behind the tub. "I will scrub your back."

"That would be lovely. *Merci beaucoup.*"

She placed her hands in the water, wetting the brush and soap, then put one hand on my shoulder and with the other started to gently scrub my back, making slow circular movements. I sat in the warmth, feeling intoxicated by the lavender-scented soap and her hands gliding over my back, when a warm rush of excitement pulsed through my body. I squirmed, trying to hide my surprise, and quickly cupped my genitals.

"Michael, relax!" Her hands glided over my pectorals as she moved to the side of the tub. She stopped moving her hands, and the soap dropped into the water.

I looked at her and then down at my chest, and my heart raced. My eyes met hers. I placed my hand over hers, pressing it tightly against my tattooed swastika.

She pulled her hand out from under mine and pointed. "The towel is over there." She stood up and left the kitchen.

The clear water in the tub had cooled and turned into a hazy broth, the lavender soap had lost its sweet scent, and no matter how hard I scrubbed, I felt that the dirt would not come off my body. When the kitchen window blew open, the gust of wind that rushed in carried the distant sound of the raging war. I reached for the towel that Catherine had hung on the back of the chair, climbed out of the tub, dried myself and dressed in my dirty uniform.

Standing at the window, I closed my eyes and tried to conjure up the sounds of Susi playing the piano but instead heard Günther singing in the hazelnut grove. I took a deep breath, inhaling the dead cold air, then closed the window.

Later I climbed the broken stairs to Wolfie's room, each step beneath me creaking, and as I reached the top, a cold wind rushed by me again, and the sound of rumbling planes made me look up. Stars were shining through an opening in the roof, and the moon was bright, making the American bombers clearly visible. I'll find something to patch that hole with tomorrow, I thought. After checking on Wolfie, I went back downstairs, grabbed my rifle, and sat in the chair by the fire, covering myself with the blue blanket and resting my feet on the ottoman. After a while I heard Catherine in the kitchen pouring the hot water into the tub, and once again I smelled the faint scent of lavender.

It was sometime later. I opened my eyes slowly, and for a moment confusion swirled around me. The fire had burned out during the night, and the lodge was quiet. I hoped that Wolfie's toes and arm would be better today because we couldn't stay here much longer. I threw the blanket off, stood up, and straightened my uniform. Then just as I had at home, I began busying myself with early morning chores. I built the fire up with the last of the wood that Veit had placed in an old cradle that stood near the fireplace.

What were we going to do with Veit? We couldn't leave him here. I put my hand gently on the well-worn wooden edge of the cradle and rocked it back and forth. I reached for my rifle, but when I wrapped my hands around the metal barrel, it felt icy, and somehow heavier. I leaned the rifle against the wall.

As I left the sitting room, the squeaking of the rocking cradle went silent. Once outside I chopped more wood, then found some lumber stored in the rafters of the woodshed that would do to repair the roof. After that, I returned to the house for the shotgun and set off for some early morning hunting. When I came back to the lodge, Catherine had made tea, and Grand-mère sat happily fussing over Veit.

I handed Catherine three dead grouse.

"*Merci*," she said, taking the birds from me and placing them in the sink.

"How's Wolfie?"

"He's still sleeping."

"Oh, what a thoughtful man you are," said Grand-mère, never taking her eyes off Veit as she spoke to me. "We'll have a lovely supper tonight, won't we, Gustav?" She turned back to me. "And will you and your friend be staying long?"

I looked at Catherine. "We'll leave as soon as Wolfie can walk."

"There is some tea for you on the table." Catherine turned away and busied herself with cleaning the birds.

"*Merci*." I grabbed two cups of tea and went up to Wolfie's room.

I pushed the door open with my foot, and to my surprise there he stood dressed in his uniform. "Nice to see . . ."

Wolfie toppled back onto the bed. Quickly I put the tea down and rushed over to him. "Are you okay?"

"*Ja*. Help me to lie down."

As I settled him back onto the bed, I said, "Wolfie, you need more rest, but we have to leave here soon."

"Where are we?"

I handed him his tea. "Not sure, but when I went out hunting this morning, I spotted what I think is our boys' tracks in the snow."

"How do you know?"

"Guess I don't know for sure, but there were a lot of them . . . unless it's the Americans?"

"I think I'll need another day or two—maybe we could stay here till it's all over?"

I laughed a little. "That would be great, but you know as well as I do that we have to get back to our unit fast."

"Wouldn't want to be stuck digging trenches on the front line without our rifles."

I nodded.

"Let's go tomorrow. I'll be better by then." He took a sip of his tea. "What about Veit?"

"He'll come with us."

"Is he better?"

"*Nein*."

"Michael, he'll get killed."

"Maybe they'll send him home."

"You know they won't do that."

"*Bonjour*, Wolfie," said Grand-mère, standing at the doorway.

Wolfie looked perplexed. "*Bonjour*," he repeated.

Grand-mère pinned some of her hair up. "It is nice that you have come to have a stay with us. Will you be with us for long?"

"Grand-mère," I said, "we'll be gone tomorrow at first light."

"Oh, what a pity. Gustav will miss you."

I took her arm, walked her down the hall, then helped her down the stairs.

When I went back to Wolfie's room, he asked, "What's the matter with that old woman?"

"I think she's kind of confused."

"Who's Gustav?"

"Her dead grandson. She thinks Veit is Gustav."

"*Ach.*"

"Wolfie, do you think you can come downstairs now?"

"I think so."

I helped him down the stairs, and we were greeted by the smell of fresh baking. The hunting lodge felt warmer. As I sat Wolfie in the armchair and covered him again with the blue afghan, I said, "That's something I haven't smelled for a long time."

Catherine came into the sitting room with a small plate of biscuits. "Nice to see you up, Wolfie."

She handed the plate to me, and I took two of the warm biscuits and put them in my pocket. "I'll save them for later."

I passed the plate to Wolfie, and he looked up at Catherine. "*Merci, mademoiselle.*"

When she left, Wolfie lit two cigarettes and handed one to me. "Is that who fixed me up?"

"*Ja.*" I took a drag of the cigarette. "I've got some work to do." I exhaled and blew the smoke out. "You'll be all right?"

"*Ja.* But I can help."

"Sure you can!" I smiled and put my hand on his shoulder. "Not today . . ."

In the shed I found a hammer and nails and a ladder and climbed the slippery roof. From way up there I got a better idea of where we were and through the trees I caught a glimpse of mortars exploding in a valley far to the west. Although the snow soon started again, by mid-afternoon I had patched the hole, and just before I came down from the roof, I spotted the two small roe deer again. Once on the ground, I collected my rifle and followed them back to a small frozen lake.

The wind had picked up, and as I stood watching the snow swirling up in intricate patterns from the icy surface, I thought back to when Wolfie and I had first learned to fish on Herr Zimmermann's farm. We had been about six years old and had made rods out of branches from his hazelnut trees, tied string on the end and made hooks for our worms out of old nails. Herr Zimmermann must have been watching us from the distance because soon he approached us holding two proper fishing poles and proceeded to teach us how to fish.

Wolfie had caught the first fish, but every time he pulled on the pole, the fish pulled back, and that scared him, not knowing what might be hanging on the other end of the line. I put my pole down and went over to help him, and we began laughing as we heaved on the rod. Then out of the water and through the air flew the fish. Wolfie jumped up and down shouting, "We caught a fish! We caught a fish!" But then he saw the fish flopping around on the ground with the hook in its mouth, and he stopped jumping and just stood staring at the poor helpless thing. Herr Zimmermann came over, took the hook out of the fish's mouth and bonked it on the head. Wolfie had cried.

The deer had stopped to browse on the bushes ahead of me. I was upwind of them so I crouched there, just watching them. Their tails flicked up and down, and the smaller one stopped eating to scratch its head with its back hoof. I thought, this is it. I took the shot and down the animal went. The other deer bolted, but I brought it down before it got too far.

I draped them over my shoulders—neither of them weighed much—and made my way back to the lodge. When I got to the front door, Grand-mère greeted me. "Oh, Monsieur, you had a good day hunting. Will you be staying with us for long?"

I smiled. "Non, Grand-mère. We will be leaving at first light tomorrow."

"Let me get my grandson, Gustav, to help you." She turned and shouted. "Gustav! Please come and help the Monsieur with his kill."

Veit came out of the kitchen and took one of the deer from my shoulder. He didn't look at me or say a word.

I followed him to the kitchen where Catherine had made a small cake, out of what I could not tell, but it had a sweet vanilla smell. When I plunked my deer down on the table, it made a loud thunk. The animal's head dangled off the table's edge, and some blood started dripping onto the floor.

Catherine glanced at me as she took the other deer from Veit. "This is wonderful. We will have a really good meal. *Merci.*"

I went to wash my hands. "Do you need some help cleaning them?"

"*Non.* Veit and Maman will help."

"How is Wolfie?"

"He is resting by the fire."

"I will sit with him. Unless you need me to do something for you?"

"*Non.*"

"As you please."

"Hello, Michael." Wolfie put a log on the fire, sat down again, and put his leg up on the ottoman. "Where did you go?"

"I had to fix the roof."

"*Ach*, that was you making all that racket."

"*Ja.* Then I saw some deer while I was up there, so I grabbed my rifle and followed them."

"Did you get them?"

I nodded. "You should have been there."

"What kind? How many?"

I held up two fingers. "Just little roe deer. Two males, one after the other—both clean shots."

"Straight through the heart?"

"*Nein!* The first one I shot between the eyes. The second one in the side of the head. They both dropped where they stood."

"You were always the better hunter, Michael."

"*Ja.*"

"Remember the first time we went fishing?"

"You cried."

Wolfie half-laughed as he pulled the blanket around him. "How much ammunition do we have left?"

"Not much." I showed him. Five grenades and one full magazine between us.

He handed me a cigarette and together we sat by the fire, chatting about home like two old men remembering the past. After a time he fell asleep again.

"Dinner is served," called Grand-mère.

I roused Wolfie and we went to sit at the dining table. Catherine had prepared a lavish meal of venison, truffles and wintergreens with pine nuts. She placed a plate of food in front of Wolfie.

"*Ach*, this looks delicious."

Catherine smiled, "*Merci*, Wolfie."

"But what's this green stuff?"

I kicked him under the table. "Just eat it."

Grand-mère, sitting next to me, touched my arm. "*Non*, Monsieur, it's all right. It's from the forest . . . ground elder."

"*Ja*," I said as if I knew what that was.

Veit shovelled more ground elder onto his plate and without looking up said, "We have this all the time. It's good."

Wolfie shrugged before taking a mouthful of the elder. "All the time?"

Veit didn't reply, but he glanced up at Grand-mère and then down at his plate.

We didn't say much else because Wolfie and I were too busy devouring every bit of food on our plates. After we finished, I pushed my plate away, even though I wanted to lick every morsel off it. Fortunately, Mama had taught me—and Wolfie—better.

"Thank you, Catherine, for a great meal," I said.

Wolfie and I excused ourselves from the table but not before we picked up our plates and put them in the sink.

As we walked out of the kitchen, Wolfie stopped beside Catherine and asked, "Mademoiselle, could I have a bath tonight?"

"*Oui.*" She looked up at me. "Michael can help you boil the water."

"*Oui, certainement.*"

After cake and tea, Catherine, Grand-mère, and Veit retired to their rooms, but Wolfie and I went back to the kitchen where I took the boiler off the stove and poured hot water into the tub.

"Michael, what's going on between you and Catherine?"

"We're Deutsch, and she's French."

"*Ja,* but . . ."

I helped him into the tub. "Guess it's good we'll be leaving."

After he finished his bath, I tidied up, then made a cup of tea and took it upstairs. Catherine's door was slightly ajar. I could see she had a candle burning. I knocked on her door and opened it. "I brought you a cup of tea."

"*Merci.*"

The night came and went too fast. I awoke to the sound of breaking glass.

I pushed the bed blanket off me. "Stay here, Catherine."

Quickly I pulled on my trousers and boots, grabbed my rifle and crept down the stairs. Wolfie must have heard the noise, too, because he was dressed and standing at the foot of the stairs with his rifle in hand. Slowly we crept toward the kitchen where the noise had come from. I pushed the door open and pointed my rifle at the woman who stood at the sink.

She raised her hands. "*Nicht schiessen!*"

I held my rifle on her for a moment but then realized who she was. "Are you Colette?" I lowered my weapon.

"*Oui.*"

"Are you by yourself?"

"*Oui.*" Colette glanced about the kitchen as though she were looking for something, possibly a knife, I thought.

I motioned to Wolfie to lower his rifle. "It's all right, mademoiselle."

Colette continued to scan nervously around, and just as I wanted to ask her if she had been seen by anyone, the kitchen door opened behind me and in came Catherine.

"Colette . . . you're back!" Catherine embraced and then kissed her sister on both cheeks.

They spoke in rapid French to one another, then Catherine put her hands up to her mouth. Her eyes had grown large with fear. "Michael, Colette saw five Americans coming this way."

"How far away?"

"About twenty minutes."

"*Ach, du Scheisse,*" said Wolfie.

Panic rose in me. "Where did you see them, Colette?"

"By the lake." Colette grabbed Catherine's hands. "Where's Maman? And why are you housing these dirty Boches?"

"They are good men, Colette. Maman is all right."

"They are Boches! Have you forgotten?"

"Let it go, Colette."

Colette continued to scowl at me, and Catherine said, "Michael, you'd better hurry."

Wolfie started out of the room, then turned back. "Thank you for all you've done, Catherine."

Catherine nodded. "Hurry!"

"Why are you helping them?" Colette shouted.

Grand-mère stood in the foyer holding Veit's hand. He was not wearing his uniform. "*Monsieur,* you're leaving?"

"*Oui.* And Veit must come with us. Where is his uniform?"

"Veit? Is he a guest here? I don't think I met him."

I ran up the stairs, grabbed the rest of my uniform and ran down again, struggling into my tunic. "Grand-mère, please let go of Veit. Veit, get your stuff! We don't have a lot of time!"

Wolfie stood at the door, holding the rest of our gear. As I pulled on my boots, Grand-mère reached out, turned my hand palm-side up and let Veit's identification tags fall into it. "Gustav found these. Maybe they belong to your friend Veit?"

Wolfie and I looked at one another, then at Catherine. She nodded and gave me a half smile.

Wolfie shrugged.

I tousled Veit's hair. "You take care, Gustav, and help Grand-mère."

Catherine pushed a small bundle of food into my chest. "You must go."

"*Oui.*" I put the bundle in my pack, and Wolfie and I slipped on our coats and helmets. We stepped onto the front porch, and the morning cold tore through me.

Catherine stood in the front doorway, a red shawl wrapped around her shoulders. "Be careful!" She gave me a kiss on the cheek as she put something in my pocket. "We'll look after Gustav," she whispered.

I took her hand, "*Merci* for everything, Catherine. When this—"

"Michael, we have to go . . ."

I turned and slung my rifle over my shoulder. "If we take the path to our left, Wolfie, it will take us down to the meadow. From there we'll have to find our way back to our unit . . . or any unit."

"We'll bypass the lake . . ."

"*Ja.*"

We hurried down the path, then made our way carefully through the forest, pausing to listen every few steps. Wolfie whispered, "What day is it?"

"Not sure . . ." Then I remembered the package Catherine had put in my pocket. "*Ach*, it's Christmas."

"Christmas!" Wolfie slapped me on the back. "*Frohe Weihnachten, Michael—*"

At that moment I heard a slight noise to my right. I whispered, "Get down!" grabbed Wolfie's arm and pulled him down into the snow. There was a huge stump nearby, and we quickly crawled behind it, but the Americans had already spotted us and their bullets ripped through the air above us. I thought about the bullets I had used up on the deer.

"Can you shoot with that bad arm?"

The wind was growing colder by the minute, and as I rolled onto my stomach, the snow beneath me crunched. I pointed my rifle, and through my scope I could see the enemy.

"My arm's okay. How many?" He was on his belly, ready to fire a round from the other side of the stump.

"Three."

"I see them. Shall we ask them to surrender?"

"*Kommt raus—Hände hoch!*" Wolfie shouted. But they just continued to fire.

"Okay, they had their chance. I'll take the two on the left, you take the one to your right."

"*Ja.*"

"Make your bullets count, Wolfie."

He nodded. "On three."

Together we slowly counted under our breath. "*Ein—zwei—drei.*"

As soon as we had unleashed our bullets, we took cover behind the stump again, and I pulled a grenade from my belt.

"We got them, Michael. Now what?"

"We wait."

"For how long?"

"Not sure . . ."

"Ahhhhhh . . . You fucking Krauts!"

More bullets rained down on us.

"Ach, Scheisse!"

I had tied the other four grenades together to make a *geballte Ladung*, and now I handed Wolfie the single grenade and took the four from my belt. I peeked over the stump and saw three more Americans running towards us. The guy in the lead was yelling, "You son of a bitch Nazi shits . . . !"

I threw the grenades. There was a deafening explosion, then all went silent in the woods, except for a slight moan from about ten metres away.

Cautiously we emerged from behind the stump and walked over to the torn-up bodies. There, amongst the blood and human remains, a kid about my age lay without his legs. He looked up at me, reaching for my hand, mouthing the words, "Help me, help me . . ."

I looked into his eyes. "I'm sorry," I said.

20

The Red Army

FEBRUARY ARRIVED, and what was to be the final push to a glorious German victory resulted in one of the biggest, bloodiest battles in the Ardennes. Even though we had surprised the Americans with our colossal offensive campaign, they had somehow held their ground, and we had to retreat, and in doing so, we had lost thousands of men. Afterwards, most of our division was redeployed, transported by rail from Cologne to Hungary.

I took great pleasure in sitting on that train with nothing to do and no one shooting at us. We were now designated as the *Baustäbe*, the SS construction staff, and were told to remove our sleeve bands to conceal our identity in case we were captured. Although we had failed in the Ardennes, perhaps we would accomplish our mission this time.

Our enemy had changed from American red, white and blue to

just plain Russian red, and we were told it was our duty to push them back. I tried not to think about what was ahead or about that day in the woods with Wolfie. The sound of the American's voice begging for help still cut through me. How often on the battlefield had I heard those words—"Help me, help me"—and all I could do to help was to shoot them dead. I had become the grim reaper's servant, his personal foot soldier.

We arrived in Hungary on February 8, 1945, at 1330, and Wolfie and I were among the group who were ordered to climb into a truck to head for Neuhäusel. Wolfie handed me a cigarette, and as I inhaled, I could feel the back tooth that had been giving me trouble off and on for the last couple of months begin to ache again. The weather had for the most part continued cold, but now the rain started to pour down.

As the heavy truck sloshed and rumbled along the muddy roads, I turned to look at the men around me. It wasn't hard to tell which of them had not fought before—the green soldiers were either young or old, and both young and old looked terrified. The soldiers with blank gazes were the ones who had seen so much blood that they had become deadly machines. I didn't know where Wolfie and I rated among them.

"Any idea where we're going?" Wolfie asked me.

"*Nein*. All I heard is that we'll be fighting Russians."

Someone at the back of the truck shouted, "We're to protect the Hungarian oil fields."

As I turned my head to see who had spoken, I spotted a frightened man in the corner hugging his knees to his chest. "Herr Kannengiesser?" I said half to myself.

He looked up at me for a moment and then turned away.

I nudged Wolfie but then thought better about telling him that our old rektor was riding in the truck with us.

Wolfie leaned in closer to me. "Michael?"

"*Ja.*"

He turned his head away and took a deep breath before he said, "If . . . if I get caught by the Russians . . . I don't want you to rescue me as you did before. I'll put a bullet in my head rather than be tortured and killed. Or worse—have them kill you."

"No one will kill you . . . or me. We're not going to think like that."

"But, Michael—"

"But nothing." I put my hand on his knee. "We'll get through this." I wiped at my eyes. "Damn rain!"

The truck came to an abrupt stop, and the small boy sitting next to me fell against me. He looked up at me with panic-stricken eyes. "I don't know how to kill."

I stared down at him. "What's your name?"

"Rupert."

"That's a good name." I put my hand on his shoulder. "That's all right. Just aim your gun at whoever is shooting at you and pull the trigger."

We climbed down from the truck, helped the old men down, and began marching to our new assembly area several miles to the east near the town of Köbölkút. At the assembly area we were told that we were to protect numerous villages and towns, but above all we were to protect the bridges in order to safeguard the Hungarian oilfields from the advancing Soviet army.

We weren't told why the oilfields were so important, but it was obvious that Deutschland was running out of fuel. Rupert didn't leave my side, rambling on endlessly about his mother and his school. I didn't pay much attention to him because I knew he would become cannon fodder all too soon, just as Oskar, Helmut and Bernd had.

"Children don't belong in war," I muttered to Wolfie.

He nodded as he sucked on a cigarette.

"Maybe we should shoot him in the foot?" I whispered.

"Ja."

On February 18 we were with the II SS-Panzer-Grenadier Regiment 26, which had been ordered to capture a small bridge over the Parizs-Puszta Canal near the village of Parkany and defend the bridgehead there at all costs. We found ourselves looking out over a large open field with the canal at our backs. A forest ran along both our flanks and facing us, several miles away, was another forest. We knew the Russians were in there, hidden among the trees, waiting to pounce. As we reorganized ourselves, I squatted beside Wolfie.

He glanced at his watch. "It's 0035."

An old man sitting beside us said, "The Russians are going to kill us!"

A verse by Carl von Clausewitz that Grandpapa Oden had often recited to me when I was very young now sprang into my head: "Russia is not a country that can be conquered . . . such a country can be conquered only by its own weakness or internal strife." Funny that now I should remember it. "What's your name?" I asked the old man.

"Friedrich," he replied as he stared out over his rifle.

I leaned over to him. "You're already dead. So don't worry."

Wolfie glanced at me and smiled. A moment later he shouted, "Get down!"

Artillery began to hail down on us, and as we tried to take cover from the shelling, we shot back wildly in the direction of the forest. After a short time several Russian T-34 tanks emerged from behind the trees, and we focussed our fire on them.

"Get into the woods!" ordered Hauptsturmführer Ott. "Go, go, go! Boii, take your section over that hill to your right!"

My section consisted of just six soldiers—Wolfie, Friedrich, three other old guys and myself. "Stay low and run like hell," I ordered. As we made our way to the hill, the old man who was running beside me fell to his knees. I tried to pull him up, then left him. He had been shot. I shouted at them to hurry, "*Schnell! Schnell!*" all the while shooting at the unseen Russians.

Once over the hill I could see a Russian anti-tank gun off to our right. I tapped Wolfie on the shoulder and pointed. "There, over to your right, see it? Stay here with Friedrich. Cover me." I leaned over to the two other old men. "Come with me."

Together we ran half-crouching until we were about fifteen metres from the gun. We dropped to the ground, I pulled out my grenade, unscrewed the bottom stick, pulled the cord and threw it. "Take cover!" I shouted. An ear-splitting explosion followed. After that, the battlefield lit up with bullets, dirt, debris and the sounds of battle. I had become the reaper's servant once more.

When the battle was over, the field was littered with smouldering tanks, weapons that lay beside countless dead soldiers—more Russians than our boys. The worst of it all was that the bridge we were supposed to guard had been destroyed by the Russians. Another defeat for our side. Still, we could have engineers come up and rebuild it while we held our side of the canal.

About ten of us settled in for the night in an abandoned barn. There were no animals in it as they had probably all been eaten. It felt good to have some shelter since it was below freezing. Wolfie and I laid our weary bodies down in a corner and covered ourselves with our woollen blankets.

My breath and that of my comrades was as foul as fermented cabbage, and we all stank like rotten meat. We had often been told that when water was not available, we were to clean ourselves with our piss. Our commander would say, "If bullets don't kill you, infections will."

Our comrades had taken a small town that day and they seemed happy about having pushed the Commies back, but what did it matter? It was always the same. Each battle meant only more death and destruction. After an unsettled few hours of sleep, I cracked open the barn door, and the sun streamed in. It felt good.

Wolfie came up beside me. "This *Scheisskrieg* is never going to end."

I glanced at him and nodded. "*Ja.*"

A good-sized creek meandered through the meadow just down from the barn, and without a word, Wolfie and I began to walk toward it, stripping off our clothes as we went. We both shivered as we stepped into the water where the creek pooled. My breath lingered at the bottom of my lungs and I cupped my hands around my genitals. And as I looked back at the barn, I saw the rest of them were trailing down to the pool too. The bitter cold did not matter as the morning sun warmed our backs. Washing the lice off our bodies was a relief. We scrubbed each other's backs, splashed about, and shivered with a feeling of normality. As I put my boots on again, I stared at the other boys, marvelling at the calm acceptance in their eyes.

Wolfie sat beside me to put on his boots. "You know, all I think about is Paula. Thinking about her and your mama, that's what keeps me going." He inhaled deeply. "Don't get me wrong, I think about my mutti too, but the memories I cling to are of the three of us when Papa was alive. After he died, I brought Mutti flowers every day for a year."

"I remember."

"And when there weren't any, I drew her flowers on rose-coloured paper."

I nodded and took a drag on my cigarette.

"I did that because Papa always did it."

"Your papa—he always had kind words for everyone."

"*Ja.*" Wolfie smiled. "Remember when I was about six and the postman . . ."

I chuckled. "And the postman, Herr Finkel, pulled you by the ear . . ."

Now Wolfie started to laugh. "And Papa saw and he said, '*Ach,* what do you think you're doing with my son?'"

I too started to laugh almost hysterically. "And before Herr Finkel could even say a word . . ."

Wolfie put his arm over my shoulder, laughing hysterically. "Papa had . . . he had Herr Finkel by the ear and . . . and . . . he started to pull him away from me, but . . . but . . ."

"But Herr Finkel wouldn't let go of your ear . . ."

Wolfie grabbed my ear, I grabbed his and let my cigarette hang from my lip. He held his cigarette in his other hand and together we tried to lead one another around by our ears, the two of us crying with laughter.

At 1700 hours Wolfie and I were given orders to escort three engineers, all old men, back to the destroyed bridge over the canal. They were part of a team that was to rebuild the crossings over the Parizs Canal. We set out on foot at dusk, and the air felt wet. My orders were to lead them through the fields, avoiding the roads wherever possible.

"Michael." Wolfie checked behind him as we followed a small, winding, muddy road that eventually led us into the soggy fields. "These old guys—they have no experience in the field. They're going to get us killed."

"Probably." I flashed him a smile. "So we better stay alert."

As I walked, the wind blew cold into my face, making my back molar ache again. My tongue would involuntarily press hard against it, sending a sharp pain along my lower jaw. Behind us, every now and then one of the old men would break the stillness with nervous chatter, and then they would demand that we stop and rest.

"I'm Max Müller," blurted one of the old men. "I gave money to Obersturmführer Werner Löbzieny for the refugees in Upper Silesia . . ." When neither Wolfie nor I answered, he went on, "You know the money collected is going to the Deutsche Red Cross . . ."

Another of the old men said quietly, "It's all insanity. We'll never get out of this alive."

I found myself thinking about Veit. His mutti, sister and brother were most likely among the refugees fleeing Silesia.

We were sitting in the muddy field, and I started to massage my cheek that by now had grown quite swollen, but even though the pressure I applied felt good for a moment, the throbbing waves of pain wouldn't subside. And Max's incessant chatter only added to my pain.

"Hush!" I whispered. I turned my head towards the sound of rustling grass.

Max and one of the other old men threw themselves flat on their bellies, covering their heads with their hands. But lightning fast, the third old guy jumped to his feet and started to shoot. I pulled him down, but I was too late. He had been shot. He was struggling for his last breath as he hit the frozen mud.

A few more shots rang out.

"Wolfie, I want you to crawl about fifty metres to the left, and I'll go right."

"What about Max?" Wolfie whispered. Max had started to crawl through the grass to get away from the shooting. Wolfie grabbed his arm. "It'll be okay, old man. Just stay put."

I put my hand on the other old man's back. "Follow me and stay low."

"My name is Friedrich," the old man whispered.

I nodded, recognizing him from the previous day.

Bullets flew over our heads. When we were in position, I whistled, the signal for Wolfie to shoot. We exchanged rifle fire with the Russians for about ten minutes then, just like that, it stopped. I looked over at Friedrich. He had been shot in the arm.

He looked up at me and with laboured breath he said, "Please . . . don't leave . . . me behind. I don't want . . . the Russians to torture me."

I knew then that he had overheard Wolfie and me talking in the truck earlier. I crawled back to the dead old man and saw that his green eyes were staring into the dark sky. I closed his eyes and took his identification tags along with his rucksack before tearing his shirt off and ripping it into strips to use as bandages for Friedrich. While wrapping the torn shirt around Friedrich, I said, "You'll be okay." Then I slung his gun over my shoulder, and Wolfie and I picked him up, dragging him as we ran, while enemy bullets began to fly like angry hornets again. Max hit the ground. I kicked him in the ribs and shouted, "On your feet, soldier, and run!"

Wolfie, not missing a beat, pulled Max up, half-hauling him along. "You can do it!"

We ran as fast as we could, dragging Friedrich's wounded body between us.

"Michael!" Wolfie said. "Max can't keep up!"

"Just hold onto him!" I could see that the old man wanted to give up, so I shouted at him. "Run, you son of a bitch . . . *Gott verdammt!*"

Wolfie looked at me, surprised at my swearing and mouthed back, "Bitch what?"

"Son of a bitch . . ."

Wolfie stopped running abruptly. "Michael . . . ! Michael, Friedrich's dead!"

I stumbled and realized that the firing had subsided some minutes before. "What?"

"Friedrich . . . He's dead!"

I gazed down at his lifeless body. He must have been shot again while we were carrying him. All I knew about him was his first name. His head dangled between his shoulders, and Wolfie and I let his arms slip through our hands. I pulled off Friedrich's identification tags, causing his body to heave up then fall back once more onto the hard ground. Leaving him there, we began running again, and this time I kept my arm under Max's body to drag him along. I wanted to escape from this hellish battle and get far away from the Russians as much as Max did.

"Michael, there." Wolfie pointed toward a derelict wooden structure ahead of us. "Let's duck into that."

But as we got closer, we could see that, while the roof was intact, the walls on two of its sides had been mostly blasted away and we could hear terrified screaming coming from inside. Wolfie turned to me and mouthed, "*Scheisse.*" We crouched down, and nudging Max with my foot, I pointed to some bushes on the side of the road, and handed him Friedrich's rucksack. "There," I whispered. "Take cover there!"

Leaving Max behind, we worked our way closer until we could see that there were a half dozen drunken Russian soldiers inside the remains of the filthy shack, and a couple of young girls were sprawled on a table in the middle of the shed. I think there may have been a third one lying curled in a fetal position in the corner. I pulled at Wolfie to come away, but he wouldn't budge. I leaned toward him and whispered. "Move! . . . Now!"

"We have to do something, Michael. They're—"

"We can't. Not now!" Again I pulled at him. "We have to deliver that old man . . . and we're outnumbered." Just then a shot rang out from inside the building. Wolfie raised his rifle. Quickly I placed my hand on it, forcing the rifle down. "*Nein!*"

"They shot one of the girls," he whispered.

"I can see that." And I felt my mind being turned around. I turned to check on Max but he was safely hidden. "On the count of three, we kick the door in and take the bastards!"

We gunned most of the Russians down, but one of them stood in a corner with his hands over his genitals. Wolfie aimed and shot him in the groin and then again in the chest. The girls sobbed, too terrified to even get up and flee.

There was nothing further we could do, so we left them there in the derelict building, and hoped for the best for them. Soon after, we delivered Max to his unit. His commanding officer thanked us and said, "What's the matter with your face, son?"

To tell the truth, I had forgotten all about my tooth by this time, but as soon as he spoke, I could feel the heat in my swollen cheek, and the dull throbbing pain returned. "Toothache," I said.

"Let me see."

I stepped closer to him, and he tilted my head back. "Open."

Reluctantly I did what he asked.

"You have one nasty rotten tooth there, boy." He stepped back. "That has to come out."

I nodded and rubbed my cheek.

As soon as we were on our way again, Wolfie said, "And where the hell are we going to find a dentist out here?"

"At the field hospital?" But by the time we were halfway back to our unit I stopped. "Wolfie, I can't take the pain anymore. You're going to have to pull it out for me."

"*Ach, nein.*"

"*Ach, ja.*"

"And how do you think I'm going to do that?"

"Not sure. Maybe take your knife and pry it out?"

"Not the best solution but it might work . . . Open up."

"Wipe your knife clean first."

Wolfie pulled his knife from its sheath and wiped it on his tunic. "Sit down and lean against that rock and open up. *Ach*, Michael stop wiggling your tongue. You don't want me to cut it off, do you?"

Saliva dripped down my chin as Wolfie forced the knife under my tooth, slowly twisting it, trying to pry the thing loose, but he hit a nerve and sent jolts of pain through my body. When I recovered, he went back to prying, and I could hear the metal from the knife scraping and clicking. Then he stuck his fingers into my mouth and started to wiggle the tooth, slowly turning it, but after a few minutes I pulled away. "*Scheisse* . . . This . . . is . . . not . . . a . . . good . . . idea!"

"*Ja.* But we have to get it out." He clenched his fist.

"I don't think punching me in the face is going to do it."

"Do you have another idea?"

I spat some blood out. "The wire-cutters!"

Wolfie pulled my wire-cutters from my gear kit. "Open wide." He clasped the cutters around my tooth, and began to twist and pull.

"Hold on." He placed his knee on my chest and with one swift motion he yanked for the last time. He fell back onto the ground, holding the wire-cutters above his head. "We got that sucker."

21

The Lake

— MARCH 1945 —

BY MARCH 30 WE WERE in lower Austria, falling back in the face of the continuously advancing Russians. We had lost Hungary, and even though more and more young boys were being conscripted to the war effort, our battalion was becoming smaller and smaller. I wondered how much younger these boys could get before they were taking them from their cradles. We had no more than a handful of tanks and were extremely low on ammunition.

We fought through the night in Ödenburg, pushing the Russians back but not without a large number of our boys dying. By nightfall we had crossed the Leitha River. We were taking refuge from the Russians as we hid in the forests of the Leitha Mountains. Untersturmführer Deganhard had orders that we were to take Hornstein. He pointed in the direction of the village. "It's approximately 2,500 metres that way. But for now we will wait."

At 0500 hours with the sky still dark we crept out of the forest. I barely breathed. I was sure my heart would explode as I led with my rifle. Wolfie, who was close behind me, pointed over my shoulder to a house about fifteen metres in front of us.

I nodded.

The silence cracked. "*Stoj! Stoj!*" a Russian voice shouted.

Swiftly I took aim and shot in the direction of the Russian voice. A hush fell and we all ran and disbursed into the village.

Wolfie, another soldier and I took cover against a house, and we began, firing at anything that moved.

"Run!" I shouted. We ducked into doorways, ran from house to house, firing our rifles. By daylight we had cleared the village of all Russians. To our delight, the local women came out of hiding and greeted us with cheese and bread, coffee and small carved wooden Easter eggs.

Wolfie and I sat on a curb as we drank our coffee. "It's Easter Sunday tomorrow," he said as he lit up.

I nodded. And after some time I said, "Do you think there's a heaven?"

Wolfie shrugged and handed me his cigarette. "I don't know."

I took it and inhaled. I wondered if, when our time came, there would be any place up there for us.

"I suppose it's a nice thought." Wolfie stood up. "We better get going before the Commies come back."

Some of our boys began to collect the extra ammunition that we had taken from the captured Russian supply carriages.

News arrived that the Russians had broken through to Vienna, and so our battalion was ordered to move back into the forest. As we left, we passed the village church, and for some reason Lorelei's words crept into my head: "Kill Hitler, kill Hitler . . ."

A group of Russians had spotted us retreating, and they quickly gave chase. We ran across fields, down country roads and across more fields, and at last took cover in the brush at the side of a field.

After a while we no longer heard their shouting or shooting and figured they had given up trying to find us. The sun's warmth soothed our fatigued bodies, and we were able to doze for a bit. We stayed there until after sunset, but just as we prepared to set out on the road from Rust and Oggau, we heard Russian vehicles approaching and quickly jumped back into the shrubbery. By now I was so sick of being chased and hiding that I took aim and shot the driver of the first vehicle in the head. Wolfie and the others aimed, fired in succession and silenced the rest of them.

Wolfie sidled up next to me. "We should take their vehicles."

For a moment I thought how nice it would be to drive and not have to be on the run. "Our guys will mistake us for Commies. They'll gun us down."

Easter Sunday fell on April 1, but there was no pause in the fighting. Like pesky flies, the Russians were still hot on our heels. All I wanted was sleep and food. Except for the bit of food the women had given us, we had been without food for three days, though the thirst was the worst.

Wolfie leaned in. "Do you have any water, Michael?"

"*Nein.*" We were all so thirsty. We were constantly in fear as we scurried across roads, hiding like hunted animals in the edges of forests, jumping into the ditches along the roadsides, and waiting for the dark to race or slither on our bellies across fields and pastures. But no matter what we did, we couldn't shake the Russians.

That night as we marched along a road, one of our men spotted lights ahead. "That must be Eisenstadt," he said.

Just then a large column of Russian vehicles approached, and we quickly slid into a deep anti-tank trench. I whispered to Wolfie, "We'll never get out of here."

He nodded.

Our Hauptsturmführer signalled for us to be quiet and to stay put until the convoy passed.

I worried that if the Russians discovered us, we would be easy pickings for them. I pressed myself into the side of the bank and felt the coldness of the earth soak into my uniform. The soil smelled musty. I kept my eyes closed.

When the last Russian vehicle had passed, I took a deep breath and was thankful for being able to march along the trench.

At last we came to a slope where we were able to climb out.

A comrade behind me said to no one in particular, "*Scheisse,* we're in a bog."

He was right, for the terrain became wetter and wetter the further we went.

Our Hauptsturmführer lifted his arm, signalling us for a stop. "Listen up, boys. Ahead is Neusiedler Lake. We'll outsmart the Russians by marching through the shallows. We'll lose those *verdammte Schweinehunde* for good."

Once we reached the lake, the full moon lit our way as we struggled deeper and deeper into the freezing cold water, which at times reached up to our chests. My nose filled with the stench of rotten reeds, and the muddy lake bottom held tight to our boots so that each step took a battle of willpower.

Wolfie, who marched in front of me, turned to whisper, "*Scheisse!* This is like the Zimmermanns' lake . . . Remember where I fell in?"

How could I forget? After all, he had almost died. "That's when you got really sick."

"But your mama looked after me."

For most of that night we slogged our way through endless kilometres of murky lake water with our rifles across our shoulders. I trudged behind Wolfie to make sure he didn't slip under the water. The air was still, and even the slightest splash rippled through the silence of the night.

"Wolfie, keep your rifle up out of the water," I whispered.

He stopped and turned to face me. "I can't keep my arms up for much longer, Michael. We must have marched over twenty kilometres by now."

"Do you have any water left?" I asked him.

He laughed softly, then waved his rifle at the water all around us. "*Ja*, lots of it, but we can't drink this *Scheissdreck*." He turned and began marching again.

The guy behind me whispered, "I'm so tired and hungry . . ."

That was the last time I heard him speak. Like so many others, he surrendered his weary self to the murky water.

I began thinking about swimming in Herr Zimmermann's lake in the summer . . . the warm water, the sunshine . . .

Just then flares lit the sky, illuminating our wretched selves. "Hurry, everyone!" shouted the Hauptsturmführer. "Those are Russian flares!"

We started to run as best we could, but being cold and tired, some of the boys stumbled and fell, and there they stayed. The first faint touch of daylight was already colouring the sky to the east as our troop reached the shore somewhere between the towns of Purbach and Breitenbrunn, and for a brief moment Wolfie and I lay shivering side by side, our drenched uniforms clinging to our bodies.

Up ahead a vineyard sloped down to the lakeshore, the barren vines planted in neat rows, and I realized from the shouting that the Russians were coming at us from both north and south of it.

"They're coming from both sides!" one of our guys yelled.

"We're cornered!" someone else yelled.

I glanced to our left and saw a grassy slope on the other side of what looked to be a road that switchbacked up the hillside. I pointed. "There!" Like wild horses thirteen of us ran across the road and up the hill, helping one another and yelling for the others to follow. But they didn't, and once we reached halfway, we lay down in the grass and listened to the gunfire. I knew we only had a few seconds before the Russians spotted us.

Wolfie rolled over to face me. "We'll get killed if we try to run across that road up ahead."

But as he said it, eight of our group started running across the road and on up the hill, disappearing into the pine forest above us.

"We have no choice," I said. I slithered up to the edge of the road, and he followed me. "On the count of three we run in a zigzag pattern."

"Okay."

We dashed across the road and helped each other up the far slope, finding safety in the thick underbrush of the forest.

Only a handful of us made it that early morning. We were out-numbered and no match for the Russians. As we stayed hidden in the safety of the forest, paralyzed by the horror unfolding in front of us, the Russians gunned the rest of our troop down. And like scavenger birds they picked through our dead comrades' pockets, claiming whatever they could.

22

Berlin

૭⁄৹

WE HAD FOUGHT the Russians for three months without a break when, without explanation, Wolfie and I were ordered to Berlin. I felt guilty about leaving our comrades, but we had orders, and on April 17, we boarded a train to Berlin.

Munching on a cheese sandwich, his feet up on the opposing train seat, Wolfie said, "Do you think Margarita is still in the city?"

"Our angel?" I gazed out the window, which had become a rolling theatre, showing snapshot after snapshot of towns in ruins. "I hope not," I said, fervently. "Maybe she's found safety in the countryside somewhere."

The train chugged along, clanking and rattling at every bend. Wolfie began chatting with a pretty girl and I dozed off.

We arrived in Berlin on the evening of April 19, and as Wolfie and I followed Hitler's personal bodyguard, the LSSAH, to a bomb shelter, we couldn't believe what we saw around us. Berlin, once such a beautiful and vibrant city, lay in ruins. The once-thriving Kurfürstendamm had vanished under rubble. Now only burned-out skeletons of the buildings stood teetering in a desolate landscape. I was struck by the sight of a mannequin standing in a burnt-out window. She was dressed only in a corset, her arm raised as if saluting Hitler. Embers smouldered at her feet.

A lump formed in my throat as I stared at the destruction. I took a deep breath and tilted my head up to the darkened sky. For a brief moment I thought I heard the soft voice of Margarita. "Hello, boys . . ."

"I can't recognize anything," Wolfie said.

"Look," I said and pointed to a bust of Hitler that lay among the rubble. We followed some Hitlerjugend children, who were now the city's defenders, into a bomb shelter, which lay two floors underground. Our footsteps reverberated on the sandstone floor, water dripped from the rusted pipes overhead, and the coughing of hundreds of people along with the crying of the young filled the tightly packed shelter.

Wolfie lit two cigarettes and handed one to me as he looked out at the sea of people. "There's probably thousands of Berliners living in cellars like this, Michael." The blue haze from our smoke only added to the stifling stench. "Wonder what this place was before the war."

A small woman wearing a long green coat and a scarf tied over her hair said in a tired but warm voice, "Here," and handed us some scratchy old woollen blankets. "It was a brewery," she said and added, "Berlin's finest." She pointed to a spot in a corner. "You two can lie down next to where that small boy is sitting."

I never slept that night. The noise of so many people kept me awake, but I thanked *Gott* that Wolfie and I had been deloused before we re-entered Reich territory. Wolfie lay close to me for warmth, but he kept me awake with his night terrors. He thrashed in his sleep, bolting up with his eyes open and screaming, only to fall back, breathing rapidly as sweat soaked him. But the small blond boy who lay beside us slept soundly. I guess he felt safe with a couple of soldiers. When early morning crept in, the Berliners began to stir.

"Are you awake, Michael?" Wolfie said, sitting up.

"*Ja.* I've been sitting here watching your pretty face for the last hour."

"Funny, *Dummkopf.*"

"Let's take a look outside."

The boy sat up and rubbed his eyes. "Can I come?"

"You'll need to ask your mutti."

He shrugged. "She's dead."

Wolfie tousled the boy's hair. "Sure, you can come, but stay close."

"I will."

As we made our way through the sea of people, I noticed two teenaged boys who huddled together. They seemed deathly frightened, and I squatted beside them. "It's going to be okay, boys."

The one boy only turned and held more tightly to his friend.

Our small new friend tugged at my sleeve. "They're girls," he said. "They're hiding."

Once out of the bunker, I was overcome by a foul stench. "What's that smell?"

"It's the dead people in the river," said the small boy.

"What?" I said.

"Well, what are people to do?" said Wolfie.

There were no birds in the hazy, burnt-lilac sky. Across from the bomb shelter was a charred tree with a single branch sprouting green leaves. The last time I saw this place, we had been mischievous boys, and Hitler had made us believe we could rule the world . . .

"Lunacy," I said under my breath.

Wolfie handed me a cigarette. "What did you say?"

"Nothing."

"Can I have one?" said the boy.

"*Nein*. You'll have plenty of time to smoke when you're older," Wolfie said. "What's your name, boy?"

"They call me Mouse."

I leaned against an old truck. It had no tires or doors, and a layer of dust covered its bullet-riddled body. We watched people scurry along the roadways carrying bundles of who-knows-what. A mutti tugged on her small daughter's arm, hurrying her along. The child carried a much too large bundle in one hand, and from her other hand dangled a little doll with long blond hair hanging over its face. Across the street was a woman wearing a beautiful hat with a red ribbon that held three pheasant feathers in place. She carried two suitcases that were clearly too heavy for her. I shifted my gaze to the squadrons of Mosquito bombers that had suddenly appeared overhead. I hadn't even heard them approach.

"Michael! Wolfie!" Mouse shouted over the wailing siren. He grabbed our hands and pulled us back towards the bomb shelter.

The RAF were bombing us, and the Russians had us surrounded. Surely this was where the final battle would be.

Once back in the shelter, I felt the walls closing in on me. Sweat ran down my face, and with each bomb exploding above, dust fell from the walls onto our uniforms. I began to see there was a very real possibility of being buried alive here, and the thought terrified me. Mouse sat close to me reading *Max und Moritz*. I thought back to Margarita and to the books she had given Wolfie and me. "You will always be my trusted Max," she had written.

"What are the Tommies bombing?" I had to raise my voice to be heard over the noise. "The city is already in utter ruins." But I knew it was an attempt to destroy the will of the people.

"I don't know!" Wolfie shouted back.

Mouse looked up from his book, glanced at us and then continued reading.

In the afternoon when the bombing stopped, we emerged from the bunker, I could hardly breathe from the thick plumes of smoke. But once my eyes adjusted to the sooty light, I looked around in disbelief. The streets were quickly filling with people crawling out of their cellars and trying to help others who were entombed. Women, small children, and old men climbed over the rubble, salvaging what they could. The surviving Berliners pushed and pulled carts and baby carriages filled with their possessions, desperation on their faces as they fled from the approaching Russians.

There lying dead at the entrance of another war bunker was the woman with the red ribbon and pheasant feathers on her hat. The contents of her suitcase lay strewn around her. "It makes no sense, Wolfie," I said.

"Why are we here?" He squinted into the sky as he wiped the dust from his face. "We should make our way back to our battalion. Surely we're of more use on a battlefield . . ."

I turned to see Hitler's personal bodyguard standing behind me. "Shut your mouth, soldier!" he shouted at Wolfie. "If you try to escape, I will shoot you myself. You'll be defending Berlin. Now move!"

He had a small group of soldiers with him, and he marched us all into the chancellery courtyard outside Hitler's office where a group of civilians, including some children, were already assembled. There we stood at attention for an hour. One of the LSSAH guards explained that it was Hitler's fifty-sixth birthday that day and we were here for the traditional celebration. It came to me that yesterday had been my sister Annalisa's birthday, too, and I tried to remember how old she would be now. Five? I thought. Was she five this year?

The same LSSAH guard who had yelled at us earlier started to shout out orders. "You are not to touch the Führer or talk to him. If he reaches for your hand, you must reciprocate. If he talks to you, you will keep your replies short."

Cameras were set up and photographers took their places. And then out of a doorway Hitler approached.

"*Achtung!*" shouted the Hitler guard.

Wolfie and I stood not moving or uttering a word. Hitler walked slowly towards us.

I couldn't believe that this small, sickly creature was the same man who once had been so proud and righteous, who had been determined to lead his country to world dominance. Instead, he had seduced a whole nation and brought it to its knees. And I had believed in him ... My face grew hot and my hands trembled. Memories flooded over me of all the people I had loved and lost, then Lorelei's words rushed in. *Kill Hitler!* My knees began to buckle and I had to concentrate to stay upright.

I saw Hitler cup a small boy's face in his hand then give a gentle tug to the boy's ear.

I felt sick. I could do it. The handle of my knife was just inches from my hand.

And then there he was standing before me, this fool teetering on insanity. I felt shame, guilt and rage as I stared into his glassy blue eyes. His hands trembled as he reached out to pin the Iron Cross First Class onto my dirty uniform. "You have made me proud and served your country well," Hitler said.

I returned his gaze. My heart beat wildly.

After Hitler greeted everyone and handed out all the medals, he quickly vanished through the same door. Once we were dismissed, Wolfie whispered, "I don't understand. Why give medals to us here?"

He was right. After all, we had already received the Iron Cross Second Class at Beverloo. "I don't know, Wolfie," I muttered, bewildered by the Führer's odd benediction. "We have been fighting for an insane fool." But the deeper truth was we had fought to stay alive.

As we were about to leave the chancellery, another of Hitler's guards approached. "Michael Boii?"

"*Ja.*" There was something familiar about this man.

He reached into his coat pocket and handed me a letter, then remained staring at me for a moment before looking at Wolfie. Finally with a half-smirk he said, "You two don't remember me, do you?"

I stepped back, and it hit me like a lightning bolt: "Jürgen Fassbender!"

Wolfie glared at him. "This sure is a coincidence."

Jürgen put his hand on Wolfie's shoulder as he turned back to me. "No coincidence. How are Paula and my son?"

I clenched my fist and through gritted teeth replied, "Paula is none of your business."

Jürgen stepped closer. "I don't think you want to take that tone with me! You see, I'm to take you to your papa tonight." He handed me an envelope. "It's all in the letter." Jürgen shoved Wolfie. "Now get back with the other boys. I'll come for you at your shelter just before nightfall." He clicked his heels and raised his hand. "*Heil Hitler.*"

We stood staring as he marched off.

"Are you going to read the letter, Michael?"

Although I wanted to tear it up, I said, "Yes, I guess I had better read it."

Michael,

It is no coincidence that Wolfie is here with you in Berlin. I know that you would never have come without him. I will explain all later. Jürgen will escort you to the Kaiser-Wilhelm-Gedächtniskirche tonight. The bell will toll when I arrive.

Papa

For the rest of the day Wolfie and I worked with other Hitlerjugend boys setting up blockades to hinder the approaching Red Army, which was now only a few days' march outside the city.

As we were moving rubble, I told Wolfie, "I'm not going to meet Papa at the church, and for certain I'm not going there with Jürgen!"

"You have to."

"*Nein*, I don't!"

"I'll come with you."

"*Nein.*"

"*Ja*, I am going with you."

"Why?"

"The Wilhelmkirche where your papa wants to meet you is close to where Fräulein Margarita lives. We can see if she's there."

"But . . ."

"Never mind. I'm coming with you."

"Okay, but we'll go before Jürgen comes for us."

"I'd like to get my hands around his filthy neck."

"*Ja.*"

Dark clouds clutched the sky as Wolfie and I set out just before dusk. We could hear sporadic gunfire on the city's eastern outskirts, marking the beginning of the Russian advance. Wolfie paused at what looked to be Friedrichstrasse.

"Remember! This was where the cabarets were, Michael."

"Yes, and my women of the night." I smiled, fondly remembering Ivy and her soft eyes. "Come on, we'd better move faster. It'll be dark soon." I pointed at an apartment building, its windows blown out. I could still see the black residue left by flames that had been long extinguished. On the third floor I could see where once a wall, now a gaping hole, revealed a kitchen table with chairs around it, a bank of cupboards and a stove. "If we cut through that building, we should come out on Fräulein Margarita's street—" I stopped as a distant church bell began to ring. "Wolfie, do you hear that?"

"The gunfire?"

"*Nein* . . . In his letter Papa said when he arrived at the church he would toll the bell."

"*Ach* so. We better hurry."

We crossed the street and cut through the apartment building, but once we were inside the burned-out building, we could see that people had been living there. There were empty food cans and old newspapers strewn about, and in the centre of the floor was the remnant of a fire pit. A baby carriage lay on its side. We heard a noise coming from behind a pillar. Wolfie walked beside me, our rifles pointing straight ahead. A gust of cold air burst through the blown-out windows, causing an empty can to roll across the floor. Wolfie fired at it.

"*Bitte, nicht schiessen!*" a voice shouted.

Slowly I moved to my right, motioning to Wolfie to move in the opposite direction.

"*Hände hoch*," I shouted.

And from behind the pillar a tall, skinny woman emerged, holding her hands up. "Please don't shoot me."

"Who are you?" Wolfie asked

"Lily Bergmann."

I walked closer, still pointing my rifle at her. "Why aren't you in a bomb shelter?"

"This is my home."

She walked over to the baby carriage and set it on its wheels, then pulled a doll out of it, kissed it, and laid it back in the carriage. Wolfie and I exchanged a look.

"Fräulein," Wolfie said, "you'd better get out of here. The Russians are coming. You won't be safe here."

"Where should I go?"

As I looked around and then back at her, she started to laugh maniacally.

Wolfie shook his head. "Let's get out of here."

"*Ja*." We stepped out of a door-less doorway. We scurried to the next street corner, I pointed across the street. "Look, that's Margarita's place."

"How can you tell?"

"See the gate?" The garden wall still stood, encircling a pile of rubble. We opened the gate. The moon peeked from behind the clouds, and for a moment I thought I saw the bathroom window that Wolfie and I had climbed out so many years before. And there standing under the back door light, Fräulein Margarita had stood in her négligée. Her slender silhouette had been so beautiful.

Wolfie nudged me and pointed. "Michael, look."

"*Ach, du lieber Gott.*"

There sniffing about was a dirty white poodle with one dirty blue ribbon hanging from its ear. I shouted, "Bunny!" For a few seconds he looked at us, then growled and ran away.

Wolfie pulled at my arm. "Come, there's nothing here for us."

"Maybe she is under that rubble."

"Our angel?"

"*Ja.*"

"I don't think so, Michael."

We left these sacred grounds, closed the gate, and became aware that the melancholy church bell was ringing again. The clouds hung heavy in the sky, but every now and then the moon appeared, casting a dull light that illuminated the remains of this desolate city.

"Michael!"

I turned and there standing at the corner stood Jürgen, pointing his Luger at us. As he moved towards us, he said, "So . . . you two decided to head off without me."

"What of it?" I said.

"*Ja* . . . what of it, Jürgen?" Wolfie echoed.

"I could shoot both of you . . ."

"Why would you do that, Jürgen?" I snarled. "For disobeying your orders . . . ?"

"*Nein.* For killing Fritz." Jürgen shot at the ground, just missing Wolfie's foot.

I slipped my rifle from my shoulder, but Wolfie was faster. He swung his clenched fist and struck Jürgen in the face.

As Jürgen stumbled back, I smashed the butt of my rifle into the side of his head. This time he fell to the ground. "*Du Pisskopf!*" I shouted.

Wolfie fired, hitting Jürgen in the leg.

He screamed and grabbed his leg. "You're dead!" And he began crawling towards his Luger.

I kicked it out of his reach and lowered my rifle to aim between his eyes. "I should have killed you all those years ago. This is for what you did to Paula, *Du Drecksack!*" But just as I was about to pull the trigger, I saw what a scared and wretched coward he was.

Wolfie put his hand on my rifle. "*Nein*—leave him. The Russians can have him. Let's go."

I reached into my pocket for Jürgen's teeth that I had carried all these years and flung them at him. "I hope you rot in hell, you piece of shit."

As we turned the corner to walk down Ku'damm, a single shot rang out.

Wolfie looked at me, stumbled, reached for his side, then lifted his hand. It was covered in blood. "That *Arschloch* . . . shot me." He slipped to the ground.

I spun around and shot several rounds into the darkness, but no one returned my fire.

Under my breath I said, "I should have taken his pistol. *Scheisse*, Wolfie." I knelt beside him. "Are you okay?"

"I think so."

"I'll take you to the first aid station."

"*Nein.* I don't want to be captured by the Russians."

"But you need . . ."

"*Nein!* Maybe your papa can help."

I hauled him to his feet. "Put your arm around me."

"I'll be okay," he said as I half-dragged him down the street.

"Listen . . . the church bell," Wolfie muttered. "We must be close."

It was around the next corner. Three of its six steeples were still standing, but the centre one had its top blown off, and the beautiful stained glass window that had graced the north face was now glassless. Only the cross bars that had held the glass remained, like a crucifix. I felt I stood on hallowed ground.

Wolfie gasped in pain as we stumbled over the rubble that lay strewn where devout congregations had knelt in prayer.

"Over here," a voice whispered from what remained of the church altar.

We moved towards the voice, guided by the moonlight coming through the hole where the stained glass window had been. Then I saw my papa. His face was sunken, and he looked a lot smaller than how I had remembered him. He wore civilian clothing.

"You look good, boy," he said as he cleared his throat. "I see you earned yourself some medals."

"Wolfie's been shot. He needs help."

"Iron Cross . . . First and Second Class. Impressive."

"They're good for nothing. We need help!"

"Where is Jürgen? He was supposed to be with you. What's the matter with your friend?"

I helped Wolfie sit against a wall directly under a large crucifix.

"Have you heard from your mama?"

"*Nein!* Papa, Wolfie needs help."

"Your two brothers—they're dead."

I held my breath, visualizing the three of us playing cards together at the kitchen table. "We need help, Papa!" I said.

"Have you heard from your mama?"

"*Nein!*"

"You're all that's left, Michael."

"Get on with it, Rudi," a voice bellowed from the shadows. "We don't have much time."

"I know. Wait for me outside," Papa shouted back.

I looked down at Wolfie as he leaned to one side and placed his hand on my boot. He smiled up at me and coughed, spitting something up, most likely blood, and my rage surged.

"Why have you asked for me, Papa? What do you want?"

"Michael, you're all I have left. You're my son. Argentina will be a place for us to carry on Hitler's work. Your blood is pure, and you are clearly a warrior. I have plans for you, Michael. Big plans."

Just then Jürgen appeared in the doorway of the blown-out side door.

Papa turned towards him, pulling his Luger, and said sharply, "What happened to you?"

Jürgen pointed at Wolfie and me. "Those two happened to me."

Papa motioned with his Luger at Jürgen's leg. "You'll slow us down."

"I'll be okay." But Jürgen looked scared as he muttered those words.

Papa never replied. He aimed his pistol and shot Jürgen in the head. His beaten body slid down the wall, blood trickling down his forehead, and with a thump his body slumped onto the church floor. The shadow from the holy cross lay like a stain just beyond his fingertips.

I stood staring in disbelief, but Papa didn't bat an eye. "Boy, we're going to Austria and then on to Argentina, and you're coming with us. This war is over. Deutschland has lost. But the Reich will continue to need us."

Quickly I stepped in front of Wolfie. "I'm not leaving Wolfie."

"Get out of the way!" He raised his pistol to shoot Wolfie.

I aimed my rifle at my papa, looking into his now faded blue eyes. "You'll have to shoot me first."

"Move, you fool!" he shouted.

A squadron of planes flew overhead, and bombs exploded nearby.

"Fuck you!" Spit flew from my mouth. "Go ahead and shoot me, you Nazi piece of *Scheisse*! Shoot . . ."

"Michael, you'll never survive the end here."

"You don't get the privilege of caring about me now!"

"Michael, I want to protect you . . ."

"Protect me? You're a little late . . ."

"Michael, you're not thinking. The Reich still needs you alive."

"The Reich! Go, Papa! Go hide away with the rest of your *Arschlöcher, Untermenschen,* pussy Nazis! . . . *Zur Hölle mit dir.* Go before I blow your fucking head off . . . ! Go-o-o . . . !"

He lowered his pistol, and for a few seconds stared defiantly at me. Then he raised his arm and clicked his heels. "*Heil Hitler.*" He turned, stepped over Jürgen's body and vanished out the door.

In the silence that followed I lowered my rifle and pulled Wolfie up, placing his arm over my shoulder.

"*Ach,* I thought . . . you were going to . . . him."

"*Ja,* me too." Together Wolfie and I slipped out of the church into the safety of the dark night.

23

Not Without You

— APRIL 1945 —

∽

"WHAT NOW, MICHAEL?"

The night air bit into me as I held Wolfie tightly against me. I could feel the warmth of his blood soaking into my uniform and his body shivering with pain.

"*Ach* . . . Michael, I don't . . . think I can make it to . . . the bomb shelter."

My mind raced. There was no one to help us. "It's okay, we'll rest in the *Tiergarten*."

"Michael, that burned-out building . . . the one we cut through . . . earlier. It's across the street . . . from the *Tiergarten*."

"Okay, we'll spend the night there."

As we stumbled down the street, I heard the high-pitched sound of Katyusha rocket launchers—Stalin's Organ as we had called them at the front—in the far distance. They were a reminder of how vulnerable we were. I held tighter to Wolfie.

"It'll be okay," I reassured him.

Finally we stepped within the safety of the derelict building, and I helped Wolfie to sit against the cold gray wall. But just as I stood erect, I felt a dull blow to the side of my head. Like a silent movie, for a second everything went quiet. Then my legs betrayed me, and I fell to the floor, though not before I heard Wolfie say, "Please don't . . ."

It must have been quite awhile before I came to. The ringing noise in my head forced me to open my eyes. I was still trying to make sense of what was happening and where I was when I heard Wolfie scream.

"Michael!"

Clumsily I rose to my feet, and for a moment the room spun around me. Then I saw the old baby carriage.

"Michael!"

Kneeling at Wolfie's side was the crazy lady who had refused to leave the building earlier, the one we had almost shot. A small fire was burning close by, providing a little light, and I could see the woman was holding a large knife in her hand. When she heard my stumbling approach, she looked up, her forehead smeared with blood. I went to reach for my rifle, but she had taken it.

"Get over here," she snapped. "Come and hold your friend down."

"Get away from him!" I shouted as I lunged at her.

She stood up, side-stepping my clumsy move, and reached into the baby carriage. Pulling out a bottle of booze, she took a swig from it. "I'm trying to save your friend's life." Then she knelt to pour some of the contents of the bottle onto Wolfie's wound.

Wolfie writhed in pain as the booze hit his wound.

I knelt beside Wolfie. "Do you know what you're doing, Frau?"

His eyes were wild, and he reached for my arm. "She's . . . trying to . . . get . . . the bullet out. Make her . . . stop!"

I shoved her away from Wolfie. "You're crazy!"

She waved her knife at me. "I'm sorry for knocking you out. It was dark and I thought you were a *Russky*. Your friend is going to die if we don't get that bullet out." She took another swig of alcohol.

The glow of the fire lit her face softly, and for a moment she looked like Fräulein Margarita. "Okay," I said, "but stay off the booze."

Wolfie squeezed my arm. "Are you sure, Michael?"

"It'll be okay." But I was thinking, *Scheisse*, what else can we do?

He gripped my arm tighter. "Then give me . . . something . . . to bite down . . . on."

I searched my pockets, then reached for my Hitler Youth knife. For a brief second I thought about the inscription on it: *Blut und Ehre*. Blood and Honour, at least it was good for something. "Here, bite down on the handle." I sat behind him, his head resting up against my chest "It'll be okay, Wolfie."

I looked at her almost fleshless old hands and saw they were trembling.

"Hold him still!" she snapped.

"I am. Have you done this before, Frau?"

"*Nein*," the crazy lady said. "But I worked in a slaughter house in Dresden for five years."

"And that means . . . ?"

"That means I know how to cut into flesh, and that's all that's necessary . . ." She began cutting into the bullet's entry wound.

Wolfie stopped squirming and closed his eyes. Beads of sweat formed on his brow, and he bit down hard on the handle.

"Be careful!" I said.

"*Halt die Klappe!* You're making me nervous. I'm only cutting him enough to get my fingers into the wound."

Wolfie squeezed my hand.

"Sorry," I said.

Wolfie winced with every jab of her exploring fingers, and his body tensed as though he were being stabbed over and over.

"It's in here somewhere," she muttered to herself, and then she looked up at me, a smile creeping over her face. "Look what we have here!" She lifted her hand to show me the bullet.

I reached out and she dropped it into my palm. "*Danke*, Frau." I went to show it to Wolfie but he had passed out, his head flopped to one side. I put the bullet in my pocket.

"Do you have a needle and thread?" she asked me.

I shook my head. "*Nein*."

The crazy lady scanned my uniform. She pointed. "Your medal."

I put my hand over it. "This?"

"Do you have a better idea?"

I took the medal off, but when I felt the point of the pin, I found it was dull. I picked up a stone and used it to sharpen the pin, then handed it to her. "At least the damned thing is good for something."

She took it, grabbed the bottle of booze, took another swig, and poured some over the pin. "Give me your hand. Now hold the wound closed like that while I pin it."

Wolfie moaned as he opened his eyes. "Michael, how long have I been out?"

"A day."

"Is the bullet out?"

I pulled it out of my pocket and showed him. "She's a beauty. You'll be okay now," I said, but I wasn't so sure because he was running a fever.

He tried to get up. "How long can we hole up here?"

I put my hand on his shoulder. "Easy there. We only have it pinned together loosely."

Wolfie reached down to his side. "What . . . *Ach, du Scheisse*." He looked up at me and laughed weakly.

"It was the crazy lady's idea," I said.

"Is there any water, Michael?"

I reached for the jug of rainwater the woman had provided and poured some into a cup. "Here . . ."

"Pretty teacup."

It was true. The teacup was pretty—it had pink roses on it—but its lip had a chip out of it. "Not so fast, Wolfie. You'll choke."

"Where is she?"

"Who?"

"The crazy lady."

"Her name's Lily." I pointed to my left. "She's over there in the corner."

Wolfie tried to sit up. "Rocking her doll?"

I pushed him gently down again. "You need rest."

Lily had a stash of Vodka bottles in the baby carriage, and she sat for most of the day rocking her doll, drinking and staring at us.

We couldn't move on until Wolfie's wound had begun to heal, but from the occasional rifle fire I knew that Russian snipers had already begun to trickle into the city, and there was only our weakened to non-existent army bolstered by Hitlerjugend boys and girls fending them off. I spent most of that day on the rooftop of the building with my rifle ready to make sure the three of us would not become carrion.

The next morning the Russians shelled the centre of the city for more than an hour. When it was over, Wolfie sat up, leaning his back against the wall. "Michael, what day is it?"

"April 22, I think. Are you feeling any better?"

"I think so."

"Good. I'm going out to look for food. Lily will keep an eye on you."

"Who?"

"Lily, the crazy lady."

"*Ach, ja.*"

"I'll be back before dark."

The sun was out and the rays struck the back of my neck. It felt good to have some warmth. I closed my eyes and for a moment I pictured Mama planting her seedlings in her vegetable garden, with Minka at her side. A cat—that's what I need, I thought. I walked the streets stepping over rubble, and then there sitting on a half–blown-up wall was a white cat—a white cat with a bell attached to a blue collar—licking itself, and soaking up the sun's rays, much like I was. For a moment I watched it lick its paw, pass it over its ear, and then do it all over again.

What I was about to do didn't feel good, but what else could I do? I drew my knife, grabbed the cat, and with one swift motion cut its throat. I picked it up by its back legs and began walking down the street, letting the blood pour onto the dusty cobblestones. The cat's bell softly tinkling.

I crouched behind a heap of rubble and I waited. And waited. And waited. Then sure enough, the dogs came sniffing around and they, too, were hungry. I aimed my rifle at one of them, and just as I went to pull the trigger, I realized that this great, dirty white poodle with one blue ribbon tied to its ear was ... Bunny. She didn't see me. As she began licking up the blood, I threw the cat at her and she shied away from it, growled, then came back to sniff at it. At last she sank her teeth into it and ran off. Just then an old brown dog limped into view, and I pulled the trigger.

The fire crackled as I laid the meat on it, and the smell of the food cooking made me think of Mama's kitchen. I could see her standing at the stove preparing Sunday dinner. I would try to sneak a taste, and always Mama would take the wooden spoon and gently shoo me away just like a pesky fly. Then she would look at me, wave me over, and let me have a spoonful. "How does that taste?" she would say. Those Sunday dinners were always special. Most often it would be Rouladen with red cabbage and potato dumplings. We kids would help make the dumplings. The fine china would come out, Mama's silver cutlery would be used, and we would all have to wear our Sunday-best clothes.

I became aware that Lily was repeating over and over, "We have food, baby, food ..." She was squatting close to the fire, rocking back and forth on her haunches, holding her doll.

Wolfie sat up, with his hand over his wound. "It smells good, Michael."

I handed him a piece of meat. "*Ja*, but how does it taste?"

Wolfie put the morsel into his mouth. "It's a bit tough, but you know what? It tastes like—mutton."

Lily gulped her share down, and as she wiped her mouth with the back of her hand, she snapped, "What do you want?"

I turned my head to see who she was talking to, but before I could say anything, a small boy had sidled up to me. "Hey, got any for me?" he said.

"Mouse?" I stood up and hugged him to me. "How did you find us?"

"I saw you shoot that dog . . ."

"What were you doing out on the street?" I cut some meat and handed it to him. "Why aren't you in the shelter?"

"There's no room," Mouse said as he bit hungrily into the meat. "What happened to Wolfie? He doesn't look too good."

"I got shot, kid," Wolfie said.

"You better get better fast, Wolfie," Mouse said, "because the Russians are coming."

"What have you heard, Mouse?" I said as I handed him more meat.

"Everyone's trying to get out of the city."

Lily stopped gnawing on the leg bone. "I'm not leaving!"

Mouse looked at Lily and shook his head. "If you stay here, you'll get killed, and so will your baby."

"We can't move Wolfie for a few more days, Mouse." I glanced at Lily, and she gripped her doll more tightly, staring at me defiantly as she took a swig of booze. I leaned toward Mouse and whispered, "That's not a baby. It's a doll."

"Oh . . . How long are you going to stay here, Michael?"

"Another couple of days," I said as I helped Wolfie to lie down again.

Mouse watched for a while, then lay down beside Wolfie and

promptly fell asleep. I sat up for most of the night worrying about Wolfie. He had a fever and I kept wondering what I could do about more food. The dog would only last us for one more day—especially with one more mouth to feed—and then what? Not that I wasn't happy that Mouse had found us, but it meant I was responsible for one more person.

I wondered what would become of us, I wondered what Mama and Annalisa and Paula and little Waldemar were doing. Were they still alive? Had they fled from the Russians in time? I tried to make sense of what this war was all about, and all that flooded my mind were the words that Mama had spoken to me: "Please stay alive." There was no out for us, only the grace of God could help, but why would he help us after all the people we had killed?

The fire burned out. The moon cast jagged shadows of several nearby bombed-out buildings across the barren walls of our building. I gazed at the deformed shapes, and as I listened to the distant gunfire, I replayed the grotesque reality of war out on the moonlit walls.

I was awakened the next morning by rapid gunfire just a few blocks away, and I knew the Russians had broken through our weakened defence lines in the night. Wolfie, Mouse and Lily had awakened at the sound of gunfire.

"We have to go," I said. I helped Wolfie to stand.

"*Ach, du Scheisse*, Michael. Leave me! You'll have a better chance without me." He reached for his rifle.

Lily sat up, grabbed her doll and placed it in the baby carriage. "We're coming with you," she said.

"I'm not leaving you," I told Wolfie. "I promised Mama."

Mouse grabbed Wolfie's rifle and slung it over his shoulder. "Where will we go, Michael?"

"Not sure," I said, handing Wolfie a long stick to use as a cane, "but we're all going together."

Mouse buttoned his blue grey coat. "One of the old men in the shelter said it was still possible to escape Berlin over the Charlotten-brücke."

I grabbed my rifle. "Okay, that's where we're heading. The bridge is only a few blocks from here. Wolfie, put your arm over my shoulder. We can do this."

Once we were outside, we realized the gunfire was very close.

"Mouse, do you know how to shoot?" I said.

"*Nein.*"

"I do," said Lily.

"Mouse, give Lily the rifle. I'll go first with Wolfie. Lily, you'll cover us. Mouse, you stay with Lily, and when I say go, both of you run like you've never run before."

"Okay, Michael," said Mouse. He nodded, keeping his big brown eyes glued on me.

Wolfie pulled out his pistol, and I held my rifle in my free hand. "Wolfie, that building across the street . . . we're going to run toward it and crouch behind the rubble that's in front of it. On three."

We ran, with me mostly dragging Wolfie. No gunfire followed us. Once we were behind the rubble, I waved for Lily and Mouse to come. But just as they started to run toward us, I saw a Russian coming around the corner. I held my hand up, signalling for them to go back. The Russian peered in our direction but we remained hidden. Lily had quickly pulled Mouse and the baby carriage back into the doorway, and the Russian ran down the side street without detecting us. After a few minutes I signalled Lily to cross the street.

"That was scary," Mouse said, as he crouched beside me.

"You did okay, kid," Wolfie whispered to him.

"Okay, Lily, we're going to do the same thing again. Only this time you'll go first." I pointed to the right. "See that old car?"

"*Ja.*"

"I want you to run with Mouse to the car, and once you're there, stay behind it. Then while Wolfie and I come, you'll cover us."

"*Ja,*" she said as she tucked the blanket around her baby before placing Wolfie's rifle on top of the blanket.

"Lily, do you think you could leave that carriage behind?"

"*Nein!*"

"Lily . . . You have a real live little boy to look after now," I pleaded with her. "Mouse needs you." But she just tucked the blanket tighter around the doll. I put my hand on Mouse's shoulder. "Stay on this side of the carriage," I told him, pointing. "Do you understand?"

He nodded. "*Ja*, Michael."

"Good then, on three." I counted. "*Ein, zwei, drei . . .*"

Lily and Mouse started running up the street. They were about halfway to the car when Lily tripped and fell, taking the baby carriage to the ground with her. It landed on its side, spilling all its contents onto the sidewalk. A half dozen bottles of booze rolled into the street, clinking as they landed. To my amazement the bottles never broke, but the doll's porcelain head shattered into a thousand pieces.

Lily crawled to her doll, whimpering. "My baby . . . My baby . . ."

"Mouse, run! Run!" I shouted.

But it was too late. Two Russian soldiers had appeared around the next corner. Unable to decide what to do, Mouse just stood at Lily's side.

I raised my gun to shoot, but it jammed. Wolfie aimed his pistol but missed. Mouse bent to pick up Wolfie's rifle, but I knew it was too big for him to shoot.

I shouted again, "Run, Mouse! Run . . ."

Lily stood up, dropped her broken baby, snatched the rifle out of Mouse's hands and stepped in front of him. As the Russian bullets hit her, she fell back on top of him. I unjammed my rifle and took out the two Russians.

All was quiet. "Mouse! Mouse!" I shouted. I ran towards him, and Wolfie trailed after me. I knelt beside Lily—on her face was a serene smile. I closed her eyes, rolled her off Mouse and scooped the boy into my arms. "Mouse . . ."

Wolfie looked into the boy's face. "Is he dead?"

But just as he spoke, Mouse took a deep breath. "Am I dead?"

I kissed his little blood-spattered face. "You're alive . . ."

"You had us worried, kid," Wolfie said. He picked up his rifle, and we ducked into the nearest doorway. "We have to keep going, Michael . . ."

"*Ja*. The bridge must be just around the corner."

"Here, kid," Wolfie said, "take my Luger."

Mouse took the pistol. "What about Lily?"

"She's gone, Mouse. We have to keep going."

Behind us I heard shouts and the clanking of an approaching tank. "Run!" I yelled. "Run like hell!"

24

Prisoners

— MAY 1945 —

❦

WOLFIE LAY SHIVERING beside me, his head in my lap. Gently I raised his shirt. The wound in his side was oozing a yellowish, opalescent liquid again.

"Michael," he whispered, "where are we?"

"Bretzenheim, near Bad Kreuznach. Remember?" After we had escaped over the Charlottenbrücke, we were able to make our way to where the Americans were dug in on the Elbe. There, they packed us and hundreds more, like sardines, into a train and took us to one of the US Army-built meadow camps in the Rhineland. Except that it was no meadow—it was a muddy field of misery. I looked up at the razor-wire–topped fence of the cage where we had been interned to await disposition. "The war's over," I reminded him. "We're disarmed enemies now."

"Not prisoners of war?"

"*Ja.* The Amis command this camp."

He was silent for a long time, then finally he struggled to sit up and looked around at the vast field of people on every side of us. "What are all these people doing here? Where's the kid?"

There were at least a hundred thousand people in this camp, and not just soldiers, but displaced civilians, from the very young to the very old. But I was most surprised that there were women soldiers and support workers there, too. And all the guards inside the fence were Deutsche soldiers. "Mouse found his Opa."

"*Ach, ja.* I remember now." Mouse talked about his grandfather. He lay back and closed his eyes.

These meadow camps were a logistical nightmare for the Allied powers because they had been unprepared for so many prisoners. Consequently, we had been given only starvation rations since we arrived. All around us people were dying, mainly from starvation as most of us were already undernourished when we arrived. And when starvation wasn't killing them, dysentery and other illnesses were. Trucks came in at night to load up the dead and take them away. We were living like animals.

"Michael, is there any water?"

A water tank was stationed near the gate, but I had no way to carry water back to him. And I couldn't stand in line for ten hours every day just to get a mouthful for myself as I couldn't risk something happening to him while I was gone. It had been a cold, wet spring, and people died each time it rained because the mud walls of the shelters they had built collapsed, suffocating them. Some people drank from the mud puddles but they became violently ill afterwards, so that wasn't an option either.

I had stopped wearing my boots because my feet had swollen, and now I dipped an old hanky in the urine I had saved in one of my boots and squeezed the liquid onto Wolfie's lips. He turned his head away.

"Remember how we did this before?" I said. "In the trenches during the battle of the Ardennes?"

"But then it was my own piss, not yours." Wolfie laughed weakly, then began coughing.

For most of that day we lay in the hole I had dug out for us with my hands. It had started raining again, and I tented one of our blankets over our heads to give us some shelter. I had no coat now—it had been stolen some weeks back. We were crawling with lice, but I did have a comb and I made sure that our hair was always groomed.

"Michael, I have to go to the latrines."

"Okay," I said. I put my arm around his waist and helped him up. As we made our way through the ranks and ranks of soldiers, I asked myself, "How long can they keep all of us in here? Probably they're hoping that we will all die off and save them from having to do anything."

We passed a group of about a hundred men who had formed a line, one behind the other, to walk in a circle to ease their boredom. Around and around they trudged, much like lions in a cage at the zoo.

It took about half an hour to get to the head of the line at the latrines. "Michael, don't let go of me," Wolfie said as I helped him to balance on the wooden railing over the cesspool beneath him. "I don't want to fall in, not like the guy last week."

It was true. If you fell into one of these toilets, you stood a good chance of drowning because no one had the strength to pull you out.

On the way back we saw four soldiers beating another soldier. They would probably kill him as he had stolen from his own.

"Let's stop at the hospital," I said. "Maybe they will have something for your infection today, Wolfie."

"*Ja*," he agreed, but I could see he was no longer hopeful of receiving any help there. "Okay. Maybe today they will have something . . ."

The hospital was not much more than a first aid station, and soldiers only went there in their last hours of life. But on this day

Frau Hildegard, the wrinkly old nurse who was in charge, came towards us, smiling. "You're in luck, boys," she said. "Pull your pants down, Wolfie. This will sting a little."

Wolfie pulled his muddy pants down, bent over, and flinched when the needle went into his bony bottom. "Auw!"

She smiled. "Michael, are you on work duty tonight?"

"*Ja*." I had been assigned to help load the dead into trucks.

At dawn the next morning, I left Wolfie sleeping while I set out to look for some food. He was awake when I got back an hour later. "How do you feel?" I asked.

"Better, I think," he said. "I was lying here remembering last Christmas in the woods."

I nodded. "*Ja*, we had the Christmas dinner Catherine packed for us." We had celebrated Christmas when we stopped in the woods on our way to find our unit.

"*Ach*, remember how wonderful that venison tasted?"

"*Ja.*"

He smiled and wiggled his toes. "Remember, you gave me these socks." I had given him the yellow woollen socks Catherine had put into my coat pocket the day we left Veit at the lodge. Now they were riddled with holes and there was no sign of colour on them. Wolfie had given me his lighter in return.

"There was a baby born in enclosure A-3 yesterday," I said. "They're going to call her Ursula."

"When were you over there?"

"Just now. I went looking for food and to check on Mouse. But they're gone—he and his Opa. They were sent home."

"That's good!" he said, smiling. "But did you find any food?"

"*Nein*. The guards have stopped people throwing potatoes and cabbages over the fence."

"Do we have any more cigarettes?"

"*Ja*, I traded one of our iron crosses to a guard." I lit two cigarettes and handed one to Wolfie.

He took a drag from his cigarette and began coughing.

"But there's a rumour that the Red Cross might be allowed to come through the camp."

Wolfie nodded. This was not the first time the rumour had circulated, but no one ever came. "Maybe we can escape?" he whispered.

I didn't answer. Anyone who had tried escaping had been shot.

"Can we send mail—has anyone sent us mail—Mama?"

"It's not allowed."

"Why can't we go home?" he asked.

As the days dragged on, our hope that someone would come to help us faded. Being hungry didn't matter anymore. Although it was late May, I was feeling the cold more and more, and the mud clung to me like a layer of dead skin. I lay beside Wolfie in our mud-hole thinking about Mama. Did she know where we were, or did she believe us to be dead? And I thought about my dead comrades, and the lives they might have lived . . .

25

Departure

— JUNE 1945 —

ᗧ

ONE MORNING AS WE lay in our mud hole, I said, "Seven hundred and sixty-six."

"What?" Wolfie asked.

"That's how many hours we've been interned here. Seven hundred and sixty-six . . ." That's when I felt a kick in my side.

"Get up, you two."

It was one of the guards, and I ignored him. There was no more fight left in me.

He kicked me again, only harder this time. "I said get up! Haven't you heard?"

I sat up and turned to face him. "Heard what?"

"All Hitlerjugend born since 1927 are to go to gate A5."

"Are we being shipped to another camp?" I asked. But he had already gone.

I shook Wolfie and yanked at his arm, "Wolfie, can you stand?"

"*Ja.*"

Quickly we pulled on our boots. Then as I helped him to his feet, he placed his arm over my shoulder and I put my arm around his waist. As we stumbled through the gauntlet of Deutsche soldiers, I remembered how Frau Silberstein had ridden her bicycle through the gauntlet of Hitlerjugend boys as they shouted, "*Jude! Jude!*" after her.

The three men sitting behind the table at Gate A5 asked us questions, examined our identification tags and handed us papers to sign, along with civilian clothing and 30 marks. Then they told us we were free to go. The gates opened, and Wolfie and I, along with about two hundred other Hitlerjugend, walked through them. I turned back once we were outside, and a sea of despair stared back at me. But as I turned to face forward again, I saw that a few local men and women were waiting to greet us with water and bread, and one man was handing out cigarettes.

A plump woman approached me and asked, "Do you know my husband, Herr Siegfried Lütz?"

"*Nein, tut mir leid,*" I said and tightened my grip on Wolfie. As we walked down the dirt road that took us away from the camp, there was not a lot of chatter among us. Our new civilian clothing hung from our skeletal frames. I felt exposed. I kept thinking, *Is it really over?* Perhaps there were snipers in the bushes waiting to pick us off? I wanted to run or hide or take cover.

Wolfie stopped. "Michael, you're walking too fast."

"Oh—sure thing." I helped him to sit on the grass and lit him a cigarette. "I guess we have to walk home."

"*Ja.* But not so fast, okay?"

As the days went by, we took shelter in the fields and on the roadsides. Sometimes people took us in and gave us food, and once we got a ride on an oxcart all the way to the next town.

We reached Herr Zimmermann's farm on the eleventh day. The

apple orchard had recovered, but the house and the big brown barn had been burned to the ground. No dog came to greet us, and the gate to the empty sheep pasture swung back and forth in the wind. I closed it. Then as we walked through the hazelnut grove, we saw that five white crosses had been placed in a row on a mound, and at the foot of each cross lay a bundle of carnations. I stopped, took Günther's St. Francis pendant from around my neck and hung it on his cross.

We walked over the old brick bridge and, as we approached my home, we could hear laughter coming from an open window. We stood in Mama's garden for a few moments in silence. Listening. Then slowly we mounted the stairs and opened the front door. I could hear Kurt's voice coming from the kitchen, and Paula laughing with Annalisa. I realized that Papa had lied when he said that *both* my brothers had died.

Wolfie closed the front door softly behind us, and we walked down the hall to the kitchen. As we stood in the doorway, I took in the whole scene—Mama stirring a pot of soup on the stove, Annalisa staring at Wolfie and me, Kurt, his left shirtsleeve pinned to his shoulder, sitting with Waldemar on his lap, Paula, her hands over her mouth, staring. All the chatter in the kitchen had stopped.

Mama turned and for a moment only stared at us. Then she placed her hand over her heart. "Michael, Wolfie?"

I wrapped my arms around her and held her tight to me as she began to cry. "We came home, Mama," I whispered, "We came home."

AUTHOR'S NOTE

Secrets in the Shadows was inspired by my need to understand how my father became the complex man he was, a man who was a product of the Nazi era with all its damaging influences, beliefs and effects. He was born in Germany in 1933, the year Adolf Hitler rose to power, and he was twelve years old when World War II ended. In order to understand my father in his totality, I had to research Nazi Germany. I realized that there were no easy answers to my questions because the complexity of human behaviour is just that, and the best I could do was try and understand what it must have been like for my father to grow up during those years.

I first researched why and how 37 percent of ordinary German people chose to elect a racist dictator. And why this nation of civilized people supported a mad man's desire for world domination. Why were citizens compliant, even complicit, and how could a government initiate laws that ultimately allowed the murder of six million Jews, along with anyone who did not follow the National Socialist (Nazi) Party's ideology? Over sixty million people lost their lives in WWII, and the German government of the time enacted laws not only to indoctrinate children but to deploy them to fight on the battlefields. By researching that dark chapter in history, I surmised what my father's childhood must have been like and how the Nazi era shaped him into the man he became.

And so I wrote *Secrets in the Shadows*, a novel in which I explored the effects that Nazism had on children in Germany. For the novel, I created two towns, Schadesdorf and Balda, along with the people who lived in them. The story follows the deployment of the Hitler Youth 12th SS Panzer Division as closely as possible, although I have altered a few events and times for the narrative flow. The names of people (except for Hitler and his close military aides, such as Hermann Göring) are a creation of my imagination, and any likeness to real people, either living or dead, is purely coincidental. I have one hope for this novel—and that is to inspire a kinder world.

ACKNOWLEDGEMENTS

I'm honoured, humbled and grateful for the help and expertise of many individuals: my publisher, Ronald Hatch at Ronsdale Press, for undertaking the publication of the novel; Meagan Dyer, for her editor's eagle eye; Nancy de Brouwer, for the cover design; and Julie Cochrane, for the novel's page design. Among the historians who helped with the historical background are Dr. Roman Töppel and David Borys. Also to be thanked are Betty Keller for her invaluable mentorship; Judith Hammill for the first copy-edit; Chris Basil for introducing me to Edmund Krawinkel, whose first-hand accounts of service at age sixteen as an SS paratrooper are deeply appreciated. For music advice and story perspective I turned to Terence Dawson, Ryan Guldemond and Patricia Hammond. Not to be forgotten are Mary Duffy, for her brilliant insights and endless encouragement over many drafts, as well as Stephan P. Mount for his wisdom and humour and early draft critiques. My writing group members— Natasha, Jo, Del, Richard, Bernadette, Cindy, Deanna and Irene—gave unlimited support. Also to be thanked for their childhood stories are Elke and Bernd Dörferdt and Ursula and Eric Bentz. For inspiration and support, I wish also to thank Francesca Hollander, Sherry Reid, Daniel Kalla, Maria Van Dyk and Wolf Wiedemann. In addition, there are my professional clients, whose constant encouragement kept me writing. My family gave much to the novel: there is my mother who filled my ears with whispers of her life, and my father who became the sorrow in my heart. Not to be forgotten are my sisters, Jurita, Carmen, Ronette, Manuela and Cécil, who formed my love of story. And to my best friend and partner in crime, Karin Smith, let me say that I cherish your honesty and the long night discussions over pilsner and wine on your front porch. And most of all to my love, Graeme Weeks: there isn't a day when you haven't encouraged, supported and inspired me to follow my dreams, no matter how crazy they may be. Much love.

ABOUT THE AUTHOR

 Heige S. Boehm's writing is greatly influenced by the stories and lives of her parents who grew up in Nazi Germany and, at the end of the war, found themselves in East Germany, locked behind the Iron Curtain. They escaped with their first two children to West Berlin in 1961, just days before the start of the building of the Berlin Wall. After living in several refugee camps they settled for a few years in Euskirchen, where Heige was born in 1964. Eventually the family relocated to Cologne. With the family living beside a thoroughfare, Heige would awake at night to hear and see army tanks rumbling down the street. There was a WWII bomb shelter across the street, and she had heard stories of how a young boy had died in that bomb shelter. Heige's older sisters discovered a secret hiding place in their basement, and they told her that a Jewish family had hidden there during the war. She came to believe that WWII was still raging, a belief that was reinforced on visits to relatives in the former GDR (East Germany), where she saw bombed-out buildings and bullet-riddled structures. It wasn't until she was nine and her family immigrated to Canada that her war finally ended. It was then that her questions about the war began. The answers lie in *Secrets in the Shadows*. Heige holds a Creative Writing certificate from the Writers Studio at Simon Fraser University. She now lives on the Sunshine Coast of Canada where she is writing and researching her next novel that follows the life of one of the secondary characters in *Secrets in the Shadows*. Visit her at www.heigeboehm.ca.